THREE MARYS

THREE MARYS

Glenn Cooper

This first world edition published 2018
in Great Britain and the USA by
SEVERN HOUSE PUBLISHERS LTD of
Eardley House, 4 Uxbridge Street, London W8 7SY
Trade paperback edition first published
in Great Britain and the USA 2018 by
SEVERN HOUSE PUBLISHERS LTD

British Library Cataloguing in Publication Data
A CIP catalogue record for this title is available from the British Library.

ISBN-13: 978-0-7278-8821-1 (cased)
ISBN-13: 978-1-84751-941-2 (trade paper)
ISBN-13: 978-1-78010-998-5 (e-book)

All Severn House titles are printed on acid-free paper.

Severn House Publishers support the Forest Stewardship Council™ [FSC™],
the leading international forest certification organisation.
All our titles that are printed on FSC certified paper carry the FSC logo.

Typeset by Palimpsest Book Production Ltd.,
Falkirk, Stirlingshire, Scotland.
Printed and bound in Great Britain by
TJ International, Padstow, Cornwall.

PROLOGUE

For Pope Celestine IV, his Wednesday morning general audiences at the Vatican were usually joyous events on his calendar – a time for him to connect with his far-flung flock in a relaxed, even festive atmosphere. On this morning he rose early, prayed in the chapel of his Sanctae Marthae residence, and had a convivial communal breakfast with staff in the cafeteria. With time approaching for him to make final preparations for the occasion, he looked up to see his private secretary and his cardinal secretary of state enter the room, both appearing rather grim.

Celestine excused himself and went to speak with them at an unoccupied table in the corner.

'What's the matter?' he asked. 'The two of you look like you have bad news.'

Sister Elisabetta, his private secretary, laid a folder in front of him. 'Holy Father, we believe you might wish to give an alternative homily this morning.'

'And why is that?'

'It's the attendance for the audience,' Cardinal Da Silva said. 'It's rather anemic.'

'How anemic?'

Sister Elisabetta had gone to one of the upper windows of the Apostolic Palace overlooking St Peter's Square to snap a few photos with her phone, and showed them to him now.

The pope put on his reading glasses. 'My goodness,' he said. 'When did you take these?'

'Only fifteen minutes ago.'

Da Silva said, 'The sun is shining, Holy Father, the sky is blue, the temperature is mild. Yet, the people have not come.'

The pope looked at the photos again. On such a day the piazza should be a sea of humanity – tourists from dozens of countries, Romans, pilgrims, clergy from all over Italy and Europe. But today, the Vatican grounds were half empty at best, with vast swathes of cobblestones visible.

A month ago the piazza had been packed for the papal audience, but each week had seen a diminution in attendance. And now, this.

Celestine scanned the homily text.

'I know you didn't write this today,' he said.

'We prepared it in advance in case it was needed,' Elisabetta said.

'It's quite tough, don't you think? Excommunications?'

Da Silva nodded gravely. 'It's the consensus of the Curia, Holy Father, that it's time to get tougher, to fight fire with fire before we completely lose control of the situation. Today is a good time to begin fighting back with greater vigor.'

Celestine closed the folder and looked off into space. He was a heavy-set man and his big chest rose and fell, sending his silver pectoral cross into motion.

'Is this my doing?' he asked. 'Did I push for change too rapidly? Did I misjudge the mood of the faithful? Did I not see the miracles that were right in front of my face for what they are?'

'Holy Father—' Elisabetta said gently.

The pope's eyes were moist when he said, 'Am I responsible for the greatest schism in the history of the Catholic Church?'

ONE

Tuesdays were clinic days at the cemetery. To an outsider it might have seemed odd that a mobile health clinic would choose a municipal burial ground as a base of operation, but to the slum residents of Malabon City in metro Manila, Tugatog was something of a safe zone. At least during the day. At night druggies scaled the walls and hung out among the concrete graves stacked in the air like condominiums, shooting up, smoking, snorting, doing deals. But daylight ushered in tranquility, and the poor and the sick felt protected and cloistered among the dead and their gentle mourners.

The Health In Action mobile van was parked in its usual spot near the main gate on Dr Lascano Street. The small staff of humanitarian volunteers – doctors and nurses dressed in the organization's light-blue polo shirts – was midway through a six-hour clinic when a teenage patient wearing thick glasses made it to the front of one of the lines. She was accompanied by her mother who looked so young she might have passed for a teenager herself. The girl was given a plastic chair under the van's shaded canopy where she sat listless, a little on the floppy side, wilted by the heat.

The nurse – a Tsino, a Chinese Filipino – glanced at the long line of patients leaning and squatting among the graves. She didn't have time for niceties.

'What's your name?'

The girl was slow to answer.

'Come on, child, do you see how many people are waiting?'

'Maria Aquino.'

'How old are you?'

'Sixteen.'

'What's the matter with you?'

Maria was slow off the mark again and her mother answered for her. 'She's been sick in her stomach.'

'How long?' the nurse asked.

'Two weeks,' her mother said. 'She's throwing up all the time.'

'Any fever? Diarrhea?'

Maria shook her head. Her hair looked like it hadn't been washed for a while. Her t-shirt was dirty.

'What time of day does she vomit?'

'Mostly in the morning,' her mother said, 'but sometimes later.'

'Are you pregnant?' the nurse asked, looking the girl full in the face.

'She's not pregnant!' her mother said, offended.

'I asked *her*,' the nurse said.

The girl answered strangely. 'I don't know.'

The nurse got testy. 'Look, have you had sex with a boy?'

Her mother pounced. 'She's only sixteen! She's a good girl. She goes to the church school. What kind of a question is that?'

'It's a question a nurse asks a girl who's throwing up in the mornings. When was your last period?'

The girl shrugged.

'When?' her mother asked.

'I don't pay attention.'

The nurse went to a shelf and took down a plastic cup. 'Maria, go inside the van and pee in this cup. Bring it back to me and wait over there. Next patient!'

The nurse blitzed through three more patients before remembering the cup of urine. She took a plastic testing stick, the kind that pharmacies sell to people who can afford them, and dipped it. Seconds later, she called Maria and her mother over.

'OK, you're pregnant.'

'She can't be!' her mother said angrily.

'You see the blue stripe. Pregnant. Remember having sex now, honey?' She didn't say 'honey' sweetly.

The girl shook her head and that made the nurse shake hers too.

'Let's have one of the doctors see you. Christ almighty, I'm never going to make it through the whole line.'

Inside the van, behind a privacy curtain, the doctor, another Tsino, glanced at the nurse's note and asked Maria to hop on to the small table. After a minute or two spent trying to see if the girl understood how one got pregnant, he gave up and raised the stirrups.

'What're those for?' Maria asked.

'Put on this gown and take off your underpants. You put your feet in those and you spread your legs. That way I can examine your reproductive organs.'

'I don't want to.'

Her mother told her it was all right. It was what women did.

The doctor put on gloves and a head lamp. He had to almost force her legs open wide.

Peering under the gown he grunted a couple of times then raised his head.

'OK, you can get dressed.'

'What? That's it?' her mother asked. 'That's not a proper exam.'

'There's no point in doing a manual exam or using a speculum,' he said. 'She's a virgin. Her hymen is intact. There's enough of an opening to let out her menstrual flow but this is a virginal hymen.'

'So she's not pregnant?'

'She can't be. It must be a false positive. We've got a rapid blood test I can do.'

'I don't like needles,' the girl whined.

'It's just a pinprick. Don't worry.'

Five minutes later, the doctor parted the curtain and came back in with the nurse. Both looked puzzled.

'The test was positive,' the doctor said. 'You're six to seven weeks pregnant.'

Her mother almost jumped out of her chair. 'But you said—'

'I know what I said. I'm afraid this is beyond me. I'm going to send her to the Jose Reyes Medical Center to see a specialist. There's got to be a good explanation.'

When mother and daughter left the van clutching the paper to present to the hospital, the nurse asked the doctor what he really thought was going on.

He confessed his complete bafflement and laughed nervously. 'It's been two thousand years since the last Virgin Mary. Maybe you and I just saw a goddamn miracle.'

TWO

Demre, Turkey

I n midsummer, the daytime temperatures on the south coast of Turkey soared oppressively but the evenings held the promise of cool Aegean breezes and easy sleeping. Cal Donovan enjoyed the fresh gusts wafting through the open windows as he showered and dressed, choosing his cleanest pair of khakis and last laundered shirt.

He stood in the sitting room of the small house he shared with his flatmate, Turkish archaeologist Zemzem Bastuhan. Zemzem looked up from his laptop and asked, 'Going out?'

'Thought I'd get a drink, Zem. Want to come?'

'Can't. Got to finish this. Have fun.'

The night air carried whiffs of roasting meat and fragrant spices. But Cal didn't walk down the hill toward the town center and its bars bulging with tourists, but uphill toward the excavation. If Zem had surprised him by tagging along it would have thrown a wrench in his plans, but it had been a good bet Zem would decline since he was a studious sort and not much of a drinker. The latter couldn't be said of Cal. Since arriving at the dig a month earlier, he had embraced the local liquor, raki, all but abandoning his vodka habit. Of course, the final common pathway for either beverage was the same: a bit of happiness, a bit of oblivion, followed by a bit of a thick head the next morning.

Cal was treated as royalty in these parts. As the co-director of the Turkish–American excavations at Myra he brought in vital funding from Harvard University and the National Science Foundation for a project that stirred national pride. Myra, a town in the ancient Greek region of Lycia, had been a pilgrimage destination for Byzantine Christians. Best known for the fourth-century church of Myra's bishop, St Nicholas – he of Santa Claus fame – recent archaeological work had begun to reveal a vast, remarkably preserved ancient Christian city beneath modern Demre.

Professor Bastuhan of Istanbul University had done much of the groundbreaking work at Myra but, short on funds, he had called on Cal to join the excavation as co-director.

Cal had leapt at the chance. He held a joint appointment as professor of the history of religion at the Harvard Divinity School and professor of biblical archaeology at Harvard's department of anthropology, but it had been a while since he'd done field work. Myra gave him the chance to oil his trowel and to give Harvard students the opportunity to spend summers working in Turkey. The only downside had been the curtailment of his usual summer research period at the Vatican.

Even in the dark, some local residents of Demre, out for an evening stroll, tipped their caps to him and murmured 'Profesör' as they passed. Closer to the dig, two Harvard grad students crossed the street to say hello.

'Working late?' Cal asked.

'Just finishing up some cataloging,' one of them said.

The other added, 'We're heading to Mavi's for a drink or three. Want to join us?'

'Maybe later. I've got a few things to do.'

'Geraldine's still up there.'

'Is she?'

He knew she was.

She was French and they had joked that all the good words to describe what they were up to – assignation, tryst, rendezvous – were French in origin. Geraldine Tison was a young archae-ology lecturer from the Sorbonne in her first year at Myra. During her first week at the dig, she had been working in the Quonset hut field office when she glanced out a window and noticed Cal climbing a ladder in a nearby cutting where he had been inspecting the remains of a newly exposed eleventh-century chapel. There was a pair of binoculars hanging on the wall and she'd been tempted to have a better look at the tall guy with muscular forearms and tousled black hair. But that would have been cartoonishly obvious.

'Who's that?' she had asked her Turkish colleague instead.

'That's the American co-director. Professor Donovan,' she replied.

'I expected someone much older,' Geraldine had said.

'Interested?'

'Perhaps. Perhaps not.'

That had been a half-lie.

The next time she saw him at the dig she left the hut and made her way toward the women's lavatories, flashing a shy smile as she passed, the equivalent of casting a lure into a pond. The fish hit the bait hard.

'Hi, I'm Cal Donovan,' he had said, stopping abruptly.

'Geraldine Tison.'

'From the Sorbonne,' Cal had said. 'Welcome to Myra. I was going to look you up. I make a point of meeting new faculty members.'

'As you can see, I'm here,' she had said melodically.

'Maybe we could grab a drink tonight to discuss the progress we've made this season,' he said. 'A bunch of us like to go to Mavi's Bar in town.'

'I'd like that.'

The dig was located at the outskirts of the town in an old olive-tree farm. Ground-penetrating radar revealed that the ancient city of Myra was vast, extending below much of modern Demre, but logistically the archaeologists could only excavate in undeveloped land on the periphery that they could buy from local farmers. The Quonset hut was a few hundred meters from the nearest cluster of cottages and on a moonless night the light from its windows was the only illumination in the area. The door to the hut was unlocked.

Geraldine looked up from the mound of pot shards on her desk. She was a specialist in Byzantine ceramics and quite adept at three-dimensional jigsaw puzzles. A pot of glue and a half-assembled pilgrim flask attested to that.

'You should lock the door when you're alone up here,' Cal scolded.

'Gareth and Anil just left.'

'I ran into them.' He bolted the door.

That was her signal to rise, switch off her desk light and approach him seductively, dangling a bottle of raki. She slowly drew closer until she was in his arms.

After the first long kiss of the night she came up for air and said, 'I needed that.'

'There's clearly more where that came from,' he said.

There was a canvas camp bed at the far end of the hut, a relic of the first years of the dig when someone would sleep there to protect the excavated artifacts from theft. Now, the decorative bronze, silver, and gold pieces unearthed during the season were kept in a heavy safe but the more pedestrian items like Geraldine's ceramics were stored in unlocked drawers. With the arrival of better funding, a security system had also been installed and wired into the police station but the bed remained. Occasionally used for a quick student nap, Cal and Geraldine had pressed it into different service. They were both single, but from Cal's point of view it would have been unprofessional to flaunt their relationship. Demre was something of a wild town in the summers but Turkey was a conservative country and, as co-director, he was leery of running afoul of the government. He couldn't bring her over to his house – Zemzem was always there – and she had roommates too, so this had been their *modus operandi* these past few weeks.

Their sex was as urgent and ferociously climactic as it had always been and afterwards, in the dark, she went to a place she had yet to venture. The future.

'You'll be leaving next week,' she said.

The bed was too narrow for side-by-side conversation. He got up and began to put clothes on to his sweaty body.

'Next Friday. It went fast, didn't it?'

'I was trying to slow it down.'

'Oh yeah? That's a trick I'd like to learn.'

'You do it by being in the moment as much as possible. It takes practice and a good deal of mental concentration.'

'Did it work?'

'Let's see,' she laughed. 'We've got another week. Back to Cambridge, I suppose? I've never been to Harvard. Maybe I could visit one day.'

Cal buttoned his shirt and looked down on her long, naked body. If he was honest he'd tell her that Demre might be their last time together. It wasn't as if he had lied to her these past weeks. They simply had never gone there, he'd assumed intentionally.

'Actually, I'm heading to Iceland before I go home.'

'Why Iceland?'

'Truth be told, I'm meeting a lady friend there.'

She sat up and crossed her arms over her breasts.

'I see. Is this a serious friendship?'

'Hard to say. I think the idea is to find out.'

She reached for her bra just as the doorknob turned and the bolt rattled. Outside a man spoke in Turkish.

'Get dressed,' Cal whispered.

A ghostly face briefly appeared at a dark window. Then a crash as a rock punched out a pane. A hand reached through, undid the latch, and pushed the broken window open.

In Turkish, the man said to his companion, 'It's OK. No alarm.'

Cal whispered for Geraldine to get under a desk.

'What are you going to do?' she whispered back but he was already creeping forward.

His plan was to make his way to the wall and get the burglar into a headlock before he hit the floor but the guy was fast as a cat and was inside in a flash.

The best way to deal with a cockroach was light. Cal threw the main switch and the hut lit up in a harsh fluorescence.

The intruder, a wiry fellow with sunken cheeks, froze when he saw Cal.

'You speak English?' Cal asked, leaning forward on to the balls of his feet.

The man was looking at Cal's hands curled into fists. 'A little.'

'Good. My Turkish isn't so good. You need to leave.'

A second man appeared at the window and said something in Turkish.

The inside man replied. Cal had hoped they would turn tail but it didn't look like that was going to happen.

He took another step forward to keep the burglar on the defensive.

'Open safe,' the man said, pointing a steady, slender finger.

'I don't have the combination. You need to crawl out that window or I'll throw you through it.'

With a practiced move, a sheath knife appeared in the man's hand and the second heftier fellow began to squeeze through the window. It wasn't going smoothly. He'd probably been waiting for his friend to open the door for him.

The thin man grinned as Cal backed away but the smile faded when Cal grabbed a push broom propped against the wall.

Cal moved toward him, bristles forward as the burglar backed toward the open window.

Cal was one of the faculty advisors to the Harvard intramural boxing club and he taught neophytes to seize the advantage whenever an asymmetry presented itself. It was better to bring a gun to a knife fight but at this moment, a broom would have to do.

He rushed the guy like a soldier with a fixed bayonet and caught him with the broom head to the Adam's apple. Grunting in pain, the man attempted to push the broom away with his free hand while thrusting the knife as close to Cal's body as he could manage. Cal backed off and charged again, bristles to face, pushing the burglar against the wall. When the man tilted off balance, Cal swung the broom in a tight arc, landing the wooden head hard against his skull. The *thwock* of wood against bone masked the sound of the broom handle splitting in a spiral crack.

Stunned by the blow, the man's hand opened. His knife fell to the ground and Cal swiftly kicked at it, sending it skittering under a bookcase.

Now the stout man's shoulders were fully through the window. He was about to let gravity do the rest. But before he could, Cal turned his attention to him and swung the broom. Unfortunately for the guy, the broom head fell away leaving a sharply pointed end that Cal used to stab a beefy shoulder. Howling, the man pushed himself back through the window and ran off into the night.

It was now Cal against the thin man and he traded one unfair advantage – the sharpened handle – for another, his fists, and tossed the spear aside. He edged toward the guy and towered over him in an aggressive stance.

That was all it took.

The burglar moaned, 'I go, I go,' and sidled toward the door, fumbling with the bolt until it gave way.

With the danger gone, Cal dropped to a crouch, sweating. He'd been rock-solid during the incident but now he felt himself shaking.

Geraldine emerged from her hiding place.

'My God, are you all right?' she asked.

'Yeah, I'm good.'

'I couldn't believe my eyes,' she gasped. 'How can you fight like this, Cal? You're a professor!'

'I get angry sometimes,' he said, breathing hard. 'It's something I've got to work on.'

THREE

The next day Cal was summoned to the police station in Demre to identify a suspect who had been detained. Cal was absolutely certain he wasn't one of the burglars although the detectives tried to convince him otherwise, to 'clear up the matter.' On his way back to the dig, walking through the town, dead quiet at this hour, his phone rang, showing a number from Vatican City. It was a monsignor asking if he was free to speak with the cardinal secretary.

The delightfully ebullient Cardinal Rodrigo Da Silva apologized in advance if he was interrupting something important.

'I always have time for you, Eminence.'

The two men were fast friends. Da Silva, a Portuguese-American, had met Cal years earlier when both of them appeared on an academic panel to discuss the history of the Catholic Church in Portugal. Da Silva had been bishop of Providence, Rhode Island at the time. Afterwards the two of them remained in contact and their friendship developed based on good food and good conversation. When Da Silva was elevated to cardinal of Boston, Cal was a personal guest at his investiture in Rome.

'How's Boston? I must say I miss it dearly.'

'I miss it too. I've been in Turkey all this month on a dig.'

'I can't keep up with you, Cal. You're quite the globetrotter. Alas, I am stuck like glue to my office chair.'

'Well, you sound chipper as usual.'

'That's because I like my boss. You know how important that is.'

'How is he?'

'He's well. He sends his warmest regards.'

It was Da Silva who had introduced Cal to Celestine. The pope had needed someone from outside the Vatican to help investigate a young priest who had developed the stigmata of Christ, and Cal had written a scholarly book on the history of stigmatics. Later, Celestine had called upon Cal from time to time to assist on other delicate matters best suited to someone working outside the groaning Vatican bureaucracy.

'Tell him I'd love to see him again soon. Unfortunately, I've got to skip my usual summer month in Rome. Hopefully I'll be coming around Christmas.'

'Ah, I see. Is there any flexibility to your travel plans? Turkey isn't a world away from Italy.'

'I'm leaving soon for Iceland.'

'Iceland! What's there if I may ask?'

'Tundra, hot springs, and a woman. And vodka, of course. Well, they've got something sort of like vodka called Black Death I'm keen to investigate. I'm meeting a friend from Boston for a getaway.'

There was a pregnant pause before Da Silva said, 'Far be it from me to interfere with your love life or your drinking life, but something has come up that's urgent enough for the pope to call an emergency meeting of the C8. He was rather hoping you'd be able to make it.'

The C8 was Celestine's kitchen cabinet, eight of his closest cardinal-advisors and confidants.

'What's going on?' Cal asked. He had to sprint past a shop blaring music on to the sidewalk. 'Is it something you can talk about on the phone?'

'Let's just say that we've got a problem involving four people. One is named George and three are named Mary.'

Cal instantly knew what Da Silva was talking about. George Pole was the American cardinal from Houston. And the Marys?

'You mean the Virgin Marys?'

'I do.'

'I thought there were two of them. The one from the Philippines and the one from Ireland.'

'There's a third girl the press doesn't seem to know about yet. She's from Peru. Pole's threatening to make some kind of open display of opposition if the Church doesn't affirm them as miraculous. The Holy Father doesn't want a public spat with the good cardinal but we don't wish to be seen as caving under his pressure.

Even if we had canonical grounds for embarking on a formal miracle investigation, you know how long that takes.'

'Pole knows that too.'

'Yes, well, we all know how George can be when he seizes on an advantageous political issue. We were hoping you might be able to quietly check into the matter and objectively advise us as to the facts.'

'Has Pole given you a deadline?'

'Two weeks from now.'

'That's ridiculous.'

'Isn't it?'

Cal sighed. 'I suppose I'd better make a call to my future ex-girlfriend.'

'Heavens, Cal, you certainly know how to make an old friend feel guilty.'

'Your Eminence, I'm half-Jewish and half-Catholic. I've got the guilt thing down to a science.'

Cal could picture the flare of Jessica's nostrils. It was a plastic-surgery nose, slightly upturned, expertly sculpted by a top man.

'I should have known better,' she seethed into the phone.

'This wasn't planned,' Cal said. 'It just came up.'

'If you only knew how many friends of mine warned me about dating you.' She used to tell him that in a teasing way but now she was being serious.

'It's hard to say no to the pope.'

'Am I supposed to be impressed that the pope is your best bud?'

'He's hardly that but we do have a history.'

Cal knew this was going to be a difficult conversation, but not because his fling with Geraldine was weighing on him. It wasn't. Sex on a dig wasn't really cheating. It was a whole other animal. Anyone in the business would tell you that digs were a free-fire zone. The call was going to be tough sledding because he knew how pissed off she was going to get about the change of plans. Optimistically he had hoped that the fact she was Catholic might help. It didn't. He held his mobile phone a few inches from his head to protect his ear drum.

'We've planned this trip for months. It's carved in stone in my calendar. This was supposed to be our first real vacation together, and here you go, fucking me up by playing the pope card. You may have the luxury of having your summers off like some kid but I don't. I've got a demanding job with a highly programmed schedule.'

She wasn't blowing smoke. She did have a big job.

They had met a year ago via one of these mutual-friend-arranged quasi blind dates, strategically choosing a restaurant in Cambridge's Central Square, halfway between Harvard Square where he worked and Inman Square, her lair. Neutral territory. The sparks didn't exactly fly on day one. It took a while for the flame to catch, sort of like lighting damp firewood. But to Cal, a slower burn wasn't a bad thing. His relationships that had started hot – too many to contemplate – tended to flame out fast. Exhibit 1: Geraldine. This thing he had with Jessica seemed to have some staying power. Maybe it was because of their symmetries. Both were in their forties and never married. Both had high-powered jobs. She was a PhD scientist, the CEO of a large biotech company, and at one time she had been the youngest female CEO of a publicly traded healthcare company. In the annals of Harvard University, Cal was one of the youngest faculty members ever to be named to a full professorship. Both were athletic head-turners and photogenic as hell. And both could hold their liquor – or in her case, wine. Her penthouse condo in Boston had something of a legendary wine cellar but she'd stocked it with a selection of rarified vodkas to keep him happy. Or maybe it was because they both traveled a lot and didn't see each other incessantly. Whatever the reason for their romantic success, with the anniversary of their first date approaching, Cal was no longer sure they'd make it there.

'Why don't you come to Rome instead? I'll take you to meet Celestine, get you a VIP tour of the Vatican.'

The line was quiet. How long did it take for blood to boil?

'I went to Italy the year before last,' she said angrily. 'I've toured the Vatican, thank you. I haven't been to Mass in over twenty years and dressing up demurely and curtsying to the pope isn't all that high on my bucket list. I want to go to fucking Iceland and I'm going with or without you.'

FOUR

The lettering on the side of the taxi said Golden Boy. Cal wasn't sure if that was the company's name or the driver's. Neither seemed particularly apt. The car was a not-new Toyota with a dent in one of the rear quarter panels and the driver looked like he needed a shave and a cigarette.

The doorman at the Peninsula Hotel in the fashionable Makati district had suggested that he might want to wait for a better taxi but Cal thought that Golden Boy was the perfect name for a vehicle to take him to a place called Paradise Village.

'You sure you wanna go there, boss?' the driver said, pulling into traffic.

'I'm sure. Why?'

'Little bit rough place. Even this time of day.'

This wasn't a revelation. He'd been warned in an email from Father Santos.

The driver wasn't finished. 'They got a lot of hitmen there. Wanna get a hitman?'

'I don't think I do. Hey, could you turn up the air conditioner?' It was only slightly cooler inside than out and it was sizzling outside.

'All the way up, boss. Gotta get some Freon. Think I gotta leak. Want me to fix it now?'

Cal rolled down the window. 'Why don't you do it after you drop me off.'

The name Paradise Village was even more ironic than Golden Boy. It was a sprawling shantytown in the Barangay Tonsuya district of Malabon City, riddled with illegal electric and water connections. According to an article he had read, and now essentially confirmed by his driver, the slum was something of a haven for Manila's contract killers.

After a slow journey through congested streets, the taxi pulled up to an iron gateway, a rusting piece of scrollwork spanning two utility poles with signage announcing Paradise Village.

'OK, boss, we're here.'

'Aren't you going inside?'

'You said you wanted to go here. Here we are.'

Cal had been told by Santos that there weren't any street names or numbers. He'd sent a hand-drawn map that Cal showed the driver.

'That's not so far. You can walk, I think. Besides, not safe to go in there and some places too narrow for cars.'

Cal reached for a few bills and went easy on the tip.

Crossing the threshold into the shantytown, Cal immediately attracted attention. Navigating by Father Santos's map, he began making his way through the narrow, unpaved streets followed by a growing entourage of children and teenagers, pointing at the tall stranger and bantering in Tagalog. Cal smiled and gave a small wave then tried to ignore the teenagers who were aggressively hey-mistering him for cash.

The streets were lined with makeshift houses constructed from a variety of cheap materials – cinder blocks, corrugated-iron sheeting, plywood. The place smelled of cooking pots and latrines. By the time he arrived at the lane that was his destination, he felt like a Pied Piper of sorts, with a large, aggressive posse of urchins in tow.

The lane was narrow; the taxi could not have passed. Halfway up the lane a gaggle of men stood guard before an iron grate that was the door of an unpainted, cinder-block house with wide, messy grout lines. As Cal approached the X on the map the gatekeepers pointed at him and moved to block his way. One man, all sinew and muscles in a tank top, angrily shouted at him.

Cal didn't speak a word of Filipino. He stopped a couple of arm's lengths from the shouting man and delivered as benign a smile as he could muster under the circumstances. The crowd of urchins behind him filled the lane and pushed forward, jamming him uncomfortably close to the shouter-in-chief. Over one of the man's powerful shoulders, Cal could see a riot of color on either side of the grate: flowers, candles in painted jars, photos of a girl duct-taped to the wall.

'Does anyone here speak English?' Cal said. He raised his voice to repeat the question then added: 'I'm here to see Father Santos. Is he here?'

One of the gatekeepers answered in English. 'No reporters allowed! Leave our Little Virgin alone. Get the hell out of here!'

'I'm not a—'

The crowd behind him surged forward, pushing him into the chest of the snarling, shouting brute.

The man pushed back with his battering-ram hands but there was nowhere for Cal to go.

The English-speaking guy had a tire iron in his fist. He pressed forward to the front of the line and raised the weapon high over his head.

Cal bellowed, 'Father Santos? I need your help! It's Cal Donovan. From the Vatican.'

Three days earlier

From the first day of his pontificate, Pope Celestine IV had lived and worked in one of the most modest of Vatican dwellings. When he announced that he would forego the traditional papal apartments in the Apostolic Palace overlooking St Peter's Square for two rooms in the Sanctae Marthae guesthouse, the wags assumed it was going to be a short-lived publicity stunt. It wasn't. The rotund and personable pontiff happily lived in a sparsely furnished bedroom, worked in an adjoining office, ate in the communal cafeteria where he chatted with Vatican staff and visiting bishops, and prayed and said Mass in the small guest-house chapel. His secretary of state, Cardinal Da Silva, one of Celestine's closest allies and confidants, opted for solidarity: after his recent appointment to the post, he too eschewed the lavish apartment provided to cardinal secretaries, opting instead for a guesthouse room close to the pope's.

Cal arrived at the Vatican after walking all the way from his hotel near the Pantheon. It was a warm, sunny Roman morning and the city pulsed with commuters going about their business amidst the alternative universe inhabited by tourists. In the lobby, several people recognized him and a few paused to exchange pleasantries. For the past few years he had been a regular visitor here but teaching and other commitments had prevented him from coming these past six months. The two men – the pope and the professor – had become more than acquaintances.

A pair of cardinals immersed in conversation passed. Cal knew the men, a Nigerian and a Spaniard. Both were members of the C8. They gave Cal knowing smiles and Vargas, the Archbishop of Toledo, paused to whisper to Cal that he was happy to see him.

'How is the Holy Father?' Cal asked.

'He finds himself challenged once again. It is not an easy job, Professor, but you know this.'

It was Sister Elisabetta who came to greet Cal, apologizing for the wait. Elisabetta Celestino – the young archaeologist who became a nun; the nun who'd been instrumental in defusing the crisis surrounding the pope's electoral conclave and in whose honor Cardinal Aspromonte had chosen the papal name Celestine; the woman whom the pontiff had elevated from her position at the Pontifical Commission for Sacred Archaeology to become his principal private secretary.

'I was early,' Cal said in reply.

Her flawless face was framed by the veil of her order, the Augustinian Sisters Servants of Jesus and Mary, a teaching congregation. He was always taken aback by a beauty so staggering that it was hard to reconcile it with the life she had chosen. But he always behaved impeccably around her, stamping out his natural urges to flirt.

'Ah, but we are running late. I do try to keep the trains running on time,' she said with a small smile. 'No easy task with the Holy Father.'

'He does like to talk,' Cal said.

Walking side by side down the corridor to Celestine's office, she told him that she understood he had changed his travel plans to attend the meeting.

'Ever been to Iceland?' he asked.

'I have not.'

'Neither have I.'

The pope was waiting with Da Silva and when he entered the small office space, the cardinal secretary stepped aside to permit Cal to bestow the pontiff with his full attention.

'It's wonderful to see you again, Holy Father.'

Celestine did what he always did when he saw Cal after the

passage of time: he reached up to clasp his shoulders and held the clench, all the while beaming and tilting his head up so he could look him straight in the eye.

'And you too, Professor. Such a pleasure to see you although I am plagued by guilt. Rodrigo has told me that I have interrupted your holiday plans. I cannot be any more sorry about this.'

Da Silva chimed in, 'How did your lady friend take the news?'

'About as well as I expected.'

'Then this is good news, no?' the pope asked, freeing Cal from his grasp.

'Actually, I was expecting it to go poorly,' Cal said, punctuating the sentence with a bit of a laugh. He caught Sister Elisabetta quenching a smile.

Celestine grimaced and let the subject die a quiet death. Elisabetta produced her notebook from somewhere in her habit and sat in the corner – her way of seeing to it that the meeting started promptly.

'So, Professor,' the pope began, 'we seem to have a problem with our dear friend, George Pole.'

Pole, as Cal knew full well, was no friend of this papacy but the way Celestine put it – without a trace of sarcasm – he might as well have been speaking of a true compatriot.

'Surely Pole can't be expecting the declaration of a miracle or even a miracles investigation,' Cal said. 'These occur during the process of beatification and canonization and that only occurs after a person's death. These girls are very much alive unless I'm ill-informed.'

'No, the three girls are certainly alive,' the pope said. 'Rodrigo asked George directly what he wanted. Tell the professor what he said.'

'He told me the Vatican must do something extraordinary in this case, even if it is without precedent. He said, "For Heaven's sake, Rodrigo, three virgins named Mary are pregnant and the Church is silent? I demand that this pope makes a spiritual declaration." So, I asked George what kind of declaration he had in mind.'

'What did he say?' Cal asked.

'He said that he wanted the beatification process to begin now. He didn't care that they were living. He said that if ever there was a case for the declaration of living saints, this was it. At the end, he's leaving it to the Vatican to decide on the form of this spiritual declaration but I got the firm impression that he wants us to formally open a Cause for Beatification and Canonization.'

Cal asked, 'And if you don't? What's his move?'

'He didn't go there,' Da Silva said. 'But knowing George it will be something loud.'

Celestine chuckled. 'What is it in English? George is media savvy.'

'But what does he expect to gain from this?' Cal asked.

Da Silva looked to the pope to answer but when Celestine remained tight-lipped, the cardinal responded. 'Above all, George is interested in making trouble for this pontificate. If we do something extraordinary he'll say he was the one who pushed us into action. If we do nothing or something less than he wants, he'll try to pillory us.'

'What can I do to help?' Cal asked. 'More specifically, what can I do in two weeks?'

Celestine stretched his arms over his prodigious belly and clasped his hands together. 'Professor, you are fair-minded, analytical, cognizant of the historical perspectives on matters of miracles and sainthood, and above all, someone we trust. It also helps that you are not part of the Vatican machinery. If I were to choose some bishop or monsignor for the task, his approach might be to seek the answer he thinks would please me. You will seek only the truth.'

'What is it you want to know?' Cal asked.

Celestine looked to the ceiling for inspiration. 'We have three Catholic girls named Mary between the ages of fifteen and seventeen spread across the globe, all allegedly virgins, and all becoming pregnant at roughly the same time. In each case we have obtained some basic information from the local parishes but the priests who are closest to these girls are not equipped to make any kind of reliable inquiry. We need you to visit these girls and their families and make your own assessment.'

'I'm not a doctor,' Cal said.

'We understand that the local priests have obtained some medical documentation,' Da Silva said. 'Collect these records, if you can, and we will have them analyzed in Rome.'

The pope nodded and said, 'It is even more important for me to get your impression of the circumstances of these pregnancies and what you think about the credibility of the girls and their families. I simply cannot properly react to this incredible situation without more information. Are we dealing with an improbable hoax with or without some nefarious purpose, or a grand constellation of miracles? This is the fundamental question.'

'Of course it's a hoax,' Da Silva said. 'Someone is behind this, if you ask me.'

The pope's mouth crinkled into a grin. 'Rodrigo, it is a good thing you were not in Bethlehem two millennia ago, in charge of the stables. You might have evicted the Blessed Mary.'

Da Silva was unmoved. 'Virgin birth happened but once in history. The Bible tells us of the second coming of Christ, not the second coming of virgin births. From what you've read of the two girls who've been reported on, what do *you* think, Cal?'

'I have no idea, which is probably a pretty good starting position for this kind of assignment. By the way, does George Pole know about the third girl in Peru?' Cal asked.

'He does,' Da Silva said, 'even though there's been no publicity about her. When I asked how he knew he told me it came to him from a South American prelate whom he wouldn't name.'

'Just so I'm clear,' Cal said, 'you're asking me to interview and research girls in the Philippines, Ireland, and Peru within two weeks?'

The pope looked apologetic. 'I know that this will be somewhat difficult, but Sister Elisabetta will get the travel office to make all the arrangements to make your journey as efficient and comfortable as possible.'

'Could I make a suggestion – well, a request?' Cal asked. 'Could I enlist the help of a trusted colleague? I have a former graduate student at the Divinity School, an Irish priest named Joseph Murphy who is now on the faculty at Harvard. Joe is a wonderful fellow, an excellent scholar, totally reliable. I bring him up because I know he's been closely following the news on the Irish Mary. She's from Gort, near his old parish. He's told me he knows the local priests. If he's available he'd be perfect. It would give me more time with the other two girls.'

'Very well, call your priest,' the pope said.

Elisabetta put her pen down. 'Where would you like to go first, Professor?' she asked. 'Lima or Manila?'

Cal shrugged. 'I'm in your hands.'

'I'll try to get you on a flight to the Philippines tomorrow,' she said, 'and I'll contact the girl's priest, Father Santos, to let him know.'

'Business class,' Da Silva told her.

'First class,' the pope said. 'It is a very long flight and I want my friend to be well rested for whatever he might encounter.'

Cal was so pinned down by the crush of bodies from the front and the rear that he couldn't even raise his arms to deflect the blow that was about to come down on him from the tire iron. All he could do was move his head to try to make the blow glancing. He forced himself to keep his eyes fixed on the weapon, black against the bright sky.

'*Itigil! Itigil! Sa pangalan ng Diyos, itigil!*'

Only later would Cal learn what Father Santos was shouting: 'In the name of God, stop!'

A large man might not have been able to work himself through the crowd but Santos was small enough to wedge himself through slight gaps and make his way to the man with the tire iron. The priest said something to him and the iron bar slowly lowered.

'Professor Donovan,' the priest said, reaching for his hand. 'I am so very sorry. You weren't injured, were you?'

'I'm fine, thanks, but this got ugly fast.'

'They are very protective of our Maria. But please, please, come inside with me.'

The phalanx of men parted obediently and Cal followed Santos inside the house. The room they entered was small, the kitchen and main living space, a threadbare rug thrown over the concrete floor, a few sticks of shabby furniture, an old propane cooker, and a sink with exposed and makeshift plumbing. Outdoors was populated by men; inside the guardians were women.

'Let me introduce you to the mother,' Santos said.

Maria's youthful mother was as brown as a hazelnut. Her

sun-baked skin seemed as tough as nut shells. She looked askance
at the tall American whose head came perilously close to the
ceiling, but gave a toothy smile when the priest explained that
this was the man they had been expecting from the Vatican.

'The Holy Father sends his blessings,' Cal said, and that was
true. After Santos translated and the woman had crossed herself,
Cal added, 'May I ask Mrs Aquino and her daughter some questions now?'

The woman nodded but insisted that Cal accept some orange
soda which he did with thanks. As he drank the sickly sweet
beverage he couldn't help thinking that it would have gone down
better with a shot of vodka. Returning the empty glass, he noticed
a bulging burlap sack beside the beat-up sofa.

'Mail,' the priest said, 'from all over the world.' A heavy woman
sat beside it snoring. 'That lady there, she's in charge of opening
the letters and taking out the money. I've no idea how much so
far but it's surely a fortune to this family.'

Maria was in a rear bedroom no larger than a closet, cross-
legged on a mattress laid out on the concrete floor, a coloring
book and a large box of fresh crayons on her lap. She looked up
briefly, cow eyes through glasses, checking him out, then lost
interest and picked out a new shade of green. Cal knew she was
seven months pregnant but it was hard to tell. Her pretty, lacy
top (a mailed gift from someone addressed only to Holy Maria,
Manila, Philippines) was billowy and concealing. He also knew
she was sixteen, but if he'd had to guess, he would have said this
tiny girl was thirteen, maybe fourteen.

Cal got down on his haunches, smiled and said, 'Hello, Maria,
my name is Cal. Can I see what you're drawing?'

The priest translated and the girl tilted the book toward him. It
was an Old Testament scene – Jonah inside the whale.

'Jonah looks pretty cozy in there,' Cal said. 'Do you know what
happened to him?'

The girl shook her head.

'He prayed to God and God made the whale spit him out.'

That made the girl giggle.

Maria's mother sat down beside her and Cal opened a recording
app on his phone. Santos also decided to squat so that all four of
them were at the same level.

'Ask if it's OK for me to make a recording. Tell them the pope would like to hear her voice.'

Mrs Aquino readily agreed and told her daughter that she must answer the questions truthfully because the Holy Father would know if she was lying. She reached for the girl's neck and pulled a small wooden crucifix hanging on a leather necklace from under her blouse so that it was visible to her inquisitors. Maria's brothers and sisters, all younger, shuffled in, one after another from their collective bedroom, obeying their mother's finger to her lips.

Cal cleared his throat and began with perhaps the hardest question while the girl was at her freshest.

'Maria, do you know how babies are made?'

She looked at her mother before replying, 'Yes.'

'How?'

'The boy plants his seed in the girl.'

'And do you know how the boy does that?'

There was another look toward her mother who nodded her permission to answer.

Maria stalled by taking the time to carefully choose her next crayon. She tested it out and said, 'He puts his penis here.' She gestured toward her privates.

'Did a boy do this to you?'

'No.'

'Are you sure?'

Mrs Aquino stepped in. 'Did no one tell the Holy Father she's a virgin? They saw this at the clinic and at the hospital. Maria is a good girl.'

Before Cal could tell her that these were routine questions, the girl volunteered an answer: she was sure.

'All right, Maria, I believe you. I'd like you to think back to about seven months ago. Did anything unusual happen to you? Something that sticks in your mind?'

'Like what?'

'Like anything that wasn't ordinary. Anything that you can remember. Just say whatever pops into your mind. There's no such thing as a silly answer.'

The girl closed her eyes and rolled her head around a bit theatrically until her mother told her to cut it out and answer the man.

She suddenly opened her eyes and said, 'There was a bright light. I remember that. Is that unusual?'

Cal had just stood to relieve a leg cramp but he settled back down to a squat to stay at eye level.

'That's for you to say, Maria. Do you think the light was unusual?'

'I guess.'

'Tell me more about the light. What were you doing when you saw it?'

'I was walking.'

'Where?'

'Here in Paradise Village.'

'Where in the village? At your house?'

'No, close to Lulu's house.'

'Where is that?'

The girl pointed in a general direction. Santos queried Maria's mother then told Cal that it was at the opposite side of the slum, maybe a fifteen-minute walk.

'Were you with your friend, Lulu, when you saw the light?' Cal asked.

'I was alone.'

'Was it during the day? The night?'

'It was dark.'

'What were you doing when you saw it?'

'I was going to Lulu's.'

'Did you see anyone on the street?'

'No, just the light. It hurt my eyes.'

'Did you hear anything? Any sound? A voice?'

'No. Not then.'

'When?'

'I don't know. Later, I guess.'

'A sound?'

'A voice.'

Cal swallowed and looked at Father Santos, who said quickly, 'She never told us this.'

'Was it a man's voice or a woman's?' Cal asked.

'A man.'

'What did he say?'

She said something but Santos didn't translate right away.

'What did she say?' Cal asked him.

'She say, "You have been chosen."'

Cal asked her to repeat that and she did.

'And were you on the street when the voice said this?'

'I don't know.'

'Where else could you have been?'

'I don't know. I don't remember.'

'Was the light still in your face when you heard the voice?'

'No.'

'OK, let's go back to when you saw the light. What did you do?'

'Do? I didn't do anything.'

'I mean what happened next?'

'I don't remember.'

'Did the light go away?'

'I don't remember.'

'Did you keep walking to Lulu's house?'

Her fidgeting turned to irritation and she shouted at him. 'I said I don't remember!'

Cal stood again and took a calculated pause to allow the girl to settle down. He sensed that Father Santos was going to berate her so he told the priest that it was OK.

He smiled at Maria and said, 'I'm sorry for all these questions. I came a very long way to see you. I have a few more to ask but when I'm done I have a gift for you from Pope Celestine.'

'What is it?' she asked eagerly.

'I'll show you soon. Can I ask more questions now?'

She nodded.

'OK, do you often go to Lulu's house at night?'

'I used to but not now. Mama won't let me out.'

Her mother said, 'Too many people. Everyone wants to touch her. The crowds are dangerous.'

'Where did you sleep that night, Maria?'

She thought for a moment. 'Lulu's.'

'You remember arriving there?'

A nod.

'Do you remember what you did when you got to your friend's house?'

'We looked at a magazine and then we went to sleep.'

'Did you tell Lulu about the light?'

'No.'

'The voice?'

'No.'

'Did the experience frighten you?'

'Yes.'

'Did you have any pain?'

'I don't think so.'

'Any pain down there, below your waist?'

'No.'

'Do you remember what you did when you woke up the next morning?'

'We played. There was no school.'

'And did you tell your mother about the light or the voice?'

'She didn't tell me,' her mother said.

'Maria, since that night, did you see the light again?'

'No, never.'

'Did you hear the voice again?'

'No.'

'And have you seen anything else that was strange or scary?'

'No.'

'Thank you, Maria. Mrs Aquino, do you remember the night Maria is talking about?'

'Not really. She used to go to Lulu's house a lot. It's bigger than ours and she has more toys. Lulu's father has a good job. My husband, may he rest in peace, got killed.'

'I'm sorry.'

'Do you think the Church would let us use the money people are sending to move to a bigger house?'

'I expect that's up to you, not the Church,' Cal said.

Father Santos concurred.

'Could we go back to that night?' Cal said.

Her mother thought and said, 'It must have been a Friday because she said there was no school the next day.'

'Do you always let her walk there on her own?'

'Yeah, it's no problem around here. They usually leave the kids alone.'

'Who?'

'The gangsters.'

'When she goes, what time does she usually leave your house?'

'After supper, maybe seven.'

Santos answered Cal's next question before he asked it. 'Seven months ago it would have been dark around then,' the priest said.

'Maria, is there anything else you can remember or would like to say about that night?'

'No, can I have my present now?'

It was a small jewelry box covered in red leather with an embossed, white papal seal. She quickly opened it, took out the gold crucifix and chain, and held it up for her mother to see.

'The pope blessed it himself,' Cal said.

'May God bless him,' her mother cried. 'Maria, you must never take it off.'

When they were done at Maria's house, Father Santos led Cal through the narrow streets of Paradise Village to the home of her friend, Lulu Ruiz. The girls were schoolmates. While it was impractical for Maria to keep attending school, Lulu was still a student and they had to wait for her to arrive home. Cal used the time to question the girl's mother and aunt about the night in question. They actually remembered it quite well because Maria had arrived for her sleepover later than usual and seemed in a bit of a daze.

'Her eyes looked funny,' her aunt said.

'Did she say something about what happened to her?' Cal asked.

'She didn't say anything.'

'She didn't mention a bright light?'

Apparently, she hadn't. Because it was late the girls had played for a while then gone to bed and that was that. The women didn't know anything more. When Lulu returned home wearing the uniform of her Catholic school, pleated skirt, white shirt and black shoes, she was even less helpful. She didn't remember a single thing about that night and she and Maria had never talked about it since.

'Maria used to come over a lot,' she said sadly. 'She doesn't come any more. I miss her.'

Later, waiting for a taxi near the entrance to Paradise Village, Father Santos passed along some of Maria's clinic records he'd obtained. He smoked a cigarette and asked Cal if he'd gotten anything of use from his visit.

'Obviously, not a lot,' he said.

'What will you tell the Vatican?'

'I suppose I'll tell them that I don't know what the hell is going on.'

'And where will you go next?'

'Halfway around the world to see another girl named Maria.'

FIVE

C al awoke in the dark, momentarily unsure where he was. The time zone changes of the last few days had spun his head like a roulette wheel. It was the sound of a street-music trio playing in the square for late-night tourists – a high-pitched ocarina, a charango, and a thumping cajón – that set him straight. He was in Lima.

He swore at the glowing digits of the bedside clock; it was too early to get up, too late to drink more vodka. He was stuck. He hated the little beggars but he popped an Ambien and waited for the chemical coma.

Predictably, he slept through his iPhone alarm – a poorly chosen one, the soothing bars of Brahms. It would take the blast of the room telephone to do the trick.

'Señor Donovan, your visitor is in the lobby.'

He squinted at the light-filled room and replied fuzzily, 'Which visitor?'

The front-desk clerk whispered, 'The archbishop, Señor.'

'Shit. Can you tell him to get a coffee? I'll be ten minutes.'

Cal flew through his ablutions and hustled down to the lobby restaurant where he found the cardinal sipping coffee and reading a newspaper.

'I'm very sorry,' Cal said on his approach. 'I broke down and took a sleeping pill last night.'

Cardinal Jaime Miranda rose to take his hand and give it a firm shake. He had been quite the athlete when he was young and, had he not blown out a knee, he might have become a professional footballer. 'God had other plans for me,' he was fond of

saying. He was young for a cardinal, only sixty-two, and he was
still lanky and muscular. He had been elevated by the previous
pope who really had no choice but to give the popular bishop
from Lima a red hat upon the death of Archbishop Aquirre.
However, Miranda had little in the way of political kinship with
the conservative pope and he had spent the bare minimum amount
of time in Rome. That had changed with the new pontificate. Pope
Celestine, the progressive lion and persistent reformer, wished to
surround himself with a like-minded council of advisors, and
Miranda was asked to join his Council of Eight, his kitchen cabinet
grafted on to the Vatican hierarchy to become Celestine's prow
of his ship of state.

'Having a few minutes on my own to read the paper was a treat,
Professor. Don't apologize.'

They had met a few times before at the Vatican and were on
friendly enough terms. Miranda knew with granularity the services
Cal had rendered the Vatican over the years and the admiration
that Celestine held for him.

Cal ordered a coffee and Miranda asked for a refill.

'You chose a good hotel in a good area,' Miranda said.
'Miraflores is highly desirable.'

'Sister Elisabetta chose it for me. I don't have my bearings yet,'
Cal said. 'It's my first time to Peru.'

'Really? When your business is done I'll have one of the monsignors take you around. Our Catedral de Lima is quite impressive
– it is not very far from here – and the city holds many wonders.
If you have several days you must go to Machu Picchu, of course,
but there are many other famous attractions.'

'I'm afraid I've got to get back to Cambridge but I'll make
plans for a proper visit before too long.'

'You've just come from the Philippines, I understand. A long
journey.'

'Very long.'

'And our Maria Mollo, she is your second or third Maria?'

'Second. A colleague of mine is investigating the third girl in
Ireland. He should be there now.'

'This is a very strange phenomenon,' the cardinal said. 'It is
hard to know what to think about it. On one hand, it is tempting
not to over-analyze and simply accept the miracle into one's

heart, but we must first make the proper investigations and exclude all ordinary explanations. That is why I am glad that the Holy Father has chosen you for the inquiry. You are his great and trusted friend.'

'I'm happy to help.'

'What was your impression about Maria Aquino?'

'Well, she's a sweet girl who seemed rather young for her age. I'm not an expert in teenage girls but in America at least, sixteen-year-olds are sixteen going on twenty. She was more like sixteen going on twelve.'

'She is from a poor family?'

'Very poor. She lives in a crowded and rather primitive slum incongruously called Paradise Village.'

Miranda leaned back and smiled. 'Paradise can be a state of mind. And what of her story?'

Cal recounted it, the cleric nodding at each beat.

'The similarities to our Maria are great, are they not? They even heard the same voice say to them, "You have been chosen."'

Cal perked up.

'Whatever are we dealing with, Professor?'

'I don't have answers yet.'

'Well, the diocese will assist you in any way we can. We have a cult of sorts forming around our virgin Maria. I consider it unhealthy and disruptive. At this point she is only a girl with a curious medical condition. She is a very long way from sainthood. The Church has but one Virgin Mary and any claims to the contrary are blasphemy. Tell me what you need.'

'Someone to take me to see her. Someone to translate.'

'My personal secretary, Monsignor Valdez, will do both. Can you be ready in fifteen minutes?'

'Of course. I'll just run upstairs and get my things.'

'Don't rush. Give me time to finish my coffee and newspaper.'

When Cal returned he saw Miranda in deep discussion with a priest whom he assumed was Valdez. The cardinal's demeanor had changed. He was frowning and making sharp gestures with his hands.

Cal joined the men and asked, 'Is something wrong?'

'This is Monsignor Valdez,' the cardinal said. 'Please tell Professor Donovan what you have told me.'

The sweat was beading on Valdez's forehead. He was breathing heavily, giving the impression he had been running.

'I received a call from the parish priest of the family of Maria Mollo not five minutes ago. The girl has disappeared.'

When the fog thinned out the mountain suddenly appeared. From a distance it looked pretty or at least festive. Hundreds, perhaps thousands of tiny houses studded the side of a steep slope, their pastel colors blending together, creating an impressionist canvas. At the peak, a large wooden cross pointed toward the shrouded sky. Below it, a huge red and white Peruvian flag was tattooed into the earth.

'That is where we are going,' Valdez told Cal. 'The San Cristobel shanty town. You see? God and country.'

The car climbed until Cal's ears popped and the pavement gave way to a narrow dirt road that rose steeply at first then more gently when the switchbacks began. The colorful houses that were dug into the mountain didn't look quite as cheerful up close. The walls were made of cobbled-together sheets of plywood and the roofs were overlapping pieces of rusting, corrugated metal. The pastels, so fetching from the valley, were peeling in the baking sun. Windows were simple cut outs covered by screens or makeshift shutters. Doors were ill-fitting.

Barefoot kids in scruffy clothes played in the dirt. When their way got blocked, Valdez leaned on his horn, waved his hand in backhanded swats, and accelerated until the kids dispersed. He did this far too aggressively and dangerously for Cal's liking but he held his tongue; after all, this was the cardinal's man.

'These peasants have too many children,' Valdez complained. 'They can't afford them. It perpetuates poverty. You know the night that Maria Mollo saw the light? Her mother has so many young ones she didn't even know her daughter was missing.'

Maybe the Church should re-think its position on birth control, Cal thought, but he kept that to himself.

A third of the way up the mountain the switchbacks ended. Valdez stopped the car and turned off the engine.

'Now we walk. Do not leave anything of any value in the car. These are very poor people.'

A steep dirt stairway cut into the mountain rose above them. The fog had rolled in again and the stairs disappeared halfway up.

'How far?' Cal asked, dodging some roaming pigs.

'Unfortunately, quite near the top. But it has not kept the crowds away. In the morning there is a steady stream of people who try to catch a glimpse of Maria. At night, they go back down. Today, with what has happened, I do not know what we will find.'

Cal wrinkled his nose at the fetid smells. The monsignor noticed and explained that toilets were merely holes dug into the ground. There were no sewers, no running water, no electricity. People had to lug their own jugs up the mountain or pay twice the going rate for bottled water from one of the little stores scattered around the slum. Maria Mollo had been heading to one of these stores the night she had been overtaken by the mysterious light.

Climbing higher, the crowds the monsignor spoke of materialized out of the fog, blocking their way.

'Move to the side, move to the side,' Valdez scolded. 'We are the representatives of Cardinal Miranda.'

The peasants tried to oblige, moving a few inches to their right on the narrow stairway, just enough room for Cal and the monsignor to advance. At the next plateau the crowd was fanned out at the next cascade of stairs and they had to fight their way through.

Nearing the end of the next run of earthen steps Valdez assured Cal they were getting close. On the plateau, the crowd was even more packed in and it took several minutes to squeeze through the throng of men, women and children, many clutching rosary beads. By the time they emerged at the entrance of the pale-blue shanty of the Mollo family, the monsignor's face was beet-red from shouting. Valdez knocked on the flimsy door with his knuckles and announced his presence.

In Spanish, an old woman told him that the virgin was not there.

'I know that,' Valdez spat back, knocking harder. 'I am Father Valdez, the representative of Cardinal Miranda.'

'Do you know where she has gone, Father?'

'I have no idea. Perhaps that is why I am here.'

The door opened a crack and a round-faced woman with black, stringy hair squinted at Valdez's face. She was cradling a baby.

'Is Father Díaz here?' Valdez asked.

'He left to go back to the church.'

'We need to speak to Maria's mother and father.'

'They are sleeping. They were up all night.'

'And who are you?'

'I am Maria's aunt.'

'Well, señora, wake them and tell them the cardinal's men wish to speak to them about Maria's disappearance.'

The woman shut the door in the priest's face and that clearly made him furious. He unleashed a torrent of grumbling. Cal's Spanish wasn't great but it was good enough; he didn't have to ask Valdez to clarify the situation. Instead he waited patiently in the sweltering heat and humidity, feeling claustrophobic from the crush of humanity to his rear.

The door finally opened and the aunt, still clutching an infant, invited them inside. The windows were covered from the inside with tacked-up towels so the room was as dark as a cave. When Cal's eyes acclimatized he was shocked at how impoverished it was. The sink was a plastic tub. The stove, a double ring attached to a can of cooking fuel. The furniture just a few sticks of salvage. Two girls and three younger, squirming boys sat on a small green rug covering a dirt floor. Cal would learn that the kids and the infant were Maria's younger siblings. All of them lived with their parents in this three-room shanty that almost made Maria Aquino's house in Manila seem affluent.

'My sister and her husband can't see you now, Father,' the aunt said, trying to shush the crying baby.

'Why is that?' Valdez demanded.

'They are too tired. Perhaps you can return another day.'

Valdez exploded, his voice rising over the baby's. 'This man is the personal representative of the pope. He has come all the way from the Vatican to investigate the case of their daughter. Now she has vanished and you want us to come back another day?'

The woman passed the baby to the oldest girl and said, 'Ask me your questions. I was here when Maria was taken. But I cannot understand your anger, Father. It was the Vatican that took her.'

Cal thought he understood but wasn't sure. An astonished Valdez translated for him.

Cal opened his recording app. 'What time was she taken?'

After Valdez repeated the question in Spanish, the woman said, 'Last night. About ten o'clock. The pilgrims had gone down the mountain. I was getting ready to go back to my own house. We had a knock on the door. It was a man and a woman.'

Cal shot her another question. 'Who did they say they were?'

'I don't remember their names. They said they were from the Vatican.'

'What language did they speak?'

'Spanish. Not Peruvian Spanish.'

'From where then?'

'I don't know. Maybe Mexico.'

'Did they show you any identification?'

'No, señor.'

'What did they want?'

'They wanted our Maria. They said that Pope Celestine sent them to take her to a safe place.'

'What place?'

'We didn't ask but her mother wanted to know if she would be able to speak to her. They said of course. They would send a man with a mobile phone to the house so we could speak to her. They said she would receive the best medical care because it was important that her baby would be healthy. They said we were too poor to protect the mother and baby.'

'How were these people dressed?' Cal asked.

'Like normal wealthy people. He was not a priest and she was not a nun if that is what you want to know.'

'After they said this, what happened?'

'They wanted to see Maria, of course. The woman gave her a fancy doll to play with.'

'OK, then what happened?'

'Maria's father said he didn't want his daughter to go. He said "to hell with the Vatican." He is not as religious as my sister, truth be told. And Maria is his eldest and he loves her a lot. He and my sister got into an argument.'

'What happened next?'

'The man gave my brother-in-law an envelope.'

'What was in it?'

'Money. Very much money.'

'How much?'

The woman whispered, 'Twenty thousand soles.'

Cal had changed currency at the airport. He did the math in his head: six thousand dollars.

Valdez whistled and told Cal in English, 'That is a year of wages for the average person in Peru. For these people it is more money than they could imagine in their lifetime.'

'And then your sister and her husband let them take the girl?'

'First they made them sign a paper.'

'What did it say?'

'I'm sorry, señor. I don't know.'

'Then what?'

'We all hugged her and they took her. They stayed up all night crying. Now finally they are sleeping a little.'

'And what about Maria? How was she when she left?'

'She was crying too. Crying a lot. She did not want to leave but the woman took her by the hand and led her down the mountain. Señores, you are from the Vatican. How is it that you do not know the pope took Maria?'

Cal looked at Valdez who remained stone-faced. It was going to be up to him to figure out what to tell her.

'The Vatican is a big place,' Cal said. 'I expect we simply were not informed. I'll make some phone calls to Rome to clarify the situation.'

'Please tell them to give our Maria lots of hugs and kisses from her family. We are praying for her,' the aunt said.

Valdez finally spoke up and said nervously, 'Yes, by all means, you must keep her in your prayers.'

SIX

It was a Saturday morning in Gort and with a little time to kill, Joe Murphy decided to pop into Saint Colman's church for Mass. He knew the church reasonably well because he had grown up in the area and had served as an assistant parish priest in nearby Galway. That assignment hadn't lasted as long as his

superiors had planned although that hadn't been a big surprise to
any of his mentors. They had suspected that the cerebral graduate
of Trinity College, Dublin might not be destined for a permanence
of parish service. Deep down, Murphy had known it too though
he had been determined to challenge his introversion and wonkish-
ness by getting out there and working with ordinary people with
real needs. Certainly, he had given it a good try. During his time
in Galway his superior had loaded up his plate with parish work
– counseling young couples as they contemplated marriage,
presiding over funerals and baptisms, talking people through bouts
of bereavement and despair. But living that life had disguised a
lie. He wasn't that priest, he wasn't that man.

One night he awoke in a panic, triggered by a dream of drowning
in water or quicksand (he couldn't recall which) and he understood
the ridiculously obvious symbolism. He was drowning in Galway.
He wanted his life of books and libraries and study back. He
investigated leading academic institutions without geographic limi-
tation, and with the blessings of his diocese bishop, he applied to
the Harvard Divinity School where he began studying for his PhD
under the tutelage of the world-renowned professor of religion,
Calvin Donovan.

During the course of Murphy's studies and dissertation work,
the two men had become friends in a chalk-and-cheese kind of
way. They amused each other. Cal the boozer and bon vivant versus
the abstemious and Spartan priest. Cal the womanizer versus the
priest who embraced his vows of chastity. Cal, the Hemingway
impersonator who pressed the squeamish Murphy to be his corner
man in amateur boxing matches. But if one were to draw Venn
diagrams of each man's passions, the intersecting area would be
scholarship. Murphy's thesis on St Benedict turned out well enough
to be published by the Princeton University Press and Cal had
used his considerable influence in securing Murphy a junior faculty
appointment at Harvard where he had recently started teaching
medieval ecclesiastical history to undergraduates. He had never
been happier. He loved his work, his music, his small circle of
friends, his prayerful quiet life. Returning to the west of Ireland
and County Galway to sort out a parish mystery did not contribute
to this happiness. Yet, when Cal asked him to jump his only
reasonable response was: 'how high?'

Sitting in a rear pew, Mass already commenced, Murphy's first thought was that he had taken a wrong turn somewhere. The priest wasn't speaking in English, or Latin for that matter. It was Portuguese. Then Murphy looked around at the sea of olive faces. Gort had changed, he would learn. About a third of the population of the small town was non-Irish, most of them Brazilian, employed in the local meat-packing industry. As a result, the cultural demands put upon the Parish of Gort and Beagh were so great that a Brazilian priest had been brought in to say Mass on Saturdays.

Murphy felt, and indeed was, conspicuous, a priest and a stranger coming up to the altar to take Communion. One man did recognize him – the Very Reverend Canon Michael McCarthy, who beamed from his spot in the chancel and approached the young priest before he could filter out with the parishioners at the end of Mass.

'Joseph Murphy! Whatever are you doing here?'

McCarthy had taught a few classes at Murphy's seminary, St Patrick's College, near Dublin, and they had bonded over their Galway connections. It was McCarthy who had helped Murphy get his parish job in his home town.

'Father McCarthy, it's lovely to see you.'

The canon pinched Murphy's black sleeve and said, 'I see you're still in our line of work. Have you come back to us?'

'No, no, just visiting. Thought my Portuguese needed some brushing up.'

'Amazing, isn't it?' McCarthy said. 'It's a small world. Our Brazilian brothers and sisters are good people and good Catholics. Fancy a little drink at the parish house or, better yet, the pub? Yes? Just give me a couple of minutes to change.'

Before long they settled into a dark booth at O'Donnell's, the older man with a creamy pint of Guinness, the younger with a half of lemonade.

'Some things haven't changed,' McCarthy said, teasing Murphy's drink. 'You haven't picked up any of the wicked ways of the Americans then?'

'Does Netflix count?'

'Well, I suppose it does.' He clinked Murphy's glass. '*Sláinte*. Tell me, how's your family?'

'Status quo, I believe,' Murphy said. 'Mum is soldiering on. She's picked up some additional grandmotherly duties along the way. Brothers and sisters still doing their farming and milking, their masonry and dry-walling. And making plenty of new future parishioners. All the things people in the west of Ireland do, I suppose.'

'Well that's fine. I expect the wounds are still somewhat raw. About your father, I mean.'

The old man had been drunk on his tractor, haying a slope way too steep – with the predictable result.

Murphy swallowed a mouthful of sweet lemonade. He'd never been much of a drinker (unlike his brothers) but since the accident he hadn't touched a drop, even feigning sips of sacramental wine during his final days of saying Mass.

'That they are. Particularly for Mum,' he said.

'Have you seen her yet? And the rest of your kin?'

He raised the canon's eyebrow by saying, 'They don't know I'm here, actually. I'm sure I'll see Mum before I leave. I'm not on the best of terms with my brothers and sisters. They accused me of abandoning her when I left for the States.'

'A man seeks to better himself and this is what he gets. Provincial thinking, if I might say so. Now then, you haven't told me why you're in Gort.'

'Mary Riordan. She's the reason.'

McCarthy took a deep breath. His mood shifted. 'Now what would you have to do with her?'

'I was sent here by my dissertation advisor at the university, Professor Donovan. He's in quite tight with Pope Celestine. He was asked by the Vatican to look into these Marys, to give an informed opinion based on the facts on the ground. Seeing as I'm a local fellow who knows the lay of the land, he thought I'd be able to make head or tail of what's going on in Gort while he's off seeing the other girls.'

'I've just read about the third Mary, the one in Peru who's gone missing now. Strange business.'

'It is,' Murphy said.

'Do you know the Riordans?' McCarthy asked.

'I don't believe we've crossed paths.'

'Well, Joe, they're not the easiest people, if you know what I mean. Kenny Riordan especially. A hard man if ever there was one. What was your plan, then? Were you going to just march over to their house and ask to come in?'

'That was my original plan. I was intending to visit this afternoon.'

'I hope you're bringing a fat purse.'

'He's charging for access?'

'He is. He and the missus are cashing in. They've got the whole family involved in the enterprise making relics and the like. Ten euros gets you a vial of water supposedly blessed by the girl. A twenty gets you a signed photo printed out on copier paper. Thirty gets you a selfie with her. A lock of her hair, or someone's hair – for all I know they're getting sweepings from the barber shop – don't even ask how much they're charging. You said it was your original plan. What's your current one?'

Murphy smiled. 'I'm hoping it's you.'

The Riordans lived in a rundown bungalow on the outskirts of town. Kenny Riordan hadn't worked in a very long while. He was on disability for a bad back. The local authority, suspecting that his back was just fine, had a man follow him around for a year trying to get a video of him playing golf or doing the tango but Kenny was too smart for them. He had the investigator dead to rights and always managed to grimace and lean on his cane whenever the fellow was about. His wife too was a benefits machine with an allowance for her diabetes and a steady stream of maternity and childcare benefits covering the eight children she had birthed. The bungalow, sitting on a nice piece of land, albeit on a busy road, was owned by the local authority and rented out to the Riordans at a fraction of the fair market rate, but really it was a matter of government money making a round trip.

Approaching the house in McCarthy's car, Murphy saw a string of pedestrians walking along the grass verge. The police weren't letting cars stop along the road so the pilgrims had to park in town and trek the half-mile or so to the house. To keep order, two police officers were on duty outside the house nearly all the time, causing Galway County councilors to grumble that the Riordans were practically a line item unto themselves in the council budget.

'You can't park here,' a policeman said, rapping on the car window.

Canon McCarthy lowered his window. 'Good day to you, Robert.'

'I'm sorry, Father. Didn't recognize your car. Is it new?'

'Indeed it is. The old lease expired, you know. May we park somewhere?'

'Just pull into the driveway behind Kenny's van.'

There were pilgrims at the front door who weren't best pleased to have queue jumpers appear, but these men were priests so what could they say? When he heard the bell, Kenny Riordan shouted through the closed door that they had to wait their turn like everyone else.

'Kenny, it's Father McCarthy. I'd appreciate a word.'

The door opened revealing a short man with a crew-cut, a generous beer belly protruding from a smart polo shirt. His boyish grin disappeared when he saw Murphy.

'Who's this?' Riordan asked suspiciously.

'This is Father Murphy. He's been sent here from the Vatican.'

'The Vatican, you say?'

'May we come in?'

Riordan had the dry-mouthed look of a man being raided by government auditors but he said, 'Course, course.'

The scene inside the lounge told the story.

Mrs Riordan, an obese woman three times the size of her husband, was sitting feet-up on a recliner, knitting, a cigarette burning in a full ashtray. In the corner, two boys and two girls, aged between five and ten, played with action figures. Mary Riordan, the star attraction, was sitting on the sofa, using a tray across her lap to sign photos for the two women gawking at her. Mary was vividly pretty, her black hair cut in a modern pudding-basin style, a silver crucifix on a chain lying over a starchy white shirt, bony knees poking out from under a pleated, plaid skirt. Murphy guessed it was her school uniform. Her mouth was fixed in a bored pout. On a sideboard were dozens of small vials filled with clear liquid, stacks of photos, a row of small cardboard jewelry boxes, presumably containing hair. There was a shoebox on the coffee table with a ten-euro note sticking out from under the lid. Kenny Riordan quickly picked it up and carried it into a back room.

The pilgrims scooped up their signed photos and asked Riordan how much they owed when he returned.

'Nothing, ladies. There's no charge.'

'What?' Mrs Riordan said, looking up surprised from her knitting.

'Hush now,' her husband scolded.

'Can we take a photo?' one of the women asked.

'Yeah, sure, go ahead,' Riordan said, looking straight at Murphy.

Before leaving, each woman touched Mary's pale hand then crossed themselves. Riordan ushered them out the door and let the people in the queue know that there'd be a bit of a delay before their turn came. Church business and all.

'So, what can I do for you, Fathers?' Riordan asked.

'Good little earner you've got going for yourself,' McCarthy said.

The man looked wounded. 'I don't know what you mean. People want to see our Mary, don't they? For good reason. If some of them want to make a small donation to support her and her family, there's no harm in that, is there?'

'We're not here to shut down your operation, Kenny,' the priest said. 'Father Murphy here has been sent by the Holy Father himself to ask Mary a few questions.'

'The Holy Father, you say? Well, ask away, Father. Just don't take too long on account of all the fine people who've been waiting patiently for their moment in the sun.'

'I'll try to be as quick as I can,' Murphy said.

Riordan cracked a smile at Murphy's Galway accent. 'You're a local fellow, are you not?'

'I am. Or at least I was. I live in America now.'

'Well, that's fine. I could tell from your name you weren't Italian but it's nice to see a local man with enough rank to get a Vatican nod.'

Murphy pulled up a chair to be closer to the girl.

'Hello, Mary, it's nice to meet you.'

Her pout remained unchanged. Murphy was just one more face. She was even prettier on second look, and she was exceedingly well-developed for just seventeen, flaunting it in a tight blouse that would have turned the heads of boys a good deal older.

'I wanted to ask about when all this started,' Murphy said. 'Can you cast yourself back to that night?'

It was her mother who answered from her recliner. 'She was out that night, in town. She and her friends were doing something of a pub crawl. She's only turned seventeen but there are landlords who'll still serve them, you know. When I was a girl they all used to serve us as young as thirteen or fourteen. I remember when—'

Her husband interrupted her, 'Jesus, Mary and Joseph, Cindy, if you go on like that the queue at the door will reach back into town.'

'Sorry,' she said. 'Anyway, after closing time, Mary and her mates split up – the other girls live on estates in town – and Mary began walking home. It's about a mile, isn't it?'

'I wonder if I might hear this from Mary?' Murphy said.

The girl sighed heavily and said, 'Like my mum said, I was walking home on my own.'

'You said goodbye to your friends. All of them girls?'

'Yeah.'

'No boys about that night?'

'I don't actually know any boys,' she said sarcastically.

'Don't be fresh,' he father warned.

She made a face at him and said, 'In the pubs, sure, but not after.'

'All right. What happened to you when you were walking home?' Murphy asked.

'I've told the story so many bloody times already!'

Her father raised his hand from across the room. 'Would you just answer the man's questions? We'll have a riot outside!'

She rolled her eyes. 'All's I remember is that I'd just gone past the SuperValu Mart when I was, like, blinded by a super-bright light.'

'What color was the light?'

'I don't know. Maybe white or yellow, I suppose. It hurt my eyes terrible.'

'Had you seen anyone on the road before that moment?'

'No. No one.'

'Did you hear anything unusual?'

'What, then?'

'Yeah, when the light hit you.'

'Not a thing.'

'But you heard something later?'

'I suppose it was later – just when I can't say – but I heard, very distinctly, a bloke's voice, a deep old voice saying, "You have been chosen."'

Murphy screwed up his face. 'Now that's a remarkable thing to hear, isn't it?'

Her mother answered. 'It is indeed. Do you think it was the Lord's voice, Father?'

'I honestly couldn't say,' Murphy said. 'After the light, and after the voice, what is it you remember next?'

'That's the thing. Nothing at all until I was walking down the Tubber Road closer to my house.'

'And no one was about?'

'Not a soul.'

'How much time had elapsed?'

'I looked at me phone when I got home. It was two in the morning or thereabouts.'

'And what time did you leave the pub?'

She wasn't sure but her father said that it was a Saturday so closing time would have been around 12:30.

'So, there's up to a ninety-minute gap to account for,' Murphy said. 'When you got home did anyone see you?'

'I woke up me mum when I came in.'

Her mother nodded. 'I like to sleep in this chair, on account of my breathing. I said to her, "What have you been up to, missy?" She looked a bit dazed. She didn't have a clue. I scolded her for drinking too much and staying out late and she went to bed. Didn't make much of it, really. Girls that age do mess about but Mary's a good girl, Father, if you know what I mean. Imagine my surprise when later on her friend stopped coming and we found out she was pregnant. Especially what with her being a virgin and all.'

'That night, Mary, could you describe how you felt when you found yourself on the Tubber Road?'

'Felt? Confused, I'd say.'

'Any pains anywhere? Any discomfort?'

'Don't recall.'

'And just to be clear, had you messed about with any lads that night?'

She became animated for the first time. 'No!'

'She's never had no relations, Father,' her mother said. 'All the doctors and nurses have said so.' Then she whispered, as if the girl couldn't hear her perfectly well, 'She was intact down there, they said.'

'Mary, this is quite important,' Murphy said. 'Can you confirm to me that you've never slept with a boy.'

'No, never,' she said quietly, avoiding eye contact. 'I think I'd remember that, don't you think? You remember your first time, don't you, Father?'

Her mother giggled but Kenny Riordan yelled at her for being fresh again.

Murphy regrouped. 'Do you know what I mean when I use the word ejaculate?'

She smirked and nodded.

'Did a boy ever ejaculate on you or your clothes?'

'Father, what a question!' her mother said, lighting another cigarette.

'No, never,' Mary said.

Murphy clicked his pen. 'Very well, are you a religious girl?'

'How do you mean?'

'I mean, do you go to church? Do you pray on your own?'

'We don't go to church, really.'

'Well, that's not true,' her father said defensively. 'Didn't we go to midnight Mass a Christmas or three ago, mother?'

Canon McCarthy felt the need to say, 'Kenny Riordan, I don't recall a single time I've ever seen you or your family inside my church.'

'Well, you're a busy man at Christmas, Father, and we were probably at the rear.'

'What about prayer?' Murphy asked the girl.

'I pray sometimes, I suppose. Lately.'

'And whom do you pray to?'

She said it so softly Murphy almost didn't hear it. 'The Virgin Mary.'

Kenny Riordan began weaving when he hit the night air, the victim of his local celebrity; these days fellows bought him pints without expecting him to reciprocate. Even though it was summer, there was a touch of a chill so he buttoned his tweed sports coat over his gut.

He hadn't walked more than half a block when he heard, 'Is that Mr Kenny Riordan?'

Wheeling around unsteadily he saw two men under a street light. Not young, not old, they wore motorcycle jackets. One tossed down a glowing cigarette stub.

'It is. Do I know you gents?' It was true. He didn't know them but he'd seen them at some of his watering holes from time to time.

'We know who you are, Kenny. What do you say we buy you a drink?'

'Well, I've had a skin-full tonight, lads, but I appreciate the offer.'

The second man was more direct. 'I've got something in my jacket that I'd like to show you. Come on over here.'

Riordan swallowed as the man undid a zipper. He half expected to see a pistol in his hand but in the glow of the lamplight he saw something else. An envelope. Curious, he weaved toward them.

'It's a thick old boy, isn't it?' the man said. 'Guess how much cash it is?'

'Wouldn't have a clue, son.'

'Hundred euro notes. Hundred of them. Interested?'

Once the priests had left that afternoon, Riordan had kept his door open into the evening, clearing all of three hundred euros from the punters. Plenty of selfies and photos but he hadn't shifted a single lock of hair. Ten grand sounded, well, exceedingly grand.

'Does a bear shit in the woods?'

'We'll take that as a yes,' the first man said. 'Want that drink now?'

'I couldn't believe my ears when you called last night. You might have told me you were coming to Galway.'

Murphy's mother looked well, he thought. A little grayer, perhaps, a little thinner, but not so different from when he'd seen her last.

'It was a last-minute type of thing. I had to come on business.'

'What sort of business?' she asked, starting the tea.

'Church business.'

'You're sounding awfully enigmatic. Church business! You're a lecturer these days.'

'Mary Riordan, if you must know.'

'Whatever does a university lecturer have to do with Mary Riordan?'

He explained how he had come to be recruited. Then she was all ears, wanting to know as much about the affair as he'd tell her. But she was disappointed. Apparently, he hadn't learned much more than what was already in the papers and supermarket gossip.

'I expect the Vatican hasn't the choice but to investigate this kind of business but I'll tell you what I think,' she said, offering up some biscuits.

'And what would that be?'

'I think she got knocked up the old-fashioned way.'

'The doctors say otherwise.'

'Local doctors. Lot of good they did for your pa.'

'A tractor rolled on to him. What could they do?'

'He was alive when he got to hospital. Don't forget that.'

Murphy didn't fight her. 'Well, anyway, it wasn't just the local quack, Mum. They bought in a consultant gynecologist from Dublin to look over her case.'

She dismissed him with a wave. 'Don't be surprised if the baby resembles the boy who sits behind her in geography class.'

'Well, we'll see about that in about two months.'

They talked for a while about brothers and sisters, nieces and nephews, two of them born since the last time he'd been in the country.

'Won't you go pay a visit?'

'I've got to go back to Boston in the morning.'

'I do wish you'd reconcile with them. You're not the oldest but you're the wisest. They could do with you in their lives.'

'Next time, perhaps. When I'm here longer.'

When he left her it was with a hug and a kiss and some tears in her eyes. Outside the quiet cul-de-sac, two Honda motorcycles were on their stands. The riders had their helmets off, straddling the bikes. They dismounted and approached him before he could reach his rental.

'A minute of your time, Father,' one of them said pleasantly enough while the other stared coldly.

'Yes, what is it you want?'

'You've been making some inquiries concerning Mary Riordan.'

Murphy glanced back at the house to see if his mother was looking out the window. The lace curtains were closed. 'And what business of yours is it?'

The question was ignored. 'You may be from here but you're not one of us anymore.'

'Is that so?' Murphy said.

'It is and we don't want outsiders meddling. Do you understand what I'm saying?'

Murphy kept his eyes on the quiet one, motionless like an obedient hound awaiting a command. He'd never been on the receiving end of violence. Surely his clerical collar would be a shield, but what if it wasn't? He suddenly wished he'd taken up Cal's offer to teach him to box.

'And how exactly am I meddling? There are those within the Church who are concerned about the girl and want to ensure her wellbeing.'

'We're not here to debate you, Father. We want outsiders such as yourself to give the girl and her family a wide berth. May I ask when you're leaving Galway?'

'May I ask you who sent you lads?'

'I'll say this directly, Father Murphy. Stay away from the Riordans or you'll be sorry. By the way, lovely house your mum's got. We weren't aware she lived here until this very day.'

SEVEN

'Come on in, Joe.'

Cal was in his office at the Divinity School, catching up on a tall stack of mail, journals, and inter-office memos. When Murphy plunked down in a chair Cal took one look at him, got up, and poured him some coffee.

'Appreciate it,' the priest said.

'You look like shit,' Cal observed.

'And you don't?'

They got the conversation about the ravages of jet lag off their chests and began comparing notes on the three girls. They were going to be Skyping with the Vatican in half an hour so they tried to keep the debriefing tight, but Cal couldn't get over the incident at Murphy's mother's house.

'What do you think was behind this?'

'Haven't a clue. It seemed to be something more than locals circling the wagons to protect a member of the clan. I mentioned the incident to Canon McCarthy and he was likewise baffled.'

'Who were they? Did you find out?'

Murphy shook his head. 'I asked around but I didn't have names, so no.'

'Did you call the police?'

'I didn't. There wasn't really a specific threat, just some free-floating menace and a surfeit of testosterone. To be honest I was more interested in coming home than launching an investigation.'

Cal's computer announced an incoming Skype call. Cardinal Da Silva and Sister Elisabetta waved and smiled from an ornate office. Da Silva must have had some formal business to conduct because they were in the secretary of state's office in the Apostolic Palace rather than his guesthouse office space.

'You haven't met Father Joseph Murphy,' Cal said.

Murphy said hello and Sister Elisabetta was quick to thank him for his assistance.

'So, Cal,' Da Silva said, 'we are anxious to hear your opinions about the girls.'

'Of course, but have you heard anything about Maria Mollo?'

'Unfortunately, nothing,' the cardinal said. 'We're told the parents haven't heard from her yet. The Peruvian police were notified and we believe they are conducting an investigation but we have no further information. It is a deeply troubling situation.'

'What about the others?' Cal asked. 'Do their parents and local authorities know what happened in Peru?'

Elisabetta said, 'We immediately contacted the parish priests in Manila and Gort to inform them about the situation in Lima.'

'What did you tell them?' Cal asked.

'To be on the lookout for anyone who offers money or any other inducements to take the girls and to be aware that the Vatican is not behind any such actions.'

Cal expressed his approval and referred to the list of talking points he had hurriedly drawn up while conferring with Murphy.

'OK. So, here's the story. Joe and I have compared notes, and the similarities among the three girls is striking, to say the least. First and most obvious is their names. Second, and equally obvious, they're all Catholic. Third, they are about the same ages. Mary Riordan is seventeen now but was sixteen at the time of the incident, as was Maria Aquino. Maria Mollo is fifteen. Fourth, they're all from poor, uneducated families. Fifth, they all disappeared at nighttime, walking alone on quiet roads. Sixth, on the nights in question, they all have vivid memories of a bright, blinding light and then hearing a disembodied male voice telling them that they had been chosen. Then nothing further until an hour or more later when they *wake up* – I'll put that in quotes – and find themselves walking again, nearer to their destinations. Seventh, when found to be pregnant, all of them had virginal hymens. This seems to be backed up by photographic evidence. The girls all say that they have never had sex of any kind. I've got to stress here that I can't vouch for the medical aspects of their cases.'

Elisabetta said, 'Sorry to interrupt but we have had a top gynecologist in Rome review the medical evidence and she tells us in her report that with the proviso that she has had to rely on the examinations of others, the hymens of the girls are absolutely incompatible with sexual relations. Furthermore, regarding the questions raised by the media and others about artificial insemination, our consultant tells us that the procedure can only be performed by inserting a speculum as one would do in a pelvic examination. That would tear the hymen in the same way that sexual relations would. And by the way, she has reviewed the sonograms and also confirms that all three babies are male. Please continue.'

'Eighth, when the estimated dates of conception were calculated based on the timing of the missed periods and the size of the fetuses on sonograms, there is, as I understand it, a high degree of confidence that conception occurred the nights that the girls saw the lights and had the unexplained time lapse.'

'Our gynecologist says the same thing,' Elisabetta added.

'Ninth, the three events described by the girls occurred within two weeks of one another. Mary Riordan was the first, followed

seven days later by Maria Aquino, followed five days later by
Maria Mollo. Tenth, the parents of the girls have all, in one way or
another, cashed in on the phenomenon. I can't say as I really blame
them. These are once-in-a-lifetime opportunities to lift them out
of poverty.'

The cardinal leaned into the camera. 'Is there any possibility
that these three families have had contact with one another before
or after the pregnancies occurred? Could there be some collusion
to pump up the noise, as they say?'

'The two families I visited don't even have telephones. They're
dirt poor and very unsophisticated. I'd put the chances at zero.
Joe?'

'Well, Ireland isn't the Third World, you know, but I don't think
that the Riordans could put pins in a map locating Peru or the
Philippines, let alone figure out how to contact someone in these
places. I'd agree with Cal.'

'Finally,' Cal said, 'with regard to the veracity of the girls'
statements – and here I had to rely on the local priests in Lima
since I couldn't see Maria Mollo – we believe the girls are telling
the truth about what happened to them the nights in question and
about their lack of sexual experience. They do not appear to be
deceitful or devious.'

'So, where does that leave us?' Da Silva asked. 'Give us your
opinions.'

Cal tapped Murphy on the shoulder and said, 'I think a good
place to start is with the Bible. I asked Joe to dip into the New
Testament to find biblical parallels to our modern Marys. Joe?'

'Well, the Gospel of Luke is where most of the action lies,'
Murphy said. 'It's Luke who tells us that the angel Gabriel comes
to Mary to inform her of her chosen status by telling her, "Hail,
favored one! The Lord is with you." Luke tells us that she was
greatly troubled at what was said and pondered what sort of greeting
this might be. Then the angel said to her, "Do not be afraid, Mary,
for you have found favor with God. Behold, you will conceive in
your womb and bear a son, and you shall name him Jesus. He
will be great and will be called Son of the Most High," etcetera,
etcetera. Now we come to this bit: "But Mary said to the angel,
'How can this be, since I have no relations with a man?' And the
angel said to her in reply, 'The Holy Spirit will come upon you,

and the power of the Most High will overshadow you. Therefore the child to be born will be called holy, the Son of God.'" Now, there's nothing in Luke or anywhere else about how Gabriel appeared to Mary – certainly nothing about a bright light – nor is there any description whatsoever in the scriptures of the moment the Holy Spirit came to her. Having said that, one might conceivably see some biblical parallels in the testimonies of our present-day Marys. Moving on, Cal also asked me to research the biblical references to the Virgin Mary's age. In short, there are none. Most biblical scholars make reference to the usual age of betrothal under Jewish law at that time in history. Jewish custom was that marriage before the age of twelve was not allowed and brides were generally no older than fifteen. So, our modern Marys are near this range. All right then, that's my bit.'

Cal smiled. 'Thanks, Joe. Any questions?'

'Thank you, Father Murphy,' Da Silva said. 'I do enjoy a good Bible lesson.'

'So,' Cal said, 'I suppose the central question here is whether we're dealing with something with a rational scientific/biological explanation versus a spiritual/religious one. We already know that these girls or their families can't be accused of perpetrating a hoax. They are very much pregnant and are very much virginal.'

'Precisely,' the cardinal said.

'Let's start with spiritual explanations. By the very nature of the beast it's impossible to find direct empirical evidence to explain an intrinsically spiritual event. As you well know, this is the fundamental issue into any miracles investigation. Essentially, conclusions on the veracity of a miracle claim must rest on the absence of a persuasive alternative explanation.' Cal realized he was sounding awfully professorial. 'Look, it's a process of elimination. If you can't figure out what the heck is going on after trying your damnedest then maybe, just maybe, you're looking at a miracle. Over the last century, nearly all of the miracles claims bubbling up to the Vatican for formal investigation have involved disease cures arising from the intercession of a putative saint. These cures generally happen in incurable diseases and they need to be spontaneous, often instantaneous and complete. Credible doctors have to certify that there's no natural explanation for what happened. Now pregnancy isn't a disease – though if it happened to one of my girlfriends *I'd* feel ill – but the approach has to be much the same.'

Cal paused to see how his unfortunate quip had gone over. Elisabetta was frowning. He was about to apologize when she spoke.

'It seems to me that we have eliminated the two rational and scientific ways that these girls may have become pregnant,' she said. 'These are sexual intercourse and artificial insemination. Their undeniable virginal anatomy excludes these. That leaves a phenomenon I know very little about other than its Wikipedia page, and that is parthenogenesis: asexual reproduction where an embryo develops without fertilization.'

'Actually, I was just going to bring this up. I'm with you on this,' Cal said. 'I looked at the same Wikipedia page. I was going to flag it as something we needed to get an expert opinion about.'

'For sure, we will find an Italian expert,' Elisabetta said. 'But as this is an important condition for us to understand and to confidently defend, two opinions would be useful. I wonder if you could also find an American expert, perhaps from Harvard or one of your other Boston institutions?'

Cal thought about it for a moment. A name came to him along with a spasm in his gut. 'I think I've got someone.' Then he said, 'The other factor I was going to raise is DNA. Once the babies are born we're going to have a lot of interesting data.'

'For sure, but we will have to wait for two months,' she said. 'Our curiosity must surely take a back seat to the small but real risks of amniocentesis.'

'Well,' Cal said, leaning back in his chair, 'I suppose it's not completely premature to talk about spiritual explanations. Aside from the overwhelming significance of virgin birth to Christianity, one of the unifying experiences each girl describes is being interrupted on her journey by a blinding light. Light is the universally defining aspect of divine presence. This is not limited, of course, to Christianity – it's thematic in most religions. One nicely representative image in Christianity comes from Acts Nine where Saul is on the way to Damascus.' Cal reached for his notes and read, '"And suddenly there shined around him a light from heaven. And he fell to the earth, and heard a voice saying unto him, Saul, Saul, why persecutest thou me? And he said, who art thou, Lord? And the Lord said, I am Jesus." Now there's nothing about the Virgin Mary experiencing a light in association with her visitation by Gabriel but the presence of blinding light in the stories of our Marys is an element that has to be included in any analysis. The girls also heard voices proclaiming their chosen status. I'd say that tilts the balance toward the spiritual end of things, but that's just me. I'll defer to the Vatican on the spiritual judgments. Could I ask what you think, Your Eminence?'

The cardinal's sigh came through the speaker loud and clear. 'What do I think,' he repeated. 'What indeed? If this is not a miracle it is a very big headache for the Church. If it is a miracle it is the biggest one since the Gabriel told Mary what was going to happen to her. Please do whatever it takes to shine a light – divine or otherwise – on this matter.'

Jessica Nelson was still angry.

A woman to her word, she had gone to Iceland on her own and, apparently, she had not enjoyed herself. Cal let her vent, shaking his head and scrunching his chin compassionately as she recounted each of the indignities she had to endure as a single woman fending off the advances of men of all nationalities at hot springs, hotel bars, and the like, but he suspected she rather got a kick out of busting balls – both theirs and his.

'I especially didn't like the food,' she said, changing the subject. 'Someone talked me into trying fermented shark.'

'Dinner tonight is but the first step in a long and arduous program to rehabilitate myself,' he said.

The tasting menu at Menton in Boston – not far from Jessica's condo – was almost three-hundred dollars a head with the wine pairing. He wasn't fooling around tonight. That was mainly because he liked her more than a little and felt guilty about pulling out of the Iceland jaunt. She was tall and brassy, an attractive motor-mouth who spewed out super-interesting facts and opinions about – well, almost everything. Cal was a confident guy but her level of self-assurance dwarfed his own not inconsiderable ego and he liked that too. Many of the women he'd dated were in awe of his accomplishments and he tired of being on a relationship pedestal. Jessica was very much his equal – athletically, financially, and accomplishment-wise.

Of course, the other reason for the hard-fought date was that he wanted to pick her brain.

'Parthenogenesis?' she asked midway through the main course. 'Why the hell are you interested in that?'

He told her what he'd been up to while she'd been touring volcanoes. The plates were being cleared for dessert when he finished.

'Trust me,' she said finally. 'This isn't parthenogenesis. I'm a geneticist. Want to know what I think?'

'I do, Jessica. That's why I'm asking,' he said, throwing back the rest of his third vodka on the rocks.

'I think these girls got knocked up the old-fashioned way.'

'Their hymens were intact.'

'Oh, and you're an expert on hymens?'

'No – although I do have a fair bit of amateur-level experience with female anatomy,' he said with a smile. 'But some real experts have examined the girls and studied the photos. Tell me why you're dismissive of parthenogenesis.'

'Because your Marys aren't insects or lizards or fish. No mammalian species is capable of giving birth without a father. First of all, mammalian eggs won't divide until they receive a chemical signal from the sperm. Second, mammalian eggs have only half the number of chromosomes they need for development. Without sperm, the embryo would end up with only half the DNA it needs to survive.'

'No way around this?'

'Well, assuming you could find a clever way to overcome both of those barriers in the lab there's a third obstacle that probably can't be. It involves something called genomic imprinting that's way more complicated than you'll be interested in, believe me. It involves the way some maternal and paternal genes are suppressed by one another. Without the sperm-cell imprint, the offspring won't survive.'

'But this doesn't matter in insects?'

'Way simpler genomes. But let's say that some way more brilliant geneticist than me – if that's even a concept – could get around all three of these obstacles, imprinting included, there's a final nail in the coffin. You said their babies are male.'

'Apparently so.'

'Theoretically, if mammalian parthenogenesis were to produce a viable embryo, it would have to be female. No sperm: no *y* chromosome. No *y* chromosome: the embryo is *xx*. A female. Game, set, match.'

'I see.' He hoped he'd be able to remember all of this for his report to the cardinal.

The waiter was coming at them with the dessert menu.

Jessica whispered to him, 'Hey, all this sex talk's made me horny. What do you say we get the check and go back to my place?'

EIGHT

Paradise Village could be a rough place at night. An outsider couldn't possibly know the invisible boundary lines but rival gangs knew exactly which blocks belonged to which posse. So, mobile phones began lighting up when a 4X4 began winding its way through the slum, blowing through territorial boundaries.

'Who's that white Toyota belong to, bro?'

'Not ours. Think it's the Sputniks?'

'Better fucking not be, bro. Only one way to find out.'

A group of a dozen shirtless and liquored-up young men brandishing machetes soon flooded into the streets blocking one of them completely. The Toyota pulled up and flashed its headlights. When that didn't disperse them, the driver laid into the horn. That only churned the waters. The youths started waving their machetes over their heads and a couple pulled small revolvers from their waistbands.

The driver and front passenger doors opened and two Filipino men got out. Both wore dark trousers and loose-fitting white, collared shirts. They weren't street gangsters and they weren't cops but what got the young men chattering among themselves were the semi-automatic pistols they were holding at their sides.

'Shit, bro,' one of them said, 'they got 1911s.'

The driver said calmly, 'We going to have a problem here, boys?'

A skinny guy with a revolver and baggy shorts said, 'You got business in our hood, man?'

'Yeah, we got business but it's not *your* business. You better put that pea-shooter away before you get yourself dead.'

The skinny kid said, 'There's only two of you fags, and those 45s got, what – eight in the mag, one in the rack? You'll be skinned before you take all of us. So get the fuck off our block.'

A rear door opened and another man got out. His firepower was more impressive – an AK-47 with a long banana clip.

'Full auto,' the driver said. 'What you boys wanna do?'

Two of the youths whispered to each other and the skinny kid who appeared to have authority declared, with a hesitant bravado, 'OK, you can pass through but don't be stopping. This is our house, understand?'

'Yeah, whatever,' the driver said, climbing back inside. He proceeded slowly as the gang made way.

When the road narrowed and became impassable the men got out. There was a woman with them, stocky with shiny black hair, clutching a shoulder bag to her side. The driver, his pistol at his hip, led the four-person procession, the man with the rifle at the rear. Most of the shanties were dark and there were few street lights so he had to use a flashlight. A solitary old man sat in a lawn chair outside Maria Aquino's house and he stood as the party approached.

'Can I be of assistance?' the old man asked.

It was the woman who did the talking, speaking English with a Latin accent. The driver translated. 'We would like to speak with Mrs Aquino.'

'But it's midnight,' the old man said. 'She is asleep.'

'I'm afraid it is important. I was sent here from the Vatican. I am the representative of the pope. I must speak with her.'

The old man blinked nervously. 'You have guns.'

'A good thing too,' the woman said. 'This seems to be a dangerous place at night.'

'It is, it is,' the old man agreed. 'Please wait. I will wake her.'

Maria's mother came to the door, droopy-eyed, in a t-shirt and shorts.

'You say you're from the Vatican?'

'I am,' the woman said. 'Your priest, Father Santos, has

advised the Vatican of Maria's situation. May I come inside to speak with you?'

'A man from the Vatican came before.'

The woman looked at her blankly. She missed a beat then said, 'And now I am here.'

Mrs Aquino stared at the men with guns behind her.

'Don't worry about them,' the woman said. 'They are my driver and security guards. We were told your area was dangerous at night. It's true, I think.'

She was invited into the dark room where Mrs Aquino lit the bare bulb hanging from the ceiling and asked if she wanted tea.

'I'm fine, dear.'

The woman wore expensive clothes and had lots of makeup and perfume. She eyed the grimy sofa and elected to stand.

'What does the pope want with my Maria?' Mrs Aquino asked, her arms folded across her chest.

'You must know, dear, that Maria is a very special girl. The whole world is talking about her. The Holy Father is concerned, very concerned about her safety. He has asked about her home situation and he has learned that there are many crowds during the day and gangs and drug dealers who roam during the night.'

'But everyone, even the gangsters, are respectful of Maria. They all love her. They call her the Little Virgin of Paradise Village.'

The woman nodded but said, 'And there is the matter of health care. She is a very young mother. Her birth could have complications. The Holy Father wants her to have the very best health care and the top doctors attending to her prenatal care and the delivery of her baby.'

'The local hospital is OK for her,' Mrs Aquino said. 'She has a good doctor.'

'The Holy Father wants his own doctor to see her. They have the best lady-doctors and the best baby-doctors in Rome.'

'What are you saying to me?'

'I want Maria to come with me now. We will fly to the Vatican tonight. The Holy Father will bless her tomorrow.'

'I cannot leave,' her mother said, shaking her head vigorously. 'I have other children.'

'You stay with them. I will take care of Maria. Don't worry.'

'No. She is staying here. I don't want to hear any more of this.'

The woman took her large purse from her shoulder and handed it to her.

'What is this?' she asked.

'Look inside.'

Mrs Aquino walked under the hanging bulb and opened it. Then she gasped.

'There's 200,000 pesos in there,' the woman told her. That was almost five thousand US dollars.

Mrs Aquino tried to push the bag back into the woman's hands but she backed away and wouldn't take it.

'My daughter is not for sale. Please leave.'

'You're taking this the wrong way,' the woman said quickly. 'It's a gift to take care of you and your other little ones. Maybe get a nice house in a better area. Once Maria has had her baby she will come back to you. We will give you a mobile phone so you can talk to her whenever you want. She'll have beautiful clothes and pretty things. It's going to be amazing for everyone.'

'No! Get out!'

Her voice was loud enough to get Maria out of bed and to summon two of the armed men who'd been waiting outside.

'What is it, Mama?' Maria asked.

'It's nothing, go back to bed, honey.'

The woman knelt on the rug and said, 'Hello, Maria. Pope Celestine sent me to take you to see him. Would you like to meet the Holy Father?'

'With Mama?'

'Only you, sweetheart.'

Her mother got in between them. 'Go back to your room, Maria,' she said.

The woman raised an arm for one of the men to help her up and when she was upright she said, 'I'm sorry, Mrs Aquino, but I have to insist. Carry the girl to the car,' she told the driver.

One man pushed the mother away and the driver grabbed the girl and lifted her up, holding her in both arms.

'Be gentle with her,' the woman said. 'Remember, she's pregnant.'

Mrs Aquino started screaming and the old man who'd been keeping vigil ran inside and demanded to know what was going on.

He got rough treatment from the second man who threw him on to the floor and that set him howling that he'd hurt his hip.

'Don't take my baby!' her mother cried.

Two young girls popped their heads out from the bedroom. The woman shooed them back and told them to stay put.

The men were prepared for this development. The man with the rifle came inside and leaned it against the wall. He had plastic zip ties and a gag and after a brief but ferocious struggle, Mrs Aquino was bound hand and foot and silenced in the corner.

Maria was crying and shouting but the woman told her to be quiet or they'd have to hurt her mother. 'Do you understand, sweetheart?'

The girl nodded.

The woman had a typed sheet of paper and a pen. She knelt by Mrs Aquino and asked her if she could write. The woman shook her head once.

'Very well,' the woman said.

She put the pen into Mrs Aquino's hand and when the woman tried to drop it, she squeezed her fingers around it and forced her to make an X at the bottom of the page.

'OK, let's go,' she told the men.

Before they left, the woman placed her purse in Mrs Aquino's lap.

'You can still keep the money,' she said.

In Ireland at this time of year it didn't get pitch black until well after ten. That's when the motorcycles pulled up to Kenny Riordan's bungalow. After the two men dismounted, a car came down the Tubber Road and turned into Riordan's gravel drive. The driver kept it running but switched off its lights.

Whether Riordan heard them or had been keeping watch, he was outside in a hurry. The taller of the motorcyclists, Doyle – he was the talker. The other fellow, McElroy, who had a pock-marked face, wasn't a conversationalist and also wasn't the brightest bulb. He relied on Doyle to handle the talking end of things. McElroy's skills were more on the physical side.

'You're punctual,' Riordan said.

'Always,' Doyle replied. 'It's how we roll.' He had a look over his shoulder. 'Have the local constabulary been about tonight?'

'They packed it in a few hours ago. They usually do a drive-by at midnight or so. That car with you?'

'It is. Chariot awaits and all that. Everything ready?'

'Depends.'

'On what?'

Riordan sniffed. 'Don't be like that, my son. Depends on the cash.'

Doyle unzipped his jacket. A legal-sized yellow envelope flopped down from his chest. It was thick and heavy.

'Mind if I count it inside?' Riordan said.

'Not a problem, friend, but don't take all night.'

Riordan went inside. His wife was barelegged on her lounger, a fuzzy blanket covering most of her nightdress. A sleep-apnea face mask lay on the side table within arm's reach, next to her cigarettes.

'Where's the girl?' Riordan said.

'Her room.'

'Doing what?'

'With her sisters, doing whatever they do.'

Riordan opened the envelope and emptied the pile of cash on the sofa. His wife tried to whistle but the only sound that came out was her lips puffing.

'Feast your eyes,' he said.

'They hundreds?'

'Yep.'

'Show me one.'

'What are you – a counterfeit expert?'

'An expert, no, but I can tell if they've been run off a copier.'

He handed her a hundred-euro note which she closely inspected. When she started to say something he told her to shut her trap lest he lose the count.

When he was done he snatched her note back and declared, 'It's all there.'

'Forty?'

'Yeah, forty grand. That plus the ten they gave us for a down payment, I'd say we're in the fucking money.'

She lit a cigarette, took a drag and parked it between two orange-stained fingers. 'Still, she's my daughter.'

Riordan repackaged the bills and slid the envelope under the middle cushion of the sofa. 'We've talked ourselves blue over this. There's no going back. There's a bloody procession waiting outside.'

Her huge chest rose and fell. 'Well, bring her to me.'

Mary was dressed in her Sunday clothes and was carrying the same small suitcase her mother had taken on her honeymoon. She was crying.

'Come here, love,' her mother said. 'Give us a big hug.'

The girl obeyed but the tobacco smoke stung her eyes making them redder.

'I don't want to fucking go.'

'I know, love, but it's for the best. For you and the baby. They said they're going to treat you like a princess and your baby like a little prince.'

'Where am I going?'

'They said they'll tell us once you get there. Security and all.'

'Who are they?'

Her father answered. 'Good people. The best, in fact.'

'Will you come and see me?' Mary asked her mother.

'I can't travel in my state, love, but maybe your pa. We'll see.'

There was a knock on the door. Doyle stuck his head in. 'All good in here?'

'Just give us another minute, son,' Riordan said. 'Saying our goodbyes.'

'Be quick. Tick tock. And you need to sign this paper.'

Her mother was sobbing and heaving and all the kids were in the lounge bawling their eyes out when Mary walked into the night air with her father. A smartly dressed, heavy-hipped woman got out of the car, her shoes crunching on the gravel.

'You must be Mary,' she said with a Mexican accent, smiling – a big, sincere-looking smile.

The girl hardly looked at her. She was glancing back at the house where pairs of eyes were peering out the windows.

'My name is Lidia, Mary. I hope we're going to be friends.'

'Say hello to the lady,' her father urged.

'Don't worry,' the woman said. 'I know this is hard for all of you. Mary, come along now. You're going to have fun. This is going to be a wonderful adventure.'

'Sod your adventure. I don't want to go,' Mary said, taking a step back toward the house.

'Can I tell you something? Your father told us a little secret about you.'

'What secret?'

'He said you always wanted a French bulldog puppy.'

The girl's eyes got big.

'Let me show you.'

The woman took a phone from her purse, opened a video clip, and handed the mobile to Mary. The girl watched a puppy frolicking on a pillow-laden, frilly bed.

'That's your puppy and your bed.'

'Serious?' the girl asked.

'I'm not joking.'

'What's its name?'

'Whatever you choose. It's a girl. Ready to go and meet her?'

Mary nodded and took her hand.

Riordan followed them to the car. The woman took Mary's suitcase and had her climb into the back. Her father leaned in and told her to behave herself. The girl nodded. That was their goodbye.

'Where're you from?' Riordan asked the woman when he straightened his back.

'I was born in Mexico.'

'She going there?'

'You know I can't tell you. Terms and conditions, right?'

'If she's leaving the country, she don't have a passport, you know.'

The woman dipped into her purse and showed him a brand-new Irish one.

'Looks like you've got all the angles covered,' Riordan said. 'How will we know when she gets where she's going?'

'We'll text Mr Doyle. He'll let you know. For the time being that's how you'll communicate with her.'

Riordan filled his cheeks and expelled the air loudly. 'Heartened to know this won't be the last time we see his charming mug.'

NINE

Cardinal George Pole was a fastidious man, bordering on obsessive. His clothes and vestments had to be arranged in his closet and laid out just so. His bathroom countertops and medicine chest were scrupulously neat and ordered. He had learned to make a perfect bed when he served as a priest in the Marine Corps and as a cardinal he insisted on doing the chore himself, demonstrating to the nuns how a quarter would bounce off his tight-as-a-drum bedspread.

On this morning, he awoke in his residence quarters in downtown Houston, prayed for a few minutes, then briskly ran through his ablutions in the same sequence as he had always done since a young seminarian, finishing with a generous splash of aftershave. Once clothed in his daily dress of black wool cassock trimmed in black silk, black wool rabat, purple silk sash, a pectoral cross suspended from a heavy chain, and spit-polished black shoes, he made his way through the diocese headquarters to his office. His work space was also meticulously organized. A folder labeled *Today's Events* was front and center on his desk. When he settled into his swivel chair and switched on his reading lamp his personal secretary, a quiet monsignor with graying temples, magically appeared through a side door.

'Good morning, Your Eminence,' the priest said.

'Good morning, Phillip. Warm outside?'

It was high summer and as usual the man replied, 'Hazy, hot, and humid.'

Pole opened the folder and glanced at his schedule. 'Here, take it,' he said.

'But that's your copy.'

'I don't need it,' Pole said. 'Cancel everything.'

'Are you unwell?'

'Never felt better,' the seventy-year-old said. He opened his top drawer and handed his aide a single sheet of paper, saying, 'We're doing this instead. Send out a media blast – use all the lists, local,

national, international – and invite them to a four p.m. news
conference at the Westin Hotel. The ballroom's already booked.
In two hours' time, send this text to the pope via that nun of his
– what's her name again?'

The monsignor, who had been trying to read the statement while
listening to the cardinal's instructions, was white as the paper he
was pinching between three fingers. 'Sister Elisabetta.'

The cardinal grimaced at her name. 'Yes, her.'

'Are you sure you want to give this to the Vatican, Your
Eminence?' he said, his voice cracking.

'I've never been more sure of anything in my life.'

Pope Celestine was head down in correspondence when Elisabetta
entered to give him the news. The pope and his entourage had
only just arrived at his summer residence at Castel Gondolfo. He
hadn't been inclined to leave the Vatican but the August heat was
oppressive and Elisabetta had prodded him incessantly about the
healthful benefits of the cool breezes coming off Lake Albano. He
chose to use a modest office rather than the cavernous and formal
one favored by his predecessors. In fact, it was the office usually
reserved for the pope's private secretary so Elisabetta had moved
to another, even smaller one down the hall. As she stood before
him to deliver the news he stared up in obvious distress and interrupted her mid-sentence.

'Both of them?'

'Yes, Holy Father, both girls. Maria Aquino and Mary Riordan
were both taken under similar circumstances with strangers
appearing at their homes, offering their parents money and guar-
anteeing the safety of the girls and their babies. In the case of
Mary Riordan, Father McCarthy is telling us that he suspects the
parents readily consented. He doesn't know how much money they
received. In the case of Maria Aquino, they told her they repre-
sented you personally but still her mother refused. They took the
girl by force and left the mother cash, the equivalent of about five
thousand euros, a huge sum for this family.'

'But this is similar to what occurred in Peru, is it not?'

'It is.'

Celestine got up and wandered over to his coffee machine
but he must have decided that his agitation would not be best

served by more caffeine. He made a round trip to his chair empty-handed.

'But who is behind this? Where have the girls been taken? *Why* have they been taken? This is all so distressing.'

Elisabetta had been furiously working the phones before informing the pope of the developments. 'From what we know from Lima, the authorities have not conducted a comprehensive investigation. Cardinal Miranda cannot prove it but he believes that high-ranking police officials were bribed to impede the investigation. We simply don't know whether the girl is still in Peru or was taken to another country. The investigations in the Philippines and Ireland are just getting underway.'

'So, what are we to do?' the pope asked.

'Wait for more information, Your Holiness. And pray. Also, I could compose an appropriate tweet for your @pontifex account.'

'A tweet,' the pope said, his voice drifting toward silence. 'A tweet—'

'I wonder, Holy Father,' Elisabetta said, 'if it might not be good for you to take some air. Perhaps a walk in the gardens. It's a beautiful, sunny day and there are nice gusts.'

'Will you walk with me?'

The Roman emperor Domitian had built the summer palace and gardens in the first century. The Vatican, ever the canny organization, had acquired the property out of bankruptcy in 1596 and it had been in continual use by the papacy since that time. The formal gardens were laid out geometrically with swathes of shade courtesy of towering cypresses, umbrella pines with crowns the shape of clouds, and blue-green ancient cedars. After a gentle stroll, Celestine took a seat on a stone bench and Elisabetta sat beside him. Here, the sun was mostly blotted out by the canopy and there was a view down on to the sparkling lake.

The girls were clearly centermost in his mind because the first thing he said was, 'I appreciate the work that Professor Donovan did for us but we're no closer to understanding the meaning of these three Marys. I don't know whether I should be praising God for sending us a twenty-first-century sign of his dominion over us, or cursing men for making cynical use of three poor girls.'

'Time will certainly tell, Holy Father,' Elisabetta said, smoothing the fabric of her habit after it billowed in the wind.

'Whatever the truth of the matter, I am fearful for these young girls. Even if some parents consented to their removal, they must be feeling scared and alone. I pray that the Virgin Mary is smiling on them in their time of need.'

Mary Riordan had hardly slept. She was at times crying and fitful, at times bored and pouting. Because of this her female companion had also spent a sleepless night. She acted like a jester trying to amuse a restive king, passing the girl fashion magazines, calling up videos and games on the in-flight entertainment system, plying her with junk food. None of it stuck for long and for hours on end the moaning continued. The woman was alone with her in the cabin of the Dassault Falcon private jet so there was no one else to absorb the blows.

She went to the lavatory to take a short break but soon she heard the girl shouting, 'I miss my mum.'

She steeled herself and returned to the cabin to say, 'I know you do, dear. We'll get her on the phone when we get to where we're going. Maybe you can FaceTime.'

The girl turned acidly sarcastic. 'That would be grand. All we'd need is for me to have a flippin' iPhone. Oh yeah, and I suppose my mum might need one too.'

That was the woman's cue to pull out the heavy artillery and maybe get an hour or two of rest before they landed for refueling. She got up and retrieved a bag from the aft storage. In it was an unwrapped white box. She walked over to the girl, placed it on her lap over the blanket covering her.

Mary's eyes lit up. 'No way! No bloody way!'

In seconds, the brand-new iPhone was in her hot little hands and before the woman was able to pull a blanket over her own tired eyes, Mary had tapped into the plane's Wi-Fi to begin to set up the device.

The woman was drifting off when she heard the girl say, 'You've got to set it to a time zone. Which time zone should I use?'

'Central. In America.'

A junior member of the press office of the Holy See had accompanied the pope to Castel Gondolfo. Her medium-height heels were not well suited for running outdoors but she did the best she could. A slow, dignified pace would not have done justice to the fax she had in her hand. The pontiff and his private secretary heard her heels on the stone path and turned to greet her.

'Emilia?' Elisabetta said. 'What's the matter?'

The young woman was a little breathless. 'This just came in for you.'

She handed the fax over without any explanation and the pope waited patiently for Elisabetta to digest the news, whatever it was, and inform him about it. He kept his gaze on the tranquil lake, perhaps sensing that the moment of peacefulness was soon to pass.

'It's Pole,' Elisabetta finally said. 'He's given his resignation.'

George Pole was a natural orator, very much at home in front of cameras. He rested his palms on the smooth podium and drank in the overflow crowd at the hotel ballroom. He recognized a good number of people in the audience. Some were well-heeled local Catholics who had donated heavily to his annual fundraisers, some were ordinary parishioners at the Co-Cathedral of the Sacred Heart in Houston and the St Mary Basilica in Galveston. Some were local politicians he had served with on panels and blue-ribbon commissions, and many were members of the Houston–Galveston media he had courted so assiduously this past decade.

Punctuality was one of the virtues he espoused and at precisely four p.m. he smoothed his gray and white, short-cropped hair then held up his hands for order. He spoke without notes.

'Ladies and gentlemen, you will surely notice that I come before you this afternoon as a simple man of God, dressed not in the finery of a cardinal of the Holy Roman Church but as an ordinary priest. As an aside, I was delighted to discover that I still fit into the clerical garments I used to wear as a younger man. Today I tendered my resignation as a cardinal. Just before I left the diocesan offices of Houston–Galveston for the last time as cardinal, I learned that Pope Celestine has accepted my resignation, surely one of fastest pontifical replies in recent memory. In my case the Vatican cannot be accused of being mired in bureaucracy.'

He paused for anticipated laughter but there was none. Looking a bit like a stand-up comic in a tough room he continued.

'My disagreements with the current pontificate are well-known. I am a traditionalist. I am proud of it. I don't believe the world stopped spinning in 1965 after the Second Vatican Council but I believe it marked the beginning of a steep, downward spiral for Catholics who believe in the bedrock values of the Church. I support the traditional Latin Mass and the traditional Baltimore Catechism. I am fervently pro-life. I support an all-male clergy and clerical celibacy. I support traditional family structures. I appreciate the beauty of traditional liturgy and the glory of Christian art, music, and architecture. The teachings of the Vatican used to be aligned with my core values but that is no longer so.'

Perhaps realizing that he was about to get into the meat of his speech, the camera flashes intensified.

'I am sorry to say that the erosion of these values has accelerated at an alarming pace under the current pontificate,' Pole said, 'and lest there be any doubt, I hold the man who holds the rudder to be personally responsible, along with his aiders and abettors. Pope Celestine has launched an ultra-liberal agenda aligning the Vatican with secular leftists who believe that the mission of the Church – my Church – is not the promotion of the word of God and the teachings of the Gospels but issues concerning so-called peace and justice. This pope has championed ambiguity on homosexuality and same-sex marriage, remarriage after divorce, marriage among certain clergy, even some contraception. In the name of social justice, he has sold off some of the great Vatican treasures of Christian art to fund his pet causes. And where will he go next? The ordination of women? Loosening of prohibitions against abortion? I shudder to think. My Church is becoming a Church I no longer recognize and it is for this reason that I can no longer serve as a bishop. As to my future plans, I may have more to say later. For the moment, I will retire to a cloistered space for a period of prayer and reflection. I will not be taking questions. Thank you for coming.'

TEN

The Dassault Falcon's co-pilot left the cockpit to find both his passengers sound asleep on their reclined seats. He made sure the girl was strapped in before approaching the woman and gently waking her.

'Ma'am, we're going to be landing in about twenty minutes. Just so you know.'

Mary Riordan only awoke when the jet landed with a bump in a heavy cross-wind. The woman had already done her hair and make-up and had the paperwork ready when the customs officer boarded the plane at the private aviation terminal.

The heat rushed in from the open door.

'Welcome to the United States,' she said. 'Passports, please.'

The woman came forward and presented her own US passport. When it was stamped, she presented Mary's passport and visa documents.

The spine of the Irish passport cracked when opened.

'Looks brand new,' the officer said. When she saw the recent issue date she said, 'Is new.'

The name must have rung a bell because she said, 'Are you *the* Mary Riordan? The pregnant girl?'

Mary stared back at her sullenly.

'That's her,' the woman answered.

'I thought she was missing.'

'Hardly,' the woman said. She'd been coached on how to handle this moment and she said confidently, 'As you can see, she's right here.'

The officer looked through her visa forms, the I-131, Application for Travel Document and the I-134, Affidavit of Support.

'These humanitarian visas are hard to come by,' the officer said, inviting some sort of reply.

'Are they?' the woman said. 'I wasn't involved in the visa process.'

That was a lie. She knew damned well how she got the humanitarian parole.

'Mary, my name is Officer Burke,' the woman said. 'Is this your first visit to America?'

The girl nodded.

'Is Boston your final destination?'

The woman gave the officer their itinerary.

Burke glanced at it and asked, 'Is your ride here?'

From the open cockpit the pilot said, 'That Cessna off our port wing.'

'OK, Mary. How long have you known this woman, Mrs Torres?'

'We've only just met.'

'Did you go with her of your own free will?'

'Sorry, what?'

'Did you want to go with her?'

'Hell no. They made me go, didn't they?'

'Who made you go?'

'My parents did.'

The woman had another document in her folder.

'Officer, this is a signed and notarized consent form from Mary's parents, authorizing this trip and the custodianship of my employer.'

The officer inspected the paper, scooped up all the travel documents, and looked through the windows at the smaller jet on a nearby stand.

'I know your plane is waiting but I want to check with my superior before clearing you. Stay on board.'

The woman sat back down, wondering whether to make an emergency call. She decided to be steady and hold off. Mary was playing with her new phone again. She'd downloaded games during the flight. To keep them cool, the pilots re-closed the door and kept the AC cranking.

Twenty minutes passed, then thirty before there was a knock on the door. The co-pilot let the customs officer back on board. She looked perturbed. Burke had argued her position against granting entry – she'd been unconvinced about parental consent for the minor – but she'd been overruled following a series of calls up the management chain of the Department of Homeland Security.

'Miss Riordan, welcome to the United States. Enjoy your stay.'

When Burke returned to the office in the private aviation terminal her supervisor said, 'I just got a call from someone very high up at DHS in Washington. It was for you and me personally. We've been told to keep our mouths shut about this entry.'

'Who am I going to tell, Frank?'

'I don't know – the whole fucking world?'

She laughed at that. 'I like this job. It's perfect for someone with a shit memory. I don't even remember who we just let in.'

Where are The Three Marys?

Cal read the headline in the *Boston Globe* and said to himself, 'That's what I'd like to know.'

Joe Murphy knocked on the door and saw the paper on Cal's desk.

'Did you read it yet?' Murphy asked.

'Not yet. I just got in.'

'You're in there. Featured rather prominently.'

Cal let out a curse and grabbed the first section.

He cursed a few more times.

Looking up he said, 'How'd this get out?'

'Don't have a clue but they missed my name so all's well with the world. It appears you've got a few voicemails.'

The voicemail counter on Cal's office phone was flashing 99, its maximum display.

'I am so screwed,' Cal said.

'That was fast,' Cal told the reporter who entered his office.

It was early afternoon. Cal hadn't left his campus office all day because of the media staking out all ways in and out of Divinity Hall. The department secretary had gone out to a food truck to get him lunch.

Earlier in the day, Cardinal Da Silva had taken Cal's call straight away.

'I can only imagine that the leak about your journeys came from someone on the ground in Manila or Lima,' Da Silva had said. 'I certainly can't rule out a source from one of the dioceses. But what's done is done. We have to find a good way to handle it.'

'I've gotten hundreds of media requests from all over the place. I'm always happy to help, Your Eminence, but I've got work to do.'

'Then do as I do during media feeding frenzies. Feed only a single shark.'

That shark was a *New York Times* reporter who laid his phone on the table to record the session and said, 'I hopped on the Delta shuttle. Door to door – four hours. So, this is still an exclusive, right?'

'Right.'

'And it's still on the record, right?'

'Right again.'

'The *Globe*'s going to be pissed.'

'Not as pissed as the *Harvard Crimson*. The editor of the college paper managed to sneak into the building with her student

ID. She begged me for an interview. I don't have the time to do more than one.'

The *Times* reporter, a diminutive man, smiled. 'So, you went with the big dog on the porch.'

Cal smiled back. 'Something like that.'

'OK, let's start. Do you know where the girls are?'

Randall Anning was not accustomed to waiting. Not for tables in restaurants. Not for his private jet to get airborne. Not for his security detail to get his car ready. Billionaires were like that, especially those with egos his size. But he was in the one place where he had to cool his heels. So he waited, his hands resting on the ultra-smooth, summer-weight cloth of his sixty-thousand-dollar Kiton K-50 suit.

He had watched the secretary typing at her desk and answering the frequent phone calls, deflecting all but one caller, the one who seemed to be the cause of the delay.

'Are you sure I can't get you a coffee or some other beverage?' she called over to Anning.

He waved her off with as much cheer as he could muster.

He was not strikingly tall, or broad or handsome, but there was something about the forthright way the seventy-year-old carried himself, his determined jaw, his sunken eyes, and his torpedo-shaped shaved head that turned heads and commanded respect.

The assistant's phone rang again and this time she rose and told him, 'The President will see you now.'

Anning couldn't recall how many times he had been inside the Oval Office but each time sent his heart racing a little. The last thing he ever wanted to do was run for office but there wasn't a President he'd met over the last thirty years whom he thought was doing as good a job as he could. And those thoughts were in abundance with respect to the current holder of the office, Llewellyn Griffith, the former governor of Florida, whom Anning considered a useful horse's ass.

'Randy,' the President boomed, rising up from his desk and flying across the room to shake his hand. 'Sorry to keep you waiting. Secretary of Defense was on the line. Shit storm brewing. There's always something to turn your hair white, not that that would be one of your problems.'

Anning wasn't sensitive about his hair follicles but it was just like Griffith to try to assert some kind of alpha-male dominance over a real alpha male.

'Mr President. Good to see you,' Anning said, his prairie accent drawing out each syllable. 'I wasn't waiting long at all.'

They sat on opposing couches, separated by the eagle of the presidential seal emblazoned on the carpet.

'You know you can still call me Lew – when we're alone that is,' Griffith said, grinning. 'How the hell have you been? When was the last time we saw each other? Palm Beach, was it?'

'The fundraiser for the RNC at The Breakers,' Anning said.

'That's right. My wife got – how do you say it in French? – drunk, and Betsy had to steady her ass out of the ballroom.'

'Drunk's a little harsh, Lew. Tipsy, I'd say, but my wife has had a lot of practice steadying the likes of me. She's strong as an ox. Got those big-boned, peasant-stock, Scandinavian genes.'

The first lady had, in fact gotten roaring drunk and way too loud on endless glasses of wine, and Betsy Anning, a Viking of a woman, had indeed muscled her back to the presidential suite. She hadn't been prompted to intervene by the President or by her husband; she just did it. The Annings took charge of things.

'So, you called this meeting, Lew. How can I be of service?'

Griffith unbuttoned his jacket to give himself more breathing room. He was a bruiser of a man, six foot five, with the body of a college athlete gone to seed, a country-club body that looked just fine in a good suit but bulbous in just about anything else. As a candidate, his principal physical attribute had been his hair, luxuriously abundant for a man of his age, naturally the color of a brilliant, uncirculated silver dollar, perennially coiffed in something of a bouffant.

'Randy, you know I ran hard on the issue of the decline of our moral standards.'

'No sir, you *won* on the issue.'

'Ha, yes. Yes, I did. And as a fellow Catholic, you know the significance of my win. I'm only the second member of our tribe since Kennedy to win the presidency. I'm proud I'm a Catholic but I'm also a proud conservative. I know what's good for this country and what's bad but I can't change things all by myself.

Sure, I've got the bully pulpit and I can work around the edges with executive orders but I need Congress to get real shit done! But it's like rowing in molasses when I keep getting hit by this kind of crap. He's got a damn-loud megaphone too.'

The latest issue of *Time* magazine was on the table. Griffith gave it a four-fingered push toward his guest.

Anning didn't have to pick it up. He knew what was inside. An open letter to Griffith from Pope Celestine harshly rebuking him for his stances on immigration, Muslims, racial profiling, crime, health care, ethno-nationalism – pretty much his whole legislative and cultural agenda.

'I read it. I'm not surprised it's gotten under your skin. I'm sure that was its intention.'

'Did you catch what that son-of-a-bitch said in the last paragraph – along the lines of the Holy See cannot sit idly by as the leader of the free world works to subvert the compassionate teachings of Jesus Christ? Then he says something like we must speak out and more. What's the more? Is he threatening to excommunicate me?'

'Hell, he's not going to do that, Lew. He's just grandstanding.'

'Well, he's publicly embarrassing me and giving ammunition to my political opponents. Did you see how George Pole handled himself the other day? He's my goddamn hero for what he did – I called him and told him that. I wish I could do something like that but I can't very well sit here in the White House and change my religion. What am I going to do, become a goddamn Baptist?' Pausing for a moment to muse, he continued, 'The evangelicals might actually go for that! Anyway, I want to know what you can do to help me through this mess.'

Anning scratched at a peeling patch of sunburned skin on his scalp. 'You know I'm not the right guy to be an intermediary with the Vatican any more, Lew. I could do it and did do it with the last pope, but I'm *persona non grata* with Celestine's crowd of Commies. I let them have it after they auctioned off half of the Vatican Museum and I haven't given the Church a nickel since then. Why should I? So they can funnel my cash into buying plane-loads of condoms for Africa or propping up leftists in South America? And yes, George is my hero too. I'm honored to call him a friend and a fellow Texan. He did something principled. I'd say he follows in your footsteps in that regard.'

'Thanks, but I didn't ask you in to feed me compliments. I need help in countering the Vatican bullshit. You've got the money and connections within important Catholic circles to muster support for me. I want you to come up with a plan to hole their ship under the water line. Maybe dig up dirt on influential cardinals surrounding Celestine. Maybe even on him. It's time to take the gloves off.'

Anning showed a row of gleaming teeth. 'What makes you think I haven't been working on something already?'

The President leaned forward, his flabby middle spilling over his beltline. 'Tell me more.'

'Lew, believe me, you don't want to know.'

'This wouldn't have something to do with the humanitarian visas for the knocked-up girls that Senator Price from the great state of Texas got me to grant? Were you the invisible hand behind that?'

'Like I said, you don't want to know. But stay tuned, Mr President. Stay tuned.'

ELEVEN

I t was Sue Gibney who had insisted that the three of them should share a room. She'd been given the assignment as den mother, with a room near theirs, and a remit by Mrs Torres to do whatever it took to make and keep them happy. When each one arrived, Mrs Torres had handed the girl over to Sue with minimal ceremony, then promptly retreated to her own quarters to recover from the ordeal.

The original plan was for them to have private rooms, three identical ones to avoid jealousy. Each had the same bedspread, the same pictures on the walls, the same dolls and toys, the same PlayStation games.

But Sue was the one who had to stay awake, particularly during their first nights, to deal with the crying and hysterics, and she had persuaded Mrs Torres to put all the beds into the same room so the girls could keep each other company.

The two women had little in common. Torres was considerably older, in her late fifties. She was regimented and proudly officious, ruling the roost with a steely attention to detail and protocol. Her features were as dark as a moonless night and she would never emerge from her suite of rooms before completing an elaborate cosmetics ritual. Bright-red lipstick was always the cherry on her sundae. She had been a naturalized American citizen for decades but her Mexican accent was still so potent that Sue had to concentrate if she spoke too quickly. Sue was fair with hair the color of milk chocolate usually tied in a retro pony-tail, and bright, lavender eyes. She eschewed make-up which made her mornings breezy affairs. And she was very much on the free-spirit side of the personality spectrum. Torres was Sue's boss. She had screened her, interviewed and hired her and had demanded a level of formality in their interactions. Their conversation about the girls' rooms had gone like this:

'Sue, we're in a thirty-room mansion and you want them to stay in one bedroom?'

'For these girls, each bedroom is like the size of their houses. None of them has ever slept on her own. They all share. On top of the shock from the sudden dislocation from their families, they've got to adjust to loneliness at night.'

'The sooner they adjust to their new lives, the better.'

'They're hysterical. They're young. They're pregnant. Do you want to be the one responsible for a miscarriage?'

And Sue had gotten her way.

The strategy was successful because the nights became quieter. Yes, there were still tears, but they came from whimpering, not wailing, and Sue got some sleep.

There were other early challenges for Sue and Torres to handle. For the Marias, there were basic hygiene issues. Maria Mollo didn't know how to use a flush toilet and neither girl had ever used a shower. The difference between the hot and cold sink taps had to be demonstrated. New personal care products had to be demoed. Mary Riordan was more worldly, insisting on using the lipstick and make-up she had brought from home and soon the other girls were curious and wanted to try them too. The Irish girl's new iPhone caused early problems. Each Maria wanted her own little machine on which to play games so Torres had to send one of the staff to town to buy a couple more. And Mary became angry because Sue wouldn't let her have the house Wi-Fi password or allow her to sign up for a cellular plan. Watching news coverage of their disappearances was forbidden. The TV in their lounge near the bedroom was restricted to videos only.

The language barriers facing the two Marias were anticipated. A local Filipino woman, a seamstress, was pressed into service after she signed an aggressive nondisclosure agreement. Torres and various maids had the Spanish covered. An English-as-second-language teacher was hired as a live-in tutor to the Marias six days a week. The cook was commissioned to do meal plans to match the girls' individual tastes and to combat homesickness.

And at the center of all this was Sue who had not seen any of this coming when she was hired four months earlier. Her first two months had been spent at the mansion, outfitting it with a seemingly unlimited budget for a purpose she hadn't fully understood. When the veil was lifted shortly before the arrival of the first girl, she had reservations. These were assuaged by additional compensation larded on from her unseen employer and meted out by Mrs Torres. In four months, Sue had earned more than the previous five years combined. Without rent, food or utility payments, her salary was pure profit and her savings account had reached levels she could never have imagined. And every two weeks it only got fatter. With the end of her paycheck-to-paycheck existence her future looked different and more interesting. She resolved to do her job as well as she could, bury her reservations, and get out of Dodge when it was done. She was keen to see what the world looked like with money in the bank.

Before long the girls settled into a routine. They got out of bed to play with the French bulldog, which Mary Riordan had named Lily. Mary had, at first, refused to share the puppy because she'd been told it was hers. But once the novelty wore off, she became less territorial and the dog became communal. Far and away the most assertive, Mary claimed the bathroom first each morning, taking her own sweet time. There were fifteen bathrooms in the mansion but Sue and the translators were unable to convince the Marias to use a different one. They chose to sit on the floor waiting, tossing Lily her chew toys.

Sue picked up a pink hairbrush from Maria Aquino's dresser and sat beside the girl. She was a tiny thing, no more than eighty pounds dripping wet, and her pregnancy hadn't added much weight. Her baby bump was slight, the smallest of the three girls. When Sue took her glasses off and began to brush her brown shoulder-length hair the girl turned her face toward her and, for the first time, briefly smiled.

'*Salamat.*'

Sue knew the word. 'Thank you.' She checked the cheat-card with Filipino phrases she kept with her. '*Walang anuman,*' she replied haltingly. Anything more complex would have to wait until Mrs Simpauco came up from staff breakfast.

The girl seemed to appreciate the small gesture and she leaned into the soft bristles massaging her scalp.

All the girls had been provided a new wardrobe. When Mary Riordan left the bathroom to begin picking an outfit for the day, Maria Aquino took her place at the sink. Maria Mollo was still in bed, awake but on her side with her head turned to the wall. Of the three, she had been the least communicative and most miserable. If Sue had been asked the color of her eyes she would have responded: red.

Torres looked in from the hall and said to Sue, 'Why is she still in bed?'

'There's no rush.'

'She's lazy, that's why,' Mary Riordan said from the walk-in closet.

'She's not lazy, she's just a little delicate,' Sue said.

Torres was less tolerant. In Spanish, she sharply told the girl to get up and make her bed. Maria reacted poorly to the harsh words and began to cry again.

'Lidia,' Sue said, 'you gave me primary responsibility for their day-to-day welfare. I'd appreciate it if you'd let me do my job.'

'Yeah, for fuck's sake, Lidia, let the woman do her job,' Mary said gleefully, emerging in her underwear to stick out her tongue before retreating into the closet.

Torres said something hateful under her breath and left.

Later she would demand that Sue call her Mrs Torres in front of the girls.

'Is the old cow gone?' Mary asked.

'You shouldn't swear and you shouldn't call her a cow,' Sue said unconvincingly.

'I'll take that with the sincerity you intended.'

'Get dressed, Mary,' Sue said. 'If I didn't know you were only seventeen.'

'How old would you have said I was?'

'Older than me probably.'

'And how old are you then?'

'Thirty-six.'

The girl whistled at that. 'Ancient.'

Sue turned her attention to Maria Mollo and sat on the bed to stroke her narrow shoulders. She wasn't much larger than the Filipino girl – a few inches taller, a few pounds heavier. She was considerably fuller in the face too, which might have made her seem more cheerful if she weren't so patently miserable, and her lips were thick and juicy. Sue had already formed her own short-hand opinion about the girls. Maria Mollo was pretty and sad. Maria Aquino was tiny and sweet. Mary Riordan was saucy and precocious. She realized that these impressions were subject to change, but she had a feeling she might have captured at first blush the essence of each one.

Sue peeled back the bedclothes, scooped the girl into her arms and tenderly lifted her. Rather than resisting, Maria put her arms around her neck and clung to her like a marsupial. Sue was not a large woman herself but she was fit with a strong core and she was able to stand easily. There was a window seat with a flat, padded cushion and that's where she lowered the girl's legs. The windows were closed and the air conditioning was working against the warm morning air outside. The girl stood there and waited for Sue to get her blue hairbrush. In her t-shirt and little shorts with their appliqué teddy bears she didn't much look like an expectant mother until she turned ninety degrees. Her baby bump was more pronounced than Maria Aquino's though less so than Mary Riordan's. As Sue began to brush her thick black hair that fell long and straight to the middle of her back, both of them gazed through the panes of glass. The landscape was flat and barren. The sprinkler-fed grounds surrounding the house were green, but stretching to an indistinct horizon, the land was scrub-brown and arid. There were white wooden fences separating the lawns and the nothingness. Between these fences, horses grazed on the stubble.

Sue's line of work had put her in front of Spanish-speakers and she reached down into her memory bank for the Spanish for horse. It wasn't a word she'd had to use before but she took a stab at it.

'Caballeros?' she said, pointing.

Something like a snort came out of Maria's mouth. 'Caballos,' she said.

'Caballos,' Sue repeated. 'Gracias.'

She didn't know how to ask if the girl liked horses and didn't want to call Torres so instead she pantomimed riding a horse, pointed at the girl and lifted her hands in a questioning gesture.

'*No nunca*,' the girl said. Then the storm cloud descended over her head once again and through quivering plump lips she moaned, '*Quiero que mi mama.*'

'*Lo sé.* I know you miss her, sweetheart.'

Mary Riordan came out dressed in a polo shirt and knee-length pleated skirt.

'She's a whiner, that one.'

Sue reproached her. 'That's not very charitable, Mary.'

'It's the truth.'

Sue looked her up and down. 'That's a skirt for formal occasions. Why'd you put it on?'

'Wanted to. Who knows, Prince Charming might turn up.'

Sue didn't want to play favorites but she had a hard time warming to the girl. She was a one-trick pony: always in your face.

'Go change into something more appropriate. Try shorts. I thought we'd go outside today with Lily before it gets too hot.'

'And where exactly is outside? And by that I mean, where the fuck are we?'

'You've been told again and again that I can't tell you that. And please don't swear.'

'Do these two know they've been kidnapped or are they too thick?'

'You weren't kidnapped. Your parents gave consent.'

'Yeah, after getting bribed by stacks of cash. If we weren't kidnapped we've been sold like livestock. Three pregger sows sold at the fair, we are.'

'Three young ladies.'

'Yeah, whatever. Did they also get in the family way absent a night of passion?'

'You're all in the same boat. That's all I know.'

'When do I get to phone my mum?'

'Soon I hope. I'll ask Mrs Torres again.'

'She's even worse than you are. You ever been pregnant?'

'Nope.'

'You Catholic?'

'Nope again. Protestant.'

'So that makes you a barren Orange hag, don't it?'

Sue sighed heavily. 'Go change your clothes, Mary.'

Later that morning the two Marias were introduced to their English teacher, Mrs White, a woman Sue had met for the first time the day before. She was only a few years older than Sue but way on the starchy side. Even so, Sue tried to be extra nice to her. After four months, she was getting lonely. Torres wasn't someone she could spend an evening chit-chatting to, or watching a film with when the girls went to bed. The huge red-brick house was a cavernous place at night when the kitchen and cleaning staff were gone. While the two girls got their first lesson, Mary Riordan got parked in front of a computer set up with learning software to continue her secondary school transition year. Every time Sue looked in she was stuck on the same page, doing her nails or playing a game on her phone and no amount of coaxing could get her to take it seriously.

'Let me call home and maybe I'll click on the next screen. Otherwise, piss off.'

After the girls had lunch they were allowed to spend an hour unsupervised in their lounge. Torres called Sue on the intercom and asked her to come down to her ground-floor office near the library.

'How did they do this morning?' she asked Sue.

'Mrs White said the Marias did fine at their first lesson. They learned some basic words. They were cooperative. Mary is on strike. She says she won't get with the program unless she's allowed to talk to her mother.'

Torres shook her head. 'I hate to let her be the one in charge. The fact is that we're on hold for a few days. They need to deliver a phone here that can't be traced. You know how security-conscious they are.'

'I don't even know who *they* are,' Sue said.

As usual, Torres ignored that kind of fishing expedition. 'Dr Lopez is coming this afternoon,' she said.

Lopez was the local pediatrician hired to be on call for the girls. He had examined them on their arrival and administered prenatal vitamins to all of them and immunizations to the Marias.

'Why?' Sue asked.

'Dr Benedict wanted to meet the pediatrician.'

'Who's Dr Benedict?'

'He's a big-shot obstetrician from Washington.'

Sue bristled at the news but held her tongue.

The Cessna jet circled overhead once then touched down on the private landing strip to the rear of the mansion. The chauffeur was waiting for the VIP passenger and gave him the one-minute ride to the front portico where Dr Benedict, a white-haired patrician of a man, emerged in a seersucker suit. He clutched a large cracked-leather medical satchel that he would later tell Sue had been passed down by his physician-father and his father's physician-father.

His greeting party in the marble front hall was Torres, Dr Lopez, and Sue. Sue inspected the business card he thrust into her hand and understood the fuss. Benedict was the President of the American College of Obstetrics and Gynecology.

Torres had him come through to the living room where she offered him a lemonade and inquired about his trip.

'Very comfortable,' Benedict said, sipping away. 'Quite a lot of secrecy,' he said. 'My lawyer actually advised against signing your confidentiality agreement without knowing the nature of the consult but you dangled a king's ransom in front of me.'

'It wasn't us,' Torres said. 'We're only employees.'

'And who is the person or persons behind the curtain?' he asked.

Sue bailed Torres out by saying, 'That's what I'd like to know.'

'I see,' Benedict said, bushy eyebrows elevating. 'When I boarded the plane, I was given a folder. That was the first time I knew whom I'd be examining today. It wasn't what I was expecting.'

'What *were* you expecting?' Dr Lopez asked.

'Oh, I don't know. Maybe the wife of a Saudi prince. I've done that kind of work before. This is rather more interesting. What's your specialty, Doctor?'

'Pediatrician,' Lopez answered.

'And are the girls healthy?'

'The Irish girl's the picture of health. The Peruvian girl is underweight and has iron deficiency. Same for the Filipino girl but she's severely underweight. We've got them both on a good diet and supplements.'

'And what do you do, Mrs Torres?'

'I'm the manager of the property, Doctor. I keep the trains running.'

'And you, Ms Gibney?'

'I'm a midwife.'

'Are you? Excellent.'

Sue didn't sound convinced. 'You think so?'

'You may know that the American College of Obstetrics and Gynecology has formally embraced the role of midwives in delivery management.'

'What ACOG says and what an obstetrician thinks can be two different things.'

'Well, it's what I think too. What's your background?'

'Masters from New Mexico State University. Twelve years of practice, mostly in New Mexico. Over a thousand deliveries. Never been sued.'

He laughed. 'No lawsuits! Now that's an accomplishment. Tell me, why the decision to do home deliveries?'

'Privacy,' Torres answered. 'They don't want a media circus.'

'You'll be in attendance, Dr Lopez?'

'That's the plan.'

'And what kind of hospital back-up will you have, Ms Gibney? You're not all that close to a local, let alone regional facility.'

'If they need a C-section, there's a helicopter on the property and a full EMT crew will be on standby,' Sue said.

'All right, I'd like to see them. Is there some place I could use for an examination room?'

Taking the elevator to the third floor, Benedict let out a 'Good heavens!' when Sue opened the double-doors.

They might as well have been in a medical complex because the room lacked for nothing.

There was an examination table with stirrups, drawers full of sterile and non-sterile supplies, a well-stocked medication cabinet, state-of-the-art fetal monitoring gear, even an ultrasound machine. All of it was Sue's doing.

'I've never seen this kind of a set-up in a private house,' Benedict enthused.

'It's a special facility for special girls,' Torres said.

'If I'm going to get back to Washington at a decent hour I'd better start,' Benedict said. 'Send them in – any order you'd like.'

Torres left to get Maria Aquino.

When she was out of the room, Sue asked him, 'Could I ask you what you were told was the purpose of your examinations today?'

'Only that an expert report was required from someone with an authoritative platform. Now that I know who the patients are, I can guess that they want my opinion on how these young ladies became pregnant. What that opinion will be used for, I've no idea. I only know that if I talk out of school about this, I'll be sued for every penny I'm worth.'

'Please hold for the President.'

Anning was in a penthouse office that gave him unobstructed views of sunrises out one wall of windows during early-morning meetings and sunsets from the opposite wall of windows when he worked late.

He suspected that someone would be listening in so he took a formal tone. 'Mr President. What can I do for you?'

Griffith was far more casual. 'Randy, how the hell are you doing? Have a good trip back the other day?'

'I did, thanks.'

'Did you see the *New York Times* today?'

'It's on my desk but I haven't gotten to it yet.'

'Well, get to it. Page one, below the fold. There's an interview with a Harvard egghead named Calvin Donovan. Ever hear of him?'

'Actually, I have. He's a personal friend of the pope. Celestine uses him from time to time to help with sticky situations. Off-the-books work when he wants to bypass Vatican personnel.'

'Well read the interview pronto. It looks like Donovan was recruited to make a preliminary assessment of the virgin girls.'

Anning reached for the newspaper. 'Really?'

'He hedges his bets and hides behind the fact that he's not a medical man but he gives the impression that this virgin pregnancy situation could be on the up-and-up.'

Anning looked at the flattering photo of Cal taken at a leafy spot on the Harvard campus. 'I'll read it right now and get back to you.'

'You don't need to call me back. I just wanted to say, Randy, that I don't know what you've got up your sleeve, and as you said, I don't want to know, but it just might be that you can use this Donovan fellow to your advantage.'

'Thank you, Mr President. I'll certainly give it some thought.'

TWELVE

D ressed in cargo shorts, pocket t-shirt, and boat shoes – the obligatory outfit for what lay ahead – Cal was finishing his second cup of coffee and trawling through his Twitter feed at his kitchen table. His Cambridge house was a large place for a single man but he needed – or more precisely, he wanted – the space for his collections. Collections of books, paintings, artifacts, sculptures – all the academic and cultural passions a good salary and a substantial trust fund could support. His father, the famous archaeologist Hiram Donovan, came from a long line of money and, upon his premature death, young Cal had become independently wealthy – trust-fund wealthy.

Social media in general and Twitter in particular was blowing up with the hashtag #wherearethemarys, something Cal very much wanted to know himself. Cardinal Da Silva had been good to pass along any information the Vatican had gleaned from its local contacts in the Philippines, Peru, and Ireland but there had been precious little information. The Vatican had the firm impression – perhaps more than that, a firm belief – that the local authorities in Manila and Lima had been paid off by unknown agents to tread lightly with their investigations. The parents of Maria Mollo and Maria Aquino clearly knew nothing. The Irish police seemed impervious to bribery but they kept banging into dead ends and admitted they had no idea whether Mary Riordan was still in Ireland or abroad. And the Riordans were unhelpful. If they knew anything, they weren't talking. So millions of people banded together as amateur sleuths, looking for the girls collectively.

Admittedly, the situation was getting out of hand. Teenage girls who vaguely resembled the photos of one of the Marys circulating on the Internet were being accosted on the streets and asked if they were them.

Maria Aquino spotted in Malaysia.

I just saw Mary Riordan in Cleveland.

Maria Mollo is definitely in El Salvador. Check out this photo.

One man who grabbed at the sleeve of a girl he thought was Maria Mollo had been stabbed by the girl's father in Honduras.

Cal thought he'd seen every conceivable conspiracy theory but was marveling at one he hadn't read – that followers of the anti-Christ had seized the girls to prevent a resurgence of Christianity – when his doorbell rang.

The caller at the door was from a courier service and asked him to sign for a legal-sized envelope pouch.

'You guys deliver on Sundays?' Cal asked.

'Looks like we do,' the guy said flippantly.

Cal took the pouch back to the kitchen. There was no sender label. He cut the plastic open with scissors and removed a large envelope with only his name printed on it. Inside were several stapled sheets and a typed memo.

> *Professor Donovan, please review and pass the enclosed expert report to your contacts in Rome. The pope may want to stick his neck in the sand but we will not. We demand that he commission the Congregation for the Causes of Saints to formally fast-track and investigate the miracle of the virgins and declare these girls living saints. If he fails to take this action with immediate effect we will rebuke the Vatican*

publicly, declare it irrelevant in this matter, and arrange for
independent examiners to investigate the girls and share the
findings at a time of our choosing.

The memo was unsigned.

Cal paged through the report to the end, slack-jawed.

'Holy shit,' he mumbled.

He quickly placed a call.

'You better not be calling to cancel,' Jessica said.

'Wouldn't miss it,' Cal said. 'Perfect weather. I'm leaving in a minute but just wanted to check – is what's-his-name, your medical director, coming with?'

'Larry? Yeah, why?'

'I may have something to talk to him about.'

You couldn't ask for a better day to sail Boston Harbor. It was late-summer warm with an intensely blue sky and moderate prevailing breezes. Jessica kept her forty-five-foot Hunter at the Charlestown Marina. She'd learned her seamanship as a girl summering on Buzzard's Bay and before becoming a scientist she'd harbored ambitions to crew on a World Cup team.

When Cal arrived the sailing party was already on board, tucking into mimosas and smoked salmon. Jessica gave him a squeeze and whispered that he would have been shark-bait if he'd been a no-show.

She asked him about the leather folio under his arm. 'You didn't bring work, did you?'

'Me? Would I do that?'

Shoving off, Cal settled into a flute of champagne on one of the padded benches in the cockpit while Jessica took the wheel, pleasantly barking orders. Four of the eight people on board were experienced sailors so Cal had no responsibilities other than drinking and being witty and charming – another of Jessica's explicit orders.

The Boston skyline began to recede as Jessica filled the sails and let the boat run fast toward the harbor islands. Cal made small talk with the passengers, a collection of professional types from Jessica's business and financial life. Cal was the trophy boyfriend. Everyone knew it and some, especially the women, seemed to know all about him.

'I was hoping to meet you,' said a heavily tanned woman in a bikini.

'Were you?' Cal asked.

'I'm Jessica's corporate lawyer. When we're not talking about deals we're talking about you.'

'I see,' Cal said, clinking her glass. 'Good things, I hope.'

'You wish,' the lawyer said, smiling broadly. 'You were a shit for backing out of Iceland. A good-looking one, but a shit nonetheless.'

'I'll take that as half a compliment.'

Approaching Georges Island and the geometrical, gray walls of Fort Warren, Cal saw an opening to sidle up to Larry Engel, at the bow.

Engel was on the heavy side. Cal had seen him maneuvering awkwardly along the railing to find his perch.

'I'm not much of a sailor,' Cal said. 'You?'

'Hardly,' Engel said. 'Actually, I can't believe I haven't barfed yet.'

'I understand you're at Jessica's company.'

'I am. I'm in charge of medical research.'

Engel countered that he understood Cal was Jessica's significant other.

'I am,' Cal said cheerfully. 'Tough job but someone's got to do it.'

'She's a demanding boss,' Engel volunteered. 'This cruise wasn't all that optional, truth be told. I was hoping to go into the lab today.'

Cal asked him about his background but he already knew it. He'd looked him up before leaving the house. MD, PhD, associate professor of surgical oncology at Brigham and Women's Hospital in Boston before Jessica recruited him for her biotech company.

Cal went for it. 'Actually, Larry, I was kind of hoping I could get you to look at something. It's an interesting medical case – well, three cases really.'

'I thought you were a historian.'

'History of religion, yeah. This involves something that borders on science and religion. Have you heard about the three missing Marys?'

'Who hasn't? You involved in that?'

'I'm doing some consulting for the Vatican. I've got a medical report on the girls. I'd love to hear what you think.'

'Yeah, sure.' He grabbed at his stomach for show. 'Beats looking at the front of the boat go up and down, up and down.'

Cal asked him to keep the information confidential and passed him the report, reading it again over his shoulder. Both of them were so absorbed that they failed to notice that Jessica had handed the wheel over to a banker friend and had come forward.

'For fuck's sake,' she said, startling them. 'You guys looking at porn?'

The page Larry was reviewing contained three close-up photos of female genitalia.

Cal began to explain but Jessica scolded him mercilessly for, in fact, bringing work along.

'At least I didn't cancel on you,' Cal said hopefully.

'This is really interesting,' Engel declared. 'I mean *really* interesting.'

'Those snatches belong to the alleged virgins?' she asked, settling down.

'You bet,' Engel said. 'This is a full work-up done by a doctor named Richard Benedict. He's not just any Joe. He's the president of the American College of Obstetrics and Gynecology.'

'So, he's the snatch-whisperer?' she said.

'Jesus, Jessica,' Engel said.

'And where, pray tell, did he examine their privates?' she asked.

'His report doesn't say,' Cal said, 'but it's a confirmation that they're all safe and together. I'm going to call him to see if he'll spill the beans.'

'So, what's the verdict, Larry?'

'Well, they're virgins, all right. There's no question in Benedict's opinion or in mine, although his opinion counts for more. And they're all early third trimester. He did the ultrasounds himself. All males. He also says that it would have been impossible to get an embryo-transfer catheter through the cervix and into the uterus without tearing their hymens.'

'Well, Cal, that should make you happy as a clam,' she said. 'Miracles abound. Now, boys, make *me* happy. Put away the work and open a new bottle of bubbly.'

Cal waited until after lunch for a time when Jessica was engrossed in her skippering. She had sailed over to Quincy Bay where a similar-sized yacht had challenged her to a friendly race back to Boston and her competitive juices were flowing. Protecting his phone as best he could from the salty spray, Cal took to the bow and called the mobile phone number listed in the report.

'Hello, is this Dr Benedict?'

The answer was gruff. 'Who's this?'

'This is Professor Calvin Donovan from Harvard. I'm sorry to bother you on a Sunday but someone gave me a copy of your report on the three Marys this morning.'

'I'm sorry, do I know you?'

'I don't believe so.'

'You're at the medical school?'

'Divinity School.' There was silence on the line. Cal explained that he was a consultant to the Vatican on religious aspects of the situation and that an unknown party had asked him to pass along his report to Rome.

'I wouldn't know about any of that,' Benedict said. 'I was hired to examine the subjects, I wrote a report, end of story. Look, I'm at my club about to tee off.'

'Could I ask you where you saw the girls?'

'You could ask. I won't say. I signed a nondisclosure agreement.'

'Was it in the United States?'

'Goodbye, Professor Donovan. I'm hanging up now.'

Cal was surprised by the lateness of the call.

It was Sunday evening in Cambridge; early Monday in Rome.

Elisabetta acknowledged that it could have waited but she volunteered that she couldn't sleep and besides, she could fully brief the pontiff before morning Mass. When Cal returned from his harbor sail he scanned and emailed Benedict's report to her.

'I sent it all of ten minutes ago,' Cal said. 'You're a fast reader.'

'I'll read it again more carefully but I understand its conclusions. You said in your cover message that you spoke with another doctor already?'

'He's not a gynecologist but he's a pretty smart surgeon. He told me the evaluation was well done and that the conclusions were supported by the facts.'

'This Dr Benedict – he's credible?'

'Gold-plated, apparently.'

'And he refused to say where he saw the girls?'

'Hung up on me when I asked.'

'You know this request, or perhaps demand, from this unknown person or persons that the matter be taken up by the Congregation for the Causes of Saints – you know that this is impossible under Canon Law.'

'I understand,' Cal said, trying to uncork an ice-cold bottle of vodka one-handed. 'An inquiry is possible only upon the death of the subject.'

'Do you think this person wouldn't know this? Does this imply we are not dealing with a Catholic?'

'I've got no idea. Anyone can Google the canonization procedure.'

'Why do you think they contacted you rather than the Vatican?'

'I suppose they saw my interview and figured I'd be a good conduit.'

'The Holy Father will surely ask me what you recommend that we do.'

'Look, it's entirely your call but if you want to keep a lid on this and discourage whoever they are from going down the publicity-seeking path they've threatened, then you could announce that you're setting up an *ad hoc* investigative panel within the Vatican, separate and apart from a formal congregation proceedings. Who knows how long that would take, if you get my meaning?'

'So, pay them lip service.'

'Exactly.'

'A tactic worthy of the Vatican,' she joked.

'Have any of the families been contacted by their daughters?'

'As far as we know, not yet.'

'Anything on the local investigations?'

'Nothing. Before you received this medical report we didn't even know they were still alive. Thank God for your news. We will make sure the parents know the girls are safe.'

THIRTEEN

When Sue asked Mary Riordan to come with her to the lounge, the girl assumed she was going to be told off for something.

'What did I do?' she demanded to know.

'This isn't about your behavior, although it could be,' Sue said.

She handed her a mobile phone. 'Here. Call your mother. The number's in the favorites list. We gave her a phone too.'

'It's about bloody time,' Mary said.

Sue went across the room – far enough to give a semblance of privacy, close enough to listen in. The phones, Sue was told, were untraceable in case anyone tried to get a bead on their location.

'Mum, it's me,' Mary said.

Cindy Riordan was talking too loudly, as if trying to compensate for the distance between them. 'They told me you'd be calling. How are you? I've been worried sick.'

'So worried you sold me off?'

'Now, don't be that way. They told us they'd be caring for you better than we could.' Then she lowered her voice to foil any eavesdroppers, 'They told me not to ask where you were.'

'Wouldn't matter if you did. I haven't a clue. Stopped at the Boston airport and then went on to somewhere else.'

'Are they treating you well, like they said they would?'

'Place is dripping with money. Big-ass mansion but there's nothing near it. Just miles and miles of what looks like a desert or some such thing. Everything's the color of corn flakes. You go outside and it's so bloody hot you want to pass out. They got horses though. There's a cook and they clean and wash up for us. They gave me new clothes, some of them are rubbish, some quite nice. They're making me do school lessons on a computer which is pathetic, really.'

'Who's there with you, love?'

'I've got a minder named Sue who's snooping on me right now. Then there's the one who came to the house. Mrs Torres.'

'She seemed nice.'

'She's not. She's a cow. The other girls are here too.'

'I figured you'd be all together but I didn't know, did I? They're going on and on about the three missing Marys on the telly and all. I'm glad you're all safe and sound. They nice?'

'They're annoying, really. They don't speak English and one of them is a real whinger.'

'Still, three peas in a pod, right? Dearie me, you'll be a mother before long and I'll be a gran.'

'They had a fancy doctor come and examine us.'

'What did he say?'

'Surprise! I'm pregnant.'

'Is the baby all right?'

'Guess so. Still got a willy.'

'You'll need to be thinking of a name for him.'

She blurted out, 'I don't want a kid! This wasn't my bloody choice.'

'I know, love. You were chosen, just like the voice told you. Voice of God, I reckon.'

'More like the cock of God.'

Sue shook her head and looked out the window at the endless, dry pastures that merged a long way off with a colorless sky. The windows were double-glazed but she could hear the machinery and clanging noises that were non-stop during the daytime, seven days a week.

'Don't blaspheme,' her mother scolded.

When the call was over Sue took her back to the communal bedroom and, one after the other, brought the Marias to the lounge to speak with their families too. Neither girl had ever used a phone before and their conversations were brief but emotional. By the time Maria Mollo had finished, Sue was also in tears. She hugged the clingy, small girl and decided to carry her back to her bed.

'Joyful reunion, was it?' Mary said. 'Mucho crying.'

'Give everyone a break and zip it,' Sue said. 'The girls have another English lesson and you've got two more hours of course-work to do. Before supper we've got a treat for all of you.'

'Treat?' Mary said. 'You gonna hang yourself?'

The sun was closer to the horizon and the blistering heat was done for the day but it was still uncomfortably warm. Sue gave each girl a bottle of cold water for the walk to the stables. Mrs Simpauco came along to translate for Maria Aquino. The stable hands were Mexican so the other Maria was covered.

'We going to see the horses?' Mary asked, skipping along.

'We are,' Sue said.

'Can we ride them.'

'That's not on the agenda.'

The stables was a large, low-slung building with a metal roof, but a quarter-mile behind it, the skeleton of a steel-framed structure was rising from the dry earth.

'Is that what's been responsible for all the racket?'

Sue said it was.

'What's it going to be?'

'I wasn't told,' Sue said. 'I really don't know.'

The girls were delighted to see the magnificent beasts. Even Maria Mollo was joyful. She immediately bonded with a stable hand named Pedro Alvarado, a small man with a winning smile, and he held her hand as they went from stall to stall introducing her to each horse by name. But it was Mary who was the most excited, asking detailed questions about the ages of the horses, their diets, their exercise regimens.

'You know a lot about horses, señorita,' the ranch foreman said.

'There's a horse farm just down the road from us. I used to help out there.'

'Maybe they will let you help here too,' he said.

'Could I?' Mary asked Sue.

It seemed like a damned good idea but Sue said she'd have to check with Mrs Torres.

After they'd gone down the row of stalls feeding the horses from a bucket of carrot chunks, the foreman said that each girl could choose her favorite and they would take them outside to a paddock to watch them run around. Maria Aquino chose a tawny mare, Maria Mollo picked a black stallion, and Mary chose a pinto mare named Sally. Pedro bridled them and led them out. The two Marias held on to the fencing, looking through the slats while Mary insisted on climbing up and sitting on the top rail.

'Careful, now,' Sue said nervously.

'Being pregnant hasn't made me spastic,' Mary said.

The horses bucked and frolicked with one another for fifteen minutes while the girls laughed and pointed. It was getting close to suppertime and Sue had to get them washed-up so she called time on the proceedings. Pedro looped the mares to the fence before leading the stallion inside first, Maria Mollo following along. Maria Aquino's horse lowered its head so the girl could stroke its cheek and Mary reached down from her perch to stroke the pinto.

'You don't want to go back in, do you, Sally?' she said.

She took the whinny as a no.

Pedro returned for the next horse and Mary begged him to take the tawny mare first. Maria Aquino and Mrs Simpauco followed.

Sue was pumping the foreman for any info he had on the steel building when Mary reached into the pocket of her shorts and fed her horse a piece of carrot that she'd reserved. While the horse munched, Mary unlooped the bridle, stood on the second-to-last rung of the fence, and swung her leg over Sally's broad back.

'C'mon, girl, let's get out of here.'

She held the reins tightly, kicked Sally's flanks with her sneakers and the horse took off through the open gate.

'Mary!' Sue screamed. 'Come back!'

The foreman shouted in Spanish for Pedro to bring a horse fast and the small man flew outside with the tawny mare. The Marias ran after him and stood beside the paddock pointing at the cloud of dust that was Mary and her horse. The foreman ripped the reins from Pedro's hand, leapt into the air and pulled himself by the mane on to the horse's back.

'Don't worry, I'll get her,' he shouted, racing out of the paddock.

'She's pregnant!' Sue screamed after him.

'Believe me, I know, señora.'

Mary was a good rider but hanging on to a galloping horse bareback wasn't easy. She bounced around and slipped to the left and the right, pinching her knees into its smooth flanks as best she could. She wasn't just blindly flying off into the prairie. She had a plan and she steered the horse toward the steel structure crawling with construction workers. She would tell them who she was and that she'd been kidnapped. She'd plead with them to call the police. She'd—

An arm reached out and grabbed the bridle by the cheek piece. Sally began to slow down. When Mary turned toward the foreman, she began to slide off. The foreman had to let go of the bridle to reach around her waist and as he did, Sally took off again.

The foreman was strong and he held her up against his mare even with her horse long gone. The tawny mare came to a halt with a verbal command and the foreman lowered the girl to the ground as gently as he could.

He dismounted and waved at Sue who was running toward them.

'Where were you going, Miss Mary?' he asked.

She was out of breath. 'I was trying to escape.'

'Why? Everyone here loves the little virgins.'

'Is that what you call us?'

'Yes, señorita. Will you come back with me?'

'What about Sally?'

'Oh, she'll come back on her own. Can I tell you something, Miss Mary?'

She nodded.

'You ride bareback real good.'

After supper Torres raged at Sue and the foreman and declared the stables off limits. The foreman was sufficiently scared by her ferocity that he kept his mouth shut and mainly stared at the floor, but Sue did her best to argue that with sufficient safeguards, working with horses was exactly what Mary Riordan needed to settle into life at the ranch.

Faced with a determined no, Sue asked whether she could appeal the decision to a higher authority. Torres imperiously informed her that as far as Sue was concerned, there was no one higher. With that, she turned her back and left the two alone in the staff room.

'Miss Sue, it's not my place,' the foreman said, 'but I agree with you. That girl loves horses and I think they love her too.'

After supper, the girls played in their lounge while Lily the bulldog frolicked. Mary was cross-legged on an overstuffed chair fiddling with her phone and the Marias were on the carpet, trying to keep Lily away from a half-done jigsaw puzzle. While Maria Mollo bent over searching for a piece, Maria Aquino, the smaller of the two, climbed on her back like a horseback rider. The Peruvian girl immediately got the joke and began simulating a bucking horse.

'Me Mary, me Mary,' the Filipino shouted to which the other Maria replied, 'I go, I go.' The two of them harvesting all the fruits of their first English lessons.

Mary looked on, po-faced at first, as they dissolved into hysterics, falling off one another and rolling about on the floor. But soon Mary was laughing too and hurling cushions at them.

When Sue came upstairs to look in on them she saw the makings of a good old-fashioned pillow fight. She quietly backed away and closed the door, letting the girls carry on being kids.

FOURTEEN

Joe Murphy lived in a sparse studio apartment in a house near Central Square. It suited him fine. It was marginally nicer than his rectory accommodations in Galway and he could walk to Harvard, rain, snow, or shine. His salary as an entry-level junior faculty member at the university was fairly modest but it was considerably more money than he'd made as a parish priest or as Cal's teaching assistant. The only luxury he afforded himself was buying the books he fancied rather than signing them out of the library. Any surplus funds were earmarked for his mother back home and a small trust fund for nieces and nephews.

It was a hot August morning and his window-box air conditioner was humming. His plans for the day were simple and pleasant. He'd finish his coffee, dress in his summer-weight clerical clothes, and stroll to the Widener Library in Harvard Yard to continue taking notes for his next book, an exploration of the medieval Church in Ireland. He'd taken Cal's advice to heart that the only way to achieve academic security was to publish, publish, and publish some more. Being a popular lecturer – and so far, Murphy was well-liked by students – was only icing on the cake.

He was dreamily streaming classical music from his computer to a Bluetooth speaker when his phone rang, showing a blocked number. He thought about letting it ring through to voicemail but he couldn't remember the last time someone called this way so he answered.

It was a woman. 'Excuse me, am I speaking with Father Murphy?'

'You are. Who is this?'

'This is Cindy Riordan, Mary's mother.'

Murphy put his coffee mug down so quickly that he spilled a little. He asked how he could help her.

'I've been worried sick about Mary.'

'Well, that's understandable,' he said.

'Do you know where she is?'

Cal had told him about the Benedict report. 'I don't, no,' he said. 'But there's an indication that she's with the other two girls who are in the same way.'

'I know that,' she replied. 'I've spoken with her.'

'Is that so?'

'They delivered this phone to me so she could call.'

'Then you likely know more than I do. What did she tell you?'

'That she was in a grand house somewhere that was very hot with the Maria girls and she was being well looked after.'

'Well that's a relief, isn't it? She didn't mention where she was?'

'She says she had no idea. She's cut off, I'd say.'

'Is there something you'd like me to do for you, Mrs Riordan?'

'There is, Father, but I don't want to talk about it over the phone. Maybe I'm paranoid but I feel someone might be listening. Do you think you could come round?'

'I'm back in America, you know.'

He heard her tutting before saying, 'Oh my, I'd no idea. I don't know what to say. It's terribly important. I've no one else I can talk to.'

'What about Canon McCarthy?'

'Don't like him. He's a cold fish. Don't trust him like I trust you.'

Murphy tried to get more out of her, finally asking, 'Look, you need to tell me more if I'm going to be getting on an airplane.'

'I'll tell you this, Father: I've done something terrible, truly terrible, and I need to make it right. I'm begging you to come.'

Later that morning Murphy called in on Cal at his Divinity Avenue office to tell him about the phone call.

'What do you think's going on?' Cal asked.

'I really don't know. The woman sounded quite emotional. I doubt it's a trivial thing.'

'What do you want to do?'

'What I want to do and what I'm obliged to do are two different matters,' the priest said.

'It's got to be your call, Joe, but if you want to make the trip let me see if I can get the Vatican to spring for the airfare.'

Murphy said, 'That would be most appreciated.'

*   *   *

Murphy's plan was to get in and get out quickly, spending a single night in Galway before flying back to Boston and his research. He hired a car at Shannon and arrived at the Riordan house well before noon. When no one responded to the knocker he leaned on the buzzer until he heard a stirring through the door.

Kenny Riordan appeared in his undershorts, glassy-eyed and smelling like a brewery.

'Father Murphy. This is unexpected.'

'I'm sorry if I woke you, Mr Riordan.'

'What time is it?'

'Just gone eleven. It's your wife I was looking for actually.'

'Why's that?'

'That's between me and her if you can respect that.'

'Oh, yeah, I've got all the respect for the collar, Father. The thing is, she's not here.'

'Oh? Where might she be?'

'She took ill last evening. Her breathing. She's got asthma, you know. They had to take her off to hospital, which isn't a small matter. Just getting her out the door and into the ambulance. She's a big girl.'

'Which hospital?'

'University. If you're going, tell her the children are with her sister and I'm tending to myself.'

'I can see you are.'

Murphy found her on the pulmonary unit. Visiting hours weren't until two but priests roamed the wards freely. She was splayed out, snoring on an extra-wide bed, an oxygen mask held to her face by an elastic band.

He closed the door and stood beside her saying her name. When that didn't wake her he lightly squeezed her upper arm through the flimsy cloth of her hospital gown. Her snoring stopped and she moaned lightly. Another harder squeeze did the trick.

'Father?' she said blearily.

'Hello, Cindy. Here I am. How are you?'

She pulled her mask away until it rested on one cheek. 'Not well, I'm afraid, as you can see.'

'I'm very sorry to hear it. I did come as quickly as I could.'

'From America?'

'Yes, all the way from Boston. You called, I came.'

'Oh dear . . .' She began to wheeze.

'Would you like me to ring for the nurse?'

She did and he removed himself from the room while a sister attended to her. When he was allowed to come back in the head of the bed was elevated and she was propped on pillows with prongs in her nostrils instead of the mask.

Before he could say anything, she told him, 'I wish you hadn't come.'

Murphy knew he probably wasn't the most compassionate priest on the planet but he could hardly contain himself. 'What in God's name am I to make of this? You called me about a matter of some gravity and I dropped what I was doing and scampered all the way back to Ireland and now you say you wish I hadn't come?'

Tears began flowing down her fleshy cheeks.

'Look, I'm sorry to be harsh, Cindy, but I'm sure you can see why I'm gobsmacked.'

She whispered something so faintly he couldn't hear it over the flowing oxygen. When he came closer, she repeated herself. 'I was right. They were listening,' she whispered.

'How do you know that?'

'They came to the house yesterday.'

'Who did?'

'Rough lads. On their motorbikes.'

Murphy could see their faces as if they were there in the room. 'One tall, one shorter, the shorter one with a cratered complexion?'

'That's them. You know of them?'

'I do. What did they say to you?'

'They told me they'd harm me and the kids if I talked to you.'

'They threatened you?'

The tears started running again.

'Did you call the police?'

'They said not to. They frightened me. It gave me a breathing fit and now look at me. So, I can't speak with you, Father Murphy, even though I want to.'

'Can you just tell me a little of what's troubling you? I do want to help.'

'Did you see anyone lurking in the corridors?' she asked nervously.

'Believe me, I'd know it if those two were about.'

She had him come even closer, so close he could smell the hospital toothpaste. 'I didn't want to do it. I didn't want to sign their paper but Kenny made me. On account of the money.'

'What money? What paper?'

'I can't say more.' She pleaded with him. 'Don't ask me to say more.'

He didn't and quietly left.

That night Kenny Riordan came to visit his wife after stopping at the pub for a few lubricating pints.

'How're you getting on?' he asked, sitting on the bed while she reclined in the bedside lounging chair.

'Much better. They've got me on the steroids by drip. Only thing is they make me put on weight.'

'Oh yeah?' he said. 'How will we know?'

She wasn't offended. She thought it was funny.

He asked whether the priest had come to visit. 'You didn't say nothing to him, did you?'

'About Mary?' she said defensively. 'I wouldn't.'

'Good, see to it you don't. We don't want no trouble. You sent the padre packing?'

She nodded her big head. 'I feel bad. He came all this way.'

'Not a total waste. He's racking up those frequent-flier miles, I'm sure.'

She visibly stiffened.

'What's the matter, love?' Riordan asked.

He heard the creak of soft-soled shoes against the pale-green linoleum tiles and swiveled his neck.

'Shit.'

'What a lovely greeting,' Doyle said. His partner, McElroy, shut the door. Doyle had the smallest bunch of gift-shop flowers one could buy. 'Brung these for you. Got a vase in here?'

She stared at him mutely.

Doyle looked around and, seeing none, plonked the nosegay into an empty urinal pan.

'Kenny, there's a pub down the block. Why don't you get yourself a pint while we have a small chat with Cindy? All right?'

'Don't leave,' she begged.

'That's awful advice,' Doyle said. 'You see, we know where your sister lives, darling. The kids are there, aren't they? You wouldn't want us riding over there later on.'

Riordan got up and mumbled to his wife that he'd be waiting in the hall.

Doyle, the tall man, bent over and whispered to him, 'Don't fret. Won't be long.'

Kenny paced the hall, making a circuit around the nursing station until he saw the men leaving her room. McElroy's face showed its usual emptiness but Doyle was grinning like he'd just heard a wicked joke. He made a point of hitting Riordan with his shoulder as he passed him.

'Done you a favor. You can step out now. And Kenny, we was never here.'

Riordan fast-walked the corridor and swung the door open. She was in the chair, her head resting oddly on one shoulder, eyes open but unsearching. He fell to his knees before her.

'Cindy. No. No. No. Nurse!'

Murphy was sound asleep in his hotel room when his phone rang. He hadn't been expecting any calls and his phone was charging in the bathroom. Aside from the unmade bed, the room almost looked unused. His small overnight bag was packed and ready to go, his clothes draped neatly over the chair.

'Father Murphy, it's Kenny Riordan.'

'It's the middle of the night, Kenny. What's the matter?'

'Can you come to the hospital. It's Cindy.'

There was a place off the hospital's ground floor called the bereavement room and well after midnight, that's where Murphy hunkered down with Riordan.

'Tell me what happened?'

'She stopped breathing. They think it was maybe a heart attack. There was nothing they could do for her.'

Murphy detected more than grief. The man was scared too.

'Are you telling me everything, Kenny?'

'Course I am. Tell me something, Father. You met with her earlier in the day. How did she seem?'

'You know she summoned me, don't you?'

'She said something about it but I don't know what she had in mind.'

'She didn't tell you?'

Riordan sputtered a denial but he looked like a tyke caught in a web of lies.

'She wanted to unburden herself,' the priest said.

'What did she say to you?'

'Even in death I can't betray a confidence but she told me a few things, perhaps not everything.'

Riordan's chest heaved a couple of times. 'Look, Father, I respect you and all but I need to know what beans she spilled. There's people about that would do us harm. I don't want my kids to be orphans.'

Murphy held a hand over his eyes while he thought. Then he said, 'Did someone do this? Did someone cause her death?'

'The doctor said it was likely a heart attack,' Riordan replied weakly.

'Are they going to do a post-mortem exam?'

'I wouldn't let them.'

Murphy couldn't stay seated. He shuffled his feet a bit and crossed his arms.

'I feel I should speak with the police.'

That got Riordan on his feet too. 'No, Father, you don't want to do that. These are bad people, really bad sorts. It'll come back on me and mine.'

'But—'

'No buts, Father. I'm begging you. What's done is done. It's the living you need to fuss over, not the dead.'

Sue's bedroom at the mansion was large and well-appointed with good furniture and tasteful pictures on the walls but it lacked personal touches. Back in Santa Fe she had decorated her condo very much to taste with southwestern rugs and bedspread, local pottery, and photos she'd taken of favorite hiking vistas in the desert and the mountains. She didn't really want to be reminded of life back home. She missed it too much. She had taken the job for the insane amount of money they threw at her but even so, she thought about quitting every day, especially now she'd met the sad little girls who seemed like wild birds in a gilded cage.

But if she left someone would only take her place. The girls weren't going anywhere.

There was a rare knock on her door, the first time she'd ever been bothered in her quarters. Torres looked like she'd hastily put on her face. The lipstick job was on the sloppy-side for her.

'Is something the matter?' Sue asked.

'You're still dressed,' Torres said. 'May I come in?'

'Are the girls OK?'

'I'm sure they're sleeping. It's late.'

She came in and sat down on the loveseat. Perplexed, Sue offered her something from the mini-fridge but the woman declined.

'I've received a disturbing call,' Torres said. 'It's about Mary Riordan's mother. She's dead.'

Sue sat on her bed, shaking her head in shock.

'My God, what happened?'

'She passed away in a hospital where she'd been taken for her asthma. I'm told she wasn't a well woman. She was quite heavy apparently.'

'From what Mary's told me, she wasn't very old.'

'Yes, it's very sad. I wanted to share the news with you. There wasn't anyone else to tell.'

'Except for Mary.'

'We mustn't tell her.'

'It's her mother.'

'Lord knows what might happen. She's pregnant. The shock.'

Sue went to the fridge and pulled the rubber cork from a half-full bottle of white wine. Torres changed her mind and asked for a glass too.

'How can we keep this from her?' Sue asked.

'I've always thought that this kind of news could cause miscarriages. Am I wrong? You're the expert.'

Sue had to admit that there was a small but real risk of emotional distress causing premature labor.

Torres drank the entire glass in a series of gulps. 'We can't take the risk. The stakes are too high.'

Kenny Riordan prevailed upon Joe Murphy to officiate at the funeral. He didn't want to do it but the fellow told him something that he knew, that Cindy disliked Canon McCarthy something awful and had said nice things about him. Murphy's sense of duty got the better of him and he got McCarthy's permission to say the funeral Mass at St Colman's. The crowd of mourners was on the sparse side. The Riordans and their grifter ways hadn't exactly endeared themselves to the local community and without Mary in attendance the curiosity factor surrounding them had diminished. Fewer still braved the lashing rain at the Rahoon Cemetery.

When Cindy Riordan's casket was lowered into her soggy grave and her children were led away by their aunt, Riordan tried to press some euros into Murphy's hand.

'Won't be necessary,' Murphy said from under his umbrella. 'I'm sorry for your loss, Kenny, I really am. So, you know, I won't be calling the authorities but if they reach out to me, I'll be honest with them. I can't be otherwise.'

'I understand, Father, but they'll have no reason to call you.'

'Was Mary informed of the death?'

'Not by me. I wouldn't know how to reach her. Cindy had a new mobile phone about but it's gone missing. Anyway, I wouldn't know what to tell her.'

Murphy parted ways with Riordan at the car park. The gravel paths were heavily puddled and his shoes were getting saturated. He had a pair of trainers in his overnight bag and he opened the boot to swap them for his wet leathers.

The next thing he experienced was the worst headache he'd ever had. He was lying on a bed or a cot somewhere that was cool and damp, a place smelling of soil and roots. His confusion was side-tracked by a powerful wave of nausea. When he tried to sit to vomit, he realized he was handcuffed to the bed frame. He rolled on to his side and barfed on to an earthen floor.

'Hello?' he shouted. 'Is anybody there? Hello? Somebody help!'

The dean of the Harvard Divinity School was a flinty Brit named Gil Daniels. He'd been introducing his faculty at an orientation session for the new crop of graduate students attending in the fall, but when he got to Cal, his true feelings about his star professor came over clearly enough. Daniels had on more than one occasion erupted in profound jealousy at Cal's Vatican access, particularly his unprecedented and unique browsing privileges at the Vatican Apostolic Library and Secret Archives, personally granted by Pope Celestine.

'Is there anyone here who hasn't heard of our illustrious colleague, Calvin Donovan?' Daniels said sarcastically. 'Contrary to what you've no doubt read, Professor Donovan does not spend *all* his time globetrotting and hobnobbing with Vatican grandees. On occasion he teaches the history of religion at this very institution.'

Cal sported a smile and was about to summarize his courses on offer for the coming year when the departmental secretary looked in and waved for his attention. He apologized and went to the door where she told him that a woman was on the phone with what she said was a life-or-death matter.

'Sorry,' Cal said to the room. 'I've got to take an urgent call. Perhaps Professor Cretien could go next.'

Daniels nodded with an expression that seemed to say that Cal had just made his point. 'I expect his bestie, the pope, is on the line.'

Cal picked up the flashing line in his office.

'Is this Calvin Donovan? Sorry, Professor Donovan?'

'Yes?'

'This is Edna Murphy, Joe's mum. I had your number over there at the university. Joe gave it to me years back just in case.' Her voice was quavering.

'Is something wrong, Mrs Murphy?'

'I've just had a call from a man who says Joe's been taken. They're asking a lot of money. I don't have any money myself but Joe always said that Harvard University was quite wealthy. I'm not to call the police or they'll kill Joe. That's what he said. I thought of calling the parish but the church in Galway isn't exactly rolling in it. That's when I thought of Joe's employer. Do you think you could help me, Professor Donovan? Joe thinks the world of you.'

FIFTEEN

Cal didn't care what the kidnappers said. He wasn't going to risk Murphy's life on a freelance effort. He'd been able to get to the airport to make the evening Aer Lingus flight to Shannon and as soon as he arrived in Galway the next morning he presented himself to the Gardai station. Minutes later he was being interviewed by an elfin inspector named Sullivan and his sergeant, a heavy-set fellow named Feeney. The two of them together evened out to an average-sized man.

'Why in God's name did his mother not call us?' Sullivan said. 'We've lost precious time.'

'She was scared,' Cal said.

'I can see that but it wasn't smart. Sergeant, get over to her house with a couple of men and set up a tap on her phone. But be gentle with the poor dear. Don't berate her. How much was their demand?'

'A hundred thousand euros,' Cal said. 'She thought the university might pay.'

'Will it?'

'That's not going to happen.'

'Well then, no ransom.'

Cal sipped bad coffee from a paper cup. 'I'm willing to pay.'

'Personally?'

'Yes.'

'That's a considerable sum.'

'Joe Murphy is a friend. And I was the one who got him involved with the Riordans in the first place.'

'Well, I don't recommend paying up in these situations but it would be up to you.'

'When we're done here I'll get to a bank to arrange for a wire transfer.'

'That's fine, Professor. Sergeant, instruct Mrs Murphy to demand proof of life the next time they call. A photo with the daily paper will do. If they're morons they'll agree to leave it in her mailbox.

If they're a notch above troglodytes they'll suggest a drop-off place. Off you go.'

The sergeant left the two of them in the interview room.

'Did Father Murphy have any enemies that you know of? Anyone who'd wish him harm?'

This was the moment for Cal to uncork the story about the menacing motorbike riders who had made threatening remarks outside his mother's house.

'A quiet one and a talkative one,' the inspector said. 'Did he say anything about their appearance?'

'Not to me.'

'And the talkative one told them to stay away from the Riordans.'

'That's what Joe told me.'

'Can you tell me your understanding of the reason that Father Murphy returned to Galway?'

'Mrs Riordan phoned him. She had something – as she put it, terribly important – to tell him and didn't feel comfortable talking about it over the phone.'

'So, he just up and hopped on a plane? That's quite the gesture and quite the expense.'

'Joe has a profound sense of duty. And the Vatican agreed to reimburse him for the trip.'

Sullivan's face turned quizzical. 'Now why is that?'

Cal told him about the consult he and Murphy had performed.

The inspector finished jotting some notes. 'So, this seems tied into the mystery of the missing girls. Father Murphy is warned to stay away from the Riordans by these two fellows and then he does the opposite.'

'That sums it up,' Cal said.

'That would make these motorcycle fellows the prime suspects.'

'That's certainly what I've been thinking,' Cal said.

'All right. We'll need to speak again in the near future. Will you be staying locally?'

'I will. Any recommendations?'

'As you seem to be a man of means, I'd say the Park House might suit your tastes.'

Cal checked into the hotel, showered and walked through the

bar on his way out. It comforted him that it was well-stocked. He had a feeling he'd be capitalizing on that by nightfall.

Doyle dropped a bag of cold fish and chips on to Murphy's cellar cot while McElroy lurked in the shadows by the bulkhead door.

'You'd better eat.'

'Toward what end?' Murphy said, swinging his feet on to the earthen floor. They'd added a chain to his restraints to give him a little more movement.

'Don't want to starve to death,' Doyle said.

'Why are you talking rubbish?' Murphy said. 'If I was getting out of this you'd have concealed your faces.'

'Oh, we'll be well away once we get paid. No chance of getting caught.'

'Who do you think's going to be paying a ransom? We Murphys don't have money.'

'All in hand, Father, all in hand.'

Outside the cottage McElroy mounted his street bike and asked the other man, 'We're not letting him go when we're paid, are we?'

'Course not!' Doyle said, swinging on to his Honda. 'They wanted him dead and that's what'll happen. They didn't say we couldn't extract some cash first. Best of both worlds.'

Kenny Riordan was well known to Inspector Sullivan. Riordan had been involved in petty crimes and scams as long as Sullivan had been on the force. Even as a fledgling Garda he'd questioned him repeatedly. He could almost close his eyes and steer his car to Riordan's bungalow.

'I'm sorry for your loss, Kenny,' the inspector said at his door.

'Well, that's grand of you, Sullivan,' Riordan said. It was still morning and he'd been drinking. 'I'll just return to what I was doing.'

'Alone, are you?' Sullivan asked.

'Me, myself, and I.'

'No wake then?'

'Fuck everyone, no.'

'I'd like a word inside.'

'Do I have a choice?'

'You do. We can chat here or at the station.'

* * *

When Cal called in at Mrs Murphy's house, she was too upset to speak with him. The Gardai were in her front room waiting for a phone call from the kidnappers and she was in her bedroom behind a closed door.

In time she emerged and said, 'I appreciate your coming but they said no police.'

'I had to talk to the Gardai, Mrs Murphy. It's too dangerous to deal with this kind of situation without professionals. Any contact from the kidnappers?'

'Not a peep. Sergeant Feeney's told me what to say. Did the university agree to pay the money?'

'It's being wired today. The Allied Bank should have it by late afternoon.'

'Thank the Lord,' she said. 'Who am I to thank? Besides you, that is.'

'That shouldn't be your first priority.'

'You're right, of course. Will you wait with me?'

'I'd be happy to.'

'Cup of tea?' She touched her hair and seemed to realize she was wearing a tatty housedress. 'Joseph never told me that you were a handsome man, Professor Donovan. I wonder why?'

Cal smiled at her. 'Hopefully you'll be able to ask him that soon.'

Sullivan took the gloves off a few minutes into his interrogation. The pint-sized inspector hadn't risen through the ranks because of his physicality. He was on his way to superintendent by dint of instinct and intellect. He was sure that Riordan was being evasive – the quick glance at the floor, the tug at the bottle of beer when asked if he knew anything about the two motorcyclists.

'A man's been kidnapped, for God's sake! A priest. A priest who said Mass at your wife's funeral. And you're sitting there, wallowing in drink, refusing to help the Gardai with their inquiries.'

'Oh, fuck off,' Riordan mumbled, gesturing toward Cindy's empty recliner, the old slab of yellow foam on the seat still indented with her form. 'You're talking to a man whose wife is fresh in the ground.'

'If you don't tell us what we need to know, Joseph Murphy will be in the ground too. Let me tell you something, Kenny, this whole business with your daughter Mary stinks to high heaven. First you turn her predicament into a cottage industry, milking the pilgrims and such, then she disappears right under your nose. And what did you tell us? That the Vatican sent for her for her own protection? That was a cock and bull story, wasn't it? Did someone pay you to give her up? Did you sell your own daughter like a prize mare?'

Riordan flashed a scowl at the cop. 'If you weren't in uniform I'd pop you one for saying that.'

Sullivan bore down. 'And then what happened? Did Cindy get remorseful? Or maybe she was never in with you. Maybe you brow-beat her into participating in the scheme. She rings Father Murphy and wants to make a confession of sorts. We know from the hospital staff that Murphy visited her in her room. What they talked about, we've no idea. But then two events follow in rapid succession. Cindy dies suddenly and two days later, Murphy is taken from the cemetery. What's your explanation for that, Kenny?'

'Sometimes bad things happen to good folks.'

'Well that's a fine platitude. Here's what's going to happen if you don't tell me what you know about these two motorbike fellows. I'll go to court to get a magistrate to issue an internment order. We'll get a post-mortem on Cindy because I'm no longer satisfied that she died a natural death.'

Riordan balled a fist impotently. 'You're a bastard. You wouldn't.'

'I would and I will. You're participating in a perversion of justice and you'll be charged if I can prove it.'

'You'd put me in jail and leave my children at the mercy of the state?'

'For Christ's sake, Kenny. Who do you think pays their way now? You?'

'I can provide for them.'

'How?'

'I've got cash,' he cried out then seemed to wish he'd kept his mouth shut.

Sullivan nodded gravely. 'I'm sure you do. I'm sure somebody with unclear intentions paid you well for your Mary. And I'm sure once I put you into custody that a search of the premises will turn up the cash. You're not the type to be putting your ill-gotten gains in a bank, are you? Kenny Riordan, I'm arresting you on suspicion of perverting the course of justice.'

Riordan gripped his beer bottle tightly, prompting Sullivan to get up and point a finger. He wasn't armed and Kenny could have thrashed him if he'd had the mind to do so.

'Don't make things worse for yourself,' the inspector said as calmly as he could.

Riordan lifted the bottle to his lips then put it down empty.

'The tall one runs his mouth a blue streak,' he said. 'I don't know his name. Never heard the short one say a word. He's the muscle of the two.'

'Names?'

'No clue.'

'What else do you know about them?'

'Seen them around from time to time. Pubs. Horse auctions. Small-timers. Someone knows someone who knows someone. That's how they come to be involved in something this big.'

'Would they be known to the Gardai?'

''Spect so. Can't imagine they're lily-white.'

'What kind of bikes do they ride?'

'Hondas, if I recall. Can't say more. I don't claim to know motorbikes.'

'All right, Kenny, I'm going to need you to come in and look at mugshots, maybe do e-fits on them.'

'Am I under arrest?'

'Not at this time. We'll see how it goes.'

The phone finally rang at Mrs Murphy's house. Sergeant Feeney sharply motioned for her to pick up but she froze. It was Cal who helped her off the settee and over to a side table where an old, corded telephone was ported into monitoring gear.

When she picked up, Feeney put on a headset.

'Galway 844772,' she said in a squeaky voice.

The man said, 'You got the money?'

'It's in hand.'

'All of it?'

'I believe so.'

'Where'd you get it from?'

'Joseph's employer provided it.'

'All right, take this down. Here's where the cash is to be left.'

Feeney scribbled and held up a note: *Proof of life.*

'I need to know if Joseph is unhurt.'

'He's right as rain.'

'I need proof of life.'

There was a pause. 'Who told you to ask for that? You didn't call the police, did you? I told you that would go bad for him.'

Feeney shook his head vigorously.

'I didn't,' she said. 'I heard the term in a film.'

The man snorted. 'A film, eh? And in this film how'd they go about it?'

Feeney pantomimed clicking a camera shutter.

'A photo with the day's newspaper,' she said.

'All right. Proof of life. Then we want the cash. You'll hear from us.'

She remembered she was supposed to ask for the photo to come to the house. 'But—'

The line was dead.

She began to fret and then get weepy. Feeney was impassive, intent on calling Sullivan to recount the call, so it was left to Cal to lend a shoulder.

Riordan complained to the young Garda officer passing him binder after binder of mugshots that the suspects were beginning to look all the same. And besides, he'd missed his midday pints and was beginning to get a bit shaky. His session with the e-fit technician had gone badly. One of the final products came out as a dead ringer for Daniel Day Lewis and Riordan admitted neither e-fit really looked anything like the men.

'Getting the face right is harder than it looks,' he grumbled.

'Here's another one,' the officer said, plonking the heavy binder down in front of him.

'Have mercy, will you?' Riordan said.

'Be brave,' she said, barely hiding her disdain. 'I'll be down the hall.'

He shifted in his chair like he'd done ages ago as a distracted schoolboy, opened the binder and yawned.

* * *

Cal was wondering if it was possible to overdose on tea.

It was late in the afternoon but the sun was still bright as midday. He'd persuaded Mrs Murphy to have a lie down and he sat in the lounge using his phone judiciously as he'd forgotten to bring his universal charger from the hotel. Sergeant Feeney, bored to the core, was at the dining room table flipping through one of Mrs Murphy's women's magazines. Then his radio crackled with the voice of the Garda officer outside the house on stakeout.

'Young male, jeans, Galway football jersey, white trainers approaching postbox.'

Feeney sprung up to peek through the gauzy curtains.

'See if he makes a drop, then detain. I have eyes on him,' the sergeant said.

The teenager pulled an envelope from his back pocket, slipped it into Mrs Murphy's post box and began to amble off.

The Garda outside shot out of his car and Feeney ran down the path. Both officers shouted at him to drop to the ground and show his hands. The teenager was immobilized by fear and soon found himself tackled and cuffed by two ask-questions-later fellows.

'What did I do?' the kid asked, face down on the sidewalk.

Feeney went to the mailbox and pinched the envelope by a short edge to avoid contaminating it with his prints. Inside, he carefully opened it with a paring knife and pulled out a color print of Joe Murphy in close-up, standing in some dark place, holding a copy of today's *Connacht Tribune* under his chin.

The teenager quickly divulged the little he possessed to the younger officer. He'd been hanging out near the Corbett Court Shopping Centre when a guy on a motorbike waved him over and gave him a fiver to deliver the envelope to this address. No, he couldn't identify him because he was wearing his helmet with the visor down. The bike was a blue Honda.

The commotion woke Mrs Murphy and Cal held her hand as she looked at the photo. Murphy looked scared as hell and she took it badly.

Feeney flipped the photo over with the tip of a ballpoint pen and called the station.

'He's alive, Inspector,' he said, explaining the photo and its delivery. 'And I think we've caught a break. Our lads aren't masterminds. The photo's printed out on Fuji paper with the store's name on the back of it. They've gone to the self-print kiosk at Corbett Shopping Centre. There'll be CCTV footage to beat the band.'

Minutes later the phone rang.

'Did you see your proof of life?' the man asked Mrs Murphy.

'He didn't look well,' she said.

'All he needed to do was look alive. It's time for the cash. You got a pencil? Cause I've got some instructions. And if we see any guards about at the drop point, the next time you see your boy he's going to look dead.'

Mrs Murphy was left in the hands of a female victim liaison officer so Feeney could see to collecting the CCTV files and Cal could pick up the ransom cash from the bank. A carrier bag with the money was to be left at a rural signpost about ten kilometers north of the city. Cal had volunteered to do the drop. Plain-clothes officers would be positioned to follow whoever picked up the bag and hopefully be led to the priest's location – at least that was the plan until Feeney came barreling into the station.

He tossed the printed images of a tall, thin man holding a motorcycle helmet at the Fuji kiosk and said, 'I know the cunt. He's Brendan Doyle.'

'What's he done?' Sullivan asked.

'More like what hasn't he done,' Feeney said. 'He's been involved in all manner of trafficking in drugs and stolen goods.'

'Kidnapping a bit above his pay grade?' the inspector asked.

'I'd say so. I've got a recollection that he's been done a number of times with an associate. Can't recall his name. Give me a few ticks.'

'See if Riordan's still here? We need to have him take a look at this Doyle.'

Riordan had left a while back. Now he was extracted from his local and shown assorted mugshots of Brendan Doyle and Keenan McElroy.

'That's them,' he declared.

The officer who had babysat him for hours was apoplectic. Riordan had passed over their mugshots earlier in the day.

'I do better with a few skins of Guinness in me,' he said.

Doyle rented a flat not far from the center of town. McElroy lived some ways out in a rural area about five kilometers from the ransom drop point. The cottage had belonged to his parents who drank themselves to death at an early age. The plan came together quickly. Cal would leave the bag at the signpost and a team of Gardai would apprehend and arrest the pick-up man or men. At the same time, two teams of armed officers from the Garda Emergency Response Unit would hit the Doyle and McElroy properties.

'You good with your part in this, Professor Donovan?' Inspector Sullivan asked.

'Drive the car. Drop the bag. I think I've got it,' Cal said.

It was overcast and at half-past ten, the N84 was pitch dark with few passing cars. With the exception of an industrial estate or two, the land was agricultural. Cal kept his eyes peeled for a red and white lettered sign advertising the sale of a plot of acreage, and when he saw it, he slowed and pulled onto the verge, perilously close to a drainage ditch. He put the car into park, grabbed the carrier bag, and swore when he opened the door. It was a straight drop down into the ditch. As he was trying to decide whether to climb over the center console to exit from the passenger side a heavy lorry rounded a bend and passed in the opposite direction. He turned his head to the left to avoid the harsh beams and saw the headlights catch something in the field. The illumination lasted only a second but it looked like a couple of people lying on the ground.

Doyle saw it too from his hiding place in the ditch.

He sprang up and got into the back seat of Cal's car and pointed a gun at him.

'Drive away. Now.'

Cal felt the barrel against his head and did as he said.

'You police?'

'I'm a friend of Father Murphy's.'

'American. Drive faster. There's police in the field.'

'I wouldn't know about that.'

At a lay-by Doyle told Cal they'd just passed his motorbike. He reached over the seat and took the carrier bag.

'Keep going while I count.' After a short while he grunted and made a call on his mobile. 'I got the cash. Slight complication. Nothing I can't handle. Go ahead and do him.'

'You don't need to hurt him!' Cal exclaimed.

'Shut up and kill your beams. OK. Now! Sharp left.'

The car was on a dirt road heading into a farm. After a bit, Doyle told him to stop and park. He exited and told Cal to get out too.

'You don't want to do this,' Cal said.

'Penalty's the same. One or two.'

Armed police stormed the two properties simultaneously, breaking down doors and lobbing in flash-bangs. The first property, a second-floor flat in town, was cleared in a matter of seconds. The second was more challenging. It was an old rural cottage with two modern additions and a root cellar with a bulkhead access. In the cellar, a team of three men shone tactical lights from their short-barreled assault rifles toward a muscle-bound fellow standing over a cot.

'Drop it!' one of them shouted.

A second later, McElroy was dead.

Two officers approached the cot slowly while the third scanned the rest of the cellar for more threats. There was a man on the cot curled into a ball.

An officer touched him and the man recoiled.

'Joseph Murphy?' the officer said.

'I'm all right,' Murphy said. 'I'm not injured. Is he all right?'

'Far from it,' the other officer said, checking the victim.

Murphy got himself to a seated position. 'If you could get me out of these handcuffs I'd like to administer last rights.'

Cal was looking down the barrel of a snub-nosed revolver pointed at the driver-side window. He played it out in his head. If he was lucky he'd live for another couple of minutes, the length of time it took to march him to a spot that the gunmen found auspicious for a murder. If unluckier, he'd be shot the second he got out of the car.

'I said get out,' Doyle said.

Cal took a deep breath. There was nothing to lose.

He pointed excitedly at the floor of the car and shouted as loud as he could, 'Holy shit! Look!'

Doyle took two steps forward to peek in and when he did, Cal opened the door into him as hard as he could, laying the full force of his shoulder into it.

When he was out of the car he fell on to a prone Doyle who briefly reached in vain for the gun that had gone loose, then used both arms to try to protect himself from Cal's fists landing on his face.

Cal presented himself at the desk of the police station and had a very short wait. Inspector Sullivan and Sergeant Feeney came running into the lobby.

'Good God, man,' Sullivan said. 'We lost you. What happened?'

Cal had a bigger concern. 'Is Murphy OK?'

'He's at the hospital getting checked out but he's unhurt,' Sullivan said.

Cal blinked in gratitude then asked them to come outside.

'Sorry, it's a no-parking space,' Cal said, fumbling for his keys. He unlocked the trunk and the officers looked down on a battered and bloodied Brendan Doyle looking up at them pleadingly.

Cal had upgraded Murphy at the airport and the two of them sidled up to the bar of the first-class lounge.

The bartender, a pretty redhead with classic Irish freckles, gave Cal the once-over but, good Catholic that she was, served the priest first.

'What can I get you, Father?'

Cal got a kick out of Murphy, the non-drinker as far as he knew, surveying the Irish whiskeys and saying, 'Bushmills. A large one, please.'

Cal asked for a Grey Goose on the rocks – 'A larger one' – and the two of them settled in for the wait. They'd talked plenty the past day and a half and they enjoyed their drinks in silence, interrupted only when Cal got a text from Inspector Sullivan.

The police had been interrogating Doyle in his hospital bed on the same ward where Cindy Riordan had met her end. Sullivan, ever cagey, had told him things might go easier for him on the kidnapping charge if he told them what he knew about Mary Riordan's disappearance.

So, Doyle started to sing like a bird – a bird, as it happened, that had little knowledge about higher-ups on the conspiracy ladder. He volunteered that he and McElroy had been the bag men between a fellow whose identity he didn't know and Kenny Riordan. He confessed that he'd gotten the order by phone from a blocked caller to get rid of Murphy. The man had an American accent. But he vehemently denied any involvement in Cindy Riordan's death. Sure, he'd been there with McElroy the night she passed but it was just to warn her to keep her mouth shut. Finally, he told the police that the last he saw Mary Riordan was the night she was dropped off at the stairs of a private plane at the Connemara Airport in Inverin.

After the interview, Sullivan sent Cal a text: *Have learned the destination of Mary's plane was Boston, Massachusetts. No further information. Keep those fists flying, Prof.*

Cal showed the text to Murphy and said, 'At least we know the Marys are probably in America, but that's all we know.'

'To the girls,' Murphy said, clinking Cal's glass.

'To the girls.'

SIXTEEN

The charity auction was in full swing at the Delamar Greenwich Harbor, a seaside hotel in one of the wealthiest enclaves in Connecticut. The ballroom was packed with bankers, lawyers, and Wall Street traders – the kind of people who paid twenty million to be on the water but rarely saw it because of their all-consuming jobs in Manhattan.

It was a tuxedo affair, the men largely indistinguishable from one another, the women in peacock mode, dripping in jewelry with designer gowns and salon hairdos. The event was in support of a women's shelter in nearby Stamford, the auctioneer a popular radio DJ with a gold-plated and barbed gift of the gab. He was on the stage, microphone in hand, sweating, strutting, cajoling and now announcing the final item of the night, a ruby and diamond necklace donated by a local, high-end jeweler.

The DJ was a Brit who tended to exaggerate his Cockney accent for Americans. He held up the necklace and had the cameraman zoom in so everyone could see it on the projection screen.

'Would you feast your eyeballs on this extravagant piece of bling, ladies and gents,' he said. 'Apparently this necklace is worth a small fortune so I want you lot to dig deep into your bottomless pockets and bid a large fortune. And gents, remember, if you win this item for your lady you'll not only go to heaven for supporting the shelter but you will so get laid tonight. Let's kick this off at two thousand, shall we? Do I hear two thousand dollars?'

The bidding climbed to fifteen grand and everyone dropped out except for two guys, both at the same table.

'You really want this?' a swarthy bond trader asked his wife, a blond with a plunging neckline that barely kept her implants in check.

'I love rubies,' she said, touching his lap under the table.

He raised his paddle. 'Sixteen.'

The auctioneer shouted, 'Brilliant! Will you look at this smashing couple? They're an advert for everything that's good and great about my adopted country. And while you're at it, would you consider adopting me? Do I hear seventeen thousand?'

The bond trader looked across the table and said with a slightly menacing grin, 'Your move, Steve.'

Steven Gottlieb refused to let his contempt for his adversary show lest he hand him a psychological victory. He vaguely knew the guy. He'd played tennis with him at a match between rival tennis clubs and had lost, which rankled him. As a rule of thumb, he despised bond traders, viewing them as carcass-feeding parasites who just moved money around the big table. Steve, on the other hand, was a venture capitalist who made his money by building companies that made great products and employed thousands of people. He'd gotten rich by creating real value for the society – at least that's how he saw it. His wife of twenty years, whom he'd met in high school, shifted her weight in her chair, uncomfortable with the proceedings. She wasn't a glitz and glamor type and she considered the auctioneer to be tacky and common. When he had announced the final item, she had whispered in her husband's ear, 'Thank God.'

'It's a nice necklace, isn't it?' Steve had whispered back.

She had done volunteer work at the shelter. 'I really don't need it but it's a good cause.'

Steve raised his paddle again.

'Game on!' the auctioneer shouted. 'You sir, with the blond appendage, how about eighteen?'

The bond trader was willing and he upped his bid.

The bidding pinged back and forth between the two men at thousand-dollar raises until it got to twenty-five thousand. Now, neither man was smiling anymore and the room was quiet until someone at another table shouted, 'Guys, you realize this thing goes for maybe five grand retail!'

'Loose lips sink ships,' the auctioneer shouted back. 'The bid is to the gentleman who's confident enough in his manhood that he's foregone a hair transplant.'

That *ad hominem* quip royally pissed off Steve and left his wife shaking her head.

'OK, let's finish this,' he whispered to her.

'Good. Let him have it.'

That wasn't what he meant. 'Thirty-five thousand,' he said, flashing his paddle.

'Well, well. Very well played, sir!' the MC shouted. 'Is that going to be the last word tonight?'

The bond trader looked across the table and said, 'You're out of your fucking mind,' before waving his hand at his neck to signify that he was out.

'Ladies and gentlemen!' the Brit exclaimed. 'Let's have a round of applause for a generous man with an age-appropriate wife.'

In the car, Gottlieb told his wife that when they got home, they should get comfortable and sit on the patio for a while listening to the waves. The gated house had a tree-lined driveway leading up to a large shingled house. Entering through the garage, he deactivated the alarm and set his keys on a kitchen counter. It was his wife who noticed that something was wrong.

'Steve, look.'

In the butler's pantry, the door to the liquor cabinet was wide open and two bottles of brandy were smashed and spilled on the tile floor.

'You didn't do this before you left, did you?'

'Absolutely not!' he said. 'Come on. We're leaving and calling the police.'

*   *   *

A pair of detectives from the Greenwich police department arrived after a uniformed officer did a sweep through the house.

One of them told Gottlieb, 'We need you to do a thorough walk-through to see if anything's missing. You got any safes?'

'Two,' he said. 'One in the bedroom, one in my office.'

'Check those. Check everything. We see you've got cameras outside. Any inside?'

'Only exterior,' he said.

'While you're looking around, we want to check your video DVR.'

While his wife sat at the kitchen table composing herself with a cup of green tea, Gottlieb began methodically checking the property. His wife kept her expensive jewelry in a bedroom safe alongside his collection of pricey wrist watches and a couple of firearms. He tried the safe door. It was locked. Her less expensive pieces were in a chest in her dressing room. They were all there. He covered every room. All the paintings and objets d'art were in place. His collection of rare first editions was intact in the library. The silver was in the dining room and nothing was amiss in the wine cellar. He checked his office last. His office safe kept some work and home documents and a little cash. He tried the door. It was locked. That left his desk. There was one highly sensitive draft contract he'd left out. Shuffling papers, looking for it, a newspaper clipping fluttered to the floor. He found the contract where he'd left it and went looking for the detectives, leaving the clipped *New York Times* article on the rug with its photo of Calvin Donovan.

Gottlieb reported back on his inspection.

The detectives told him the video feed didn't show anything but advised him that there were a few blind spots he might want to address.

'You sure the alarm was on when you came in?' one of the detectives asked.

'It was on. I deactivated it.'

'Was it set for home or away?'

'Away mode. We don't have pets.'

'Have there been any malfunctions?'

'The alarm's been perfect,' Gottlieb said.

'You positive the alarm was on?' the other detective asked.

Gottlieb's temper was getting short. 'Look, I'll show you.'

He had an app on his phone that showed the system history. The detectives passed the phone between themselves.

'Does anyone else have the alarm code? Cleaners, handymen?'

'No, and besides, the history shows all the activations and deactivations. No one but me entered codes today.'

'This is a new one on me,' one of the detectives said. 'We'll dust for prints but I suggest you contact your security company and see what they think. This seems to be more along the line of a prank than a burglary, what with the brandy bottles and all. Anyone you can think of who'd pull a stunt like this? Your kids, their friends?'

'No, nobody,' Gottlieb said.

'We don't have children,' his wife said.

Gottlieb's mood turned darker after that night. He missed work the next day waiting for the security company technician to arrive. After the fellow declared that the system was operating correctly he said he couldn't offer any explanation for how someone could have pulled off the break-in. Gottlieb threw a fit and demanded the chief technician make an appearance. The security company was a local smart-home outfit that Gottlieb had paid a small fortune to fit out his house so they obliged him quickly. The head man came over in the afternoon and spent a couple of hours trouble-shooting with his laptop computer.

'Your system is A-OK, Mr Gottlieb. There isn't a single fault.'

'How the hell did this happen then?' Gottlieb said. 'My wife and I don't feel safe. If this is a result of shoddy work by you guys, I swear I'll light you up with a lawsuit. I'll be getting another company in to check your work.'

The technician, an older fellow who gave the impression of having been around the block a few times, said evenly, 'You know, the only thing I can think of is radio waves.'

'Radio waves?'

'Yeah, I've never seen it but I've read about it. It's theoretically possible to generate the right frequencies of radio interference to jam the system and trick it not to trigger to an open door or window sensor-circuit or a glass-break sensor. It wouldn't show up in the system history files because none of the sensors would have fired. For a top-of-the-shelf system like yours it's not something a coked-up neighbor kid is going to be able to pull off or even a professional burglary crew up from the city. It's real black-hat stuff. Government agencies can probably do it. Sophisticated hackers. You need a lot of hardware and software.'

Gottlieb frowned and sat down ungainly on the nearest chair.

'You OK?' the technician asked.

'Yeah, I'm fine.'

'You can get other people in to look at your system, Mr Gottlieb, but no one in the area knows more about this shit than me.'

Gottlieb began drinking more and sleeping less. When he did go to bed he transferred a revolver from the bedroom safe to the top drawer of his night table. He spent another thirty grand getting a second security company to install a redundant alarm system, beefing up the coverage of the exterior cameras and adding interior ones. His wife told him he wasn't looking well and asked why he was taking the intrusion even harder than she was. He told her that he was fine but she didn't believe him.

Five days after the break in Gottlieb was working at home. He'd drunk half a bottle of scotch the night before and was too hungover to slog his way into the city. Besides, he had a telephone board meeting with one of his west-coast portfolio companies and whether he did the call from his home rather than his office made no difference. He had been at his desk in his home office for an hour, multitasking on his computer, listening to the call on speaker mode and chipping in comments from time to time. He'd been vaguely aware of something out of the ordinary – something olfactory – and as the call progressed he became more convinced that something was giving off a bad smell.

With the company's VP of accounting droning on in the background, Gottlieb got up and started sniffing like a blood hound. He convinced himself that the foul odor was strongest at the bookcase wall and he kept sniffing until he was standing in front of the wall safe, hidden behind a section of books. He shifted an armful out of the way, entered the digital code, and opened the door.

'Fucking hell!' he shouted, falling backwards on his ass.

He heard some board members asking over the line whether he was all right.

'Yeah, I'm fine,' he said, 'but something's come up. I've got to sign off for a while.'

He ended the call and crept toward the safe again. The smell was putrid, gagging. There was something in there but it took the flashlight from his phone to see what it was.

The exterminator held it with a gloved hand by its long, gray tail.

'How do you figure it got in there?'

Gottlieb was holding a wash cloth over his mouth and nose. Through it he said, 'No idea. What is it?'

'It's a possum. There's plenty of them around. I see them getting into a house every so often but I've never seen one crawl up into a safe and close the door behind it.' He looked over his glasses for a reaction but got none. 'This one's been in there a while. She's pretty ripe.'

Gottlieb looked strung out. 'Can you get it out of the house, please.'

'Sure thing,' he said dropping it into a canvas bag. 'One thing's kind of interesting about this one. She's pregnant as hell.'

SEVENTEEN

Two months later

Maria Aquino was a tough little cookie but Sue could tell she was scared. Up to the moment of her first contraction she'd been the phlegmatic one. She had handled her protruding belly and changing physiology without the drama of the other girls. She never missed a language lesson. She took her dishes and silverware to the kitchen and her dirty clothes to the laundry room without complaining and obliged the female staff whenever they wanted to reverently touch her abdomen. Sue called her the trooper.

But when that first contraction came she winced hard, moaned, then went quiet and fearful.

It was nighttime and the girls were in their lounge watching a video. Mary Riordan and Maria Mollo noticed her changed behavior and Mary knocked on Sue's bedroom door.

'I think something's happening with Maria.' Lily the bulldog was with her, excited to see Sue.

'Which one?' Sue asked, slipping on shoes.

'The Minion.' She had the big eyes and glasses. Mary's nickname for Maria Mollo was Eeyore, the depressed donkey from *Winnie the Pooh*. Sue had once asked what the Marias called her and Mary had said, 'Don't know. Her Royal Highness most likely.'

Sue stayed up with Maria after the other girls went to bed. She didn't bother to put her up in stirrups. An exam would come later. A quick palpation of her belly while she reclined on the sofa was enough for the experienced midwife. The next contraction was the real deal, real enough for Sue to wake up Mrs Simpauco. Maria's English was coming along but Sue wanted communications to be perfect. After telling the girl what the next several hours would be like, Sue let Mrs Simpauco return to bed until needed again.

Maria spent the interval between contractions quiet and tight-lipped, arms folded over her tight abdomen. The girl had seen her mother birthing her brother and it had traumatized her – the screaming and crying and pushing and groaning and all the bodily fluids.

The third contraction came an hour later and with that, her lip began to quiver and her eyes welled up.

'Don't worry, sweetie pie,' Sue said, stroking her hair. '*Tama lang*. It's OK.'

Six hours later, in the wee hours, her water broke and the girl briefly lost it and became hysterical. Sue thought it was as good a time as any to bring her into the delivery room to clean her up and do a pelvic examination. She had been planning for this moment from her early days of work for Miracle Ranch LLC, the name of her employer that appeared on her paycheck. Although she had learned her craft in modern hospitals, she worked in people's homes and the idea of clinic-level facilities in a private setting was something different.

She calmed Maria down, got her into a gown festooned with teddy bears and cleaned her with a sponge and warm water. When she was comfortable on the table Sue called down to Mrs Simpauco's room and told her it was time.

When the woman arrived, Sue got Maria into stirrups and inserted a speculum. Previous exams had obliterated her virginal hymen. She was dilated only a centimeter. It was going to be a long haul.

'Let's check on the baby,' she said via the translator.

She had already introduced the girls to all the gear in the room so they wouldn't be frightened come the day. External fetal monitoring required two belts wrapped around the abdomen, one to detect the baby's heart rate, the other to measure the contractions. Maria tensed as Sue strapped her in but nodded solemnly when she was told the baby's heart was good and strong.

'You see that number – a hundred and twenty-four? That's how many times your baby's heart is beating every minute,' Sue said. 'He can't wait to meet you.'

The girl was too scared to smile.

It was dawn and the sky was pink when the contractions came every five minutes. Sue made a call on her mobile to Dr Lopez.

'Maria Aquino is at four centimeters. The fetal heart rate is good, no decelerations.'

'Be there in an hour,' the pediatrician said. 'Think I've got time for a Starbucks?'

It was a joke between them. There weren't any Starbucks in these parts.

'You've got time to roast your own beans.'

Mrs Torres stuck her head in after breakfast and greeted the pediatrician in Spanish. Maria was listless and drained, sucking on the straw of a juice box being held by Mrs Simpauco. Torres wanted to know where they stood and when Sue told her she thought the baby would crown within the hour the woman said something that caught Sue off guard.

'I'll have the videographer get set up.'

Sue stared at her for a moment then asked to speak outside the room.

'What do you mean, videographer?'

'They want the delivery recorded. Didn't you know?'

Sue had to work hard to control her temper. Of course she didn't know because Torres had never mentioned it.

'Who wants it recorded?'

'They do. The people paying for all this. Your employer.'

'Why do they want to do it?'

'It's not my place to ask.'

'You can't just record people without their permission.'

Torres was prepared. Her omnipresent clipboard had release forms for Sue and for Lopez.

'What if we don't want to give permission?'

'Dr Lopez is good with it. I already talked to him.'

'What if I'm not good with it?'

Torres gave her one of her passive-aggressive smiles. 'Then I guess Maria will have to have the baby on her own.'

'For Pete's sake,' Sue said.

'Don't worry, no one will know it's you. They want you and Lopez wearing surgical masks. They don't want anyone recognizing and contacting you.'

Sue threw this development on the smoldering bonfire of all the reasons she disliked this boss of hers.

While she was signing the release she said, 'What about Maria? Doesn't she have a say in whether she's taped?'

'She's a minor. I'm signing for her.'

It turned out the videographer was a man in his fifties who Sue already knew. He had joined the staff a month earlier and had spent his time closeted away in a basement room near the security office. One day, over lunch, when Sue asked what he did, the guy looked a bit guilty and had said, in a rehearsed way before excusing herself, that he'd been hired to do special projects.

Maria was too spent to pay the videographer any notice but while he was setting up a tripods and lights at both ends of the birthing table, Sue said, 'Special projects?'

The man shrugged. 'That's what I was told to say. Sorry.'

'Film a lot of deliveries?' Sue asked.

'Only my own – my wife's I mean – but it was a long time ago. Shot it on film. That dates it.' He pointed at Maria. 'She's young.'

'I've got to go back to work now. Stay out of my way, please.'

When the contractions were coming every two minutes and eliciting ever-high-pitched yelps, Sue had her pull up her knees to have a look.

'OK, she's fully dilated. I can see the head. Tell her I can see the baby's head.'

The translator told her and the girl gave a single eyes-closed nod.

'Is it show time?' the videographer said.

'No, it's delivery time,' Sue replied icily.

'Masks on, please. And you, translator lady, I need you out of the shot. Just scoot your chair back a little more, little more. OK, good.'

Sue donned her mask and got back to it. 'Maria, I want you to start pushing.' She put her hand over her lower abdomen. 'Push from there really hard when I tell you to. OK? We'll begin with the next contraction.'

The contraction started and the girl did her first push, a good effort but not what Sue wanted out of her. Over the next several cycles Maria got more effective but she was tiring rapidly and that had Sue worried.

'She's so loud,' the cameraman complained. 'It's blowing out my sound levels. Are you going to give her something for the pain?'

Sue turned to him and said, 'Will you please shut the fuck up?'

Maria recognized the word – Mary Riordan had taught her all the good ones – and she giggled for the first time that night.

'OK, kiddo,' Sue said, 'time for a big fucking push.'

Maria yelled and bore down hard.

'That's it, that-a-girl, you're crowning. Mrs S, tell her to stop pushing! I don't want her to tear herself.'

Tufts of brown scalp hair poked out of the dilated birth canal. Maria's sweat-drenched head slumped to one side of the pillow.

'OK, honey, the next push is going to be the golden one. Tell her that.'

And Sue was right. One more contraction, one more push, and the baby slipped out smoothly into Sue's gloved hands. The placenta followed a few seconds later and Sue laid the infant on Maria's bare belly.

'Here's your baby boy, baby girl,' she said.

Maria looked down on it, her eyes really as big as a Minion's, her lips parted in awe.

'OK if I let the cord pulse for a while, Doctor?' Sue said.

Dr Lopez shrugged. 'Cut immediately. Wait a few minutes. I'm nothing but flexible on the subject,' he said, watching the baby take its first breaths. 'Looks like a nice, healthy baby. Easily seven pounds. Nice job, mom. Nice job, midwife.'

When Sue was ready, she told the girl to hold the baby while she milked the cord, clamped and cut it. Untethered, Maria pulled the baby higher, on to her chest.

The videographer had a hand-held camera for the occasion. He came in tight and before Sue could stop him from almost poking the baby with his lens, he asked a question which Mrs Simpauco immediately translated.

'What will you call him?'

Maria looked into the camera then at the wriggling infant and said in English, 'His name Jesus Ruperto. Ruperto is name my father. Jesus is name my savior.'

When the lights and the cameras were off, Sue asked the translator what had just happened.

'Mrs Torres had me tell Maria what she should name the baby. I've been practicing with her how to say it in English. She did good, don't you think?'

Cal was meeting with one of his two new PhD candidates, a Nigerian student with an interest in the history of Catholicism in Africa. Gil Daniels, Cal's dean, rapped on the open door.

'Sorry to interrupt but have you seen the video?' Daniels said.

'What video?' Cal asked.

'One of the girls you investigated – the Filipino one, has just given birth. Someone released a video.'

'Of what?'

'The birth of the baby.'

'Jesus,' Cal muttered.

'Yes, exactly,' Daniels said, waving off. 'How did you know?'

Cal asked his student if she minded if he went online to check out the video.

'You were involved with the girls?' she said, impressed.

'I did a consult for the Vatican,' he answered, opening his Twitter feed.

'Everyone back home is deeply immersed in this story,' she said.

'Tell me why.'

'It's a matter of hope and inspiration, a sense that the fundamental tenets of the faith are relevant to our lives today.'

'I've heard that view. You're saying it's percolated to the grassroots of the Church?'

'In Africa, yes, certainly.'

His feed was packed with news on the birth. The YouTube video released only thirty minutes ago already had over a million views. His student stood behind him at his desk to watch it. Two minutes long, it was professionally shot and edited, showing young Maria Aquino in the final stages of labor accompanied by a subdued soundtrack of ecclesiastical music. She was in a birthing suite attended by two masked healthcare workers and a Filipino translator off screen. The music rose as the baby was delivered and placed on her belly. Then, a close-up of the baby clutched to her chest and the declaration of his name. Jesus Ruperto. The shot faded to black with a final musical crescendo.

'Nothing more?' the student said. 'Nothing about where she is, who has taken her, anything about the other girls?'

Cal closed his laptop. 'One has the sense that we're all the audience of a giant reality TV show.'

EIGHTEEN

The addition of baby Jesus Ruperto, or JR as Mary Riordan dubbed him, changed pretty much everything around the ranch. The ranch staff, down to the stable hands and gardeners, chefs and cleaners, went about their jobs proudly with a new sense of purpose. Even the saturnine Mrs Torres had a much-improved temperament; one day Sue caught her standing over JR's crib, staring down and singing to him in Spanish. It turned out, the woman had a lovely voice.

It was the girls who changed the most. Maria Aquino floated on a cloud of new motherhood, so buoyant that Sue was worried she might come crashing down when her hormones stabilized. But the other girls were also smitten by JR and wanted to take turns washing and changing him, preparing for their own moments in the sun. It seemed that the only melancholy one was Lily, the dog, who likely felt neglected.

In the evenings, when the heat was manageable, the girls and Sue took JR for circuits around the house, taking turns pushing his pram. Every time they got to the stables-side of the mansion they would look to the sky.

'Still don't know what's it for?' Mary Riordan asked.

'They don't tell me anything,' Sue replied, shielding her eyes from the setting sun.

'I reckon it's for them,' Mary said, reaching in to tickle JR. 'It's for you, little man, isn't it?'

Sue might have been the only employee of Miracle Ranch LLC who wasn't giddy. Her work was only a third done. She worried about the two impending births, particularly little Maria Mollo, she of the tiny hips. The closer Maria got to her due date, the more frequently Sue talked to the helicopter pilot to make sure he'd be ready to fly her into town for a C-section if it came to that. And Sue fretted about Mary Riordan, poor thing, who still hadn't been told about her mother's death.

Ten days later it was Maria's turn. Her water broke while she was watching a morning cartoon show, immediately followed by her first cramp. Afterwards, the contractions came at breakneck speed and Sue had to scramble to prepare the birthing room for action and to get Dr Lopez to drop his morning clinic schedule and hurry out to the ranch.

The small girl was scared out of her mind when Sue carried her into the suite and placed her on to the table. Torres, impassive as she was, had a bit of a soft spot for the girl and was the designated translator. She arrived with the videographer as Sue was having a look at Maria's cervix.

'Holy smokes,' Sue mumbled, adjusting her headlamp.

'What's the matter?' Torres said.

'She's already six centimeters. We need Sam.'

Sue and Dr Lopez were now on a first-name basis. The pediatrician arrived while the baby was crowning, all of two hours since her first contraction.

'I thought you were worried about her pelvic diameter,' he said, throwing on a mask. 'She's a rocket.'

'The baby's really small,' Sue said. 'Come on, Maria, time to push, push, push!'

With an ear-piercing shriek, Maria gave it her all and the baby squirted into Sue's sure-handed grasp.

With the videographer standing over her, Torres asked the panting girl what she would call the baby.

Maria was nervously ready with the answer. She wasn't an attentive student. Her English wasn't as good as Maria Aquino's, and she was exhausted, but she said, 'Baby Jesus Juan. Juan my padre. Jesus my—'

Torres whispered the word in her ear.

'Jesus my savior.'

Baby JJ looked like a peanut beside JR. He was one and a half pounds lighter and had to spend his first few days under a phototherapy lamp for mild jaundice. The two Marias began to do everything together, harmonizing their maternal schedules using whatever common English they could muster to chat and joke about poop and pee and breast milk. Mary was on the outside, looking in, getting bigger and bigger and more and ever more irritable.

'When's my time?' she asked Sue.

'It's going to be soon, honey.'

'Better be or I'll burst like the bloke in *Alien*.'

There was another problem in Mary-Riordan-land. The two Marias would come back from their phone sessions with their mothers, giddy and talkative. The women had been shown the birthing videos and photos of JJ and JR. But Mary Riordan had been cut off from her mother for over two months and had received shifting explanations.

First there was a problem with the special phone they had to use, then one of her sisters dunked it in the toilet and they had to wait for a replacement. Then her mother had to go to hospital for an operation. That's when Mary had her first chat with her father who assured her that all would be well with her mum, though, typical Kenny, he was drunk and never asked how Mary was getting on.

A month later, it was her father again on the other end of the line. He'd been drinking again – he'd gotten boozed up in anticipation of the call – and told her that her mum, brothers and sisters were visiting with Cindy's sister.

The next time, her aunt was the one who answered. Kenny had pressed her into service, telling her that he'd gotten firm instructions to keep hiding the news of Cindy's death until she'd had her baby.

'Aunt Cathy, tell me what's the matter with Mum,' Mary had demanded.

'Well, to be honest, dear, she's had a bad case of the phlebitis. Her weight, you know. She's been back in hospital but she sends her love. Your sisters and brothers are here with me. Say hello to Mary, children.'

And Mary had heard the shouted hellos through the phone and had felt a touch better.

Sue argued repeatedly with Torres over the subterfuge, telling her it would permanently scar the girl. But the woman stubbornly refused to budge and warned Sue not to go off the reservation. The powers that be were insisting that her baby's physical health was more important than Mary's emotional health.

A knock on Sue's door marked the beginning of Mary's turn.

The girl was standing there in her oversized t-shirt and elasticated shorts, her face screwed into a grimace.

'You weren't all that interested in sleeping tonight, were you?' Mary said.

Mary had already decided she'd be calling the baby Jesus David. Torres told her the first name was mandatory – house rules. The middle name was up to her. 'Sod Kenny,' Mary had said of her father. 'My granddad, David – he was a nice man.'

Sue gave Mary a hug and said, 'Let's go next door and have a welcome party for JD.'

If Maria Mollo's labor was yin, Mary's was yang.

It dragged on all night, throughout the next day and into the following night. Dr Lopez spent hours napping in a guest bedroom. The videographer came and went. Torres dropped by every so often, scurrying off to make phone calls from her office. But Sue maintained the vigil, fueled by coffee and adrenaline, refusing to leave Mary's side. She even endured the girl's favorite pop-song playlist on a loop.

Twenty-seven hours into labor, Mary was eight centimeters dilated. She was panting like a hot dog and was pale as a ghost and glistening with sweat despite a shivering-cold AC setting.

Fatigue caused Sue to take a few extra seconds to process the beeping of the fetal monitor. The cobwebs cleared when she saw the baby's heart rate had slowed to ninety.

The videographer was dozing in a chair. Sue woke him and calmly had him call over to Dr Lopez's room.

'What's the matter?' Mary asked, panting and steeling herself for the next contraction.

'JD's heartbeat's a little slow.'

'What's that mean?'

'Just keeping an eye out.'

Lopez came in and conferred with Sue over the tracings.

'I agree. Late decelerations,' he said quietly. 'I think we should scramble the helicopter.'

The next contraction hit and Mary groaned in agony.

The monitor beeped again. This time the fetal heart rate dropped to eighty.

'I don't think we've got time for the chopper, Sam.' Sue unwrapped a sterile forceps kit and an episiotomy kit in case she needed to make an incision.

'What's happening?' Mary cried out.

Sue went to the head of the table and mopped Mary's wet forehead. 'We think JD's not getting enough oxygen. I'm going to do a routine procedure called a forceps delivery.'

'You done it before?'

'More times than you've had porridge with milk and brown sugar.' It was the girl's favorite breakfast.

Sue got ready and the videographer asked if he should be recording this.

She still couldn't stand the guy. 'Only if you want to film the birth.'

Sue placed her fingers into Mary's vagina and probed the cervix for the baby's cranium. Then she slid one forceps tong along one side of the head and another tong on the other side, then locked them in place.

Torres came in just then, froze in fear, and crossed herself.

Sue said with a contained urgency, 'OK, Mary, at the next contraction I want you to push really hard.'

An 'Arghhh!' came out of Mary's mouth and Sue tugged hard on the forceps. The baby's head emerged from the cervix face-down and made it almost out the vagina when the progress abruptly halted.

'Heart rate is sixty and falling,' Lopez called out. 'Speak to me, Sue.'

'Shit,' she whispered. 'Sam, hand me a couple of clamps. Stat.'

'Nuchal cord?' he asked.

'Big time.'

'Didn't see it on the ultrasound,' Lopez said, coming to the foot of the table.

'JD decided to pull a Houdini on us at the last minute,' Sue said, grasping the first clamp.

The umbilical cord was double-wrapped as tightly as a hangman's noose around the baby's neck and his face was turning blue.

'Is my baby all right?' Mary cried.

'Relax, honey. Just relax,' Sue said.

Torres took hold of one of Mary's hands.

Sue slid a clamp around one loop of the purple cord and the second clamp close to it. Lopez handed her a scissors and she made the cut. The baby still didn't budge.

'Double knot,' Sue said, her voice getting a half-octave higher. 'Give me another couple of clamps, please.'

Lopez passed them over and Sue positioned a second set of clamps. When she cut between them, the baby positively hurtled out of the birth canal as if shot by a cannon.

This wasn't the time for maternal fulfillment. Sue bypassed Mary and handed the infant to Lopez who carried it over to his work station.

He talked while he worked, his reassuring tone aimed at the mother.

'I'm just going to give him a little extra oxygen, Mary, a blend of room air and oxygen. I've put this little clamp on his finger to measure the oxygen in his blood. Here we go, that's a nice breath, big boy. He's getting pinker already.'

'Can I see him?' Mary asked.

'Just give me a minute or two.'

Lopez was being optimistic. He wasn't ready to let the baby breathe room air alone for ten minutes and then he waited another five before he was comfortable handing him to Mary.

Sue and Lopez put arms around each other's waists and looked on as the cameraman came in for the money shot.

Mary held the baby like a fragile piece of china and at Mrs Torres's prompt said, 'Hey there, world, say hello to my baby, Jesus David. David was my granddad on my mum's side. Jesus – well, you know who he was, don't you?'

Sue slept until late the next morning. If she had dreams she couldn't remember them; she told Torres later in the day that it felt more like being in a coma than sleeping. As soon as she showered, dressed, and gulped a cup of coffee she went to see Mary who was alone in the communal bedroom. The girl was so sore and shattered she hadn't gotten out of bed.

'Hey you,' Sue said. 'How're you getting on?'

'Don't need to get hit by a freight train no more,' Mary said. 'I know what it feels like.'

'You had the roughest time. Don't rush it but don't stay in bed all day. I don't want you getting blood clots in your legs.'

'I'll be up and about soon enough. Got to pee something wicked.'

'Where's JD?' Sue asked.

'Minion and Eeyore have him.'

Sue helped her to her feet and left her in the bathroom to clean herself up. The scene in the lounge was one for the ages. While Maria Mollo looked after babies JR and JJ who were lying in a playpen, Maria Aquino was breastfeeding Mary's baby.

The girl looked up at Sue and smiled like an angel. 'Baby JD very hungry,' she said.

Sue was waiting for Mary when she hobbled back to bed wearing a t-shirt and tracksuit bottoms. She told her that JD was feeding like a champ.

'Minion's a good egg,' Mary said. 'Even Eeyore's growing on me. So, what's next for us Jesus mums?'

'I wish I knew,' Sue said. 'Look, Mary, there's something I want to talk to you about. Some people – not including me – felt it needed to wait until you had the baby. Well, you've had the baby.'

'It's about my mum, isn't it?'

Sue nodded and Mary began to blubber.

'How did you know?' Sue asked.

'Because it was bloody obvious? No word in months. Everyone making lame excuses. How'd she go?'

Sue only knew what she'd been told. 'Breathing problems.'

'She had the asthma.'

Sue had armed herself with tissues stuffed into her pockets. She began to deploy them.

'Why didn't you say anything?' Sue asked.

Mary broke down hard. 'Because I knew and I didn't want to know. Does that make any sense?'

Sue found Torres doing paperwork in her office.

'I told Mary about her mother,' she said. 'She already knew.'

Sue had expected Torres to lash out and accuse her of acting unilaterally. But she didn't.

'She's a smart girl,' Torres said. 'She's got a good intuition. Is she OK?'

'She cried a river. She's been bottling it up.'

'I see.'

'There's something else I want to talk to you about,' Sue said.

'I know what you're going to say. I've got good intuition too.'

Sue hadn't had a cigarette in years but the cravings hit her in the solar plexus like she'd just quit. Fortunately, there were none at hand.

'Look, you're good at keeping things close to the vest,' she said. 'I have no idea what the grand purpose of all this is. I don't know how the girls got pregnant. I'm not like a lot of the people around the ranch. I don't see holiness when I look at their faces or their babies' faces. But I'm not the least bit religious so maybe I'm not seeing what you can see. All I see are three wonderfully ordinary girls and three wonderfully ordinary newborns. I don't have any idea what you have in mind for them or what that thing is out back. I was hired to do a job. You paid me a shitload of money to do it. The job is over. You've got three healthy babies and three healthy moms. It's time for me to go home.'

Torres had been nodding during her monologue. She rolled her chair back and reached into a desk drawer. The envelope had Sue's name on it.

'There have been discussions about your role going forward,' Torres said.

'Discussions? With whom?'

'The powers that be.'

Sue scoffed at the phrase. 'Why don't you just call them the

Wizards of Oz. The men behind the curtain. This is all such bullshit. These girls are being manipulated for something by somebody.'

'I'm sorry,' Torres said, 'but I can't agree with you. People believe these girls are holy vessels, that they were touched, that they were chosen.'

'Well, obviously, I don't.'

'I know you're not a woman of faith, Sue. I understand what you think you know but maybe you don't know everything. You weren't hired for your beliefs. You were hired for your skills as a midwife but your role has certainly gone beyond that. Read this letter, please.'

Sue opened the envelope and read the pages. It was ostensibly from Torres as the representative of Miracle Ranch but the language was written by a lawyer. It was a contract extension for another six months of employment. There was enough additional money for Sue to buy a house, travel the world for a few years, do whatever the hell she had always wanted to do, if she had a clue what that was.

'I don't need the money,' Sue said in a breathy exhale.

'Everyone needs money.'

Sue ignored her and handed the letter back.

Torres seemed to be prepared for her reaction. 'The girls need you. All of them, especially Mary. It's more than needing you. They love you. You have a bond with them.'

Sue looked like she wanted to interrupt.

'What did you want to say?' Torres asked.

She sighed. 'Nothing. I learned a long time ago not to bother asking questions you're not going to answer.'

Torres nodded. It was true enough. 'Listen to me, Sue, there's no one else here who can take care of them like you. Definitely not me. They do not love me. They've no reason to. I'm not warm like you. I never had children. I don't know how to take good care of them. If you left they'd be in turmoil. They couldn't cope. Just six months. After six months, it will be different. Believe me, I know things. They'll be able to let go of you. Take the money, but don't do it for the money. Do it for them.'

The academic year was about to start and Harvard was in its cycle of autumn rebirth with the arrival of freshmen and returning students. Cal planned to spend Labor Day weekend with Jessica at her beach house in Nantucket for a placid end to the season. While he was packing he got a call from Joe Murphy that concerned him. Murphy could never be accused of being ebullient but he sounded flat – actually more than flat.

'I'm thinking of telling Mary Schott that I need to take some time off,' Murphy said.

Schott was the chairman of the history department. Murphy had only been on the faculty for a year but he'd already made a good initial impression for his undergraduate course on medieval history. The student ratings on Harvard's Q Guide had been rather stellar. Of course, Cal had wanted Murphy on the faculty of the Divinity School but Gil Daniels had blocked it in an act of spite and jealousy over Cal's celebrity status as the pope's fair-haired academic. At least that's what Cal had suspected. So, Cal had persuaded Mary Schott to take Murphy on and the maneuver had been a win-win.

'Why, what's up, Joe?' Cal said.

He knew what was up. Murphy was having a rough time. You didn't come through a brutal kidnapping unscathed. Cal had gotten a call from one of his former grad students who did an overlapping year with Murphy at the Divinity School before getting his degree. Andy Bogosian was now an associate professor at the University of New Mexico, a rising academic star in the Department of Religious Studies.

'Hey, Cal, I talked to Joe Murphy yesterday,' Bogosian had said.

'How'd he sound?'

'Like shit. I'm worried about him.'

'We all are.'

'He should see someone.'

'I know. I'm going to talk to him.'

'He's going to tell you he wants to take a leave of absence.'

'I'm not sure that's a great idea,' Cal had said.

'I don't know. Maybe a change of scenery would be a tonic. I'd love to get him to come to New Mexico. A New England winter's a-coming. Bad for the psyche. I could pull some strings and get a position opened up in my department. I mean, what the hell's he doing in the History Department anyway?'

Cal knew that Bogosian probably could pull all sorts of strings.

He was from New Mexico political royalty. His father had been attorney general. His brother was the lieutenant governor.

'Don't be poaching talent from Harvard,' Cal had said. 'You'll anger the gods. I'll look after Joe the best I can. Don't worry. I'll call you soon with an update.'

Murphy sounded mechanical. Cal could picture his downcast face. 'I don't know. I've had trouble focusing on my new lectures.'

'You went through a lot, Joe. It's understandable.'

'Well I don't know about that. I thought I should tell you first.'

This needed more than a phone call. Cal went out on a limb, not for the first time in his life. 'What are you doing this weekend?'

'I've got an impressive watch list on Netflix.'

'Throw some clothes in a bag. Civilian clothes and swim trunks. You're going to the beach.'

Jessica's idea of a romantic weekend on the beach didn't comport with entertaining a depressed priest but Cal used all his charms and got her ex-post-facto sign-off. That proved to be easier than snagging a last-minute ferry ticket for the busiest weekend of the summer but he pulled that off too.

Hanging on the railings, and taking in the choppy waters of Nantucket Sound, Murphy told Cal and Jessica he felt like a gooseberry.

'What's a gooseberry, other than the obvious?' Jessica asked.

'Ah, it's a term from the old country,' Murphy said. 'The ugly friend who tags along with a couple.'

'You are so not ugly,' Jessica said unhelpfully.

On the first morning Cal left Jessica asleep in bed to do a beach jog where he found Murphy, sitting with his back to a dune, contemplating the dawn.

'Nice here,' Murphy said. 'Thanks for the invite.'

Cal sat beside him.

'Not running?' Murphy said.

'You're giving me an excuse not to,' Cal said, slipping off his sneakers and digging his feet into the sand.

'You're welcome.'

'So, tell me something,' Cal said. 'If someone – say a parishioner when you were in the business – came to you with a story that resembles yours, where they were coshed on the noggin, kidnapped, held in a cellar, marked for execution

– and they told you they were feeling adrift, what would you say to them?'

'I expect I'd tell them similar things to what you're about to tell me.'

'There you have it. I rest my case.'

'That was easy. Go for your run then.'

'Look, Joe, I don't know if you've got PTSD or just plain-vanilla angst but I think you ought to see someone.'

'A priest, mayhap?'

'No, my friend, a psychiatrist. This is not a spiritual matter. It's biological. Let me get you a name of someone at the medical school. See someone a few times before you blow up your semester.'

'Maybe.'

'That's better than no.'

'It's not like there are zero spiritual issues on my mind,' Murphy said digging a shell from the sand. 'Haven't you been troubled by the implications of our virgins?'

'Troubled? I don't know, Joe. It's hit me more in the head than the heart. I'm fascinated. I'm curious. I'm just not getting big-time spiritual vibes. You know Mary Riordan. You saw the videos of Maria Mollo and Maria Aquino. If you didn't know the back stories you'd think you were looking at regular teenage girls with their regular babies.'

'Do you suppose the Virgin Mary and her baby Jesus looked so extraordinary?'

'Wasn't there.'

'Well now, I wasn't either but here's the thing. If you buy into the religious canon of the Gospels and the New Testament – as I do – then you're confronted with the lack of prophesy regarding these Marys. There's plenty to chew on regarding the second coming of Christ, but nothing about a new wave of virgin births and three new baby Jesuses. What does it mean? Have we missed something fundamental about the fabric of Christianity?'

Cal's phone beeped with a text message.

'Jessica wants to know where I am.'

'You should go to her.'

There was another beep.

'She's not looking for my companionship,' Cal said. 'She says there's another video.'

'Mary Riordan,' was all that Murphy said.

Cal clicked on the link and the two men watched her birth video, the soundtrack of organ music working nicely with the waves breaking on the sand.

'Jesus David,' Murphy said after Mary, looking into the lens, announced his name. 'Good on her for picking her grandfather. Kenny Riordan's a bastard.'

This third video didn't fade to black as the others had. It dissolved to a shot of all three girls sitting side-by-side on a sofa, each one holding her infant and smiling sweetly, almost beatifically. When this image turned to black two words were displayed.

THE BEGINNING.

And then a scroll unfurled with these words translated into other languages – not a dozen or three dozen but perhaps a hundred.

'Something's coming,' Murphy said.

'Please hold for President Griffith.'

Randall Anning was not the type of man who owned a Caribbean estate. He had a Caribbean island. When the call came in he was driving a golf cart from his house down to the harbor where he was expecting a yacht-load of children and grandchildren for the long weekend.

'Randy, how the hell are you?'

'I'm good, Mr President. Are you in Washington?'

'God forbid. I'm down in Florida on Jupiter. Bill Finke lent me his estate. You know Bill, don't you?'

'Sure I do. We're on the Business Roundtable together. What can I do for you?'

'You've seen the newest video? This third girl, the Irish one, with her own Baby Jesus.'

Anning smiled. 'Yes, I've seen the video.'

'What do you make of it?'

'Stirs the heart of this old Catholic,' Anning said. 'We seem to be awash in miracles.'

'The last time I got such a rise out of religion was when Sister Veronica was spanking my bare bottom. Still think about that damned nun.'

'We all have a Sister Veronica in our past.'

'So, here's what I want to know,' Griffith said. 'What do you think Pope Celestine is making of these latter-day Marys and Jesuses? Do you think he's shitting himself?'

Anning's motor yacht was approaching the dock. He waved to the children waving at him.

'I expect he is, Lew.'

'That all you have to say to me?'

'For the moment. Stay tuned.'

'I'm the goddamned President, Randy. There's only so many times you can tell me that.'

NINETEEN

Cal, Jessica, and Father Gooseberry, as Jessica had taken to calling Murphy, were having oysters on the patio of Cru on Nantucket wharf when Cal got a call from a blocked number.

'Is this Professor Calvin Donovan?' the caller asked.

'It is. Who's this?'

'It's George Pole, Professor.'

'Cardinal Pole,' Cal said in surprise, catching Murphy mid-oyster and causing the priest to stare.

'I'm not a cardinal any longer. Call me George.'

'All right, George.'

'Is this a good time?'

'Yes, of course.'

'Excellent. I know the Vatican's gotten you involved with the virgin girls. You've been following all the recent developments, I trust.'

'Of course. The newest video. The Beginning, whatever that means.'

'Theatrical, don't you think?' Pole said.

'That's *exactly* what I think.'

'So, Professor, how'd you like to play a part in this drama, visit the Marys, kiss a few babies, and see for yourself what's going on?'

*   *   *

Jessica's picture window was glowing orange in the setting sun. Cal was doing his best imitation of a bartender, shaking up frosty batches of ultra-dry vodka martinis and trying to avoid the second coldest thing in the house: her icy glare. The moment he told her that he'd be cutting the weekend short and departing the island in the morning on a private jet, he had become the gooseberry and Murphy had become her preferred partner in conversation.

'Do you want me to fire up the grill?' Cal asked.

She was a little drunk by now. 'I think I heard a voice. Joe, do we want this man to fire up the grill?'

Murphy had declared that his goal for the evening was to acquire a taste for vodka and he reached for his martini glass. 'Is it a requirement as your house guest, Jessica, that I be in the middle of this domestic spat?'

'Yes, it is,' she said, wrinkling her nose at Cal.

'Then yes,' Murphy said. 'I do think that you should light the grill, Cal. I'd do it myself but I see you're on gas here. I'm not a propane man. Now if it had been charcoal you wanted then that would have been a bird of a different feather.'

Over steaks Cal tried to worm his way back into Jessica's good books.

'DNA,' he said suddenly.

'What about it?' she asked, deigning to acknowledge him.

'If I'm going I should try to get DNA from the babies, don't you think?'

'I don't care about the babies,' she replied, not very helpfully.

'Well, putting that aside, how would one go about getting the DNA?'

'If I tell you, will you do the dishes while Joe and I drink dessert wine under the stars?'

Cal was the only passenger on the private jet that came for him the next morning at Nantucket Memorial Airport. The pilot and co-pilot cheerfully informed him that their skills at serving food and drink weren't all that wonderful and that he might do just as well helping himself to whatever he wanted from the well-stocked galley.

'So, guys,' Cal said, checking out the empty cabin, 'want to tell me where we're headed?'

'They told us you're not supposed to know that, sir. We've also been instructed to keep the window shades down for the entire flight.'

'I promise not to peek.'

The flight lasted four and a half hours and Cal managed to do some prep work for the courses he'd be teaching the coming semester and fire off an email to Cardinal Da Silva and Sister Elisabetta about his unexpected invitation from George Pole. Before landing he got a reply from Da Silva expressing a high level of concern that Pole was in some way involved with the girls. He asked Cal to contact him immediately, any hour of the day or night, when he had information to report.

When the plane touched down, the door was opened, and the stairs deployed, Cal got a blast of hot, dry air. He hardly got a chance to check out the brown, featureless landscape because an SUV with blacked-out windows was waiting a few feet from the stairs.

'Long drive?' Cal asked the driver, settling into the back seat.

'Not very.'

The guy must have been a comedian because a minute later the SUV stopped and the driver opened the door for Cal. Standing at the front portico of a red-bricked mansion was George Pole, wearing a lightweight, tan suit.

Cal had never met him although he knew a lot about him, particularly his unabashed conservative politics and his penchant for picking public spats with the pope.

'Your Eminence,' Cal said, extending a hand.

'Just George now,' Pole said. 'Welcome, Professor.'

'So, judging by the flight time and the weather I'm guessing we're in Texas or Oklahoma,' Cal said.

'Well, we just call it the ranch,' Pole said lightly.

Beyond the circular drive Cal saw a convoy of landscaping trucks heading down an access road loaded with mature trees with huge root balls wrapped in canvas.

'Please come in. It's hotter than Hades although we're certainly not there.'

Pole took him through a marble-floored entry hall into a formal living room decorated with southwestern art and Frederic Remington bronzes that looked suspiciously like the real thing. A

Latina woman with a black uniform and white apron came in, asked Pole if they wanted something to drink and she left with an order for a couple of coffees.

'Make yourself comfortable, Professor. I expect you'd like to know why I asked you to come.'

'I expect you're right. Are the girls really here?'

'They are. And three special little fellows. I'm sure you were among the billion or so people who watched the birth videos.'

'I was.'

'Then you saw the message. The beginning.'

'A teaser if ever there was one.'

'Yes, but truthful. We wanted you to see the Marys and their infants because in the coming days, weeks, and months people will question many things about them. We live in an age of conspiracy theories. People still believe the moon landings were faked. We wanted someone with impeccable credentials and impartiality to see firsthand what has happened here at the ranch. We want you to bear witness.'

'You keep saying "we."'

'I'm but a cog in a wheel, Professor. There are others, of course. This is a large endeavor.'

'Seems to me you're a pretty big cog. Was your resignation tied up with this?'

'I don't want to get off on the wrong foot with you by lying. I was aware this was coming, yes.'

'I'm happy to hear you aren't going to lie,' Cal said. 'Tell me what you have to say about the allegations that the girls were kidnapped.'

'I've read the reports. I don't believe they are credible or correct. Yes, the parents of the girls were given money but this was done to support them and make the girls comfortable in the knowledge that their families were taken care of in their absence.'

'Cindy Riordan isn't comfortable. She's dead.'

'Again, I'm aware of the investigation into her death. My understanding is that the autopsy was inconclusive. Natural causes are still very much on the table.'

'She begged a colleague of mine to come and see her and when he arrived she refused to tell him the full story. She was scared and she wasn't the only one.'

'How is Father Murphy? He had an ordeal.'

'He's doing fine,' Cal said, hitting Pole with an arctic stare.

'These men who held him. It's true they were hired to provide a measure of local security for the Riordans but they undertook the criminal act against Joseph Murphy wholly on their own. I deeply regret their involvement.'

'Tell me why the girls were taken in the first place?'

'Isn't it obvious?' Pole said. 'We live in the twenty-first century, Professor. The world is fully interconnected and information flows seamlessly and instantaneously. And then suddenly, we have three teenage girls in our midst, all with a shared name, the evocative name of Mary, all who are blessed with virgin conception. You've seen Dr Benedict's medical assessment. The evidence is incontrovertible.'

'You're the one who sent it to me.'

'Not me personally but, yes, it came from us. We've thought for a while that you were someone we might be able to work with. It's the one thing the pope and I agree on. You visited Manila and Lima. You saw the crowds of jostling pilgrims, the slums, the inadequate security. These very exceptional girls and their precious progeny were at risk. Thank God there were those with the vision and resources to keep them safe and ensure that they came to healthy, full terms. These girls and their sons belong to the world, just as the Blessed Mother Mary and Jesus Christ do.'

'Could the girls leave if they wanted to?'

'Why don't you ask them that?'

'I will.'

'Any other questions before you're brought to them?'

Cal chuckled. 'Yeah, I've got a few. Beginnings beget middles and middles beget ends. What's your role going to be in the next phase of whatever this is?'

Pole opened his arms to the ceiling. 'All will be revealed.'

'Tell me, is all this intended to be a stick in the eye of Pope Celestine?'

Pole had been sporting a benign smile up to this point. He put his cup and saucer down and said, 'I wanted the Vatican to open a formal miracles investigation. Did the pope convene the Congregation for the Causes of Saints? No, he did not. Did he pay lip service with some kind of *ex officio* panel that as far as I know hasn't even met? Yes he did.'

'Since we're being honest with each other, the informal panel was my recommendation and I believe the term "lip service" was actually used during the conversation.'

The smile returned to Pole's face. 'Honesty is so cleansing, don't you think?'

Pole saw Mrs Torres passing through the entry hall and gave her a thumbs-up sign. Shortly afterwards Sue arrived.

'Professor Donovan, I'd like you to meet the woman who works particularly closely with the girls. I've only just met her myself although I'm familiar with her wonderful work. She'll take you upstairs. Feel free to ask her anything except for our location. Everything else is fair game.'

'I'm Sue,' she said, ignoring Pole and taking Cal's hand.

'And I'm Cal.'

It was a familiar feeling, that tingling in his chest when he first set eyes on an interesting woman. Beauty would always turn his head but it took something else to trigger that chest sensation. Sometimes it was intangible but with her it was her duality, a look that simultaneously expressed confidence and fragility. And there was something about her swinging pony-tail and piercing eyes.

Pole told Cal he'd see him again at the end of the visit and went off in search of Torres.

'Are you comfortable with a couple of flights of stairs or would you prefer the elevator?' Sue asked.

'I think I can make it.'

He followed her up the marble staircase and, half a flight up, he figured out what it was about her hair. 'You were the nurse in the videos, weren't you?'

'Midwife, but yes.'

'Sorry for my ignorance. I've successfully avoided everything to do with pregnancies and their aftermath.'

'How did you know it was me?'

'Your hair.'

'Dead giveaway. One more flight. Some of the staff live on the second floor. The girls and I are on the third. They told me you were a professor from Harvard.'

'Do I look the part?'

'Not really. I figured you'd be older.'

'Listen, is there somewhere we could talk before I see them? I want to get some background on their last few months.'

'We can use my room if you're comfortable with that. I made my bed.'

She left the bedroom door open and had him sit on the sofa in her TV area. She opened her mini-fridge and said, 'Limited choices. Water or wine? It's a bit early for wine, I suppose.'

'Is it?' he said but when she reached for a bottle of Riesling he said, 'Just joking. Water's fine. Tell me, were you with the girls from the beginning here, wherever here is?'

'I was here when they arrived, setting up for their blessed deliveries.'

'Blessed, huh?'

'Sorry, that's just me being me.'

'When you talked to the girls, did you get the idea that their parents went along willingly with their leaving?'

'There's a language barrier with the Marias and I didn't want to upset them so I guess I don't really know the details. I wasn't there. Mrs Torres was. Maybe you should ask her.'

'I haven't met her. What does she do?'

'She's the manager of the ranch.'

'Does Mary Riordan know about her mother?'

'She only found out after the delivery. She's very sad, of course. They were worried the shock would cause a miscarriage.'

'Who's they?'

'I really don't know. You may hear me say that a lot. I haven't met anyone in charge beyond Mrs Torres. I never saw the man you were talking to downstairs. Maybe he's the "they." My contract's with a company called Miracle Ranch. I'm sort of in the dark. That's probably why they let you talk to me. I only know about the girls.'

'How'd they find you?'

'I answered an ad. One thing led to another. I had no idea what I was getting into.'

'Where were you before?'

'I'm a New Mexico girl.'

'Could I ask? Are you religious?'

'Funny question.'

'Is it? I'm sorry. I've got religion on the brain. I'm a professor of religious studies.'

'I wasn't told about you. Look, it's not as if I don't understand the significance of what's going on here. It's just that I'm not sure why you want to know about me.'

'I withdraw the question. It was intrusive.'

'It's OK. I'm a Christian but I'm not religious. You're probably wondering if I've been affected by them. Honestly, I've been too busy to think about it. Maybe it'll hit me later.'

'How do you think the girls have adapted to being here?'

'I think they've done really well. It hasn't been without its little dramas. They were plucked out of their normal environments, away from their families, and pretty much forced to live together. Each one has her own personality and cultural frame of reference but you'll see – they've bonded in a kind of sisterhood. This place has been a cocoon. They're unaware of most of the fuss going on around the world. They've just heard a few snippets when they've called home. Now they're all mothers, the bond's gotten even stronger. Ready to meet them?'

Rising, something caught his eye out one of her windows.

'Jesus, what the hell is that?' he said.

'Probably what it looks like. They've been building it ever since before I arrived. A few hundred men at times but it's almost finished. I don't go up there. It's not my department.'

'Does it worry you?'

'I don't know. Maybe it should. Ready?'

The girls were waiting for them in their lounge. They had all participated in making a colorful sign pinned to their cork board: Welcome Professor Donovan.

Mrs Torres and Mrs Simpauco were in the room to translate for the Marias. The older babies were sleeping in a communal crib. Mary Riordan was holding her newborn.

On cue the girls all repeated the sign in English.

'Hello, girls, I'm very pleased to meet you,' Cal said. 'What a lovely greeting.'

He went to each girl in turn, shaking hands, exchanging some personal words. He told Maria Aquino it was good to see her again and asked after her mother. The girl told him that she spoke to her mother every week and missed her very much. To Maria Mollo

he said that he'd met her parents in Lima. That surprised her no
end. She too spoke by phone with them regularly.

'And you must be Mary Riordan,' Cal said.

'Process of elimination,' she said, not making much in the way
of eye contact.

'I wanted to tell you how sorry I was to hear about your
mother's passing.'

'Yeah, sucks,' she said, concentrating on the baby. 'You met her?'

'Not me, a friend of mine told me about her.'

'The priest?'

'Yeah, Father Murphy.'

'Priests have friends?'

'The friendly ones do.'

She laughed.

'So, this is where you all hang out?' Cal asked.

It seemed like the girls had been rehearsed. Maria Aquino got
up and with Mrs Simpauco translating, showed Cal their
PlayStation and their collection of DVDs. Torres helped Maria
Mollo give a tour of their art supplies and board games and took
him down the hall to see the classroom where they had their
English lessons.

Returning to the lounge, he saw that Sue had climbed on to
the sofa next to Mary and that the girl was resting her head on
Sue's shoulder.

'I don't suppose you need English lessons, Mary,' he said. 'Are
you studying anything?'

'I'm meant to be doing course work online to keep up with
where I'd be back home.'

'Meant to be?'

She looked at him and fluttered her long lashes. 'What are they
going to do? Beat me when I refuse?'

'Sue doesn't seem like the beating type.'

'Oh, I don't know about that,' Sue said, playfully holding a fist
to the girl's jaw.

'The school work is bollocks. All they care about is the baby.
My job was to have him,' Mary said, sullenly, 'and here it is.'

'I don't know much about babies but he's a nice-looking one.'

'You want to take him? I could use a pee.'

Cal stuck a hand in the pocket of his khakis, like he was fishing for change. With both hands free he bent over and awkwardly took hold of the baby. Sue counseled him to hold it to his shoulder and quickly placed a towel underneath to protect his shirt.

'He's a barfer,' Mary said.

'Hello, there, Jesus David,' Cal said. 'Pleased to make your acquaintance.'

He did things he'd seen people do with babies in the movies like bouncing around on the balls of his feet. Then he took a chair and cradled the baby on his lap, wiggling his forefinger over his mouth. JD took the bait and began vigorously sucking on his finger.

'Wow,' Cal exclaimed, 'you're strong.'

'Tell me about it,' Mary said, returning. 'Cripples my nipple.'

Sue scolded her but the two Marias had already learned the expression from their friend and began giggling.

Cal handed JD back and asked if he could hold the other babies.

'Which one is this?' he said pointing to the one in the crib with the thickest shocks of brown hair. 'I'm the worst. They all kind of look the same to me but all babies do.'

'They do look similar, don't they?' Sue said, causing Mrs Torres to shoot her a sharp look.

'*Akin.*' Mine, Maria Aquino said. 'JR.'

Cal sat down with the robust-looking infant, played with him and tested his sucking strength too. He caught Sue staring at him and self-consciously handed JR to his mother and went for Maria Mollo's JP. The baby was still a bit of a peanut compared to the others but was catching up.

'He was really small at birth and had some jaundice but he's doing great,' Sue said.

Cal was going to do his finger-sucking again when JP puked on Cal's midsection.

'I sorry. Please excuse,' Maria Mollo said, garnering praise from all the women for her excellent language skills.

'You speak English very well,' Cal said, ignoring the spit-up and giving the baby to Maria.

'Come on,' Sue said to Cal. 'Let me help you clean up.'

She took him to a bathroom down the hall and surprised him by going inside with him, closing the door.

'What the hell are you doing?' she demanded, turning the faucet on full and loud.

'What do you mean?' he asked.

'Don't give me that. The finger cots.'

Cal simply said, 'Busted.'

He had a little rubber sheath on his pointer finger that he dipped into the spittle, rolled it off, and placed into a baggie he pulled from his pocket.

'It's for their DNA,' he said. 'You going to turn me in?'

She wet a sheet of paper towel and set about cleaning his shirt.

'No.'

'Why not?'

'I've wondered how they'd test,' she said.

He mouthed the words, thank you and said, 'I'm supposed to get samples from the girls too if possible. Hair from brushes, tooth brushes, that sort of thing.'

'You're not going to stick your finger into their mouths too?'

'I'm not good at this. I really am just a professor of religion.'

'Any more baggies?'

He dug into another pocket.

'I'll get you some hair,' she said, 'On one condition.'

'What's that?'

'You let me know the DNA results. You're not the only one who's curious.'

They exchanged numbers on a piece of paper towel and he used the rest to blot his shirt dry.

When he returned to the lounge he asked the girls if he could pose some questions about life at the ranch. The Marias nodded and Mary, who had put JD into the communal crib, ignored him and played with her phone.

'So, what's the best thing about being here?' he asked.

'Her!' Maria Mollo said, pointing at Maria Aquino.

'Her!' Maria Aquino reciprocated.

'What about her?' Cal asked, playfully pointing at Mary.

'I don't give a toss what Minion and Eeyore think about me,' she said.

The Marias explained their nicknames and Cal asked them if Mary had one too.

'Baka!' Maria Aquino said.

'Baka?' Cal asked.

'It means "cow" in Filipino,' Mrs Simpauco said.

Mary Riordan feigned insult then cracked up and threw a pillow at the girl and soon all three of them were laughing.

'OK,' Cal said. 'What's the worst thing about living here?'

Torres started to object but Cal said that George Pole had told him he could ask the girls anything he wanted.

Soon they all agreed that being away from home and their families was by far the worst.

'Would you go home tomorrow if you could?' Cal asked.

'If we could take our babies with us, we'd be gone,' Mary said. 'We all think that.'

Sue came back in and sat with the girls on the sofa.

'What would be the next best thing?' Cal asked.

Maria Aquino said in Filipino, 'To bring our families here to live with us. This is a big house. There's room for all of them.'

'Is that something that's been discussed?' Cal asked.

'Not with me,' Mrs Torres said acidly.

Cal looked to Sue who added, 'If it hasn't been discussed with her it definitely hasn't been discussed with me.'

Torres felt a need to say, 'Sue always thinks I know more than I do.'

'But you must get your instructions from someone,' Cal said.

'That I can't discuss.'

Turning back to the girls, Cal asked, 'What is your biggest hope for the future?'

Each girl said the same thing. They wanted their babies to be healthy and they wanted to go home.

'But we'll miss Sue,' Maria Mollo said.

The other two girls agreed.

Sue went to each one, planting a kiss on the forehead.

'I'm curious,' Cal said, 'Do any of you feel holy, like you've been touched by God?'

'No, sir,' Maria Aquino said in her language, 'we don't feel special. We feel like girls with beautiful babies.'

Cal knew this would be his last question. He knew the grim-faced Torres would shut him down but he asked anyway. 'OK, one last question. Did all of you want to come here or were you forced to come?'

Mrs Torres took a series of short steps forward and turned herself into a physical barrier between Cal and the girls.

'That's an outrageous question, Professor Donovan. The girls will not be dignifying it with an answer.'

'George Pole did tell me—'

'I don't care what you were told. The girls are my responsibility and I won't have them subjected to objectionable questions.'

Cal smiled. 'Well, I did say it was my last question. Thank you all for your time. As he was saying his goodbyes, Mary Riordan silently mouthed a word to him. He was certain it was: 'Forced.'

When Sue escorted him downstairs he asked her, 'Would it be possible for me to spend a few minutes with Mrs Torres? To talk about her experiences when she picked up the girls?'

She gave him a smile that seemed to say 'fat chance,' but asked him to wait. A few minutes later she returned.

'She says she's tied up,' Sue said. 'She apologizes.'

He grunted in frustration. She broke the uncomfortable silence by asking what he thought about his visit.

'The girls seem well. But obviously, it's a weird environment for them.'

'Weird is a word that rattles around my head a lot,' she said. 'I think something's going to happen. I don't think things are going to stay the same.'

'What's going to happen?'

'I'm in the dark but that man you were talking to?'

'George Pole.'

'Yeah, he creeps me out. A lot about this place creeps me out.'

'You could leave.'

'They persuaded me to stay another six months. For the sake of the girls.'

'What happens in six months?'

'Mrs Torres told me the girls wouldn't be as dependent on me after that.'

'You're here by choice. I don't believe the same is true for the girls.'

'I don't go there,' she said. 'Maybe I should but I don't.'

'I don't think anyone could legitimately criticize you for your role here,' he said. 'It's pretty clear how much the girls love you.'

She teared up fast. Cal had the sense she wouldn't mind it if he touched her hand. She didn't and he kept his fingertips on her knuckles.

'Thank you for your help. The DNA testing is ultimately for them.'

'What are you expecting, Professor of Religion? God's DNA?'

'I'm in the dark too,' he said, sliding his fingers away. 'I'll text you when I know.'

'Will you be coming back?'

'If they invite me. I don't know where we are.'

He thought she might volunteer their location but she didn't. Instead she smiled at him. 'If you do maybe we could have that glass of wine.' Then she caught herself. 'I'm sorry, that wasn't cool.'

'Don't be sorry,' he said.

She left him in the great room and George Pole came in to see him off.

'Mrs Torres tells me you had a productive visit with the girls,' he said.

'I think it was. I asked them if they wanted to leave. They said they did.'

'You also asked them what the next best thing would be. They answered, bringing their families here.'

'Were you listening in?'

Pole smiled and nodded. 'We have baby monitors for safety.'

'More honesty,' Cal said. 'Are you going to send for their families?'

'It's something that's under consideration. You'll be reporting back to the Vatican I assume?'

'I will. Do you want me to carry a message?'

'Please give Celestine my regards.'

'What shall I tell him about what's going to happen after this beginning of yours?'

'Tell him that all will be revealed.'

'And what do you want to tell me about the structure I saw out the window?'

'I'll tell you the same thing. All will be revealed.'

TWENTY

After Labor Day, Cal made a pilgrimage to Jessica's office armed with a box of roses.

'What are these for?' she asked, clearly fully aware of the offering's purpose.

'Shit, Jessica, for being me I suppose. For ditching you on Nantucket, for leaving you with a depressed priest on a holiday weekend.'

'Actually, we got along famously,' she said, 'and he wasn't the least depressed – at least with me. He bordered on merry. Joe's my new BFF. I used to say that gay guys were the best friends a girl could have. Now I'll tell anyone who'll listen that priests are even better.'

'Good to know,' Cal said. 'Anyway, to paraphrase Caesar, I went, I saw, I didn't exactly conquer. But I got samples for DNA. Can I give them to you?'

Jessica took the baggies with finger cots and hair and told him it would take a few days.

'Was it a religious experience?' she asked tartly.

'It was more like visiting a girl's boarding school.'

'I'm awfully glad I wasn't there,' she said. 'It might have given me unpleasant flashbacks.'

'So, can I make it up to you with dinner on Friday?' he asked.

'Actually, Cal, I'm booked. Joe and I have a dinner date.'

Cal thought he'd be speaking to Cardinal Da Silva and Sister Elisabetta but it seemed the interest in his report was so great that the pope wanted to participate directly. George Pole, the proverbial thorn in his side, was back sticking him again and Celestine wanted to understand his intentions. While Da Silva and Elisabetta asked questions, the pope stayed silent.

'The infants, how did they seem?' Da Silva asked.

'Like infants, I guess,' Cal said. 'I haven't been around many babies so I don't have a good point of reference. To be honest, they looked pretty much the same to me.'

'I see,' Da Silva said, a bit deflated perhaps.

Cal added, 'If you were expecting that I'd say they all had little halos over their heads like a Renaissance painting, then no, they didn't.'

'I really don't know what I was expecting you to say,' Da Silva said.

Finally, the pope's voice came down the line sonorously. 'I am more interested how George Pole seemed.'

'Self-satisfied,' Cal said. 'A bit like the cat who ate the canary. Picture him with feathers coming out of his mouth.'

'That is an image I can easily imagine,' the pope said. 'Did you get the impression that George was the one who conceived of the taking of the girls?'

'He alluded to the involvement of other people but it was hard for me to judge whether he's a pawn or a king.'

'The only thing we know for sure,' Celestine said, 'is that he is no longer a cardinal.'

Elisabetta asked, 'Professor, did you get any sense of the timing of Pole's next move?'

'None. He said "all will be revealed" a couple of times. Does that mean days or weeks or months? Your guess is as good as mine.'

'We can share something with you, Professor,' Da Silva said. 'Since Pole resigned as cardinal, we have received notice of a trickle of resignations of priests mostly from American dioceses with petitions for the dispensation of their clerical obligations. However, just within the past few days we have become aware of fifty resignations of priests and two American bishops, one from Missouri, the other from Louisiana, both ardent conservatives. One gets the idea that something is brewing.'

Cal heard a series of sounds coming from the Vatican end of the call.

Someone knocking on a door.

A chair scraping as someone got up.

Elisabetta talking to a man in the distance.

Her saying something in Italian he couldn't quite make out and the pope replying, 'What did you say?'

Cardinal Da Silva said into the speakerphone, 'Sorry, Cal, could you just hold on a second?'

Then he heard a TV transmission in the background that sounded like a news program.

Then Elisabetta came back to the speaker and said, 'I'm sorry, Professor, but we've got to hang up now. I'd suggest you turn on your television. There's a picture of what is probably the building you told us about on George Pole's ranch.'

TWENTY-ONE

C al didn't have a TV in his office so he logged on to CNN from his computer. An anchorwoman was talking over an aerial shot of the structure Cal had seen from Sue's window. The chyron at the bottom of the screen read: BREAKING NEWS: VIRGIN BIRTH GIRLS TO APPEAR TOGETHER.

The footage appeared to be shot from a drone or a helicopter sweeping over the structure. The scale of the building was much greater than what Cal had appreciated from his myopic window view. What he saw that day was a section of a spike that suggested a church spire, but from his vantage point he hadn't been able to take in its full character or visualize its peak. Now it was clear that this was a church – more than a church, a cathedral, its spire tipped by a giant cross of gleaming steel.

It certainly wasn't the first modernist cathedral that Cal had ever seen. Brazilians have an affinity for building outsized, provocative Catholic cathedrals on a grand scale, but the ones in Brasilia and Rio de Janeiro were so futuristic that they barely resembled churches. Likewise, for the Cathedral of St Mary of the Assumption in San Francisco. This ranch cathedral was an unusual hybrid of a classic Gothic European design and modern architectural aesthetic. Instead of medieval stone, it was built with glass and steel. It had the traditional cruciform ground plan of a long nave crossed by a transept and a soaring central spire but instead of the rather small and narrow windows of Gothic churches, the cathedral walls were all glass, greenish and mirrored, and it was in a mirrored surface that Cal caught the reflection of the helicopter that was shooting the live footage.

After a short while the architectural parallel hit him. The client must have told the architect: build me a twenty-first-century version of England's Salisbury Cathedral.

It looked like it could accommodate several hundred worshippers but so far, all broadcasted shots were exterior. As the helicopter continued to circle the structure, the anchorwoman referred to briefing material the network had just received indicating that at any moment they would be receiving a live feed from inside the church, its location undisclosed.

The anchorwoman said, 'I want to stress that ordinarily we don't run video that isn't ours or that we haven't previously vetted but because of the extraordinary level of interest in these missing girls, we are airing it with a brief delay to give us the opportunity to cut the broadcast if we deem the material is inappropriate. Let's bring in our religious affairs correspondent, Henry Capriati, to get his views on what we're seeing.'

The reporter started commentating about the size and scale of the church, stressing that whoever built it was intending it to be used by large numbers of people. Then he said, 'Clearly there is a high level of interest in seeing the three Marys and perhaps hearing from them for the first time. And now there will be a high level of interest in learning who are the individuals behind this construction.'

Cal felt a tap on his shoulder. He'd been so glued to the computer that he had failed to see Joe Murphy coming in.

'Thought I'd swing by to watch this with you,' Murphy said. 'You mind?'

'Have a seat. Sorry there's no seat belt.'

'You think it's going to be wild?'

'How could it not be? Reached a decision on this semester?'

'I'm not going to take a leave. Business as usual.'

'Does that mean you're feeling better?'

'I am. Jessica's been a help, if you must know. Thanks for making the introduction.'

'I'm delighted, Joe, and somewhat amused. Jessica's done nothing but bust my balls lately. I never pegged her as being the supportive type.'

'I dare say your dynamic is different,' Murphy said with a smile. 'She's been a good listener and a good sight cheaper than a shrink. She's also funny. Turns out I respond well to humor. Who knew? It's also refreshing that she's a she. I haven't had a female friend since my days before the seminary.'

'Well, I'm—'

Cal didn't get 'glad' out of his mouth because the video feed abruptly switched to the interior of the cathedral accompanied by Bach's Prelude in C Major for the organ. For all the modernity of the exterior, the interior was muted and strangely traditional. The tinted glass filtered out the brightness of the sun and bathed the interior in a greenish hue. The ceiling was vaulted and pale with wooden coffering evocative of flying buttresses. The floor was a green, mottled marble, the empty pews dark and lacquered. The altar, built of similar dark wood, stood in a polygonal apse decorated with a giant painted panel, a modern work paying homage to a Renaissance style of the Virgin Mary holding the baby Jesus in her arms, except that there were three Marys and three babies.

The camera smoothly zoomed on to the apse until a man appeared from a wing and approached the altar.

'Holy shit,' Cal said. 'Holy, holy shit.'

'Is that . . .?' Murphy asked.

Cal answered, 'You're damn right it is.'

It wasn't all that surprising to see George Pole making an appearance. Cal already knew he'd be involved in some way. What was eye-popping was what he was wearing. The man was climbing the altar dressed in papal vestments. But not fully modern ones. Some of his regalia and vestments had not been worn by pontiffs for ages, including his triregnum, a triple-tiered crown, his broad old-fashioned pallium worn over his white chasuble, and a red mantum, a cape that was so long and impractical that it hadn't been used since the Second Vatican Council. And the staff he held in his right hand was not the modern papal ferula capped by a crucifix, but the ancient crozier, the bent pastoral staff fashioned on a shepherd's crook.

'What is happening?' Murphy muttered.

Standing at the altar, Pole surveyed the empty church. His audience was not there with him. It was in the ether, fed by TV cameras.

The music faded and he spoke into a microphone. 'Good day to you,' he began. 'My name is George Pole. Until recently I was a cardinal of the Holy Roman Church. I resigned my position out of love for the Church and its glorious history. But it was no longer the Catholic Church I knew. I began to stop recognizing it when, as a youngster, it abandoned the Latin Mass. I began to stop recognizing it when it made a purposeful turn to so-called modernity and ecumenism that changed Catholicism in large ways and small. I particularly stopped recognizing it during this papacy when the Church became a vehicle more for social welfare than the welfare of the everlasting soul. Because of my abiding love for the deeply rooted traditions and theological underpinnings of the Church I could no longer be a cog in the wheel of what it has become.'

Cal grunted a laugh. Pole had used the same phrase to describe his role in whatever *this* was.

'As I contemplated my fate I did not have a clear vision of what might follow. I just knew that I could no longer keep on walking down the same path. And then something miraculous happened, something that points so emphatically and definitively to the glory and the wisdom of our almighty God. The Lord looked down from Heaven and reached out to touch three teenage girls from far-flung reaches of the globe. These girls were young and pure, virgins all. They were simple girls. They did not come from wealth and privilege. And despite their virginity – verified not only by experts within their own countries, but by Dr Richard Benedict, the president of the American College of Obstetrics and Gynecology, in a report I intend to release today – I say despite their virginity, these girls, all named Mary, became pregnant. They saw a divine light and they heard the voice of God tell them, "You have been chosen." And now these girls have given birth to infant boys they have decided to call Jesus. Jesus Ruperto, Jesus Juan, and Jesus David. How, I ask you, do these Marys differ from Mary of Nazareth, the mother of Jesus Christ? I for one, see no difference. Two millennia ago the world needed a savior and the Holy Ghost delivered him unto us. Jesus Christ still walks among us but most are blind to his presence. So, what has the Holy Ghost done? He has given us three new Sons of God to verily walk among us and counsel us, three new Sons of God to renew the Church and reinforce the message of the Gospels. We cannot be blind to these infants. I will not be blind to them. For they come at a time when the mother Church needs a renewal and I no longer believe that renewal can come from within. It must come from the outside. The Holy Roman Church is no longer relevant. That is why I have accepted the position as pope of a new Church, a Church steeped in ancient traditions, a Church that cares about your soul, not your politics; a Church for rich and poor; a Church for a new era, dedicated to Jesus Christ our Savior, dedicated to Holy Mary, Mother of God, but also dedicated to Jesus Ruperto, Jesus Juan, and Jesus David, and the three Marys, their Holy Mothers. For myself, I have taken the name of Peter, pope of the New Catholic Church.'

Murphy spat out, 'What a fucking asswipe.'

Cal was thinking much the same thing but he said, 'I've never heard you swear before, Joe. That has to be coming from Jessica.'

'She's bringing out the Galway in me.'

Pole took a pause, perhaps imagining a crowd somewhere erupting in applause. When he continued he looked to the wings and said, 'And now, I would like the world to meet the font of our inspiration: our Marys and their infant sons.'

The organ music picked up again as Maria Aquino, Maria Mollo, and Mary Riordan each entered the apse holding on to their babies. The girls were dressed in identical outfits of long-sleeved white button-down blouses, black skirts coming well below the knee, and black flat shoes. The babies were likewise dressed identically in white shirts and the light-blue blankets that swaddled them. The Marias were smiling but Mary Riordan looked fed up and shirty.

'Get a load of our Irish lass,' Murphy said. 'She looks as joyful as I did in my proof of life photo.'

Pole came down from the altar to be among the girls. There must have been a Lavalier mic clipped to his vestments because he was perfectly amplified.

'The Old Catholic Church as we will now call it will be outraged. They will be baying for our blood. They will condemn us as heretics. We will be called sacrilegious. But we will not be silenced and we will not be cowed. Our foundation is made of thick and everlasting bedrock. Our foundation is our new Virgin Marys and our new baby Jesuses. Now I, Pope Peter of the New Catholic Church, invite members of the Old Catholic Church including its priests, monsignors, nuns, bishops, even archbishops and cardinals and all its devoted faithful to join us. I also invite members of all Christian Protestant and fundamental faiths to join us. In fact, I invite members of any faith – Jews, Muslims, Buddhists, anyone – and people who have been agnostics or non-believers, to open their hearts to the miracle of virgin birth you can see with your own eyes. Join us.'

'You going to sign up, Joe?' Cal asked.

'Where do I enlist?'

'Before too long, this magnificent cathedral that we stand in today will be sanctified by me as the Cathedral of the Blessed New Virgin Marys. I will be conducting Mass on that day, a Latin Mass. The location of our cathedral will be made public and we will welcome the attendance of the faithful. Our Marys and their babies will be there to celebrate Mass with us. Have a blessed day.'

The transmission ended and Cal blurted out, 'Holy shit. What did we just see?'

Murphy stayed in his chair, shaking his head in disbelief. 'I've developed a taste for strong drink lately. Is it too early?'

'It's too early even for me,' Cal said. 'Wouldn't you like to be a fly on the wall at the Vatican about now?'

There was indeed a pesky fly on the wall of Pope Celestine's guesthouse office and Cardinal Da Silva swatted at it with his hand when it buzzed his face. They had watched the broadcast with Sister Elisabetta who had asked another of the pope's secretaries to hold all the calls. The constant ringing as Church officials and government ministers tried to reach the pontiff was driving them to distraction.

'The only person I want to hear from is Carla Condorelli,' Elisabetta had said. 'Find out where she is.'

The head of the Vatican press office, it seems, was out for the morning attending a school meeting for one of her kids.

'One had the impression that we had not heard the last of George,' the pope said.

'But no one expected this,' Da Silva said.

'It's not completely unexpected,' Elisabetta said. 'He was behind Professor Donovan's meeting with the girls.'

'But a pope?' Da Silva cried. 'He not only has the gall to

call himself a pope but he takes the name of Peter? Not even Peter II!'

The pope sighed and got up to make himself a coffee. Elisabetta offered to help but he waved her off. He enjoyed the simple task of choosing a pod and placing it in the machine.

'I can see you are upset, Rodrigo,' he said, 'but we must put this into perspective. This is not the first example of breakaway Catholicism. The last report I read had it that over twenty million people belong to schismatic Catholic denominations. And George isn't the first of the *episcopi vagantes,* the wandering bishops.'

'His choice of names for his sect is rather curious,' Da Silva said. 'The New Catholic Church. Shouldn't it be the Old Catholic Church if he's moaning that we've strayed from our traditions?'

'Well he's calling *us* the Old Catholic Church,' Celestine said, loading up his cup with sugar and whole milk under Elisabetta's disapproving eye, 'which I agree is curious and also uninformed. Perhaps he is unaware that this was the name taken by one of the breakaway sects formed in the nineteenth century. The Old Catholics were unhappy about the First Vatican Council. They thought it was too conservative! The world does spin, does it not?'

'Yes, but has a breakaway group ever tied its formation to a new crop of baby Jesuses?' Da Silva said.

The pope smiled, either in response to the cardinal secretary or the sweet, milky coffee. 'I'll admit that *is* a wrinkle.'

'What would you like us to do, Holy Father?' Elisabetta said. 'We must make a response.'

As if on cue, Condorelli arrived and apologized for her absence.

'You are aware of what just happened?' Elisabetta asked her.

'I was listening on the car radio,' she said. 'I almost crashed. It's quite the situation.'

Elisabetta challenged her. 'That's all you have to say?'

'That's all I have to say in front of the Holy Father.'

The pope spoke up. 'We must be firm, of course, even stern in our response. But I feel it would be a mistake to seem over-wrought. We must avoid words like heresy or blasphemy or apostasy. We must be respectful, not so much to George Pole, but to the girls. Their status remains an open question. What is not in question is that they are young and innocent. We are in no position to say how they conceived their babies. Carla, write a press release and circulate the draft. And Elisabetta, let me know as soon as you hear from Professor Donovan about his DNA samples.'

Cal was ending his long day in his preferred manner by sitting in a high-backed leather chair in his library, reading a book in Latin, and tugging on a vodka from a pleasingly heavy cut-crystal glass. His Cambridge house on a tree-lined street – populated by more professors than perhaps any other street in America – was dead silent. It was the time of year when neither heating or cooling was needed; houses were dead quiet and vibration-free.

His insistent ringtone broke the mood. He took another gulp of vodka when he saw it was Jessica. Clearly, he had not done enough in the way of penance and for his sins he prepared for another flogging.

'Hello, Jessica, I'm still sorry about Nantucket.'

'I am so over that, Cal. Was that why you thought I was calling?'

'Thought crossed my mind.'

'Well it shouldn't. Joe Murphy told me I should forgive you and I have.'

'He told you that in confession?'

'No, over drinks. So, I just got the DNA results.'

'Yeah?'

'Are you ready for some seriously weird shit?'

TWENTY-TWO

When he was alone, as he was this night, Cal usually crawled into bed by one in the morning or later, and assisted by his spirit animal, the goose – as in Grey Goose – he would quickly tail off. But the DNA results he got from Jessica had jazzed him up and were too provocative to put into an email, so he stayed up until two thirty to place a call to Cardinal Da Silva at a time he would be arriving at his Vatican desk.

'Yes, the Holy Father has been asking about the DNA results,' Da Silva said. 'But it's awfully late at your end.'

'I couldn't sleep.'

'All right then, tell me.'

'Recall that I got saliva samples from each baby and hair samples from each mother.'

'I remember.'

'OK, here it is. All the babies had identical DNA.'

'Not similar – identical?'

'They are identical triplets, born to different mothers,' Cal said.

'Well I wasn't expecting that.'

'Me neither.'

'And the mothers?'

'None of them shared any DNA with the babies. They were all complete biological strangers. Genetically unrelated.'

'What can this mean?'

'It means you can understand why I couldn't sleep. I guess the only way to start to answer the question is by asking another one: what would Christ's DNA look like if we could have tested it?'

There was a longish pause that Cal didn't step into. He figured the cardinal was composing his thoughts. 'We may go back to the fourth century for the answer to that,' the cardinal said.

'The First Council of Nicea,' Cal interjected.

'That's correct,' the cardinal continued. 'From that gathering, the doctrine of incarnation was elucidated, holding that Christ was fully God, begotten but not created by the Father, and fully human man, his flesh arising from the Virgin Mary. So the first thing I'd say, Professor, is that Christ would have indeed had DNA! He was flesh and blood. He was born, he grew to manhood, he practiced his vocation as a preacher and he was killed for it in a most mortal way. Now, as to the matter of maternity and paternity, we can be sure that Mary was his mother. The Bible is clear as glass on the point. And we are certain from the Gospel of Matthew that Mary's husband Joseph was not the father and that the Holy Spirit was.'

Cal had his Bible open to the section which he read aloud, 'Matthew verse twenty: "But after he had considered this, an angel of the Lord appeared to him in a dream and said, 'Joseph son of David, do not be afraid to take Mary home as your wife, because what is conceived in her is from the Holy Spirit.'"'

'Yes, there you have it,' Da Silva said. 'So, you'll have to indulge me in a thought experiment that I can honestly say I have never before performed. To give effect to the science of genetics, there can only be these possibilities: the Holy Spirit's DNA combined with Mary's DNA to produce Jesus, the mortal being; all of Jesus's DNA came from Mary; all of Jesus's DNA came from the Holy Spirit; or all of Jesus's DNA came from somewhere or someone else entirely.'

Cal had a note pad by his side with the same possibilities.

'So, we can scratch the one where all the genetic material comes from Mary,' he said. 'Jesus was male. Mary could only contribute X chromosomes.'

'All right,' the cardinal said, 'I see that.'

'So, what about the idea that all the DNA came from the Holy Spirit?' Cal said. 'Well, I suppose it's not a stretch to impute a maleness to God – that's a traditional if sexist view. But what about the Holy Spirit, which is conceptually a breath, a wind, God's animating force in action? There are no theological interpretations that imply that there was some kind of actual physical contact between the Holy Spirit and Mary. Otherwise the conception couldn't be virginal. But, can a breath or a wind be said to have something as mortal as DNA? Can God be said to have a genetic code? Seems like a bridge too far, but what do I know? And what if the answer is otherness, that Jesus's DNA came from somewhere else entirely? This too seems outside the realm of science as we know it.'

'So, what are we to make of your DNA results, Professor?'

Cal looked wistfully at his empty vodka glass. 'That the results of these Marys and these Jesuses are probably as unfathomable as the results would have been if Holy Mary, mother of God, and Jesus Christ had been tested.'

Da Silva agreed and said, 'Now we must wait for the next shoe to drop. Who knows where Pole is going with this and how many people will follow him?'

'I'm not prepared to just sit and wait,' Cal said. 'I want to find out where the cathedral is. I want to go back there and confront Pole about the girls. I think they were coerced into coming to America. I think they're virtual prisoners. I think the whole thing stinks to high heaven.'

'If the stink reaches that high,' the cardinal said, 'then perhaps God will assist you.'

Before he finally went to sleep he fulfilled his promise and texted the DNA results to Sue Gibney. He also threw in a question. He asked her to divulge where the cathedral was located.

For whatever the reason, she never replied.

The key to finding the girls had to be George Pole. That's what Cal concluded over his morning coffee. He knew he needed help. He was good at tracking down clues to medieval mysteries in the dusty archives of the world, but finding a man wasn't high on his list of skills. What kind of person *was* good at this? Private detectives and investigative journalists came to mind. He hopped online and quickly got disillusioned about detectives. Mainly, they were local players. He scanned the detective agencies in Houston, Pole's home city, but the cathedral (or Pole) could be anywhere. Then he gave newspaper journalists a try. A few papers had a national reach, but like detectives, most worked their local patches. He thought about the reporter from the *New York Times* who'd interviewed him in Cambridge but then, on a whim, he went to the *Houston Chronicle* website and searched for George Pole. The search window lit up with dozens of articles about Pole and one reporter's name. Amanda Pittinger.

He clicked on Pittinger's link and shot her an email telling her who he was and why he was contacting her. He ended with his phone number. No more than a minute later, it rang.

'This is Amanda Pittinger calling for Cal Donovan.'

'Wow, that was fast,' he marveled.

'You typed the magic words,' she said.

'And what were they?' he asked.

'George Pole.'

Amanda Pittinger had covered George Pole for years. A veteran reporter for the *Houston Chronicle*, Pittinger had always found Pole to be a reliable newsmaker. Pole and the media had always had a mutually beneficial relationship. Journalists found his controversial positions and outspoken views fodder for their stories and Pole found them to be convenient megaphones. Perhaps no one in the Houston media scene was closer to the former cardinal than Pittinger who often got exclusives in return for front-page, top-of-the-fold stories – accompanied by a flattering photo, of course. The symbiosis was so evolved that she even had Pole's mobile number which she used freely.

Pittinger spilled plenty of front-page ink covering the cardinal's resignation but in the past two months he hadn't rated a single story as he faded into the no-man's land of yesterday's news. That changed in dramatic fashion with his appearance at the altar of the mystery cathedral and her assignment editor literally begged her on his knees – the man actually fell to his knees on the newsroom floor – for her to track him down and get an interview or, absent that, find out where the cathedral was located, who built it, who funded it, etcetera.

Pittinger had had to help her portly editor to his feet. 'Find Pole, find the church, find the girls, Amanda, before he makes his announcement and everyone knows,' he said. 'Someone's going to get the Pulitzer for this story. Why not you?'

Pittinger told Cal she knew who he was. She'd read the *Times* article about him and the girls.

'As it happens,' she told Cal, 'I've been looking for the good cardinal, or should I say, pope?'

'Any luck?' Cal asked.

'None. I started at the obvious place and called his mobile number and got a voicemail-box full message – apparently, he's given his number out a little less exclusively than he led me to believe. Then I called everyone I know who knows him. Nothing. I've been wracking my brain but I really don't know where to go.'

'I was there,' Cal said.

'Where?'

'At the cathedral. With the girls.'

'Then you know where it is!'

'Actually, I don't.'

He told her about the pains taken to prevent him from learning the location.

'All I can tell you is that we were airborne for about three hours forty-five minutes from Nantucket,' he said.

'And you're sure you stayed in the United States?'

'Didn't need a passport.'

'OK, let me get a map,' she said, continuing to talk. 'Your

typical private jet flies about five hundred miles an hour and if you flew three and three-quarter hours, that would have been a trip of about eighteen hundred miles. From Boston that would have taken you to the Dakotas to the north, or down to Nebraska, Kansas, or my fair state of Texas. I did tell my editor that George would probably stay close to home.'

'That's still a lot of ground to cover,' Cal said. 'It's hard to believe that you could build a cathedral without anyone talking about it.'

'Exactly,' she said. 'You've got banks and lenders, architects, suppliers, hundreds of builders. Everyone involved must've been wrapped up tight in confidentiality agreements.'

'Suppliers,' Cal said.

'What?'

'Suppliers,' he repeated. 'How do you build a cathedral?'

The line went quiet until she said, 'This cathedral? Steel. Lots and lots of steel. In Watergate they followed the money. Here, we're going to follow the steel. Aren't you the clever one?'

'That's what my mother tells her friends.'

'Let me jump on this. Give me a little time.'

'Okay, but I want you to promise me something.'

'What's that?'

'If we find it, I want to go there with you.'

'And why is it you want to go back?' she asked.

'I want to see the girls again. I think they're being held against their will. I think their parents were strong-armed into letting them go.'

'You're something of a white knight, aren't you? All right, Cal. I'll work with you. We'll be in touch.'

Pittinger dropped everything else she was doing and ran down to the editor of the paper's business section. He steered her to an online roster of all US steel manufacturers and foreign-steel importers but a fruitless morning of calls left her adrift. No one would violate customer confidentiality and tell her whom they were supplying. Then, in one conversation, someone mentioned steel brokers, people who put bulk steel purchasing deals together. While a broker involved in a particular deal might not squawk, a rival broker who had wind of it might. And that's how, eight hours into her quest, she had a call with Dwayne P O'Connor, a broker from Pittsburgh whom she knew was a cigar-chomper because she could hear the end of it squishing over the phone.

'Oh, I know exactly who placed the order,' the broker said, 'because I got shafted in the process. I was negotiating on behalf of a client in New York City who wanted to build a condo project in Tribeca and the deal was almost there with a German supplier when we got shut down. Someone came along and offered a significant premium for rush product. Same thing happened all over the map. German steel, Japanese steel, domestic steel. It got vacuumed up by one buyer with a super-rush job and very deep pockets.'

'Who was the buyer?'

'Hillier Construction.'

'And where are they?'

'Vernon, Texas.'

Pittinger called it up on Google Maps. It was in west Texas near the Oklahoma border. About eighteen hundred miles from Boston.

'Do you have contact info for Hillier you could give me?' she asked.

'Sure do, but don't tell them where you got it. I can't say for absolute sure but I've got a nose for it and I think that church on the news is where that steel went.'

The general manager of Hillier hung up on her, not once but twice. She had a nose for it too and that told her that Hillier was almost certainly involved. Buildings require permits, and large projects like public churches require a raft of permits, so her next call was to the Vernon City Hall where she was soon talking to the manager of the Building Services Department.

She asked about any large construction projects and occupancy permits recently granted in Vernon or surrounding Wilbarger County, of which Vernon was the county seat.

'I was wondering if someone was going to call about that,' the manager said. 'It appears you're the first. I suppose you'll want to know the details. I may not want to but I'm obliged to cooperate with you. Matter of public record.'

Cal was at the George Bush Airport in Houston by 10:30 the following morning. Amanda Pittinger was holding a little sign with his name at baggage claim. He immediately liked what he saw – a pretty, frizzy-haired blonde, maybe about his age, with thigh-high boots and a short denim jacket bedazzled with rhine-stones. She had a wicked smile and she used it to let him know she liked what she saw too.

'Hey partner,' she said, 'you're as handsome as your online photos.'

'Good to hear. I'd hate to start our relationship by disappointing you.'

This had the potential to be a big scoop so Pittinger had pulled out all the stops and got approval from the paper's publisher to hire a private jet from Houston to Wilbarger County Airport where a charter helicopter was waiting to take them plus a *Chronicle* photographer further on.

'You been here before?' Pittinger asked the helicopter pilot, showing him the paperwork.

'Can't say as I have, but I know where the ranch is at.'

'ETA?' she asked.

'Not long, maybe fifteen minutes. We're not putting down, right?'

'Can we?' Cal asked.

'I don't know, mister. Not if it's private property. Now if you've got permission, that's another thing.'

'No permission,' Pittinger said. 'We'll just circle around and take some photos.'

The land was flat, featureless and a patchwork of tan prairie land and green, irrigated cotton farms. Flying in from the north the pilot saw it first from a distance of maybe five miles. The sun was low in the western sky and its reflection in the panels of glass hit his eyes through polarized sunglasses.

'There it is,' he said, and the photographer started working two cameras, shooting stills and video.

The money shot wasn't the cathedral. The earlier video broad-cast had told that tale. It was what surrounded it. There was an enormous red-brick mansion house and a large stables complex. Horses grazing in a paddock. The vast stretch of surrounding cattle land, brown, non-irrigated, with herds of long-horns grazing in far-flung tracts.

'That's the house where I met the girls,' Cal told Pittinger.

'Big-ass ranch,' the pilot said. 'Got to be over two thousand acres judging by the boundary fences. Who'd you say owns it?'

'I didn't,' Pittinger said. 'It's registered as the Diamond Bit Ranch. I'm still trying to pierce its ownership structure. It's wrapped up in shell companies. The newspaper's lawyers are working on it.'

'From the name, I'd guess your owner's into oil and gas exploration. What else do you want to see before sunset?'

Then the photographer pointed to something going on at one of the outbuildings. A bunch of men were getting into a row of white SUVs and driving toward the mansion house. There they got out and began pointing rifles toward the sky. The photographer aimed back at them with his long lens.

'Shit,' the pilot said, 'they're getting a bead on us.'

'This isn't a restricted area, is it?' Pittinger said.

'We're legal but this is west Texas, lady.'

They heard the rifle blasts. Tracer rounds streaked into the darkening sky.

'Fuck me!' the pilot shouted. 'Those were warning shots and I am duly warned.'

He pitched down, throttled up, and beat a hasty retreat.

Back at the Wilbarger County Airport they bid adieu to the rattled pilot and headed to the waiting jet for the trip back to Houston.

'I'm not going,' Cal announced.

'Don't tell me,' Pittinger said, using her wicked smile again.

'I'm telling you,' Cal answered.

'I'm coming with you,' she said, then told the photographer to upload the pictures to the photo editor and enjoy the solo flight home.

They waited at the tiny terminal for a local rental company from Vernon to deliver a car and got some soda and pretzels from a vending machine. There, Pittinger bore down on him like he was the subject of one of her stories. By the time the car arrived she knew his life history including the fact that he'd never been married and was decidedly heterosexual.

While he drove toward the ranch, in the interest of parity, she told him about herself. Her first marriage had lasted all of two months but she'd been nineteen so, as she put it, that one didn't count. The second one lasted twelve years and that one counted big-time because she still had two years on the spousal support she was paying.

'I don't want to sound sexist,' Cal said, 'but you're paying him?'

'I most certainly am. The situation arose because I have something called a job and he has something called laziness. The State of Texas is gender blind to the particulars. My advice to you is never get married or, if you do, marry a gal who's richer than you are.'

'I'll stick with the latter.'

Eventually she asked the question he'd been waiting for. 'So why is it that you're on this crusade? I've known a fair number of university-types but not many of them crawl out of their ivory tower and get their hands dirty.'

They were getting close to the ranch and she was the one with the map open on her phone. It was dark now. The land was flat and featureless and he doubted there would be any signs.

'Tell me when to turn,' he said. 'Look, I don't pretend to know how these girls got pregnant but they're just girls. It makes me mad as hell that they're being exploited. They want to go home and I want to help them get there. It's not complicated.'

'Man alive,' she said, blinking at him incredulously. 'Are you sure you don't want to consider getting a pre-nup?'

'Why's that?'

'Because I so want to marry you.'

Pittinger was hoping the turnoff from the highway would get them to the cathedral and at the end of a long, unmarked road a guard house manned by a couple of armed men seemed to confirm they were in the right place.

Cal lowered his window.

'Hey, good evening. My name is Professor Cal Donovan. I was here a little while ago. I wanted to see George Pole.'

The nearest guard leaned out the window and said, 'I'm sorry, sir, there's no one by that name here.'

'All right, how about Lidia Torres or Sue Gibney?'

The two guards looked at each other and the one hanging out the window gave the same answer. These people weren't there either.

'Look, I know the score, fellows, and I know the three girls, the three Marys are here and that Torres and Gibney are here too. George Pole invited me up to the ranch and there's going to be hell to pay when your people find out that you turned me away tonight.'

After the guards exchanged more glances Cal was told to shut off his vehicle and wait. Ten minutes went by and a pickup truck rolled up. A large man with alligator-hide boots, a big lone-star belt buckle and a cream-colored cowboy hat got out and loped over to the rental car. Clay Carling was the director of security at the facility, an ex-Texas Ranger who wore a serious case of swagger on his sleeve.

'Howdy. My name's Carling. I'm the head of security here. What can I do for you?'

Cal repeated what he'd told the guards.

'I know who you are, Mr Donovan. We didn't meet the day you flew in but I was advised about the visit. No one's advised me about this one.'

'It was on the spontaneous side,' Cal said.

'And who are you, Miss?'

'I'm just a friend of his along for the ride.'

'I see. Well, I'm sorry to disappoint you but we're not going to be able to let you on to the property this evening.'

'George Pole might not like your decision very much,' Cal said. 'Could you call him?'

'Already did. He suggests you write him a letter and he'll be sure to send you a reply.'

'I don't have his address. Could I get it from you?'

'I don't have it either. Now if you'll turn your car around and go back the way you came, that would be fine. Otherwise I'll have to call the sheriff and have you folks arrested for trespass.'

Heading back to Vernon, Pittinger said that she could see how disappointed Cal was. She told him that as a journalist she was used to getting the door slammed in her face.

'Maybe we could try to find another way in.'

'If we do those boys will light us up like a Christmas tree. I'm not real interested in dying out here, if you must know.'

'Now what?'

'Well, it's one helluva drive back to Houston. What do you say we do it in the morning?'

'If that's what you want, sure.'

'I also want a good steak.'

'I can handle that.'

'Then I want us to check into a motel with a bottle of excellent booze and we'll see what happens after that.'

'I can handle that too.'

Randall Anning was up before sunrise working out at the private gym at his Houston headquarters. His personal trainer was stretching him out when he got a call from his chief of staff.

'I don't suppose you've seen today's *Chronicle*,' his aide said.

'What's it say?'

'It ties you to Pole, the cathedral, the girls, you name it.'

'They didn't get the location, did they?'

'Yes they did, complete with their own fly-over photos.'

'Damn it to hell. We're a week away from releasing that. OK, end of workout, beginning of shitstorm. Let me know when President Griffith calls.'

'Are you expecting a call?'

'I am now.'

'Randy, you are one sly fox,' Griffith said.

Anning was getting out of the elevator when the White House rang.

'I thought it was best you didn't know before the fact, Mr President.'

'That's what everybody tells me when they don't want me to know something. Plausible deniability. Well, that ship has sailed. How long have you been planning this?'

'Pretty much as soon as I heard about the girls. I'm old enough that I didn't expect to see another miracle like this in my lifetime.'

'You worked with George Pole on it?'

'From the beginning.'

There followed a giddy torrent. 'I had a feeling George had something lined up when he resigned. He's a genius. The guy traded up from cardinal to pope! And not just any pope. Pope Peter! Can you imagine what the hell's going on inside that motel room that Celestine calls his office?'

'You saw the Vatican statement, I'm sure. It was fairly

reserved. He's keeping his powder dry, to see if our venture gets traction.'

'Well count me in – unofficially of course. I don't want to lose too many Old Catholic votes. God, I love the name: the New Catholic Church. Was that you leaking to the papers?'

'Actually no. It's going to complicate life. We weren't planning for crowds at the ranch for another week but we'll adapt.'

'Hell, Randy, just throw some more money at it. One of these days you've got to tell me how much a cathedral costs.'

His hand forced by the *Houston Chronicle*, Anning had to move up his public announcement. The hastily issued press release provided the salient details. In ten days time, Pope Peter of the New Catholic Church would celebrate Mass at the Cathedral of the Blessed New Virgin Marys at Miracle Ranch in Wilbarger County, Texas. All were welcome. Eight hundred people could be accommodated within the cathedral. Overflow crowds could watch the Mass on big screens inside event tents. The press release provided directions from Interstates 40 and 44 and GPS map coordinates.

Not six hours after the press release hit the wires, the first vehicle approached the security gate at the ranch. A guard at the checkpoint radioed to the security headquarters located in the basement of the mansion house.

Clay Carling had his cowboy boots up on his desk, watching an array of screens.

'What you got?' he asked. He knew full well what the guard had. He could see the minivan and its passengers.

'Appears to be a load of nuns,' the guard radioed back.

'Well, why don't you ask them where they're from and what they want?'

The guard leaned his head in, had a chat, and got back to Carling.

'They're from Oklahoma City. They're – what is it – Caramel nuns – sorry, they corrected me – Carmelite nuns – who wanted to make sure they got seats in the cathedral for the service. They want to see the girls and the babies. They've got food and water with them. Say they won't be any trouble.'

'Hang on a minute,' Carling said, picking up his phone. 'Gotta make a call.'

The guard bided his time engaging in chit-chat with the driver, a woman in her sixties who was the youngest of the five. As a non-Catholic, the young man was nervous around nuns and the best topics he could come up involved questions like, did their clothes got too hot in the summer?

Finally, his radio crackled to life. 'Mr Anning says it's OK to let them in.'

'To the tent village?' the guard asked.

'Send them up to the big house.'

Torres was waiting at the portico of the mansion.

'Hello, my name is Mrs Torres,' she said to the minivan driver.

'I'm Sister Anika. Bless you for letting us in.'

'I expect you'd like to meet the Marys.'

Anika and some of the others began to cry. 'It's like a dream.'

'It's not a dream,' Torres said. 'Please follow me inside.'

It wasn't long before the next car arrived. Then the next. And the next. None of them would get the same star treatment as the minivan of nuns but they would all be let in and shunted toward the tent and RV city, a proto-village that within a day became a proto-town on the way toward becoming a proto-city. It helped to have a billionaire behind the venture. Anning spared no expense providing for electricity, water, and even sewer hookups. For those without their own (or enough) provisions a local superstore was rushing to set up shop in a warehouse-sized building on ranch premises to sell everything from food to propane. The ranch was so vast that the budding community wasn't even within eyeshot of the mansion although the spire of the cathedral was visible to all. On the day of the Mass, if people couldn't walk the mile, a fleet of shuttle buses would provide transport to the church and the overflow crowd could stay in the village to watch the proceedings on stadium-sized projection screens.

At the mansion, Torres took the nuns by elevator to the third floor. She neglected to tell the girls of the visit, which in retrospect, she admitted, had been a bad idea.

Each girl had her own reason for becoming upset at the sight of five nuns shuffling down the hall. For Maria Aquino, it was because the nuns at her school often beat her and her classmates for all manner of transgressions. For Maria Mollo, nuns would visit her slum to take away unwanted children for adoption to wealthy families in Lima, Arequipa, and Trujillo. For Mary Riordan, it was because she simply didn't like them. They annoyed her for reasons she probably couldn't articulate arising from her father's categorical denigration of authority figures.

When the girls scurried away like cockroaches fleeing a switched-on light, Torres called out, 'Sue, go get them and bring them to the lounge. Why are they hiding?'

'They weren't expecting visitors,' Sue said. 'They haven't had any since they arrived. Maybe that's why.'

'Well, I didn't know the sisters were coming either. They wanted them to meet the girls.'

They again. The concept of *they* and *them*, the people behind the curtain, grated on Sue. Now that this man, George Pole, had surfaced, she assumed he was one of *them*. After her first brief encounter with him at the mansion the day Cal Donovan arrived, she had seen him again while the cathedral video was being filmed and he'd given her the willies. She didn't like smarmy men and he, with his oppressive cloud of aftershave and painted-on smile, was smarmy as hell. Even worse, he hadn't showed a dot of interest in her as a person. She was a mere servant.

Torres took the nuns into the lounge while Sue negotiated. The girls were a unified front in their opposition to a command performance. Not only were they against seeing the penguins – Mary's term – but their babies were napping and they wanted a rest. They conferred among themselves for a minute in the combination of a bit of English, a bit of Spanish, sign language, and the facial expressions that they had developed as a way of communicating and then Mary Riordan took the fore as designated negotiator.

'We'll do it under certain conditions,' she told Sue.

'I'm happy to relay your terms to Mrs Torres,' Sue said, feigning gravity.

'First, we want double puddings for the next three days,' Mary said.

'Noted.'

'Second, we want to go horseback riding in the morning.'

'Check,' Sue said.

'And third, we don't want to go to Mass next Sunday.'

Sue set her ponytail shaking. 'Number three is going to be tough. In fact, from what I've been hearing from Mrs Torres, it'll be impossible. This is supposed to be your big coming-out party.'

'It's a bloody Mass, not a party,' Mary said.

'Figure of speech. Still, forget number three.'

'We don't want to be stage props for this creepy pope-guy. Did you smell him? I think he was wearing perfume.'

'I hear you but forget number three. Believe me.'

Mary huddled with the others and came back to the negotiating table. 'Minion and Eeyore are with me on this. We'll do it for double puddings for a week and horseback riding every morning for a week too.'

'I'll run it up the flagpole,' Sue said.

She buttonholed Torres, pulling her away from the nuns to discuss the deal.

'Look, Sue, I think it's a bad idea to give them concessions. It will simply embolden them to make more demands in the future.'

'These are small things,' Sue said. 'I got them to back off their demand to skip Mass.'

'My God. That would be a disaster.'

'The girls are captives and they know it. They're getting rebellious. It's understandable. Give them a little control over their environments and you'll see the benefits.'

After a sharp inhale/exhale Torres said, 'Tell them yes and bring them and the babies to the lounge.'

The girls marched into their audience with the geriatric nuns like prisoners to their inquisitors with their eyes cast downward at the infants in their arms. The nuns fell to their knees as if felled by lightning and began praying in adulation. Sister Anika seemed quite agile but as to the three septuagenarians – particularly the especially fat one – and the frail octogenarian, Sue suspected she'd have to help them up.

The nuns began chanting the Angelus and while they did Torres caught Sue and Mary quickly exchanging an eye-roll.

> *Anika*: 'The Angel of the Lord declared unto Mary.'
> *All*: 'And she conceived by the Holy Spirit.'
> *All*: 'Hail Mary, full of grace, the Lord is with thee. Blessed art thou among women, and blessed is the fruit of thy

womb, Jesus. Holy Mary, Mother of God, pray for us
sinners, now and at the hour of our death. Amen.'

Anika: 'Behold the handmaid of the Lord.'

All: 'Be it done unto me according to thy word.'

All: 'Hail Mary, full of grace, the Lord is with thee. Blessed
art thou among women, and blessed is the fruit of thy
womb, Jesus. Holy Mary, Mother of God, pray for us
sinners, now and at the hour of our death. Amen.'

When they were done, Sister Anika looked up and said, 'Blessed
Marys, to be in your presence and the presence of your infant
boys is the greatest moment in our lives.'

Mary Riordan blinked at her, her mouth curling wickedly. 'You
might have begun with hello.'

Maria Mollo and Maria Aquino understood Mary well enough
to giggle.

Torres mumbled something about the Irish sense of humor and
Sue began hoisting the nuns off the floor.

The eldest one, Sister Consuela, once on a chair, pointed an
arthritic finger at Maria Mollo and said in Spanish, 'Are you the
one from Peru?'

Maria had a brief conversation with the nun about how beautiful a girl she was and how handsome a baby Jesus Juan was.
The old woman reminded Maria of her great aunt and she was
respectful.

Sister Henrietta, a huge woman sweating through the air conditioning, found the coolest place directly under a vent. She waved
her hand in blessing toward each baby. 'Jesus David, Jesus Juan,
Jesus Ruperto. They are glorious and handsome babies! To think
that we are in their holy presence.'

Mary Riordan was not going to furnish the same respect as her
comrade. 'Can you tell which is which? I mean if we scrambled
them like a Rubik's Cube, could you put them back in their right
places?'

'I hope I could but I don't know!' the nun said.

'Cause now that they're all almost the same size, us mums
would have a task if they weren't in their outfits.'

Mrs Simpauco had come in and was translating for Maria
Aquino.

'I could,' Maria said. 'Jesus Ruperto is the most clever and has the best smile.'

'Not bloody likely, Minion,' Mary said. She stepped on the Filipino girl's foot just hard enough to elicit a screech and a retaliatory thigh pinch.

Sue sensed that things might go sideways from here. She'd seen their playful competitiveness turn nasty. She positioned herself in between the warring parties.

Anika asked if she could touch Maria Mollo's baby and when the girl agreed, the nun laid her hand on its head.

She closed her eyes and whispered, 'They will die for our sins and our faith will be reborn.'

Sue heard her and snapped angrily, 'What did you say?'

'I'm sorry,' the nun replied, withdrawing, 'I didn't mean to offend.'

Sue was trembling. The girls had never seen her genuinely angry and they stared. 'Don't ever say that again,' Sue warned.

'Again, I am sorry I offended, but my faith is strong.'

Mrs Torres changed the subject. 'Did you come a long way, Sisters?'

'From Oklahoma,' Sister Nancy replied, giving off a high-pitched wheeze with each breath.

'Will you be heading back soon?' Sue asked flatly.

'Oh no,' Sister Anika said. 'We plan to stay for the Mass. We wanted to make sure we got seats inside the cathedral.'

Mrs Torres said, 'I'm sorry but I wasn't told your situation. What kind of community are you from?'

'We're a closed community of Carmelites,' Anika said. 'We left a note for our Mother Superior.'

'She didn't know you were coming?'

'Oh no. She wouldn't have permitted it. We told her in our letter that regretfully we were leaving the Old Catholic Church and joining the New Catholic Church. The words of Pope Peter resonated with us no end.'

'Mother Catherine probably had a fit,' Sister Nancy said.

'So, you intend to stay here for nine days?' Sue asked incredulously.

'We passed by the tent city. We'd be very happy there,' Anika said.

Anika's fellow nuns all agreed.

Then Mrs Torres stunned Sue by saying, 'Nonsense. You can all stay in this house. They want this to happen. We have extra rooms.' Then she looked straight at Sue. 'They think the girls would do well to be around women of faith.'

TWENTY-THREE

Randall Anning wasn't camera shy. He regularly appeared at trade fairs, investment conferences, and financial television shows as an advocate for oil and gas drilling interests, particularly his own firm, Anning International. But even though this interview was on familiar ground in his Houston office, and wasn't live, he had butterflies as the pancake make-up was being applied to his face. This was *60 Minutes*, after all, the most venerable and most watched interview show in the country, and his interviewer was none other than Harry Stone, the godfather of the program, whose silver tongue distracted his prey from the stiletto he might suddenly thrust. And Stone was a well-known New York liberal whom Anning expected could turn openly adversarial to an arch-conservative Texas oil and gas man.

The lights were on and the lead cameraman checked to make sure Anning's bald head wasn't showing glare. He gave a thumbs-up to the producer who asked if Anning was ready to go.

'Yeah, let's do it. I haven't got all day, you know,' he said gruffly.

With that, Harry Stone entered, his silver-streaked hair magnificently wavy, his suit and tie natty, his red pocket square jaunty.

'Pleased to meet you,' Stone said, extending his hand. 'Don't get up. They've got you where they want you. Sorry for being just in time. I was taking an important call.'

'Maybe you just wanted to spring yourself on me at the last moment for maximum effect,' Anning said.

Stone showed his capped teeth. 'Would I do that? What would you like me to call you?'

'How about Mr Anning?'

'Mr Anning it is. You can call me Harry. Let's begin, if that's all right with you. If you want to take a break at any time just say so. We'll edit it out.'

'I'm sure you'll edit the hell out of it to get the story you want,' Anning said.

'It's your story, Mr Anning. We're just helping you tell it.'

Stone took his seat opposite Anning and winked at the producer who simply said, 'Go,' to the two cameramen.

Stone: So we have three young women – teenagers, girls really – one from Galway, Ireland; one from Manila, Philippines; one from Lima, Peru. All named Mary or Maria, all ostensibly virgins, all pregnant. Why is a Texas oil and gas tycoon getting in the middle of this?

Anning: Not *ostensibly* virgins. Proven virgins, certified by a leading expert.

Stone: Dr Richard Benedict, President of the American College of Obstetrics and Gynecology. We talked to him and yes, he does believe they are virgins.

Anning: I got involved, as you say, because I've taken seriously – very seriously – the notion that this is a sign, a sign that needed to be heeded.

Stone: You're a man of faith, are you not?

Anning: I believe I am. I'm a Catholic, an observant one.

Stone: And three years ago, that faith was tested. You were in a plane crash in a remote wilderness. Multiple people died. After an ordeal, you were rescued. How did that test your faith?

Anning: I prayed like hell and God heard me. I was saved, literally and figuratively.

Stone: You said that these girls are a sign. A sign from whom? God?

Anning: Absolutely.

Stone: And what does this sign say to you?

Anning: That God sees fit to renew the tree of Christianity, particularly Catholicism, by once again sending the Holy Spirit down from Heaven to bring unto us not one but three of his sons.

Stone: And why do you think God feels Catholicism needs renewal?

Anning: Isn't it obvious? We have a pope in Rome who is turning the Church into a global social service agency instead of what it's meant to be.

Stone: And what is that?

Anning: A religious institution. An institution that provides moral and spiritual teaching, that gives the faithful a path to salvation based on the principles of Jesus Christ.

Stone: Don't you mean *your* admittedly conservative interpretation of Catholic doctrine?

Anning: Not just mine. I am not alone in feeling that leftist, socialist values have permeated the Vatican and have perverted its core, foundational principles.

Stone: You don't like liberation theology, the notion that people – poor people – first need to be liberated from social, political, and economic oppression before they can be saved?

Anning: I despise it.

Stone: And you despise Pope Celestine.

Anning: I don't despise him. I pity him. I think he's misinformed, misguided, and has surrounded himself with yes-men.

Stone: Cardinals.

Anning: He promotes his friends and alienates those who don't agree with him.

Stone: Like Cardinal Pole, or should I say, Pope Peter of the New Catholic Church?

Anning: That's right.

Stone: You didn't like it when Pope Celestine sold off artwork and statues from the Vatican collection to aid the poor.

Anning: I thought it was a betrayal of Catholic traditions.

Stone: Even though Jesus had plenty to say about charity and helping the poor.

Anning: There are other ways. I, for one, have given millions to Catholic charities and millions of other lay individuals have contributed mightily. The Church's cultural heritage is not something, in my view, that ought to be sacrificed for any reason. For me, it was among the last straws.

Stone: Last straws. All right. So, you see a sign – three girls who become pregnant by, let me just say it, virginal conception, and you use your considerable resources to remove these girls from their homes, from their families, from their countries, and bring them to a ranch in west Texas.

Anning: I wanted to make sure they had the best possible care, that they had the best chances of delivering healthy babies. And that has come to pass.

Stone: You made that decision on your own. Not with George Pole?

Anning: He is a friend of mine and a spiritual advisor. I discussed my intentions with him.

Stone: And now he's a pope. What does that make you?

Anning: A friend of the pope.

Stone: Mr Anning, don't you think this is awfully in your face? You've formed this entity, the so-called New Catholic Church, you install a friend as Pope Peter, you build a mega-church, a cathedral in west Texas of all places – hardly a bastion of Catholicism. Isn't this just a stick in the eye to the Vatican?

Anning: No, it's an appropriate reaction to the greatest miracle that's occurred since the birth and resurrection of Jesus Christ. It's a miracle that's occurred right under our noses, that's real and verifiable. And it's not a single miracle but three, simultaneous ones. And why west Texas? I'll tell you why. I own the land. Permitting was easy. There's a lot of hard workers in these parts. You're right about not being all that many Catholics in the area but here's the thing. We don't see the NCC—

Stone: The New Catholic Church.

Anning: That's right. We don't see it as a church that only Catholics will gravitate to. Pole said as much in his national address. We see it as a destination for all the faithful: Catholics, Protestants, Jews – you name it. All are welcome.

Stone: All are welcome to your new cathedral next Sunday.

Anning: Where our pope will celebrate his first Mass in the presence of the girls and their infant sons.

Stone: How much did you spend on the Cathedral of the Blessed New Virgin Marys? By the way, who came up with the name?

Anning: Our pope named it. Cathedrals don't come cheap.

Stone: Millions of dollars.

Anning: Certainly.

Stone: Tens of millions.

Anning: Certainly.

Stone: A hundred million or more?

Anning: It was worth every penny.

Stone: President Griffith is a Catholic. He hasn't made a statement yet. Have you talked to him?

Anning: The president and I are friends. We talk on occasion.

Stone: He's no fan of the Vatican either, is he?

Anning: He, like me, is a conservative.

Stone: Have you talked to him about the NCC?

Anning: I wouldn't ever discuss the subject of a conversation with the President.

Stone: How did these three girls get visas to enter the United States?

Anning: Usual channels.

Stone: Really? Usual channels. We checked with the State Department and the Department of Homeland Security and their spokesmen said they had no information on how visas were issued. Did President Griffith personally intervene on your behalf? Was the President in on this scheme to bring them here and stick it to the Vatican?

Anning: This would be a good time for a break, Harry.

Cal had one hand on a vodka on the rocks and another on Jessica's right breast. He was accomplishing this feat of ambidexterity on a Sunday evening seated on a sofa at his house, an arm looped around her back.

'You want to make out or watch TV?' she said.

'Both, obviously. I'm on next.'

They'd just watched the Stone–Anning interview and after the commercial break, the Stone–Donovan interview was coming. Harry Stone and the *60 Minutes* crew had filmed him in Cambridge

only three days earlier so the edit had been a rush job and Cal
was keen to see how it turned out. He thought it had gone all right
but one never knew. He now had a pretty firm opinion on how
Anning's interview had turned out. He and Jessica agreed that the
brash, unsympathetic Texas billionaire came across like a brash,
unsympathetic Texas billionaire.

'He was kind of a prick, don't you think?' Jessica said.

'Not a guy I'd want to have a drink with,' Cal agreed.

'Christ, Cal, you'd have a drink with anyone.'

'Yeah, probably. What do you think people will think of me?'

'Probably that you're kind of a prick too. A cuter prick but
a prick nonetheless. And let go of my tit so I can get more
potato chips.'

He didn't love watching himself but he thought he did pretty
well. It wasn't hard to work out that Harry Stone liked him a hell
of a lot more than Randall Anning. The journalist's face was more
benign during his interview, his smiles more frequent, his questions
generally friendlier. The idea was for him to be a counterpoint to
Anning, an objective academic with a view of how this breakaway
sect figured into the history of Church schisms, a confidant of Pope
Celestine, and someone who had met the Marys. While watching
the segment, Jessica told him he was coming across sober as a
judge – 'As opposed to the way you are now' – and he toasted the
comment with a refill of his glass. But when Stone asked him a
question about the girls he had become more passionate.

'Look, I don't have a rational explanation for their pregnancies. Are they miracles? That's not for me to say. But after
meeting with them and their families I can tell you this: these
girls were taken from their homes against their wishes. Their
extremely disadvantaged families were coerced and bribed to
part with them. Mary Riordan's mother died under circumstances
that are being investigated by the Irish police. I believe they are
being used as props by the people behind the New Catholic
Church and I think it stinks.'

'Stinks,' Stone repeated.

'To high heaven.'

'Well that got a rise out of you,' Jessica said, slipping her hand
on to his crotch. 'Bravo.'

'They wouldn't let me in to see the girls again. I was pissed off.'

'Come on then,' she said, pulling him off the sofa. 'Use some of that aggression on me.'

They were in a post-coital mood of lethargy when his landline rang.

'Aren't you going to get it?' Jessica grumbled at the fourth ring.

'I mostly get junk calls on the house phone.'

'On a Sunday night?'

He reached for it on his nightstand. The phone showed an unknown number.

It was a man. 'Hello, is this Calvin Donovan?'

'Yeah, who's this?'

The caller sounded nervous. 'My name is Steve Gottlieb. I'm sorry to bother you. I found your home number online. I just saw you on *60 Minutes*. I think we should meet. I don't want to say too much on the phone.'

'What are you talking about?' Cal said. He was on the verge of hanging up. 'Meet about what?'

'The girls. The Marys. I have something you need to hear.'

TWENTY-FOUR

Cal wasn't much of a mall guy and, to his eyes, the Connecticut Post Mall in Milford, Connecticut was no different from any other big, soulless jumbles of big-box stores and parking lots. The day after the *60 Minutes* piece ran, he gave a lecture at Harvard then jumped in his car for the two-hour drive to Connecticut. Steve Gottlieb had sounded credible. He wouldn't have blown half a day if he had the smallest notion that the guy was a crank. Gottlieb had steadfastly refused to give Cal any idea about what kind of information he possessed or who he was, repeating that he didn't trust the phones. What convinced Cal to make the trip was his voice. Unless you're a trained actor, he'd told Jessica, you can't fake fear. As they lay in bed afterwards, they'd Googled him and, lo and behold, there were a ton of Steve Gottliebs, including over a dozen in Connecticut – if that's where he lived.

The traffic was light and the drive down from Massachusetts had been quick. He arrived half an hour early and parked in the lot in front of the store Gottlieb had mentioned: Buybuy Baby. Did the guy have a sense of humor? He'd ask him that by way of breaking the ice. Inside the mall he found a Sbarro and a Starbucks and, loaded up with pizza and coffee, he returned to his car to wait for the mystery man's arrival.

Cal scanned the arriving cars for the black Acura he'd been told to look for and at precisely the appointed time, the car came into sight and parked a couple of rows from him.

Cal got out of his car and waved in the Acura's direction. Through the windshield he saw that Gottlieb was a middle-aged man with sparse hair. Gottlieb waved back and opened his door.

The amnesia was retrograde to the pizza and coffee.

The EMTs found Cal sitting beside his car, his face and forearms peppered with small cuts from flying fragments of safety glass. When questioned, he knew who he was, the day and date, and why he was there but he had no recollection of what had happened.

'I had a slice of pizza,' he said, looking around, confused. 'It was greasy as hell.'

'Don't you hate that?' a medic said, checking his blood pressure. 'It's normal. Want to try and stand?'

'Why not?'

He got his legs under him and had a look around. The parking lot was filled with emergency vehicles. A fire truck was foaming down a twisted black car.

'What happened?' Cal asked.

'There was an explosion,' the EMT said.

'Anyone hurt?'

'Looks like there was a casualty.'

Cal picked a tiny piece of glass out of his forearm. 'I was supposed to meet a guy in a black Acura. Is that an Acura?'

The EMT said, 'Why don't you sit back down while I get a cop to talk to you.'

Cal waited inside his car with the AC running until a detective knocked on the glass. Cal rolled down the window.

'Mr Donovan, Detective Brancatio here, Milford police. I understand you were supposed to meet the victim here. Let's have a chat.'

Brancatio asked for identification and Cal gave him his driver's license and Harvard ID. The detective must have figured a Harvard professor was in a low-risk category because he climbed into the passenger side to do his interview in a cool place.

When the detective sat down Cal got a glimpse at his clipboard: Steven J. Gottlieb, Greenwich, CT. Age 49.

'So, the EMT tells me you don't remember the incident.'

'I didn't,' Cal said. 'Sitting here, it's coming back to me.'

'OK, what do you remember now?'

'I got here early. We were supposed to meet at three. I went inside the mall and got something to eat, then I came back out to wait for him.'

'For who?'

'Steve Gottlieb.'

'OK. Go on.'

'He arrived in a black Acura. He told me that's what he was going to be driving. It was how I was supposed to recognize him.'

'You didn't know him?'

'No. We talked on the phone last night for the first time.'

'OK. What happened when he pulled in?'

'I got out of my car and waved. He was parked where the car is now, I guess. He saw me and waved back. I think he was getting out of his car when there was a fireball. I don't remember the sound. The next thing I remember the EMT was standing over me. You said victim. Is he dead?'

'Oh yeah, he's most definitely dead. So, tell me why it was that you decided to drop whatever it is you do on a Monday to drive down from Massachusetts to meet a guy you don't know in the parking lot of a mall.'

Cal didn't hold back. He told the detective everything Gottlieb had told him – which wasn't much – then poured out the story of the three Marys and his involvement up to and including the *60 Minutes* broadcast. Brancatio wrote a lot slower than Cal talked and the interview dragged on. The detective obviously knew about the girls (who didn't?) but for a guy with an Italian name, he seemed to have remarkably little interest in the theological aspects of the story. He kept getting interrupted by email notifications and radio calls from his headquarters and Cal got the idea that he was jammed up with work and needed a big case like a hole in the head.

'So, you have no idea how Gottlieb figures into all of this?' the detective finally asked.

'That's why I was here. To find out.'

'And I suppose you have no idea why anyone would want to put an explosive device inside his car.'

'Absolutely no clue. You're sure it was a bomb?'

'I did three tours in Iraq. Trust me, it was a bomb.'

Cal declined to get checked out medically in Connecticut and after a headachy drive home he was hoping for some TLC. But Jessica was already in California on business and he had to settle for the tender graces of the Grey Goose. A quarter-way into a fresh bottle, his nerves were sufficiently settled to find out what he could about Steven J. Gottlieb of Greenwich.

Gottlieb's fingerprints were all over the Internet. It seemed he was a significant player in the world of finance and venture capital. Tilos Capital, his company, was a large technology investment firm based in Manhattan and Gottlieb was a senior partner who served on a mind-numbing number of corporate boards. Cal downloaded the list, wondering how one man had the time for all those meetings. He also seemed like a philanthropic type with multiple awards and recognitions for his charitable contributions, including a ten-million-dollar gift to his alma mater, Carnegie Mellon, where he'd gotten a degree in engineering. He and his wife belonged to a Jewish reform congregation in Greenwich where he served as a trustee. There were no links Cal could find to any Catholic groups or causes.

Cal took a break and took stock. Nice guy, at least from what people said about him publicly, and a wealthy guy.

After peeling off all the little Band-Aids from his face and arms he showered and freshened his drink before doing one of those Internet searches for criminal and arrest records. Without knowing Gottlieb's social security number, he had to settle for a superficial result but it was unrevealing. Next up, he checked for postings on Twitter and Facebook. Gottlieb did operate a Twitter account but it consisted entirely of retweets of corporate news for his portfolio companies. His Facebook account was public but it had only occasional posts. There were photos of him and an attractive wife on vacation, hiking, at sporting and charity events. He had a powerboat. He looked fit. If there were kids he didn't post about them.

The bottle was getting light and Cal's eyelids were getting heavy. That night he would dream of Facebook pictures of a seemingly sweet, suburban husband and successful venture capitalist, and giant orange fireballs.

Cal waited two days. What was the decent length of time to wait to make a call like this anyway? It probably wasn't two days but he felt he had to find out more so he rang the listed home number of Steven and Beth Gottlieb.

'Hello, is this Mrs Gottlieb?' Cal asked after a small-sounding hello.

'Yes.'

'I'm terribly sorry to call at a time like this but I'm Professor Donovan from Harvard. I was there. When your husband was—'

'What do you mean you were there? Sorry, who are you?'

'Calvin Donovan. Your husband called me on Sunday night after he saw me on *60 Minutes*. He said he wanted to speak to me.'

'About what?'

'About the Catholic girls, the virgins.'

There was a pause that left Cal hanging. 'Steve? Catholics? I don't know what you're talking about.'

'If I could—'

'Professor Donovan, you should talk to the police, not me.'

She hung up.

He thought about calling again but he didn't. The woman sounded terrible and he didn't want to make her evening any worse.

TWENTY-FIVE

When Sunday arrived, the girls were almost unmanageable. Led by Mary Riordan, they formed a bloc and refused to put on the white outfits laid out for them by Mrs Torres. Their infants were to be dressed in white too.

'First of all,' Mary told Sue, 'we're not going to put on these ugly-ass dresses, and second of all we're not dressing our boys in these poncey little suits.'

'Ugly dress,' Maria Aquino said, nodding. She seemed pleased with her English and high-fived Maria Mollo.

'It's just for a couple of hours,' Sue said. 'It's not negotiable, I'm afraid.'

'Oh, you're afraid, Sue, but it's us who'll be mortified,' Mary said.

'Try the dresses on. I'm sure they'll look lovely.'

'Is Perfume Pope going to be there?' Mary asked, holding her nose.

She'd taught the phrase to the Marias and the two of them started marching around the room, holding their noses, chanting, 'Perfume Pope, Perfume Pope.'

'I'm sure he will. It's Sunday Mass.' But she grinned in solidarity. 'Hopefully he'll go easier on the aftershave.'

'Will it be on TV?' Mary asked.

'I don't know. Probably.'

'Then we're not doing it.'

The electronic cathedral bells began to peal.

Sue was prepared for the eventuality. It was bribery time. 'All right, ladies, if you go along like nice little soldiers I'm authorized to offer you a very special reward.'

'What?' Mary asked.

'This afternoon, Pedro will take you for a trail ride into the countryside. He says you're all good enough riders now. There's a pond a good long way from the house and you can have a picnic there and go swimming. You can feed the babies before you go and Mrs Torres and I will look after them.'

Mary and the Marias withdrew to a corner and after one of their pantomime conversations Mary came back.

'We want one more thing.'

'What's that?'

'We don't want the penguins hanging about up here when we get back.'

'I can make that happen. Deal?'

'Deal.'

'Then please, put—' she almost said, 'your Virgin Mary dresses,' but checked herself and said, 'your pretty white dresses on. I'll help with the boys.'

*   *   *

The bells kept pealing right up to the ten a.m. service.

Once the girls were groomed and dressed, Sue quickly got herself together. She hadn't brought many good clothes to the ranch but she did the best she could to look smart for the occasion.

When she came to get the girls from the lounge there was a gaggle of people in the hall, most of them unfamiliar, many in clerical dress.

With a series of 'excuse me and pardon me' she wriggled herself into the lounge where the girls and the babies were surrounded by the Carmelite nuns, Mrs Torres, several priests, and three bishops one of whom was speaking to Maria Mollo in Spanish. The clerics were dressed in vestments for the service of Mass. There was also an imposing bullet-headed man in a black suit who knew her even if she didn't know him.

The man approached with a meaty, extended hand. 'You must be Sue Gibney. I'm Randall Anning. This is my ranch.'

'Pleased to meet you,' she said, wincing at the crunching hand-shake. 'I figured someone owned it.'

'You figured right. According to Mrs Torres, you've done good things here, Sue. Of course, I saw you in action on the videos. You seem to know your birthing beans.'

'Can't complain about three healthy babies,' she said.

'Three healthy, happy, and holy babies,' he said.

'Who are all these people?' Sue asked.

'Well, these priests and bishops here have defected from the Old Church. Some of them are local, from Texas and Oklahoma, but they're from all over the States. This bishop talking to Maria, well he's come all the way from Peru. He's a defector too, one of our highest-ranking fellows, along with these other bishops. I think you know the nuns.'

'Yes, I know them.'

'The rest of these folks work for me at my company, my senior executive team. I do energy exploration. Meeting the girls and babies is a perk for them. Gotta keep the oil and gas flowing. There's a lot of new bills to pay around here. Now, if you'll excuse me, it's time we all move on down to the cathedral. Don't want to keep our pope waiting, do we?'

On the ground level of the house, Sue tried to walk with the girls but Mrs Torres had a particular choreography that shunted her toward the rear of the procession with Mrs Simpauco, Mrs White, the English teacher, Dr Lopez, the pediatrician, and the mansion staff of cooks and cleaners. Anning, Mrs Torres, and the bishop led the way under the watchful eye of Clay Carling, Anning's head of security. The girls came next looking eerily similar in their white dresses, white shoes, and white hair bows, each one holding identical-looking placid, blue-eyed babies. The nuns followed them like religious ladies-in-waiting, then the bishops, the priests, Anning's favored employees, dressed in their finest, and finally Sue and the staff.

It was a hot, late-summer morning and the sun shone brightly. Those with sunglasses slipped them on. On the walk to the cathedral the procession passed the stables. Pedro and the other stable hands were also in suits and they waved at the girls who would have waved back if not for the infants in their arms.

The shiny green facade of the cathedral reflected the arid landscape.

The last time Sue had been inside the church it had been almost empty.

'Do you think they'll fill it, Sam?' she asked Dr Lopez.

He pointed. 'I think so.'

A long line of people snaked from the entrance doors, down the stairs, and into the prairie. A group of security guards in blue blazers were working crowd control and informed those on the cathedral steps that they weren't going to get in. They began instructing, then gently pushing people away from the building toward a field of giant video screens in the distance where it seemed a large crowd was already assembling.

Someone on the stairs saw the procession coming and shouted out. Soon people were calling excitedly at the girls and, seemingly from nowhere, blue-blazered men appeared and flanked the Marys in a protective cocoon. The procession headed to a side entrance at the transept and once inside they were bathed in cool air and tranquil organ music. Every seat was filled except for the first two rows, cordoned off with a white rope that was removed as they approached. A hush fell over the crowd and all talking ceased. There were camera flashes.

The Marys were seated front and center along with Anning,

Torres, and the nuns. Sister Anika was assigned the position beside Mary Riordan who moved as far away from her as she could without sitting on Maria Aquino's lap. The girls looked around for Sue and found her in the row behind them. She gave them a wan thumbs-up. The priests and the bishops peeled off to the sacristy to assist George Pole in his final robing. Video cameramen scanned the crowd and set up their shots from multiple positions.

While waiting for the Mass to begin, Anning chatted amiably with Torres.

'I talked to a bunch of TV executives early this morning,' he said. 'Guess how large an international audience they're expecting today?'

'Is it going out live?' she asked.

'You bet. Guess?'

'Fifty million?' she said.

'You've got to be joking. Try half a billion. Maybe more. This is going to be the biggest TV event in history. By far.'

'I had no idea. The crowds here are amazing.'

'Carling tells me that we've got over five thousand people on the ranch now. It's insane. I think I've rented every portable toilet and generator in west Texas. We've got the county coming to string up more utility lines coming into the property. I thought this was going to be big but not *this* big and not this fast.'

'Well, it's a very big miracle, Mr Anning.'

'Yes, it is, Lidia. It most certainly is and I'm blessed to have the resources to make all this happen.'

Mary Riordan flicked Maria Aquino with her finger.

'Ow.'

Though she was sitting she made her pantomime of a waddling penguin and set the Filipino girl giggling. Then Maria passed the mime down the line to Maria Mollo and the three of them were in stitches before the nuns ganged up on them and sternly whispered them to order. Mary Riordan got Sue's attention again and the two of them engaged in a bit of face-playing before Anning turned around. His scowl shut Sue down cold.

Then the organ music stopped and the cathedral was deathly quiet. Even baby JJ, who'd been a little fussy, fell silent.

A priest carrying a thurible of burning incense entered first, followed by priests carrying lighted candles. One of the American bishops bore the cross. The Peruvian bishop acted as lector, elevating the Book of the Gospels, and finally, Pope Peter, in full papal regalia took up the rear of the processional.

There was no music, only the simple chanting of a short introit, the Gloria Patri.

Gloria Patri, et Filio, et Spiritui Sancto. Sicut erat in principio, et nunc, et semper, et in saecula saeculorum. Amen.

Pole had vowed to resurrect the old religion, the Latin Mass, and this was exactly what he was doing.

When Pope Peter had taken his place at the altar he began in a clear, proud voice:

'In nómine Patris, et Fílii, et Spíritus Sancti.'

The congregation had been given the printed Order of Mass and they invoked an *Amen*.

And Peter called out:

'Corpus Christi, salva me. Sanguis Christi, inebria me. Aqua lateris Christi, lava me. Passio Christi, conforta me.'

The Mass droned on in Latin for the better part of an hour and since few in the cathedral had participated in the old Tridentine Mass, the congregants, particularly the children, became restless, none more so than the Marys and their babies who fidgeted and murmured despite the best efforts of the nuns to keep them still. Throughout, a camera was trained on the girls. The production director, holed up in a small studio in the basement, was operating under Anning's strict instructions, and chose only the most flattering shots to make the broadcast. Even Anning seemed relieved when Peter, after a brief homily laying out, in bullet-point succinctness, his objections to the current state of the Church of Rome, moved on to consume the body and blood of Christ. Putting down the chalice of Communion wine, the pope addressed the congregants in English.

'Good people, it is time for you to receive Holy Communion. Before you come forward, I'm sure you will wish for us to first extend Communion to our beloved Holy New Virgin Marys. Holy Mothers, please come to the altar.'

Mary Riordan whispered to the Marias, 'He means us,' and did a pantomime of drinking wine and eating a wafer. Mary rose and leaned back over the pew to Sue. 'Did you think that was ever going to end?'

With that, Sister Anika pulled the Irish girl toward the altar by the sleeve of her white dress and the cathedral erupted in the wash of camera flash.

The afternoon sun was blazing while Anning and Pole went for a stroll near the mansion house.

Anning was Texas-casual in jeans, cowboy hat and boots, and Pole was papal-casual in a simple white cassock and red slippers.

'So how do you like being pope so far, George?' Anning asked.

'You might want to call me Holy Father or Your Holiness,' he replied.

'I have my answer,' Anning said. 'You like it a lot. How long do you think it's going to take you to recruit a college of cardinals?'

'Not long. I have stacks of letters and hundreds of emails from priests and bishops. Bishop Ticuna, our friend from Peru, will likely be among the first. But I'll tell you this, Randy, we're not going to have any homosexuals joining the clergy of the NCC. We're going to have a litmus test and that means background checks – good ones.'

'You know I'm fine with that.'

'And unrepentant homosexuals and women who had abortions won't be getting Communion or NCC burial rites.'

'You know I'm more than good with that too. You've got your work cut out for you. Lot of work to build a worldwide organization from scratch. You can't do it alone. Take it from me. I've built companies. You're going to need good people.'

'I completely agree,' Pole said. 'When are you breaking ground on my Apostolic Palace? We're going to need it sooner rather than later plus buildings for the NCC's administrative offices and living quarters for officials. And a more immediate need is Confessional booths. We've got a tent city full of the new faithful who will want Confession.'

'Confession booths are cheap – we can move on them. The other stuff isn't. I've got deep pockets but I want to lay off some of the funding of your grand vision on to donations. We're going to raise a lot of money, believe me. But don't fret, I've got my architects working on a site master plan for – what did you want to call the place?'

'New Vatican City.'

'OK, sure. Good name. Trips off the tongue. Your Holiness.'

As they got near the stables Anning swore.

'I hope what's going on isn't what I think is going on,' he said.

The girls were talking to one of the stable men while others were saddling up horses.

Anning quick-walked the rest of the way with Pole just about keeping up.

'What is happening here?' Anning shouted.

Sue was with the girls while Torres was with the babies.

'They're just going for a picnic and a swim with Pedro, Mr Anning,' Sue said.

'On whose authority?'

'Mine, I guess. It's a reward. They've been really good.'

Mary Riordan had been helping to cinch her saddle. She looked up and said, 'Yeah, in keeping with the religious theme of the day, we've been bloody little angels.'

'I don't like your tone, young lady,' Anning said.

'That's Holy Mother,' to you, she said, sticking out her tongue.

'Now, now,' Pole said. 'That's no way to behave, Mary. Mr Anning has given you so much.'

'Whatever,' she said, returning to the saddle cinches.

Anning was fuming. 'Miss Gibney, I'm not going to allow horseback riding. It's far too dangerous. What if one of them were to fall and hurt herself? No, it's out of the question.'

Pedro stepped forward a pace. 'Excuse me, señor, but the girls are good riders. These are the most gentle horses. I'll make sure they are safe.'

'What's your name?' Anning demanded.

'It's Pedro, señor.'

'OK, Pedro, pack your bags, you're fired. No one talks back to me on my own damn ranch. I want you off my property by sundown. And Miss Gibney, report to Mrs Torres's office in an hour. We'll speak then.'

When it was time for her to go downstairs to face the music, Sue told the girls she'd be right back. They were all crying, even tough-as-old-boots Mary Riordan.

'That's the last bloody time we go to one of his fucking Masses,' she sobbed.

'Don't swear, Mary,' Sue said, wrapping her up in a hug. 'You're way too holy for that.'

That kind of a comment usually got a laugh out of the girl but not this time.

'What happened to you, Sue?' Maria Mollo said through her tears.

'I'll let you know when I know. Mary, make her understand that.'

Mary did a silly pantomime and both Marias got it.

'Be back as soon as I can,' she said.

In the hall, the nuns were lurking. Sue told them if they knew what was good for them they wouldn't enter the girl's bedroom right now.

Anning was sitting behind the desk while Mrs Torres stood, her arms folded, her lip trembling, from what Sue assumed was a dressing-down.

'Sit down, Miss Gibney,' he said.

Sue spoke first, 'I want you to know that Mrs Torres has had nothing to do with the girls and horseback riding. It was always my idea to get them to behave. A carrot on a stick. They behaved, they got to ride.'

'Well, I understand, but this is Mrs Torres's show. She's my manager here. You work for her. Ultimately the safety of the girls and their sons are her responsibility. So, she's not absolved, are you, Lidia?'

'No, sir.'

'Now I can see the girls are fond of you, Miss Gibney, and well they should be. You were there from the beginning. You delivered their babies. I'm sure you're a good, reliable person. I wouldn't have hired you unless you checked out as well as you did. But here's the thing. I can't have you making unilateral decisions that affect their safety and welfare. I need you to be a team player. Are you willing to be a team player?'

'Look, Mr Anning, I can leave if you'd like me to. I was supposed to go already. Lidia persuaded me to stay.'

'No, I don't want you to leave. You're an asset for the girls and I recognize that. I simply need your assurance that you'll act like a member of the team and consult Mrs Torres on all significant decisions.'

'All right,' Sue said. 'Team player.'

Anning's phone rang. He answered it and turned his back on Sue and Torres.

'Yes, Mr President, how are you? Good, good, did you watch the service? Well, I'm glad you enjoyed it. No, we don't have the ratings yet. Yes, I'm sure, you're right. They'll be huge.'

TWENTY-SIX

The ratings were, in fact, huge. All told, the Mass was seen live by 540 million people, including 90 million within the United States.

'Look at these numbers,' Anning said, waving the papers at Pole. 'Biggest TV event in history. And it was in Latin! Wait till I tell Griffith.'

President Griffith did indeed take note and he took action. At noon on Monday the White House put out a presidential statement.

Along with millions of his fellow Americans, President Griffith watched Pope Peter of the New Catholic Church celebrate Mass at the marvelous Cathedral of the Blessed New Virgin Marys in the great state of Texas. Today he issued this statement: 'As you know, Kristy and I are Catholics. We have steadfastly maintained our faith even as the arch-liberal policies of Pope Celestine have changed the Church for the worse, pushing a failed political agenda and de-emphasizing its bedrock principles of theology and morality. We maintained our faith because we felt we had no other place to go to worship within the traditions of Catholicism. That has changed. We now have another place to go. As of today, Kristy and I are uniting with Pope Peter and will join the New Catholic Church. We intend to travel to Texas next Sunday to celebrate Mass at the Cathedral of the Blessed New Virgin Marys.'

Later in the day Cal got a text from Murphy.

Murphy: See the statement from Pres Griffith?
Cal: Yeah. Can you believe it?

Murphy: Believe what? That he's a giant tool?

Cal: I think we knew that already.

Murphy: Not that I needed another reason to hate the fellow
but this is the icing on the cake.

Cal: Worst President in history. Thank your lucky stars you're
not American.

Pope Celestine was rarely given to flashes of anger but his old friend Cardinal Da Silva was seeing it in spades tonight. The day before, Celestine had endured the entirety of Pole's Mass, which he watched with Sister Elisabetta in his lounge, drinking cup after cup of coffee and getting increasingly agitated, to the point where she cut him off by unplugging his coffee machine. He had fielded urgent calls all day from cardinals across the globe, informing him of impending defections of parishioners and asking for direction. And Elisabetta had given him a copy of President Griffith's statement earlier in the evening.

Celestine was florid, his neck veins bulging. 'Rodrigo, we are in the midst of a crisis. We have the beginnings of a true schism on our hands. Everything we are trying to achieve must be put on hold as we deal with this. Disaster!'

'I cannot disagree with anything you say, Holy Father.'

The pontiff sagged on to a chair and flopped his arms on to his lap. 'This is of my making. Perhaps I went too fast with my reforms.'

'No, Holy Father. I emphatically say no. The Church you and I love is a compassionate Church, a loving Church, an inclusive Church. How can reaching out to the poor, the displaced, the disenfranchised be anything but actions that Jesus Christ himself would champion? Pole and this wealthy man behind the curtain, Randall Anning, have built a sinister version of the Church. People will see through it.'

Celestine nodded. 'What should we do?'

'First, we must put out a papal encyclical, condemning the schismatics and affirming the primacy of the Holy Roman Church over matters of faith and dogma. We must lay out a firm framework under canon law in case the matter becomes more serious and we must take further steps.'

'Fine, yes.'

'Second, we must accelerate the formal investigation of the girls. If their pregnancies are miraculous then we must declare them so and embrace the girls and their offspring within the Holy Roman Church. If they are not miraculous, we must make that declaration and lay out the evidence.'

The pope nodded his assent. 'Please have the Congregation for the Causes of Saints formally take this up on a fast track and assign our best people.'

'Third, I've summoned Mrs Abernathy, the American Ambassador to the Vatican, for an urgent consultation tonight. I will lodge a formal protest concerning the intemperate remarks and actions of President Griffith.'

'And what will that accomplish?'

'Practically nothing. It is a matter of form and protocol. Also, she is quite useless. She is the wife of one of Griffith's political allies who has no background in diplomacy or international affairs. Her sole credential seems to be her Catholicism.'

'Is that it, Rodrigo?'

'No, there's a fourth item – and this is from Sister Elisabetta – you must have your blood pressure checked. Imagine how I would feel if I lost my dear friend? And imagine having to conduct a conclave with all of this going on?'

Cal felt his mobile buzzing in the jacket of his sports coat while he was giving a lecture on the causes and ramifications of the First Crusade. When the lecture was done he glanced at the missed call notification then moved as rapidly as he could through the questions put to him by the scrum of undergrads swarming the lectern. Most were more interested in hearing what he had to say about the NCC than the Crusades.

'Guys, I've got to run,' he said finally. 'Come to my office hours and we can keep going with your questions.'

Back at his office, he ignored the telephone message slips the departmental secretary left on his desk and a hundred new emails, many of them media requests. He returned the missed call.

'Mrs Gottlieb, Cal Donovan here. I got your message.'

Her voicemail had sounded urgent and her voice now had lost none of its tremulousness. 'I think I need your help.'

'Talk to me.'

'Someone broke into my house.'

'When?'

'Last night. A girlfriend had me over. You know, to take my mind off of things. When I got home I heard someone in the house. I shut the door, got back in my car and drove away.'

'Did you call the police?'

'Yes. They came and found a back door was forced. Someone went through Steve's desk. I don't think anything is missing but I'm scared.'

'I'm sure you are.'

'I feel so stupid. I didn't set the alarm when I left. My brain's been scrambled. Steve told me to use the new alarm every time.'

'New alarm?'

'He had the system replaced a few weeks ago because of the previous break-in.'

'You had another burglary?'

'It wasn't exactly a burglary. Nothing was taken. Someone broke in and left something. In Steve's office safe.'

'What did they leave?'

'A dead animal. An opossum. It was very pregnant.'

Cal tried to process what he was hearing but it wasn't making a lot of sense.

'Mrs Gottlieb, why do you think your husband wanted to see me?'

'I'm not sure.'

'He said it had something to do with the Marys, the Catholic girls. They were pregnant too. Could there be a connection?'

She began to cry. 'I don't know. I don't know what to think.'

He didn't have a clue how to calm her down over the phone. 'Look, Mrs Gottlieb, your husband called me after seeing my interview on TV. He knew I was involved with these girls. So here's the question: did he have any involvement?'

He heard her blowing her nose. 'I don't think so. How could he have? We're Jewish. He was in finance. He didn't have anything to do with pregnant girls.'

'Please, think about it. There must be some connection. He called me because he wanted to tell me something he knew.'

'I watched *60 Minutes* with Steve. He knew him.'

'Who?'

'Anning.'

Cal tightened his grip on his phone. 'Randall Anning? How did he know him?'

'That plane crash that he talked about surviving? Three years ago? Steve was there. He was the only other survivor.'

Cal's phone hand was hurting. 'Did your husband see Anning since then? Did they talk or communicate in any way?'

'I don't think they did. Steve would have mentioned it. I'm sure he would have. We talked about everything, even his work.'

'Mrs Gottlieb, I want you to think hard and tell me everything you know about that plane crash.'

Over the next week, the situation at the ranch deteriorated.

Sue knew it. Mrs Torres knew it. But Anning didn't want to hear about it. 'Handle it,' he told Torres, 'or I'll find someone who can.'

The girls were on a rampage. They were relieved, of course, that Sue hadn't gotten the chop, but they were beside themselves over Pedro's dismissal and their loss of horse-riding privileges. They wouldn't get dressed in the morning, they wouldn't shower or make their beds, and they sure as hell weren't going to do their school lessons. Of course they took care of their babies – breastfeeding, bathing, changing diapers – but otherwise they were on strike.

As Sunday approached, the girls sensed they had more leverage and Mary presented Sue with a list of demands, written out in her schoolgirl handwriting.

Sue read the page and shook her head.

'They're not going to re-hire Pedro,' she said. 'I've been lobbying all week for it and it's a done deal. Anyway, I doubt he'd even want to come back after being treated like that.'

'He's not the only one who can take us riding,' Mary said, softening. 'The other fellows are nice too but Eeyore really likes Pedro. She's the most upset about him.'

'Maybe I can get them to agree to let you ride only in the paddock. I think it was the trail riding that really freaked them out.'

'Riding in a little circle is bollocks,' Mary said, returning to a hard-line position. 'No Pedro and no trail rides means no Mass on Sunday. You tell them we're serious. And what about the third item?'

Sue looked at the page again. 'I didn't think the white dresses were all that bad.'

'Mary said *what*?' Mrs Torres asked.

Sue had gone to her office to argue the case for the girls and had dutifully relayed Mary's threat.

'She said that if they were forced to go to Mass against their wills, they would get up and moon the pope during the service.'

Even repeating it out loud struck Sue as funny, but Torres clearly was not amused.

'Look, Sue, I've had several conversations with Mr Anning this week and he's adamant. He'll never take Pedro back and he won't let them ride. When he makes a decision he sticks to it. I've worked for him for a long time. He's a successful man and an uncompromising one.'

'Is he married?'

'His wife is in Houston. Betsy hates it up here. She's from Los Angeles originally and can't stand the cowboy way of life.'

'She wouldn't even come for the Mass?'

'She's not Catholic. I don't know what she is. I don't think she cares about religion.'

'Well if she came here and saw how miserable the girls are, maybe she could have some influence.'

'I met her once and she's a very unfeeling person. Anyway, it's not going to happen.'

'Well we've got to do something,' Sue said.

'Do you have any other ideas?'

'I do, actually. I don't know if Mr Anning would go for it but what about this . . .?'

Torres knocked on the library door. Anning had returned to the ranch from Houston that afternoon for the Sunday Mass and was immersed in a book and a bottle of bourbon. He invited her in and offered her an adult beverage, as he called it. She politely declined and said she was having ever greater concerns about the mental and physical health of the girls. They were taking care of the babies but little else, and all of them were only picking at their food.

'What is it, a collective hissy fit about this Pedro fellow and their horses?'

'Being a teenager isn't easy, Mr Anning, and being a new mother isn't either. Then you mix in the special pressures they have being away from their homes and families and suddenly being considered holy women with holy babies and being put in front of crowds and TV cameras.'

Anning reached for a toothpick and went after a bit of steak from dinner. 'There's another way to look at their situation, Lidia. These girls, each of them, were poor as church mice. They lived like cockroaches and now they're in a mansion and are adored by a minimum of the five hundred and forty million people who saw them last Sunday live on television. I'd say they're spoiled brats on easy street.'

'Mr Anning, I'm sure you're right but I think there's something we can do, a small thing to make them feel better and behave better. I'm concerned that if they don't want to cooperate they may make a scene on Sunday inside the church.'

She mentioned the mooning threat.

'They wouldn't.'

'Oh yes, they would.'

'Christ. On live TV? What is it you have in mind?'

That evening, Sue gave the girls the news with Mrs Simpauco and Mrs Torres on hand to properly translate. As she talked she cradled JJ in her arms and cooed at him every so often. The other babies were sleeping but JJ had been a little colicky. The bulldog was curled up in her little bed under the cribs.

Anning had said yes to Sue's proposal. He had agreed to bring their families from overseas to stay with them in the mansion.

'My whole family?' Maria Mollo asked.

'Your parents and your brothers and sisters,' Sue said.

'Me too?' Maria Aquino asked. 'My mother and the kids?'

'Of course.'

'I don't want my dad to come,' Mary Riordan said. 'Trust me, Kenny will try to sell anything that's not nailed down. My brothers and sisters would be good, though.'

'When they come?' Maria Aquino asked.

'He said it will take a few weeks to arrange for the visas but he'd start to work on it in the morning,' Mrs Torres said.

'What about Pedro and the horses?' Mary asked.

'Not part of the deal, kiddo,' Sue said. 'But this is good, no? I mean how much fun will it be having your families here?'

All of them smiled and asked if they could get cheeseburgers.

'Fuck it,' Mary said, when the cook came up with a big tray of food. 'Kenny can come too.'

TWENTY-SEVEN

An even larger audience – more than 600 million people – watched the next Sunday Mass broadcast from the Cathedral of the Blessed New Virgin Marys and, over the following two Sundays, the ratings climbed ever higher. The girls dutifully wore their white dresses and behaved themselves in front of the cameras. During the week, they did their schoolwork, ate the food put on their plates, and stopped complaining about Pedro and the horses. They were even civil to the nuns.

But every few days they would ask Sue about the arrival of their families and Sue would pass their questions up the line. Mrs Torres assured her repeatedly that the visa applications were in process and that when she had definitive news she'd let her know. The girls had Sue take them down to the second floor of the mansion where, with the bulldog trotting along, they made inspections of all the empty guest rooms and drew maps of which member of whose family would stay where.

After the second Mass at the cathedral, activities at the ranch ramped up. There had been constant meetings. County public health officials had grown alarmed about the burgeoning population of the tent and RV village, which had come to be called Miracle Village. When the census hit seven thousand, they had threatened to pull a variety of permits. At first Anning had fussed and fumed about this being private property (not to mention Texas) and his rights to do whatever the hell he wanted to do on his own land, but then he and Pole had concluded that this wasn't an all together negative development.

'Randy, we don't need to be overly focused on the numbers of followers locally,' Pole had said, 'just the way that the Vatican has never been overly focused on the numbers of people who come to Mass at St Peter's. The only metrics that count are the numbers of parishioners we have. We need NCC churches all over the world. We need an NCC church in every parish there's an Old Catholic church. We can't effectively compete otherwise. The local numbers are wonderful, the TV numbers are amazing, but that's not where the action's at.'

'Hell, I don't disagree with you,' Anning had said, sipping a bourbon on the porch. 'It just rankles me when a bunch of pencil-necked geeks come on to my land to tell me what I can and cannot do. All these damned people in Miracle Village are a logistical and security nightmare. I don't really mind capping off the population, to be honest. You're right, we ought to concentrate on monetizing the six hundred million folks in TV land.'

Pole arched an eyebrow. 'Monetize? Really?'

'Maybe not the best word but you know what I mean. We've got to get them contributing to the charities that we think are worthy and get them to pay *our* Peter's Pence at *our* collection plates on Sundays. You can't separate money and influence, you know.'

Pole had been nursing a bourbon too. It was a fine autumn evening and he had been feeling rather buoyant. 'I do know that. I'm putting the finishing touches on a document I'd like to share with you soon. It's a proposal to support renting worship spaces in all major cities in all fifty states to push the celebration of Mass down to the grass-roots. We're just getting to the critical mass – no pun intended – of priests defecting from Vatican control to populate the effort. I think it can serve as a blueprint for international expansion.'

'That's fine. I look forward to reading it. Our numbers are up, Celestine's numbers are down. Happy days.'

'Indeed they are. And Randy, I've made some scribbles on the architectural plans for my Apostolic Palace. I think you'll like my suggestions.'

'Oh, I'm sure I will, Your Holiness. I know it's your number one priority – after saving souls, that is.'

*   *   *

Cardinal Da Silva was used to maintaining a challenging schedule of official duties, but the past few weeks had taxed him to the point of exhaustion. His own staff at the secretariat was concerned about his health and one of his most trusted monsignors had contacted Sister Elisabetta to see if the pope might persuade him to have a bit of a rest – even a couple of days off might be beneficial.

She called on him at his formal office in the Apostolic Palace where he had just concluded yet another crisis meeting of Curia personnel.

'Sister, how nice to see you,' the cardinal said. 'How is the Holy Father?'

'Tired, like you.'

He laughed. 'And you don't also look like you could fall asleep in that chair?'

'It's an occupational hazard these days,' she said. 'Seriously, I wonder if I can prevail upon you to take a small vacation. It might be an inspiration to the Holy Father.'

'It's difficult to see my way clear to doing so,' he said. 'Have you seen the latest figures? We've had hundreds of resignations of clergy and nuns from all over the world. We lost three more cardinals this week – OK, all right-wingers, but still. Attendance at Mass is steadily down on a week-by-week basis. Contributions to Catholic charities are also way down. Even attendance at the papal audiences and the pontiff's Sunday Angelus is down.'

'I know, I know,' she said wearily.

'And Pole's numbers are up, up, up. This so-called New Catholic Church is gaining traction.'

'People do like a good miracle,' she said.

'Speaking of which, how can I contemplate taking even a single day off when the Congregation for the Causes of Saints is formally meeting tomorrow? They need to make a determination fast – one way or another.'

'I've spoken to Cardinal Vaughn,' Elisabetta said. 'He's not used to working under this kind of timetable. He usually has years for his deliberations, not weeks!'

'Tell me something I don't know,' Da Silva said ruefully. 'Listen, while I've got you, I had a conference call with the C8 earlier today. They're not in a panic but they're not far off one either.

They want to recommend a drastic escalation of undertakings to the Holy Father. They want to wield the ax.'

'Excommunication,' she said, rubbing her face.

'Excommunication *latae sententiae*, those excommunications reserved for the pope,' he said, nodding. 'The thinking is that we need to act now and issue the decrees against Pole and all the priests and bishops who have celebrated Mass with him.'

'Under what grounds?'

'Multiple grounds. Under canon law they are schismatics who have willfully withdrawn from the authority of the reigning Roman pontiff. They are apostates. They are heretics. Cardinal Della Queva would be the one to draw up the charges. I've already commissioned a draft.'

'When would we release it?'

'Let's see what the crowds look like during the papal audience this Wednesday. It's as good a barometer as any.'

'All right. What else?'

'They recommend the pope make written and video statements on denouncing the schism, announcing the excommunications, and reaffirming the values of the Holy Roman Church. He must also warn clergy who might be contemplating leaving the Church that excommunication will also be their fates. Finally, he must warn parishioners that any confessions, absolutions, Christian rites administered by a priest in the so-called New Catholic Church, are without weight and are null and void. We must metaphorically burn these heretics at their metaphorical stakes. Celestine is a fighter. Let's give him powerful weapons.'

Sue was walking down one of the rear halls at the mansion where George Pole had been given a temporary office when she heard Anning's voice through a half-open door. It was a Saturday night and Anning was back at the ranch for Sunday Mass. She wasn't a natural snoop but she picked up a few alarming words so she stopped, dropping to the floor and pretending to tie her sneaker laces.

'So you have no intention of bringing their families to the States,' Pole said.

'Hell no. I just told Torres I would so she could quiet them down and prevent a ruckus. The last thing we want is their mamas and papas here, treating them like little girls. And they'd probably all be pains in the asses too with this demand and that demand. These girls have to grow the hell up. They're mothers. They're more than mothers; they are religious icons. You think Holy Mother Mary behaved like a prima donna two thousand years ago? The hell she did. And she was probably younger than them.'

'What will you say to them when they don't arrive?' Pole asked.

'Visa problems. I'll keep moving the timeline.'

'And what if they stop believing you and revolt like Mrs Torres said they might? If they refuse to cooperate on public events? If they disrupt Mass?'

'I've been thinking about it, George – goddamn it, there I go again – Your Holiness. I think in the short, medium, and long run we're going to be better off if we ship these girls back to where they came from. They did their jobs as holy vessels. It's the baby Jesuses that are important to our church. Sure we venerate the Virgin Mary but it's Jesus Christ who's the foundation of Catholicism.'

'We can't just separate mothers from their children,' Pole said.

'Sure we can. Happens every day. Social services comes along, makes an assessment about unsafe parenting, and children are made wards of the state. Betsy and I will adopt them in a New-York minute. Well, I'll have to bribe her to go along but that's my cross to bear. I'll bring in a team of psychiatrists and social workers to attest to the instability of the girls and a friendly judge will do the right thing. I am so sick of their whining, I can't wait to see the back of them. I will raise the boys right. We'll get the nuns to help. When they're older the boys will understand what is required of them. When they're older, they can go back to their own countries, go to wherever it makes sense and preach their gospels. It'll be a beautiful thing and the NCC will just explode in popularity.'

'You certainly have thought this out, Randy. Of course I'll back you on this. When do you want to pull the trigger?'

'Soon.'

Sue heard a shuffling from inside the room, stood up, and fast-tiptoed down the hall.

When she got to her room, she let her anger out in a rush of bitter tears. After she collected herself, she washed her face and poured a wine from her mini fridge. It took her less than five minutes to make a decision.

She poked her head into the girls' bedroom to see if they were still awake. They were in bed playing on their phones. The babies and Lily were asleep.

'Hey guys,' Sue said. 'Can we talk?'

'Is there news about our families?' Mary asked loudly.

'Sort of. Can you keep your voices down?'

'Why?'

'In case the nuns wander past. Here it goes. I made a decision tonight. I'm going to leave.'

'Sue not go,' Maria Mollo cried, throwing off her quilt.

'You can't leave,' Mary said. 'I will burn this fucking house down if you leave.'

'Don't swear,' Sue had said. 'And please don't burn down the house.'

'I love you,' Maria Aquino told her, climbing off her bed and wrapping her skinny arms around her neck.

'Look,' Sue had said after calming them and sitting them down on the carpet. 'Here's the thing. I'm definitely going but I want you to come with me.'

They looked bewildered.

'What about our families?' Mary asked.

'They're not coming. I just found out.'

'Why not?' Mary asked.

'I don't think Anning ever intended to invite them. He lied to get you to behave.'

'Then tell that bald-headed wanker we're not going to his fucking church tomorrow.'

'At this point I almost think that's what he wants you to do. Oh, Christ, Mary, the Marias aren't going to understand everything I'm going to say about your families, the babies, and you guys. You're going to have to make them understand in your own way.'

'Go on,' Mary said. 'You talk and I'll act it out for them in living color.'

For the next several minutes Sue talked and Mary, wide-eyed herself, translated a story to the wide-eyed Marias of their babies being yanked out of their arms and the girls being sent back home without them. Sue was impressed at how masterfully Mary was able to communicate something this complicated to the other girls. Using simple words like, 'Mamas and papas no come,' and pantomimes involving babies being snatched from their arms and being booted out of America, the girls grew frantic.

When she was done Sue asked them if they understood everything. Then she told them they couldn't cry and tomorrow they had to act like nothing was wrong. They were mothers now and their most important job was protecting their children.

Mary had one more question. 'What about Lily?'

'We can't take the dog, I'm afraid.'

'Why not?'

'She barks, remember?'

'Could we leave her to Mrs White? She likes her a lot.'

'That'll work,' Sue said.

Sue returned to her bedroom and unplugged her phone from its charger.

'Hello, Professor Donovan, this is Sue Gibney, the midwife. Yes, I know I've ignored all your texts. I apologize. You came back to the ranch? When? God, I'm sorry, I had no idea. Do you have a moment to talk now?'

TWENTY-EIGHT

S ue waited until after breakfast.

Mrs Torres usually ate alone in her office and that's where she found her.

'Got a minute?' Sue asked.

'Sure, what's up?'

'I need to take a few days off.'

'Oh?'

'It's my sister. She's in the hospital. I need to go back to Santa Fe.'

'You never mentioned a sister.'

'We're not that close but, you know, when someone gets sick . . .'

'I understand.'

'It's just for a little while. It's serious but not that serious.'

'When do you need to go?'

'I thought I'd leave late tonight.'

'Oh good. I thought we'd have to get them to Mass today without you.'

Sue showed some mock horror. 'Heaven forbid.'

After Mass, the girls had as ordinary an afternoon as they could. They played games in the afternoon, they breastfed the babies, and had a wash before dinner. Meanwhile Sue's afternoon was anything but ordinary. She packed a few things of her own but mostly furtively gathered up some bare-minimum essentials for the girls and their babies when no one was looking, interspersing them among her own things in her case. Her plan involved getting the babies as tired as possible and the girls kept them out of their cribs well into the night.

Over dinner, staff members were curious about Sue's departure but she played it down and asked Sister Anika if the sisters were ready to hold down the fort with the girls.

'I believe we're up to the task,' she replied stiffly as there was no love lost between the women.

Over dessert, Clay Carling, the security head, slipped into the room and cut himself a hunk of pie.

'Sorry I was late,' he said. 'There was a fight in the tent city I had to sort out,' he said. 'It's supposed to be alcohol-free, but it's not.'

'I thought your men were checking vehicles at the gates,' Sister Anika said.

'They are, but this ranch is massive. There's almost two hundred miles of perimeter fence. There's a black market in people bringing beer, booze, pot, you name it to the fence lines and selling it to the good Christians who drive their trucks from the tent city and RV park.'

'Human nature,' the chef said.

'You got that right,' Carling agreed. 'So what time in the morning you taking off, Sue?'

She smiled at him maybe for the first time ever. She didn't like the man one bit. He was a humorless ex-lawman with a macho-bullshit swagger that utterly turned her off.

'Many of you may have noticed how uncharacteristically limited I've been in my wine consumption,' Sue said. 'That's because I'm leaving tonight.'

'What time should I tell the boys at the gate you'll be pulling out?' Carling asked.

'I've still a bit of packing to do. Sometime between one and two,' she said.

'Well, you know the alarm code,' Carling said. 'Deactivate it when you exit and reactivate it on your way out.'

'Of course,' she said.

The mansion was dark and quiet except for some hallway night-lights on the bedroom levels. Sue made a dry run with one of her bags, disarming the alarm and putting it inside the van she'd parked by the kitchen entrance.

She went back upstairs using the elevator and in the glow of a nightlight she saw her hands were shaking. This was the point of no return. She could tell the girls it was all a terrible idea. Or she could plunge ahead into the unknown.

She quietly entered their bedroom and saw them dressed in jeans and t-shirts, standing by their unmade beds holding their sleeping babies.

'So ladies, you ready?' she asked.

They were crying. Each one in turn hugged Lily. The bulldog had also stayed up late playing and was so tired in her bed that she hardly wagged her tail at them. Mary was the last. Snorting back her sadness, she made sure her note to Mrs White was sticking out from under the bed.

Heading down in the elevator, Sue whispered that they had to be extremely quiet. The elevator stopped in the downstairs hall. Sue stepped out and stared.

'Miss Gibney,' Anning said. 'Sorry to startle you. I was just having a midnight feast. The chef had some nice leftovers.'

Sue reached behind her and closed the elevator grate and door.

'Well, I'm off now,' she said. 'Heading home for a couple of days.'

'Mr Carling told me. Drive safely. Lot of idiots drive drunk at night in these parts.'

'Thank you. I will.'

'That your camper by the kitchen?'

'It is.'

'I had one of them when I was young. Wish I still had it. I'll

set the alarm after you,' he said, moving to follow her toward
the kitchen.

She thought fast and patted her pockets down. 'Oh heck,' she
said. 'I left my keys in the bedroom. Please don't wait for me.'

'All right then,' he said. 'You take care. Back in time for Mass
next week?'

'Definitely.'

She re-entered the elevator and hit the button for the third floor.

'I think I shit myself,' Mary said. 'Minion looked like she was
going to puke.'

This time when the elevator opened, the ground-floor hallway
was empty. Sue led the girls through the kitchen and bundled them
into the back of the van and covered them with bedding. Then she
noticed something she'd failed to take stock of before, a rear
security camera. She didn't care if someone reviewed the playback
in the morning but if the camera was being actively monitored,
the game was up.

There was nothing to do but climb in and drive off.

The ranch was so large that it took almost ten minutes to get
to the main gate. The gatehouse lights glowed ominously in the
distance. Sue swallowed hard and slowed to a stop at the barrier.
The guard slid the window open and looked her over. Inside, she
saw a bank of video screens including a view of the back of the
mansion near the kitchen. The guard looked sleepy; maybe he'd
been napping.

'I'm Sue Gibney.'

'I've got you. Mr Carling said you were taking off tonight.'

'Well, bye then,' she said.

The young man seemed to get more alert. 'You live around
here?'

'Why do you ask?'

'Maybe we could get a beer or something.'

'Unfortunately I live in New Mexico.'

He was leaning out the window now, making time. 'That's a
cool van. You got a bed in there?'

'Tell you what? Why don't I give you my number. You can call
me if you're ever in New Mexico.'

'Well, I'll have an excuse to go there now. I'll take that number,
Sue Gibney.'

She was five miles away before she spoke again.

'Oh my fucking God, we made it,' she said. She had wanted to scream it out but she remembered the sleeping babies.

Mary threw off her blanket and imitated the young man. 'You got a bed in there?' Then she dissolved into laughter. 'Pretty smooth, girlie. Why don't I give you my number? Was that your real number?'

'What do you think?' Sue said.

Sue hadn't told the girls the next part of the plan in case they were caught. She didn't want anyone else to get into trouble. At the small town of Quanah she took Highway 6 north toward the Red River and the Oklahoma border and, just after a bridge over the Groesbeck Creek, she pulled the van over on to the verge.

'We stop?' Maria Aquino said.

'Sue's got to pee-pee in a bush-bush,' Mary said, sending the girls into a paroxysm of sniggering.

'Not exactly,' Sue said. 'We're meeting a friend.'

There was a flash of headlights from a vehicle parked on the opposite verge a hundred yards away. Sue flashed it back. The vehicle slowly approached and did a U-turn to pull alongside.

'Come on girls, out you go,' Sue said.

'Pedro!' Maria Mollo cried, running into his outstretched arms.

She began to chatter in Spanish but the stable man warned her to keep it down so as not to wake JJ.

He dangled a set of keys at Sue. 'Your camper is really nice, a real classic. You sure you want to swap? My friend's van is a junker.'

'As long as it runs.'

'It runs fine. I put mattresses inside to make it more comfortable for the ladies. The shocks kind of suck too, to be honest.'

'Tell your friend not to drive the camper for a while. Until things settle down.'

'I'll tell him. Sure thing. Where you going to go?'

'It's best if you don't know. And Pedro, thank you.'

She gave him a hug and a peck on the cheek.

'OK, Sue. No problem. Just be safe, OK? I don't want to see you or the girls get hurt. Señor Anning's a tough guy. He's going to be pissed. You know how to shoot?'

'A gun?'

'Yeah, a gun. I put a pistol in the glove box for you. It's old but it works. Like the van.'

'I don't know how to shoot a gun.'

'It's a revolver. You pull the trigger, it fires.'

Pedro's friend's van was, in fact, a piece of junk. It rode rough, it smelled of oil, and the speedometer was pegged at 30 mph even in park. But the AC worked and so did the radio. They'd survive. Before long, the Marys were curled up, spooning the babies, and Sue was putting miles between them and the ranch.

Sister Anika was knocking on Torres's bedroom door. 'Mrs Torres? Mrs Torres? Do you know where the girls are?'

Torres answered in her nightgown. 'I'm sorry, I don't understand.'

'I looked in after morning prayers and they weren't in their bedroom.'

'Did you . . .?' She was about to ask if she checked with Sue, then remembered that the Sue era was over. 'Are the babies sleeping?' she asked.

'They're not in the room either. Only the dog seems to be there.'

Torres ran up the flight of stairs and did a frenzied inspection of the floor, including Sue's empty room, before calling down to the dining room and even the stables. Then in a panic, she literally pressed the panic button on the alarm panel and all hell broke loose on the ranch.

Anning and Pole were too agitated to sit. They both paced Anning's library, coffee cups in hand, waiting for Clay Carling to give them an update.

'Right under my goddamn nose, George. The girls must've been in the elevator when I saw her last night.'

Pole chose not to admonish Anning for calling him George.

'I will make sure she spends the rest of her life in jail for kidnapping. She fucked with the wrong man.'

Pole had a registered letter he suddenly produced.

'Look what they sent me, Randy. I've been excommunicated! The bastard excommunicated me. My priests and bishops got letters too.'

Anning looked at him askance. 'George, we've got a six-alarm fire going on and you're talking to me about getting a mean letter from the Vatican?'

'I'm sorry. I knew Celestine would do it but when it actually happens – well, it's still a shock, that's all.'

'Wear it like a badge of honor, damn it. And don't be bitching about that nonsense now.'

'You're right, of course,' Pole said, dabbing at a spot of coffee that had slid from his lips on to the cassock he'd hastily thrown on. 'Let's just pray the babies are safe.'

Carling came in looking deathly, followed by Torres who didn't look any better.

'The man on the main gate missed it,' he said. 'There they were, plain as day on the kitchen-rear security cam at one eighteen a.m.'

'Fire his ass,' Anning said.

'He's already gone. He got Sue's number as she was leaving. He wanted to ask her out. I checked it. It's bogus. We have her home address in Santa Fe. I've got a team on the way to stake it out.'

'She won't go there,' Anning said.

'Probably not, but we've got to cover all the bases. I've already notified the State Police. They've got Gibney's plate number.'

Pole said, 'You didn't mention the Marys and the babies, did you?'

'Of course not, George,' Anning said. 'We've got to keep this quiet or we'll have a scandal on our hands. This needs to be done quietly and efficiently.'

'But an amber alert could help,' Torres said.

'I said quietly!' Anning said.

'I told the police she stole sensitive documents from the ranch,' Carling said. 'They all know who you are, Mr Anning. If they spot her, they'll call us first. We'll get one of our judges to issue a warrant for them to monitor her credit-card use. She buys gas or a Snickers bar and we've got her. And one more thing. I don't know Gibney all that well but she doesn't strike me as a criminal mastermind. She knows she's going to need help if she's going to elude us.'

'Who would help her?' Anning said.

'Pedro Alvarado might,' Torres said.

'Who's he?' Anning asked.

'The ranch hand you fired the other day,' she said. 'He lives in the county.'

'I'll personally pay him a visit,' Carling said. 'Anyone else?'

Torres thought. 'When that professor came here – Donovan – Sue and he seemed to hit it off.'

'Check the ranch phone logs,' Anning said.

'She never once used the ranch lines,' Mrs Torres said. 'If she called outside she used her cell phone.'

'You know our policy. No personal mobile phones on the premises.'

Torres seemed ready for a tongue-lashing. 'I searched her room. She had one in her medical bag. She must have smuggled it in.'

Anning didn't pounce or swear. He calmly asked Torres if she knew the phone number. She had anticipated the question and gave him a slip of paper.

'OK, clear the room,' Anning said. 'Let me make a call.'

In five minutes, Anning had made his connection.

'Mr President,' he said, 'we've got a bit of a problem over here. Is this a secure line? Good. What's the chance we can get the FBI or some other agency to check on the cell-phone calls of one of my former employees? Hell, yes, it's important.'

TWENTY-NINE

'Circle the airport and pick me up in ten minutes,' the man said to his partner.

They had been following an Uber driver's Volvo as it made its way from Cambridge to Logan airport. Inside the terminal, the private detective kept Cal on a tight leash. Surveillance in an airport was a piece of cake. There was usually enough of a crush that you could get close to a mark without getting made. So when Cal made his way to an automated ticked kiosk to get his boarding pass, the detective joined the line right behind him.

He looked over Cal's shoulder and picked up the flight numbers. When Cal took off for the boarding gate, a check on the departure board showed that Flight 193 was bound for Dallas.

He placed a call. 'Mr Carling, he's going to land in Dallas in about five hours.'

* * *

When Cal left the terminal and stepped into the Dallas heat, another pair of men was waiting, and watching him approach a taxi stand.

'That's him,' one of them said, checking the photo on his phone. 'I'll grab a cab so we don't lose him. Get the car and follow. Call if you lose contact.'

The taxi dropped Cal off at a recreational vehicle sales and service center midway between Dallas and Fort Worth.

'Hi there,' Cal said to the woman behind the counter. 'I called yesterday to book an RV rental. My name's Donovan.'

She checked her computer. 'Oh yeah, we got it all fueled and prepped. It's the 2010 Damon Sport thirty-two-footer. Sleeps six. It's a nice vehicle.' She gave him an obvious once-over. He was looking on the preppie-side with tight jeans, Oxford shirt, and blazer. 'You know how to handle a vehicle this size?'

Cal grinned back. 'Is the pope Catholic?'

She squinted at him. 'Which pope you referring to?'

Clay Carling brought two of his men with him in case Pedro had company. It hadn't been necessary. The young man was alone in his small house, his wife at work, his kids at school. Pedro knew Carling by sight, but if he was scared, he didn't show it. He stood at his front door defiantly upright.

'You know who I am, right?' Carling said.

'I know who you are, señor.'

'You on your lonesome here?'

'Yeah. What do you want?'

'I just want to talk.'

Pedro looked at the other fellow standing in the front yard, one of the security men he'd frequently seen at the main ranch gate. He had spotted three men getting out of the pickup. The third must have gone around to the back.

'About what?'

'Can we go inside? Hotter than hell out here.'

A table fan was running inside. Children's toys littered the floor. Carling had a peek into the kitchen.

'See you got a pot of coffee on.'

'Want some?' Pedro said.

'How'd you know?' Carling said, showing some teeth.

Pedro gave it to him in a chipped cup.

Carling helped himself to an armchair. It was Pedro's. No one else in the family was allowed to use it. The small man said nothing.

'You find new work yet?' Carling asked.

'Not yet.'

'Too bad you got cross-wise with Mr Anning.'

'These things happen, I guess.'

'Sure they do. Say, did you hear what happened at the ranch yesterday?'

'I didn't hear nothing.'

'Oh yeah? You know Sue, right?'

'I know her.'

'Well, for some damned reason, Sue decided to kidnap the girls and their babies. Can you imagine?'

'I don't know nothing about that, señor.'

'Well, I think you're lying, Pedro.'

'I'm not lying.'

'You talk to Sue since getting fired?'

'No, señor.'

'See, that's another lie. We checked her phone records. She called your cell phone day before yesterday. That call was really short, probably only long enough to leave a voice message. Well, you called her back not two hours later. That call lasted six whole minutes. Remembering now?'

Pedro was eyeing the closet where he kept a hunting rifle on a shelf out of reach of his small kids.

'Oh yeah, I forgot. She offered to give me a reference for a new job. We talked about that.'

Carling put his cup down. 'That's not what you talked about.'

'Yeah it was. She's a nice person. She's going to write me something.'

Carling stood up and towered over Pedro. 'I think you helped her, maybe swapped a vehicle with her so she could evade detection. Know that camper of hers?'

'The VW? Sure, I've seen it.'

'I see you've got a lock-up garage. That VW's not in there, is it?'

'No.'

'Mind if I take a look-see?'

'This is private property, señor.'

'Well, I respect that, but what we have here is an extraordinary situation. What that means is, your private property ain't shit to me. Let's go have a look inside, all right?'

Outside, Pedro looked for the right key on his keychain. Carling and the two security guys looked on.

'Haven't got all day,' Carling said.

Pedro unlocked it and gave the door a tug. The garage had some tools, kids' bikes, a bunch of junk.

'See, señor, I told you I didn't have a camper.'

'OK, then,' Carling said. 'You've gone a little bitty way in gaining my trust. Let's go the rest of the way. Let's go inside here and finish our talk.'

Pedro made a quick dash toward the road. The nearest house was a hundred yards away. Maybe he hoped to flag down a car but it didn't matter. Carling's men blocked his way and grabbed him, pulling him inside the garage.

'I'll handle this,' Carling told them, stepping inside the hotbox. 'Keep a watch.'

The garage door was closed for ten minutes.

When Carling emerged, he didn't have a dry patch on his shirt and there was a broad swath of sweat around the band of his cowboy hat. There were drops of blood on his tan boots. He closed the door behind him.

'Son-of-a bitch didn't talk,' Carling said. 'Tough little guy.'

One of the guards asked, 'We need to dump him somewhere?'

'Nope. Didn't see fit to finish him but I told him he'd be dead and his family'd be dead if he called the sheriff.'

'What now?'

'It's all eyes on this Donovan fellow.'

The Marias were being stoical but Mary Riordan was having a moaning fit.

'How long are we going to be driving around inside this piece of junk? My insides are like scrambled eggs. I didn't sleep a wink. It's not healthy for the boys neither. Smells of old diapers.'

It had been a long night and a boring, hot morning. None of them, except for the babies, had gotten much sleep. The girls had crammed together on the mattress. Sue had hoped to recline one of the front seats but none of them would go back so she napped upright. For safety, if there was such a thing for women alone on the road at night, she had parked in a Walmart Supercenter across the border in Oklahoma. It was well lit and there were a few campers and RVs parked there. There was no point in driving through the night and no need to get an early start the next day. She needed to wait for Cal and he wasn't going to be flying out until the morning.

'We'll stop soon for a bathroom break and dispose of the diapers,' Sue said.

'You still haven't said where we're going.'

'If I said Midland would that mean anything to you?'

'Not a bloody thing.'

'That's why I didn't say.'

'You're getting more and more hilarious, Sue. Why are we going there?'

'To meet someone who's going to help us.'

'Who?'

'You met him. Cal Donovan.'

'The egghead from the college?'

'That's the one.'

'Is he single or married?'

'How would I know?'

'Could've looked him up.'

'Why would I do that?'

'Because you fancy him.'

'Why do you say that?'

'Saw the way you were looking at him, that's why.'

'That's ridiculous.'

'Is it?'

'Yes, it is.'

'So how's he supposed to help?'

'He knows someone who'll take us in while he arranges something.'

'Do you know how vague and stupid that sounds?'

Sue squeezed the steering wheel hard in lieu of screaming. 'Mary, do you have any idea how annoying you can be sometimes?'

'I've been told as much by my teachers. Teachers I hate. Why don't we just go to a police station?'

'And tell them what?'

'I don't know. How 'bout that the Perfume Pope tried to diddle us? They'll have to take our word, won't they?'

'More likely I'll get arrested for kidnapping and you'll be returned to the ranch. Mr Anning's a powerful man.'

They drove on. Baby JJ started crying and Maria Mollo couldn't get him to settle down. The crying set off JD, and JD set off JR.

Mary put her fingers in her ears and Maria Aquino announced, 'None more.'

'None more – I mean no more what?' Sue asked.

'Pampers.'

Mary pulled her fingers out. 'Can't hear you. What did you say, Minion?'

'Pampers.'

'Shit,' Sue said.

'Very good, Sue,' Mary said. 'Shit is right.'

'Why didn't you guys say something before when we were at the Walmart?' Sue asked.

'I think Eeyore may have been trying to say something about that last night but it was all just Spanish jabbering.'

'Wonderful,' Sue said. 'Are we having fun yet?'

'He's in a big-ass RV, Mr Carling,' the private detective said.

'Where's he heading?'

'I-20 westbound toward Abilene.'

'You keep him in sight,' Carling said, 'and text me the RV's particulars and plate number.'

Cal was getting the hang of driving the big machine but when he first got behind the wheel he had muttered to himself, 'Lord, please don't make me have to back this thing up.' He was high off the road in a captain's chair, listening to the AM radio because the FM band didn't seem to work. His only choices were pop music, country, or shrill radio preachers who all sounded the same. Even a professor of religion couldn't stomach their spiel. He opted for country and watched the long, straight highway and the brown scrubland, low, green hills and very large, very blue sky.

His mobile rang and he fished for it in the blazer draped over the passenger seat. He didn't recognize the number.

'Hello, Donovan here.'

'Professor Donovan, this is Beth Gottlieb.'

He wasn't expecting to hear from her again. She had told him what she knew about Anning and their plane crash. It was tantalizing but circumstantial. He hadn't known what to make of it and he still had no idea what Steve Gottlieb had wanted to tell him.

'Beth. Hi. Can I help you with something?'

'It's the other way around,' she said. 'Maybe I can help you.'

THIRTY

I t was hard for Cal to get a handle on Beth Gottlieb's state of mind. She seemed to be a cauldron of bitterness and sadness. At times, her speech was pressured, flowing too fast. Then she would downshift into a dull, slower pace. Then it dawned on him. She'd been drinking. It was mid-afternoon on the east coast but Cal could recognize the sound of alcohol.

'What are you supposed to do when you find out your husband was having an affair?' she asked.

He didn't answer. He didn't think she was looking for one.

'You think you know someone and then, all of a sudden, you don't. If he were alive, I'd wring his neck. I would, you know. I didn't know it but I think I'm the type of woman who would have taken a knife to all his suits and shirts and poured paint all over his fucking shoes. Do you have any idea how many pair of shoes that man had?'

'How did you find out?'

'I had to have his safe drilled open. I never knew the combination. I found letters. Not many. They were fucking love letters sent to his office. She marked them personal and confidential because his assistant would've opened them otherwise, I guess. She didn't sign them. Just the letter B. There was no return address. They had a New Haven postmark. They were full of sex stuff. Sex stuff! I love your body. I love to feel you inside me. I vomited. I literally vomited.'

Cal wanted to vomit too. 'I'm sorry, Beth. I'm wondering what this has to do with me.'

'I'm getting to that but I ask you, what am I supposed to do with this now? Steven is dead. Murdered, and the police don't know why or by whom. I can't yell at him. I'd feel like a crazy person if I went to the cemetery and shouted at his grave. I mean, what am I supposed to do?'

'Maybe you should speak to someone. A therapist maybe?'

She turned angry again. 'I wasn't asking for your advice. It was rhetorical. I thought you were a Harvard professor. You can't spot rhetoric?'

'Sorry.'

'So, his email folder and calendar – everything work-related – was there on his office computer. As long as I don't log out I don't need the passwords. Understand? I had a good long browse last night with a bottle of wine for emotional support. You're not a drinker, are you?'

'As a matter of fact, I am.'

'Then you understand. I was looking for who this B was, the times they met up to do the dirty, anything. He was careful. Very careful. Probably because his assistant had access. But I did find one calendar entry from a year and a half ago. And this is why I thought about you.'

He was traveling in the fast lane and had failed to notice a car on his bumper trying to get him to move over. It flashed him and he slid into the right lane. He would have preferred using two hands to steer the sluggish beast but he wasn't going to hang up now.

'I see. What was it?'

'It was for a teleconference. He didn't put the numbers down or the subject. It just said "Telecon, Monday, three p.m., Anning and BH at YSE." You were interested in Anning, weren't you?'

'I was, yes. And you think BH might be your B?'

'Not *my* B, *his* B.'

'That's what I meant.'

'Yes, *his* B! If he wasn't trying to hide her from the world he would've put her fucking name down.'

'OK. Does YSE mean anything to you?'

'Steven never gave me credit for my mind. I was a Romance Languages major in college. I graduated with a 3.7 GPA. That's good, isn't it?'

'Very good.'

'So, this mind of mine put two and two together. New Haven postmark on the sex letters. Yale is in New Haven. The Y in YSE is for Yale.'

'What do you think YSE stands for?'

'Yale School of Engineering, of course. Steve went there for grad school. Didn't you know?'

'Maybe. I forget. So, who is BH?'

He heard a doorbell.

'I haven't gotten that far. Say, I've got to go. A friend is taking me for a pedicure. I helped you, didn't I?'

'Quite possibly. Thank you. I mean it.'

'Maybe you could come and thank me personally. I thought you were a very attractive man.'

Cal got off the call fast.

Anning. BH. YSE.

Maybe it meant something, maybe it didn't.

He was making good time and he was hungry so he decided to pull off the highway at the next exit and find some fast food. And make a call without having to take a hand off the wheel.

'He exited the highway, Mr Carling.'

'Where?'

'Merkel,' the private detective said. 'Just west of Abilene a bit.'

'OK. Any sign of Gibney and the girls?'

'Not yet. Hang on, he's pulled into a McDonald's. We're just going to follow along and park on the other side of it.'

Carling was in his security office in the basement of the mansion house. He tapped a pen on his desk blotter.

'He's gotten out of the RV,' the detective said.

'And?'

'We've got eyes on him. It looks like he's ordered food.'

'OK, what else? Are they there?'

'Hang on. My partner's going in.'

'Don't get made.'

'He won't.'

There was more pen tapping, faster.

'My partner's back, Mr Carling. He's eating a burger. Alone. The other parties aren't there.'

'Well, thank you so much for the burger-and-fries blow by blow,' Carling said, ending the call in disgust.

Sue was northwest of Cal on I-27 midway between Amarillo and Lubbock, heading south toward Midland. She'd lost track of all the bathroom breaks the girls had required and now Maria Mollo was begging for another one. Besides, the van was smelling of ripe diapers again. She usually only pulled off the highway at exits marked with multiple roadside services but the sign for the one coming up only had a gas station sign. Maria was almost howling so she took it.

The small road passed through a nothing of a town, just a few small houses – not even a general store. At first, she thought the gas station was closed. The pumps were empty, the garage doors were closed. She didn't even recognize the brand of gas they sold. It was as if they'd gone back in time. Then she saw a light on through the door marked, office.

'I'll fill the tank,' Sue told Mary. 'You know the drill. Only one girl at a time. This is Maria's turn. You're too recognizable together.'

'Yeah, tons of paparazzi around here,' Mary said, moving into the passenger seat and having a look through the grimy window of the van.

Sue got out, picked a grade and began fueling. She looked around for a restroom sign and didn't see one so she knocked on the office door. When no one answered she opened it and said hello.

The garage door lifted and a lanky man in overalls came out into the forecourt. He looked her up and down and asked her what she needed. She saw that a second mechanic was underneath a car up on a lift.

'Just looking for a bathroom for my daughter.'

'Through the office, first door on the right. It's good you're buying gas.'

'Why's that?' she asked.

'Because we don't let people use the facilities unless they're paying customers. Cash or credit?'

'Cash.'

'That's good, 'cause our credit-card thingy's busted. Something about a modem or some such shit. I don't know.'

Sue didn't like the look of anything about this place but the van was filling and Maria needed emptying. She opened the back and let her out, walking her into the office and checking out the bathroom. It was halfway between clean and filthy but there was toilet paper and Maria was eager. She waited outside the door until she was done.

When they got back outside, both mechanics were standing by the van, trying to get Mary Riordan to roll down the passenger window.

Sue's mouth got dry. She quickly opened the rear door and pushed Maria in. The pump had stopped. She removed the nozzle and cradled it.

'How much do I owe you?' she asked.

'Could be free,' the second mechanic said. 'This is my place. I can make that happen.'

'How much?' Sue asked again, this time with an edge.

'Tell you what?' the owner said, wiping his hands against his jeans. 'I will even check the oil of your shitbox because I expect you know it's burning oil and I'll clean your windshield which is splattered with half the bugs in the county. Why don't you and these girls come inside with us? We got beer in the cooler. It's just about happy hour anyways.'

Sue reached into her pocket and took out a twenty-dollar bill, folded it a few times, and tossed it on to the asphalt.

'We're going,' she said, backing along the van.

The other mechanic walked toward her showing a mouthful of tobacco-stained teeth. 'We think you girls ought to stay a while.'

Sue was trying to keep calm enough to figure out something to do when she saw the owner slowly retreating toward the office and the other guy stopping in his tracks. The van had manual-crank side windows. She heard the passenger-side squeaking open.

Mary Riordan pointed Pedro's revolver out the window.

'I will fucking pull the trigger, you shit-for-brains pair of fuckers,' she said in the strongest Irish accent Sue had ever heard.

Sue ran around to the driver's side, started the ignition and burned what little rubber the worn tires still had speeding away toward the interstate.

'Put the gun back, Mary,' she said in a shaky voice.

The girl returned it to the glove box. The Marias were wide-eyed and confused in the rear. They hadn't seen what had happened and hadn't understood the English. But they'd seen the gun and Sue wasn't sure whether they were scared or impressed.

No one spoke again until they were back on the highway when Sue said, 'You wouldn't have pulled the trigger, right?'

'What do you think?'

Sue didn't answer.

'How come you didn't chew me out for swearing?' Mary said.

Sue shook her head. 'Because I think it was the most beautiful thing I've ever heard you say, Mary Riordan.'

Cal finished his McDonald's. He remained in the booth frustrated with his slow Internet connection, then gave up and called Joe Murphy.

'Yeah, I'm in Texas, on my way to meet them,' he said. 'I've only got one bar. Can you do a search for me? Steven Gottlieb's wife drunk-called me about something she found in her husband's calendar. It's a meeting he had a year ago with Anning and someone with the initials BH from, she thinks, the Yale School of Engineering. Can you go on their website and have a look?'

'Not a problem,' Murphy said. 'Got my computer right here. OK, any idea what department?'

'No clue. How many do they have?'

'Several. I'll just have a look-see. There's a couple hundred faculty, it appears. BH, eh?'

'BH. A woman, I think.'

'All right. Here's a woman. Belinda Hartman. How's that sound?'

'Promising. What's her department?'

'Biomedical Engineering.'

'Do me a favor, Joe? Dig into her background. See what you can find out about her professionally and personally.'

'I'll ring you back when I'm done. Be careful out there.'

It was five o'clock in the afternoon and Randall Anning was itching for a drink. He'd been holed up all day in his library getting inconsequential updates from Clay Carling, and he'd been getting angrier and more agitated as the day dragged on. He finally broke down and poured himself a small bourbon just to take the edge off and dialed down to the security office.

'Where is he now?'

'The last update had him approaching Midland,' Carling said.

'No sign of the girls?'

'None, Mr Anning. You know I'll tell you as soon as there's contact.'

'Make sure you do.'

Anning hung up and poured another measure. Knocking it back, he reclined in his big leather chair and swiveled it around to run his eyes over the wall of photos behind his desk.

He settled on a modest one. It was small, the color wasn't vivid, and it was shot from a distance, making it almost impossible to make out who was in the shot. That made it very different from the other photos in the gallery, most of them beautiful portraits of Anning with celebrities and politicians, including the last six Presidents.

It was a picture shot from a helicopter of two men waving their arms on a snow-covered mountain peak beside the wreckage of an airplane.

THIRTY-ONE

Three years earlier

It was winter in the Andes and the conditions for skiing were nothing short of perfection. Waves of snowstorms had deposited a firm base and waist-deep, pillowy powder over the best of the ski peaks. In between the storms the temperatures were relatively mild and the sun shone brightly. It was the group's last night in the Chilean mountains at Nevados de Chillán and the spirits of the nine guests were as high as the altitude. They occupied a private dining room at the five-star Gran Hotel Termas de Chillán where their host, Randall Anning, rose to give a toast.

'Oh hell,' said Kincaid, an oil man from Dallas. 'Randy's going to talk again.'

'Well you just button it, Bruce,' Anning said, grinning ear to ear. 'Last I checked, I was picking up the tab for the week so you've got to listen up when I pretend to be a toastmaster.'

Kevin Fox, an investment banker from New York who was tipsy from pisco, the local brandy, clinked his water glass with a knife for quiet.

'Thank you, Kevin,' Anning said. 'That gesture alone is going to win you my next M&A deal over you, McGee, since you're more interested in whoring for Gottlieb's IPO business than showing your host – i.e. me – some goddamn courtesy.'

McGee pretended he wasn't listening and said, 'Sorry, Randy, were you saying something? I was just talking to Steve about a hot IPO.'

Over laughter, Anning said, 'You're making my point, you bastard. Now, gentlemen – and needless to say, I'm using the term loosely – tonight marks the midway point of our skiing adventure. We've had three marvelous days of off-piste helicopter skiing here in Chile and I think we all have learned enough about each other's athletic talents – or lack thereof – to make some awards. The awards committee consisted of all the billionaires in our group – hey wait, I'm the only one – and the judgments of the committee are final and are not going to be questioned. Understood? OK then, the first award is for the skier who's got the best form, is the fastest down the mountain, and is far and away the best-looking. Hells bells – that's me!'

Amidst booing, Anning reached under the table and pulled out a bottle of liquor that he put in front of his place setting.

'The prize is a bottle of Pisco Puro, which is kind of like a Chilean single-malt scotch. It's from a single grape variety. Don't say you didn't learn anything this week. All right, the next award is for the skier who's least likely to find another skier buried in an avalanche. And that award goes to Phil Alexander, who couldn't find the buried beacon on three tries.'

Alexander, a corporate lawyer, protested, 'Sue me. I contend that my earpiece was defective.'

Anning presented him with an identical bottle of brandy and said, 'The next award is for the skier who moaned the most about his altitude headache – and that would be Steve Gottlieb. Steve, here's your brandy plus a couple of Advils.'

Gottlieb got up, bowed, and clutched his head.

Anning kept it up. 'Here's an award for the guy with the most garish ski suit and that goes to Mr Yellow and Pink, Neil Bartholomew.'

Bartholomew, a natural gas pipeline builder, took his bottle and said, 'You fellows only wish you had my sartorial taste.'

'What the hell does sartorial mean?' Kyle Matthews, a refinery CEO said. 'That a pansy word to match your pansy clothes?'

'No, Kyle,' Bartholomew said, laying it on thick, 'it's a word I learned in a place called school. Ever been there?'

Anning gave a couple more awards and said, 'Oh hell, the rest of you mugs deserve honorable mention. Come and get your brandy but don't get too damned drunk tonight. It's wheels-up at eight a.m. for the real pièce-de-resistance of the week, Cerro Catedral in Argentina. The Cathedral, gentlemen, where you're going to experience the best off-piste skiing of your soon-to-be enriched lives.'

It was clear that not all the men had heeded the warning about drinking too much because the courtesy van to the airport was uncharacteristically quiet. A private plane, a King Air 350 turbo-prop, was waiting to ferry them to Argentina. They filled all the available nine seats. The pilot came back to chat with them after he and the co-pilot had finished their checklist.

'I'm honored to be your pilot today,' the captain said. 'My name is Joaquin Araya. My co-pilot, Matias Espinoza, and I will fly you and all your expensive skis down to Carlos de Bariloche, a distance of nearly 800 kilometers. Flight time today will be just under three hours. The conditions are overcast but we won't be flying into any heavy weather. I recommend you keep your seatbelts fastened when you aren't at the refreshment center or heading to the lavatory just to be safe. Enjoy your flight, gentlemen.'

Anning, whose head was crystal clear, was in the front-most seat, the only one that swiveled, holding court and doling out plastic cups of coffee when the aircraft leveled off at 27,000 feet. Before they were socked in by clouds, the Andes peaks were a sight to behold, crisply scalloped and pure white.

Steve Gottlieb was seated beside Neil Bartholomew. The two

of them hadn't talked all that much on the trip and they used the opportunity to get to know each other better.

'So, Steve, how is it you know Randy?'

'We met a couple of years ago when he was looking at acquiring one of my portfolio companies.'

'Oh yeah? Did the deal happen?'

Gottlieb laughed. 'He wanted too low a price.'

'He's a cheap bastard, isn't he?'

They were in the row behind Anning who swiveled, said he heard the remark, and swiveled back to the book he was reading on his tablet.

'Well, let's just say we saw more value than he did. Anyway, he's sniffed the butts of a few of my companies since then. We'll see if we ever make a marriage.'

'What kind of companies do you invest in?'

'Our fund isn't monolithic. We do all sorts of technology plays from med-tech to robotics to software solutions.'

'You an engineering type or a finance guy?' Bartholomew asked.

'At this point, both, I guess, but I've got a Masters in mechanical engineering from Yale.'

'Nice, very nice.'

'How about you, Neil?'

'Business major, Texas A&M. I'm an Aggie, through and through. Went to work in nat-gas right out of college and never looked back. Kids?'

'Does a wife with temper-tantrums count?'

'I think it does, Steve.'

'Then yes, I've got a kid.'

They were ninety minutes into the flight when everyone in the cabin heard it.

A plink, then a loud pop.

The cockpit door was open and everyone in the front could see and hear the pilot and co-pilot reacting to the situation.

'What's happening?' Phil Alexander said from the rear.

Anning was the closest. 'Fucking hell,' Anning said. 'It looks like the pilot-side windshield's cracked.'

'That's not good, is it?' Kevin McGee said.

'Firmly in the category of not good,' Anning said. 'Let's all pipe down and let these boys up front do their jobs.'

The pilots, maybe due to stress, reverted to Spanish, and while the co-pilot was about to radio for permission to make an altitude change, there was a much louder pop and then an almighty whoosh when the windshield leaf catastrophically delaminated and flew off.

The cabin immediately depressurized.

Oxygen masks deployed.

The roaring sound was deafening. No one could hear each other's shouts.

Then the plane lurched to the left and banked down hard.

The failed windshield leaf had been sucked into the left turboprop and had shredded the blades. A blade fragment had become shrapnel, shearing off the left horizontal stabilizer and elevator.

Anning pulled a dangling mask to his face and peered into the cockpit. The co-pilot was reaching over to the captain who was slumped against his harness. A spray of blood flowed out the open window from the wound in the pilot's chest where he'd been pierced by a chunk of the shattered propeller.

The plane began corkscrewing, nose down through the thick cloud cover. The co-pilot pulled on his oxygen mask and shifted his attention from the pilot to the controls. He wrestled with the control yoke and rudder pedals and managed to marginally get the nose up. But they were losing altitude fast.

The clouds cleared.

A mountain was looming.

Anning lost sense of time. The side of the mountain was getting closer and closer. The roar of the wind was too loud for anyone to hear the co-pilot shouting, 'Brace! Brace! Brace!'

Gottlieb became aware that his face was cold and numb. His eyes were closed. He tried to wriggle his nose but it was too stiff.

'Ow!' he cried. His right elbow and right knee hurt terribly.

He opened his eyes and blinked in abject confusion. He was sitting in his airplane seat, seatbelt in place, but there was no airplane. His shoeless feet were sunk into snow. Everything surrounding him was pure and white and very cold. Flurries of snow swirled around him.

He looked to his left. His seatmate was also strapped in but

Neil Bartholomew's head wasn't there and his powder-blue sweater was red with blood.

Gottlieb screamed.

Anning awoke. He heard a scream in the distance.

He was looking into the remains of a cockpit. Both pilots were as mangled and twisted as the metal. He looked behind him and saw snow, only snow. The fuselage had been ripped from the front of the plane at a point just behind his seat. He did a quick inventory of his person. Everything seemed to work and he wasn't in any significant pain.

'Hello!' he shouted at the man who had screamed. 'I hear you!'

'Help!'

'Who is it?' Anning shouted.

'Steve Gottlieb!'

'It's Randy, Steve. Who else is with you?'

'Neil's dead.'

Anning said, 'Jesus Christ,' way too softly for Gottlieb to hear. Then he shouted, 'Are you hurt?'

'Yes!'

'OK, let me come to you! Just hang on a minute!'

Anning unbuckled his belt and stepped through the partially collapsed opening into the cockpit. He thought both the crew were dead. Bones showed through trousers, but the co-pilot was breathing.

'Hey, wake up!' he said, pulling on the man's ear.

There was a low moan.

He couldn't remember the fellow's name. 'Hey, we've crashed. Did you radio a mayday? Did you radio our position?'

The man opened his eyes a bit and tried to speak.

'No radio. No time,' he rasped, closing his eyes.

'Is there an emergency beacon on board?' Anning said, pulling on his ear again.

His eyes opened one last time. 'No ELT.'

'Is that the beacon?' Anning said, but the co-pilot's breathing shuddered then stopped.

Anning swore and turned toward the snow. His first step sank him to the middle of his thighs.

'Steve, where are you? Call to me!'

'Here!'

Anning squinted and looked around, trying to pin the direction the voice was coming from. He was on a slope, a steep slope. He saw something silvery quite a distance downhill.

'Call again!'

Gottlieb's voice wasn't coming from that direction. He had to be uphill; Anning began slogging against gravity until he saw the incongruous sight of two men strapped into side-by-side seats, one with a head, one without.

He made it to Gottlieb's side and tried not to look at Bartholomew's corpse.

'Who else is alive?' Gottlieb asked.

'I don't know. The pilots are dead. I think a section of the cabin is down the mountain a way. What hurts?'

'My arm and my knee.'

'Do you think you can walk? We should get down there.'

'I can try.'

'The snow's deep. I'll help you.'

They had no way of judging how far down the mountain the rear of the fuselage had landed but it took an agonizing hour of walking and sliding to get there.

It was missing the wings and tail but it was largely intact. It had sheared off behind Anning's seat. Gottlieb's row of seats had spilled out on impact. Gottlieb collapsed in exhaustion and pain and he rested his back against the hull while Anning had a look inside. The rest of the seats and their occupants were intact. Anning grimly walked through the cabin, taking stock of six dead men until he got to Phil Alexander, the lawyer, in the last seat, just forward of the lavatory and luggage space.

Alexander was conscious, his eyes staring wildly.

'Phil, I'm here.'

'Where am I?'

'We crashed.'

'We did? I don't remember. Fuck, it's cold.'

'We're on the side of a mountain. Steve Gottlieb's alive. That's it.'

'I can't feel my legs. My belly hurts.'

'Shit. Let me think. Stay there.'

'Randy, you asshole,' Alexander said, grimacing in pain. 'You think I'm going to get up and dance the fuck out of here?'

Outside the wind had picked up and it was snowing harder, coating the silver fuselage in a white skin. Anning sat beside Gottlieb and gave him the score. For the first time since the crash, Gottlieb cried.

'We are so fucked,' he said.

'It's not good, my friend,' Anning said. 'No two ways about it.'

'Maybe the pilots radioed a mayday before we went down.'

'The co-pilot was alive for a minute when I got to him. They didn't.'

'Hopefully the plane was equipped with an emergency transponder,' Gottlieb said.

'Is that an ELT?'

Gottlieb nodded vigorously. 'Emergency locator transmitter.'

'Shit out of luck, Steve. They didn't have one.'

'Then we're dead,' Gottlieb said. His cell phone was in his jacket pocket. 'I just tried my phone. No bars.'

'We're not dead yet,' Anning said. 'I'm going to need your help to get Phil out of there.'

'Why?'

'Because it's filled with bodies.'

'It's snowing out here, Randy. There's no shelter. We should move inside.'

'What about the bodies?'

'I'm no doctor but I don't think dead men need shelter. Let's drag them outside and figure out how to cover the opening of the plane. Then we can try to get a handle on Phil's injuries and see if there's any food on the plane.'

Anning agreed with the plan and then said, 'I'm telling you right now, Steve, if we have to eat human flesh to survive, I will do it.'

Gottlieb groaned, 'For fuck's sake, Randy, we've been on the side of this mountain for less than two hours and you're already talking about cannibalism?'

THIRTY-TWO

Cal was ten miles outside of Midland, Texas when Murphy called with a data dump on Belinda Hartman. He steered the RV into the slow lane and plastered his cell phone against an ear.

Hartman had a large online presence, at least academically, but Murphy wasn't sure that it was all that illuminating. Cal had to agree. Her CV was pure-bred. Undergraduate at Yale. Masters at Yale. PhD at Yale. Straight on to the Yale faculty and currently an associate professor at the Yale School of Engineering. Hell, she probably peed Eli-blue, Cal thought. She taught courses in mechanical engineering, bioengineering, and even a seminar in entrepreneurship. She was in the double-century club with over a hundred published papers and over a hundred patents.

On a hunch Cal asked Murphy, 'Can you check when Steven Gottlieb got his engineering degree from Yale?'

Murphy told him to hang on and went to the website of Gottlieb's venture capital firm. His bio was still there even though he had well and truly departed.

Murphy told him.

'Was that when she was there?' Cal asked.

'There we have it,' Murphy declared in a minute. 'Classmates.'

'So, the two of them knew each other in school,' Cal said. 'Maybe they were an item back then, maybe the affair started later in life after Gottlieb was married. He goes on to fund engineering companies, she's an inventor. A year and a half ago they have a meeting with Randall Anning. What's this meeting about? That's the question.'

'You can't ask Mr Gottlieb,' Murphy said. 'At least not in this life. That leaves Anning and Hartman. But what evidence is there that it had anything to do with our Marys? Gottlieb's a venture capitalist, she's a technologist, Anning is involved in drilling for oil and whatnot. Maybe it's simply to discuss a business venture.'

'We don't have any evidence that it had something to do with the girls. None whatsoever. But it's intriguing, don't you think? We know that Gottlieb wanted to talk to me about them and someone killed him before he had a chance. We know that he and Anning endured something awful together up in the Andes. I'm betting this meeting the three of them had was significant.'

'Doubtful that Anning is going to be a font of information,' Murphy said.

'That's why I'm calling Hartman the second I hang up with you.'

The number listed on the YSE website was an office line. It rang through to voice mail with an instruction in Hartman's voice that if the call was urgent to dial zero for the departmental secretary. It was late in the day, five thirty on the east coast, and Cal figured he'd come up empty. But a young man picked up and said, 'Engineering.'

Cal told the secretary that he was a colleague of Hartman's from Harvard and that he had an extremely urgent need to speak with her. After a brief hold, the man told him that it looked like she'd left for the day. Cal persisted and managed to get him to cough up her mobile number.

She sounded like she was on a car speakerphone.

'Hartman.'

'Professor Hartman, this is Professor Cal Donovan from Harvard. I'm sorry to bother you.'

'Do we know each other?' she asked.

'We don't,' he said. 'I—'

'Are you at the School of Engineering?'

'Actually, I'm at the Divinity School.'

Her tone turned decidedly suspicious. 'I'm sorry, what is this in regard to?'

'It's about Steve Gottlieb.'

The line went quiet. He wasn't sure if she'd hung up until he heard the sound of a car passing hers.

'What about him?'

'Steve contacted me recently,' Cal said. 'He told me he wanted to meet to discuss something.'

'What?'

'He said it was about the virgins, the Marys.'

There was another pause. He thought she was choosing her words carefully. 'Why do you think he called you?'

'I've been involved with them. He saw me on TV.'

'That was you? On *60 Minutes*?'

'It was. I was there, Professor Hartman. I was in the parking lot when his car blew up.'

'Jesus, you were there?'

'Unfortunately, yes.'

'Did you speak to him?'

'I didn't get the chance.'

He heard her swallowing. Her voice became lachrymal. 'I don't know what to say. I don't understand why you're calling to tell me this?'

'Look, I'm not in the least interested in your personal life but—'

'What are you saying?'

'His wife, Beth Gottlieb, was going through his papers and found your letters.'

'Shit. Look, this is none of your business.'

'I know. It's something else she found that's the reason for my call. It was a calendar entry from about eighteen months ago. A telecon at your office with Steve and Randall Anning.'

The line was quiet again.

'You know who he is, right? The man who's been funding the New Catholic Church?'

Her nasal passages sounded drier now, her tone formal. 'I'm sorry, Professor Donovan. I've just arrived at my next appointment. I'm afraid I won't be able to help you. Goodbye.'

Anning's mobile phone rang showing a blocked caller. He had a feeling who it was and what it was about. Some spook somewhere in the alphabet soup of federal agencies had been tasked with anonymously helping him track cell phone calls. First it was Sue Gibney, but she'd gone dark for the past twenty-four hours. Now it was Cal Donovan.

'Anning.'

'Mr Anning, he's made calls to one Massachusetts number and two Connecticut numbers.'

'Who are they?'

'The Mass number belongs to a Joseph Murphy.'

Anning grunted. He'd read all about his kidnapping in Ireland. 'And Connecticut?'

'One was the Yale School of Engineering, the other was to a Belinda Hartman.'

Anning thanked the caller, put his phone down and snapped his eyes shut.

The sun was getting lower and the western sky was becoming mellow and golden. Sue had arrived at the meeting point two hours early. There wasn't any point in just driving around aimlessly. She was bone-weary. The girls were tired and the babies were restless, especially JD, who seemed warm to the touch. She felt safe at the parking lot at the Walmart in Midland, which was located just off of I-20. It was bustling with cars and families but at the same time was perfectly anonymous.

Sue didn't trust the exhaust system of the old van but she needed to keep the AC running in the heat. As she cooled her brood down she kept the windows cracked, fearing carbon monoxide. There wasn't enough Freon in the pipes to neutralize the hot air so it was still pretty warm inside. She took the girls and their babies, one-by-one, inside the store to properly cool off, use the restrooms and changing facilities, and buy ice creams, cold drinks, and sandwich fixings.

When she took Mary and JD inside, the girl asked Sue to check him again.

'He's still warm, isn't he?' Mary said.

'I'm going to buy a thermometer,' Sue said. She found an infrared thermometer, took it out of its packaging before paying for it and aimed it at the baby's forehead. His temperature was mildly elevated.

'He's got a runny nose,' Sue said. 'It's probably just a cold. Acetaminophen drops should help.'

At the checkout, the cashier looked at the thermometer and the medicine and the baby in Mary's arms, too intently for Sue's comfort.

'Is the little fellow under the weather?' the cashier said.

'Just a tad,' Mary said.

Sue wasn't pleased that Mary had opened her Irish mouth.

'What an interesting accent you've got, honey?' the woman said, eyeing her. 'Where are you from?'

'She's Canadian,' Sue said, handing over some bills.

'Oh yeah,' the woman said, nodding and bagging the items. 'I thought you sounded French.'

Back inside the van, the girls occupied themselves playing with the thermometer, taking readings of everything animate and inanimate within the scope of the beam.

'How long now?' Maria Aquino said.

'Soon,' Sue said. She checked her watch one more time. Where was he?

The private detectives were keeping to a quarter-mile separation behind Cal. The RV was big and lumbering; there was little danger of losing sight of him.

'He's signaling,' one of them said.

'Bathroom, food, or bingo?' the driver said, getting ready to exit too. 'Let Carling know what's what.'

Carling had just stubbed out a cigarette and when he got their call, he lit another one. Mr Anning didn't let people smoke anywhere inside the mansion but down in the basement with his office door closed, Carling took his chances. His ashtray, a Styrofoam cup half-filled with old coffee, was swimming in butts.

He looked at his wall map. 'Midland, you say? Where the hell's he meeting up with them anyway?'

'Could be Mexico,' the detective on the phone said. 'Or New Mexico.'

'Or maybe right here in Texas. Stay on the line and tell me what he's up to.'

Cal had seen the sign for the Walmart from the highway and headed there from the exit. He had no way of knowing if Sue had even made it there and if so, what she was driving. When she'd called the day before they had hastily sketched out the barest outline of a plan. And once they had agreed on the meeting place he'd chosen from a glance at Google Maps, he'd warned her to turn off her mobile phone and remove the SIM card. Anning seemed like the kind of man who had the resources to find people. All Cal could do was loop around the parking lot with the RV, the equivalent of waving a big old flag.

There were a dozen double rows of parked cars at the front of the store. Cal could only manage to make every other turn in his long rig. He was in the middle of the lot when he spotted an old van flashing brights. He slowed to a crawl as he passed and saw the driver, one extremely happy woman with a long ponytail.

He parked at the end of the row, taking up several empty spaces. Sue pulled in next to him. They got out at the same time. Although they barely knew each other, their spontaneous embrace seemed like the most natural thing in the world.

'Mr Carling, it's her!' the detective said.

'You sure? You absolutely sure?'

'It's definitely Gibney.'

'The girls. Do you see the girls?'

'Not yet. They're probably inside her van. It's a black Dodge van. Let me try to get the plate for you.'

'Screw the plate. They're going to ditch the van for the RV. I don't want them getting inside the RV. Do you understand?'

'What do you want us to do?'

'Stand by and keep this line open, goddamn it.'

Carling put the detective on hold and called up to the library. His boss picked up on the first ring.

'They just called,' Carling said. 'They have eyes on them.'

'Where?' Anning said.

'A Walmart in Midland. What do you want them to do?'

'Do? Get them to take the girls and the babies back, for Christ's sake!'

'They can't force them. They're not law enforcement, they're private investigators. By state law they aren't even armed.'

'For Christ's sake, Clay, these men we hired are tough guys, no? We're talking about some teenagers, a midwife and a college professor!'

'Why don't we just get the police involved, Mr Anning? We can say they were forcibly taken from the ranch.'

'I do not want the police involved, Clay. They'll have to do some kind of investigation at a minimum. We can control the police around here, but the State Police? The local police in Midland? Don't you forget that Calvin Donovan was there when Gottlieb got killed. I don't know what he knows or what he thinks he knows at this point. He called Belinda Hartman today! Did you hear me?'

'I heard you.'

'No police. Just tell your fellows to strong-arm the girls into their car and drive them back here.'

Carling got back to the detective and gave him a set of instructions. He and his partner listened on the speakerphone. When they pushed back, Carling hit them with an incentive: he'd double the fee for a successful conclusion.

'If we've got to use muscle, Mr Carling, we're putting our PI licenses in jeopardy,' the driver said.

'Triple your fee,' Carling said.

'Triple? That's a deal,' the driver answered.

The shadows across the parking lot were getting long. The detectives watched from a nearby parking spot as the girls and their babies emerged from the van and climbed into the RV. Cal and Sue started transferring their belongings from the back of the van parked right behind the RV.

'OK, get the shit from the trunk and let's move,' the driver said. 'I'll box them in.'

The guy in the passenger seat got out and retrieved a tire iron and a baseball bat from the trunk and climbed back in for the ten-second ride over to the front of the RV. The driver braked hard, slammed the transmission into park and left the car running. Both men jumped out and began menacing Sue and Cal. They were big men. The bat and tire iron made them look larger.

'We work for the ranch,' the driver said. 'We know what you did, Miss Gibney. You kidnapped those girls. We're taking them back. Bring them and the babies out here and you and your friend won't get hurt. If you don't we'll have to work you over. You'll both be spending tonight in a hospital and we'll still bring the girls back where they belong.'

Cal stepped in front of Sue. He was a big man himself but they didn't look all that intimidated.

'These girls left because they wanted to leave,' Cal said. 'You'd be the ones doing the kidnapping. If Mr Anning thought she'd broken the law it would be the police here, not you.'

The man with the bat pointed it and said, 'This isn't a debate, mister. Back the fuck away.'

'I'm not going to let you take them,' Cal said, getting ready to take a hell of a beating.

First the guy with the tire iron took one step back. Then a second. The guy with the bat dropped the lumber and also took a couple of steps to the rear.

Cal was feeling pretty damn smug about his ability to intimidate until he looked behind him at Sue, who was pointing a revolver.

'Get back in your car and get the hell out of our way,' she said.

'Yes, ma'am,' the driver said, holding his hands up a little. 'Just be careful with that gun, all right.'

'I want you to give a message to Mr Anning.'

'Yes, ma'am. I will.'

'Tell him to go fuck himself.'

Carling ran up the steps to the ground floor of the mansion, the soles of his boots skidding down the marble hall. He flew into the library without knocking.

'Do we have them?' Anning said.

'Sue pulled a gun on them. They got away in the RV.'

'Where the hell did she get a gun?'

'Maybe she had one all along. Maybe she got it from the stable guy. I told our guys to keep following them. Do you want to reconsider calling the police?'

Anning got up and took his cowboy hat from an elk antler on the wall. 'No! Scramble the chopper and bring a rifle. We're going to take care of this ourselves.'

THIRTY-THREE

As soon as he cleared the parking lot and got back on the highway, Cal floored the RV. It was a sluggish beast but it eventually picked up speed. Sue sat beside him, the pistol resting on her lap, a trembling hand resting on the gun.

'Where'd you get that?' Cal asked.

'A man on the ranch.'

'I'm glad you had it. Know how to use it?'

'Mary Riordan taught me.'

He looked at her quizzically.

The girls were splayed out on the bench seats, clutching their babies and trying to make sense of the craziness.

'Girls, you remember Professor Donovan,' she said.

They nodded but he wasn't what they wanted to talk about. They'd just seen Sue pull a gun on some men and now they were throttling down the road in an exotic vehicle with beds and a kitchen.

'Sue go gun,' Maria Aquino said.

'Sue kill fuckers like Mary?' Maria Mollo asked. Mary Riordan had taught them well.

'No!' Sue said. 'I was just trying to scare them.'

'It worked,' Cal said.

Mary Riordan was looking out the large rear window. 'Excuse me, guys, those blokes are following us.'

Cal confirmed it in the rearview mirror. 'They look like they're keeping their distance.'

'Where are we going?' Sue asked.

He had his phone on map mode. 'We're taking the next exit. We're going north. To New Mexico.'

'Home,' she said softly to herself.

'We should cross the border in an hour and a quarter,' he said. 'We'll pass through Roswell, avoiding UFOs if possible, then up to Albuquerque.'

'Why there?' she asked.

'I've got a colleague at the university who's going to give the girls sanctuary until we figure out what to do next. I'm thinking about something public, maybe a press conference. I don't know yet.'

Sue was repeating the word 'sanctuary' absently. Then she said, 'Thank you. I didn't know who else to call.'

'I'm part of this now,' he said. 'I'm glad you did.'

'We have to protect them,' she said. 'Anning and Pole have turned them into circus performers. And the babies. The beautiful, beautiful babies.'

He checked his mirror again. 'We'll protect them.'

She took her hand off the gun and touched one of his hands wrapped around the steering wheel.

Mary saw the gesture and said, 'I told you, you fancied him.'

'Oh, Mary,' Sue said. 'You and your mouth.'

Maria Mollo asked what fancied meant and Mary made a kissy face and smooching sounds, sending the girls into a fit.

When they had laughed themselves quiet, Sue turned around to try and spot the following car herself.

'I'm afraid for them,' she said, too quietly for the girls to hear. 'Maybe we should call the police. I don't care if I go to jail.'

'You're not going to jail but I don't think we want Texas police involved. Randall Anning's got a long reach in this state. Maybe we'd be safe. Maybe we wouldn't. I'm going to feel a lot better in New Mexico.'

Anning's AgustaWestland AW189 helicopter was one of the fastest civil models you could buy. It was rated at over 300 kilometers per hour and could carry up to nineteen passengers. With only the pilot, Anning, and Carling on board it felt cavernous and empty. There would be plenty of room to ferry the girls and their infants back to the ranch in speed and comfort.

Carling was in the seat behind Anning and the pilot, keeping up a running dialogue with the two detectives pursuing the RV. Anning had been a nervous flyer since his accident in the Andes, but he put that out of his mind by focusing on the map display in the cockpit.

'They're here,' Anning said to the pilot, pointing to a spot. 'State Road 385 heading north toward Seminole. How long before we get to them?'

'Assuming he stays northbound at the speed limit, I'd say we're going to intersect with him in about an hour.'

Carling asked, 'What are we going to do when we get to them?'

Anning turned and dressed him down harshly. 'You let me worry about that.'

Cal couldn't get comfortable as long as they were being followed. The road was flat and featureless with little traffic in either direction. There were no trees, no vegetation at all taller than a few inches. It was all stubble and sandy earth. Dusk was coming and the car behind them was easy to keep tabs on, especially when its headlights switched on.

'What the hell are they doing?' he asked. 'They're keeping a respectful distance but they're not letting go.'

'I just want this to be over,' Sue said. 'I'm so tired.'

'You never told me where you live.'

'Santa Fe.'

'Nice city.'

'I love it. I wish I hadn't left.'

'The girls would've been in a sorrier state if you hadn't been there for them.'

'Maybe, but I paid a price. I sold my soul to the Devil.'

'You mean Anning.'

'I mean him, all of it.' She looked over her shoulder to see if the girls were listening. They were in the back, inspecting the bunk beds and the bathroom. 'What's going to happen to them?' she asked.

'They have families.'

'They'll be freaks back home. They'll never have peace. You know about these things. Did the Virgin Mary have peace? Did people let her be?'

'The Bible is sketchy on her life. If you believe the accounts in the Gospels, there's a suggestion she stayed involved with her son throughout his life. She was said to be there when Jesus performed his first miracle, turning water into wine. She was said to be among the women at his crucifixion. There are a few other oblique mentions. Beyond that, there's nothing.'

She was teary and gulped. 'Will that happen to the boys? Will they be murdered one day too?'

'God, Sue, history doesn't always repeat itself. If they're really the product of miraculous conception then all I can predict is that they'll have remarkable and closely watched lives.'

'Do you think they are? Do you think they're miracle babies?'

There was a box of tissues in the center console, left there by the last person who rented the RV. He pulled a few out and handed them over.

'I really don't know. But hey, some people say that all babies are miracles.'

'What about you?' she asked. 'Do you say that too?'

He deflected the question with a joke. 'Hell, Sue, I just think it's a miracle I've been able to avoid having any of my own.'

*   *   *

They were flying directly into a setting sun that was slowly sinking into the horizon, turning the desert sky shades of pastel.

'Mr Anning,' Carling said, 'they're telling me they're still on State Road 62 heading west, about ten miles from the New Mexico border.'

'She's from Santa Fe,' Anning grumbled. 'Maybe she's got people there she thinks are going to help her. How long till we're over them?'

'Less than five minutes,' the pilot said. 'Clay, if you could get the pursuit vehicle to tap its brakes every so often, we can make them out by their brake lights.'

'I'll do that,' Carling said.

Anning grabbed a pair of binoculars and scanned the road. In a minute, he declared that he thought he could see flashing red brake lights. In another minute, he was more certain, and a minute later, Carling confirmed the sighting with his naked eyes.

'That's them for sure,' he said.

'I see the RV,' Anning said. 'I see the son-of-a-bitch.'

'We'll be over it in sixty seconds,' the pilot said. 'What altitude do you want?'

'Low,' Anning said. 'I want you to get their attention.'

'Then what?' the pilot asked.

'Get ahead of them and get them to stop.'

'How?'

'Land the damn chopper on the road if you need to.'

'Mr Anning, if I do that without declaring an emergency then I could lose my pilot's license.'

'Then declare a goddamn emergency if you get caught. You work for me. Remember that. Got it?'

'Yes, sir. I copy. Descending to a hundred feet. There they are, right in front of us.'

The roar of the helicopter engines was so loud that Cal nearly froze at the wheel. He instinctively let up on the gas as the chopper passed overhead and it filled the big windshield as it passed over, heading west.

Sue recognized the distinctive red and white markings. It was going to be her medevac vehicle at the ranch in case any of the girls needed it during labor.

'That's Anning's,' she said.

'I guess we know why those guys were following us,' Cal said. The sudden roar had scared the girls and babies something fierce.

'Why won't he leave us alone?' Sue said.

'Guys like him don't let go easily,' Cal said, checking his position on the GPS map. He looked down for only a couple of seconds. When he looked up again he saw the helicopter setting down about half a mile ahead.

'Christ almighty,' he said. 'Girls, do you have your seat belts on?'

Mary fastened hers and the Marias followed her example. All of them held their sons tightly to their chests. Cal heard Maria Mollo praying in Spanish. Mary Riordan, always so tough, began to cry.

Anning turned to Carling and said, 'Get out there and wave at them to halt. Use your rifle to make them stop.'

'You're not asking me to fire on them, are you?'

'I am not. We can't risk hurting the babies. Just scare them to a stop.'

Cal and Sue saw a man on the road standing in front of the chopper. He had a rifle.

'Oh God, Cal.'

'I'm not going to stop,' he said.

'What then?'

'This. Hang on. Girls, duck down!'

Mary Riordan reached over to the opposite bench seat and pushed her friends' heads down.

The median strip was level with the road and flat as everything else around them. At the last, safe moment Cal slowed a little to keep control of the bus then steered left onto the median, bypassing the helicopter and rejoining the highway to the west. The detectives' car slowed and stopped.

'Shit, Carling's standing there with a fucking gun,' the driver said. 'This job is ridiculous, man. Stick a fork in me, I'm done.'

With that, he did a slow U-turn on the median strip and took the highway back east.

Carling just shook his head and re-boarded the helicopter.

'Get back after them,' Anning said to the pilot.

Cal heard the engines roar over them again.

'Open the door and fire a warning shot,' Anning said. 'Make him stop.'

'I don't think that's a good idea,' Carling said. 'Once a round goes downrange, there's no accounting for it.'

'Do it, goddamn it!'

Carling sighed hard and slid the side door open. 'Hover and keep it steady,' he told the pilot.

By the glow of the cabin lights, Cal saw the profile of a shooter aiming down at them. He braked hard. There were no cars coming from either direction. They were alone on a deserted stretch of Texas highway. The rifle shot sounded like a clap of thunder. Cal saw the round spark about fifty yards ahead as the lead met asphalt.

Sue screamed and so did the girls.

Cal said as calmly as he could, 'Sue, take my phone and find Andy Bogosian in my contacts. Call him on his mobile number and give me the phone.'

Cal sped up again and the helicopter flew ahead westbound to once again double back.

Sue handed him the ringing phone.

'Andy, this is Cal Donovan. I'm with the girls. We're on State Road 62 in Texas about five miles from the New Mexico border. We're in trouble. That's right. Big trouble. I need you to pull every string you've got.'

'Again,' Anning said. 'Closer this time. That bastard's going to stop for me.'

The chopper got into position again and Carling leaned out, sighting through the rifle scope. This time his round slashed the pavement about twenty yards ahead of the RV. A piece of asphalt pelted the windshield.

There were more screams and Cal drove on.

'I'm not fucking going to stop,' he muttered, clamping his hands around the steering wheel.

'Again!' Anning shouted. 'Get in for another shot.'

'He's not stopping,' Carling said. 'We can't stop him without crashing them.'

'I said, again. Closer. He'll lose his nerve.'

The pilot headed west for another swing.

The pilot pointed. 'Mr Anning, look at that, about three miles away on the other side of the state line.'

A conga line of blue flashing lights was heading east. Then

suddenly, the lights became stationary. Blue flashes lit up the darkening sky.

Anning wasn't sure what to make of it but Carling knew.

'Those are New Mexico State Police! They're holding at the border.'

'Why?' the pilot asked.

'They don't have jurisdiction in Texas, that's why,' Carling said.

'Shoot a tire out!' Anning shouted. 'It's now or never.'

'He could lose control,' Carling said. 'We might flip it.'

'We've got to take the chance. Do it, for Christ's sake.'

The chopper hovered no more than twenty feet above the road and Carling did as he was told. They were so close that when he took the shot Cal could see into the cockpit and the look of hate on Anning's face.

The heavy slug ripped into the front passenger-side tire, shredding it. Cal felt the bus violently lurch toward the right. He struggled to keep it on the road but it drifted too far and began traveling on the scrub. He braked as it bumped over the vegetation until it dipped hard and came to a jarring stop when the right rear tire slid into a shallow drainage ditch.

The girls shrieked and the babies wailed.

'Everyone OK?' Cal shouted. He'd been holding his breath for so long that now he was panting for air.

'Yes, we're all OK,' Mary cried, 'but they're fixing to kill us!'

'Are the babies all right?' Sue said, about to unclick her belt and go back.

Cal saw the blue lights flashing ahead of them no more than a mile away.

'It's Andy. He came through.'

He gave the rig some gas and it rocked hard. Sue kept her belt on.

'They've stopped,' Carling said, relieved as hell.

The helicopter was hovering a few feet off the ground, yards away from the stalled RV.

Anning looked out one window. The bus was bucking as Cal tried to free the rear tire from the ditch. Out the pilot's side window he saw the flashing police lights close by.

'He's going to free himself,' Anning said. 'We can't let him get loose. Shoot the engine block. Disable it.'

'I'm not putting a round into that RV,' Carling said. 'Someone's going to get shot if I do it.'

'Then give me the fucking rifle,' Anning said, turning back and almost ripping it out of Carling's hands.

Anning slid the passenger door open and pointed the rifle at the grill.

Cal saw the rifle barrel, threw the transmission into low gear, and buried the gas pedal into the floor. The RV rose up like a whale breaking the waves.

Anning pulled the trigger as the RV came down, free of the ditch.

The RV regained the roadway and Cal fought to keep it on a straight line as the front rim sent showers of sparks on to the road.

The pilot had to lift up precipitously to prevent a collision with the throttling RV. He hovered a hundred feet above the highway. Anning watching helplessly as the bus fought its way to the west.

The state line was looming. The police lights were getting brighter.

A sign said: Leaving Texas. Another sign said: Entering New Mexico.

Cal pulled over on to the verge and the police cars converged.

'Sue, we made it. We're safe.'

She was staring straight ahead. One hand was still on the pistol. The other hand was over her diaphragm. Her shirt was soaked in blood.

He whipped off his seatbelt and got close.

She said to him in a soft, breathy voice, 'Don't let them see me.'

'Girls, stay in your seats,' Cal shouted.

'Is everything all right?' Mary said.

'Just stay put!'

State troopers opened the doors.

'We need an ambulance,' Cal shouted. 'Please take the girls out.'

Cal put pressure on her wound. He felt pulses of hot blood against his palm.

'You're going to be OK, Sue,' he said. 'The ambulance is coming.'

'I'm not OK,' she said weakly. 'Not OK.'

'Come on, stay with me. I want to get to know you.'

'I would have liked that. Cal?'

'Yes?'

'Are the babies safe?'

'They're safe.'

'Don't you think they have the loveliest eyes?'

'Sure I do.'

She shut her own eyes and whispered ever so faintly. 'I think they're my eyes, Cal.'

'Sue.'

Then she uttered her last words. 'She knows. Mrs Torres.'

THIRTY-FOUR

L ooking back on it, Anning and Gottlieb would agree that the hardest night on the mountain wasn't the one when they were the hungriest or the one when they had lost the last thin reeds of hope. It was the one when Phil Alexander died.

The third night.

They had left him strapped to his seat. His back was broken and something very bad was happening inside his belly. It had slowly ballooned to three times its normal girth and the skin had become drum-tight and turned the color of an eggplant. The man had been one of the sharpest corporate lawyers in America and also wickedly funny. The sense of humor departed on the first night, his lucidity left on the second, and his life force faded to black on the third. What persisted up to the point of death was the pain. Intermittent moaning turned into a roaring groan. Near the end he was howling like an animal caught in a steel trap.

That night, Gottlieb used his good arm to try and give him some snow to eat but he kept turning his face away like a child refusing a spoonful of spinach.

'Don't waste your time,' Anning said from under the pile of parkas he'd stripped off the dead. 'He's done.'

'Maybe dehydration is making him more uncomfortable,' Gottlieb said.

'Dehydration's the least of his problems.'

The two men were only a few feet away from one another but it was so impossibly dark inside the fuselage they couldn't see each other.

'He needs to be quiet,' Gottlieb said. 'I can't stand listening to him anymore.'

'Stick some wadding into your ears.'

'I tried it. It didn't work.'

'Then sleep outside.'

'I'll freeze to death.'

Anning was getting testy. 'Then maybe we should help him with his pain!'

Gottlieb understood the meaning. 'We could be rescued tomorrow.'

'He's already dead.'

Gottlieb felt his way back to one of the blood-encrusted seats.

The lawyer howled long into the dark night. Anning was able to nap intermittently but Gottlieb couldn't sleep a moment. Then, as the first blue-gray mountain light was washing the blackness away, the howling abruptly stopped. The sudden quiet had the effect of waking Anning up. What he saw was Gottlieb kneeling beside Alexander, his good arm bearing down on the lawyer's face.

The two men didn't say a word about it then, or later.

They just fell into a deep slumber and slept through the morning and into the afternoon.

When Alexander was consigned to the row of dead men outside the plane, the fuselage became more livable. They had made an inventory of the crash site, scouring the cockpit and front section, the fuselage and baggage compartment, and the pockets of the dead for anything edible and usable. The small galley contained a drawer of cellophane-wrapped pastries and breakfast bars but they had spilled out when the front of the plane ripped apart on impact. But they found a half-dozen breakfast bars scattered in the cockpit where the pilots must have squirreled them away, and a large bar of chocolate inside McGee the banker's duffel.

'One-quarter breakfast bar in the morning, one-quarter in the night per person,' Gottlieb had suggested. 'That way we'll have a little something to eat for six days. If we're still here after that, the chocolate bar should get us another three or four days.' For a time, Anning kept his mouth shut about another source of protein and fat in their midst but Gottlieb suspected that he hadn't heard the last of the subject.

For better or worse – Anning contended for better – among the luggage, they recovered three unbroken bottles of Chilean brandy from their last night at the resort.

Again, Gottlieb had an opinion. 'I don't think drinking alcohol's such a good idea in freezing thin air.'

'Nonsense,' Anning said, having a swig. 'What do you think St Bernard dogs carry in their collar flasks? Brandy, for Christ's sake. It's got calories. Food of the gods.'

Gottlieb was more interested in getting warm. All the ski clothing was valuable, of course, and each man had donned as many layers as humanly possible, but fire would have been life-saving. A generation earlier, some of the passengers or crew would have been smokers and carried matches or lighters, but there weren't any fire-starters to be found. Gottlieb, the engineer, got the idea to find a battery to make a spark and light some goose down from parka linings. In the cockpit was an empty set of clips where a flashlight had been mounted but it must have hurtled down the mountain. There had to be some kind of battery back-ups behind the instrument clusters but they spent an entire two days exhausting themselves pulling at the tangled metal and banging away without finding what they were looking for.

The luggage area was filled with skis and poles, of course, and they even had an absurd little conversation about the feasibility of the uninjured Anning trying to ski down the mountain. It would have been a very fast suicide mission.

So, they fell into a tedious and highly uncomfortable routine.

During daylight hours they took shifts, one of them always remaining outside the fuselage, scanning the skies for rescue. They had pried off a reflective piece of cockpit aluminum and while one man tried to keep warm, the other braved the strong winds that swept the mountainside, catching the sun on its surface and bouncing light toward the sky. At night, they tied cargo-hold webbing woven with parka sleeves and ski pants over the jagged fuselage opening to insulate them as best they could from plummeting temperatures.

And they marked the passage of time, in the age-old way: a line for each day scratched into the burled wood of an interior piece of trim.

Within a few days it became apparent to both of them that they had remarkably little in common beyond a narrow slice of business interests. However, it was hard to come up with a topic more trivial than buying and selling companies when one was marooned on the slippery slope of a desolate mountain peak. Each of them would have, perhaps, chosen any other man in their party as a survival companion. Anning, a son of Texas ranches and oilfields. Gottlieb, a son of Manhattan private schools and Broadway plays. As long as there were a few morsels of civilized food to eat and any hope that a civilian or military aircraft would find them, they were able to keep their conversation to practical matters of survival.

But when ten days had passed and they were down to the last square of chocolate and a thimbleful of brandy, when their energy levels redlined and apathy set in, they turned philosophical in search of common strands of humanity.

It was a heavily overcast afternoon and snow was falling heavily. There was no point in watching the sky on a day such as this so they both huddled inside their aluminum tube. Usually they chose seats as far apart as they could to carve out a bit of privacy but Gottlieb had been so exhausted that he fell into the seat opposite Anning on the way to the rear.

They had established the outlines of each other's domestic lives early on. Anning was Gottlieb's senior by twenty years. He had a wife who led the existence of a Houston socialite and country-clubber. She rarely accompanied him to the place on earth he liked best, his horse farm and ranch in west Texas. They had two daughters, one married to a fellow in Texas who owned a bunch of automobile dealerships, the other to a pharmaceutical executive in New Jersey. Neither woman had ever had any serious career aspirations. Anning had a couple of pictures of grandchildren in his wallet but he showed them to his companion in a perfunctory way, without a grandfather's pride. Gottlieb was married to a girl he had known in high school. They met up again after college and had a prosperous, childless, suburban life in Connecticut. Anning suspected that Gottlieb was a New York liberal and Gottlieb suspected Anning was a Texas conservative. They didn't talk about politics. Why make a bad situation worse?

Anning took the pilot's folding knife from his jacket pocket and weakly held it up.

He said, 'You know we're going to have to get some protein soon. We're starving to death.'

Gottlieb shook his drooping head. 'I'm not with you on this, Randy.'

'You will be.'

'I don't think so.'

'Hell, Steve, all they are is slabs of meat in a cold locker. They don't have names any more. Their souls have departed. I knew some of them better than others but I'd say they were all good people. The parts of them that matter now are in Heaven.'

Gottlieb was too fatigued to laugh. The most he could muster was a sharp exhale. 'You really believe that?'

'What? That they're in Heaven? You're damn right I believe it. You're Jewish, right?'

Another sharp exhale. 'Did my name give it away?'

'I've known plenty of religious Jews. I take it you're not one of them.'

'You take it right.'

'Well, I'm Catholic. I'm a deeply religious man.'

'I haven't heard you praying.'

'I pray silently. I don't choose to wear it on my sleeve. Not here. But if you were to find some faith up here on this mountain and you wanted to pray to God, I would join you. Just putting it out there.'

The sharp wind was splattering snow against the skin of the plane. Gottlieb let his chin fall on to his chest. 'I'll let you know.'

Two nights later, as it fell dark, Gottlieb was sitting in the same seat. Despite more threats, Anning had kept the knife in his pocket, unused, and Gottlieb suspected he wasn't really all that committed to carving into a frozen arm.

'You go to church?' Gottlieb asked.

'When I'm in Houston, I do. I like our Cardinal. George Pole. He's old school. I admire that.'

'What does that mean? Old school?'

'He's a traditionalist. A theological conservative. As am I.'

'I guess you're not a fan of Pope Celestine then.'

'If you must know, I can't stand him.'

'That's strong.'

'My views are strongly felt. I think this pope has done more to harm the Church than any pope in my lifetime. Cardinals aren't infallible. They made a mistake in the last conclave. They thought they knew their fellow cardinal, Aspromonte, and they didn't. Even my friend George Pole fell into the trap. Once Aspromonte was elected, he showed his true colors. He's a flaming socialist – maybe even a Communist – a liberation theology stooge who's more interested in his social agenda than maintaining the ancient traditions of Catholicism.'

'Gee, Randy, you're not too worked up over him, are you?'

'It's something I take very seriously. You should hear the conversations I have with Cardinal Pole. We share the same fears about where the Church is heading. Gay marriage – check. Birth control – check. Ordination of women – check. If Celestine lives long enough and appoints enough of his people to the College of Cardinals, then you won't be able to tell a Catholic from a Methodist.'

'Or a Jew,' Gottlieb said.

'The one good thing about dying on this mountain,' Anning said, 'is that I won't have to bear witness to the wholesale destruction of the institution I love.'

They entered the third week on the mountain, too drained to spend more than an hour a day outside the fuselage. The meager rations of chocolate and brandy were a distant, fond memory. Everything they did, they did slowly and painfully. Even talking seemed like hard work.

Anning had been returning to the subject of the Church in the Celestine era, as if the anger it stirred up inside him gave him energy. Gottlieb was sick of it but he didn't have the strength to protest.

'If we get rescued, you know what I'd like to do?' Anning said.

'Get a cheeseburger and fries?'

Anning ignored him. 'I'd like to bring him down. Burn Celestine's Church to the ground.'

'Oh yeah? Sounds violent.'

'I'm not a violent man.'

'Then how?'

'Oh, I don't know. Maybe by giving Catholics an alternative.'

'I'm not sure the Jews will let all of you in.'

'I'm serious.'

'OK.'

'The Church needs to be reinvented.'

'How would that happen?'

Anning closed his eyes. Gottlieb thought he'd drifted off and he decided to take a nap too. But Anning wasn't sleeping, he was thinking, and suddenly he spoke, startling Gottlieb.

'You'd need to re-create the formative events of Christianity, that's what,' he said. 'You'd need a new Holy Mother, a virgin. You'd need a new infant Jesus born from that virgin. You'd need a new clergy dedicated to the core values that made the Catholic Church powerful and great. You'd need to convert the faithful to a new Catholic Church, stir them up like crazy with new miracles. Hell, why only one Mary and one Jesus? Have more than one. From different parts of the world. Inspire the faithful with a vigorous new religion that makes them leave the old, corrupt one in droves.'

Gottlieb was watching him get more and more animated. It seemed like the mental exercise was doing him good and he was almost apologetic when he pointed out the obvious.

'It's a great plan, Randy, except that it's hard to dial up a miracle. Virgin birth was a big deal because it was a big deal.'

The talking had made Anning's mouth dry. They kept a tray of snow inside the fuselage for water and he scooped some into his mouth.

'You could fake it,' he said.

'Fake what? Virginal conception?' Gottlieb asked.

'Why not? You could take a virgin, knock her out, and plant an embryo inside her. Hell, I'd even go for girls named Mary. Why not? Mary gets pregnant. Boom. Virgin birth. Names the baby Jesus. The boy is raised to be a prophet. He's convincing as hell because he thinks he's the son of God. What's to say that couldn't work?'

Gottlieb tried to straighten himself in his seat. 'Randy, aside from all the bullshit ideas you're spouting, do you even know how *in vitro* fertilization works?'

'No, do you?'

'As a matter of fact, I do. Beth and I tried it. Many times. I don't know how many embryos we transferred. None of them took. We moved on. But here's how it's done. The woman is put up in stirrups. The doctor inserts a speculum to get a good look at the cervix. The embryos get sucked into a catheter and the catheter gets threaded through the speculum into the cervix and guided with ultrasound into the uterus where the embryos get deposited.'

'So?'

'So, what do you think happens when you insert a speculum into a virgin? It busts the hymen and you can't prove she's a virgin anymore.'

'That's a problem, isn't it?'

'To your diabolical scheme? Yeah, Randy, it's a problem.'

'You're an engineer. Isn't there a way around it, some way to preserve the virginity and still get the embryo in?'

Gottlieb helped himself to some of the snow. 'It's not an engineering problem that's ever been in need of a solution. No one's ever had a problem with speculums before.'

'What would you have to do?'

'Well, you'd need to invent a new kind of catheter with exquisite tip control that you could thread in through a gap in the hymen under fiberoptic guidance and deliver an embryo payload into the uterus.'

'I don't have any idea what you just said. Would it work?'

'Maybe. I mean I don't think embryo transfer works a hundred per cent of the time. If you wanted one virgin Mary you'd probably need to do two or three procedures. If you wanted three Marys you'd need to do five or six. But it's stupid, Randy. Why are we even talking about it?'

'Do you know anyone who could design this catheter?'

Gottlieb snorted. 'You're still talking about it.' But after a while he said, 'My mistress probably could.'

'Your *what*?'

'Don't look shocked. I've been having an affair for years. Her name's Belinda.'

'Your wife doesn't know?'

'I've been careful. Maybe they'll meet at my memorial. Belinda and I were at the Yale School of Engineering together. Years later, I looked at licensing some of her patents for one of my companies. The rest is history.'

'She could design my virgin birth machine?'

'Randy, enough already. I'm going to take a nap now.'

They were both sound asleep when the fuselage began to vibrate. Gottlieb blinked himself awake. Their mountainside abode, so quiet besides the occasional sound of wind and snow whipping against the aluminum skin, was weirdly noisy.

'Randy! Get up. Get up.'

He pulled Anning to his feet by a padded sleeve and the two men stumbled from the fuselage into a deep drift of pristine snow.

As they began waving furiously at the Chilean Air Force Huey helicopter hovering overhead, a military photographer looked down on them and snapped their picture.

THIRTY-FIVE

Sue Gibney was at the kitchen table in her sunny Santa Fe condo, placing a Skype call to a person she had never met and whose name she didn't know. She was bemused by the anonymity of the process and wasn't taking it all that seriously. It was a harmless, intriguing lark. The advertisement sought healthy women between the age of twenty-five and thirty-five to donate their eggs to a couple with fertility issues. The successful candidate would be Caucasian or Hispanic, college-educated, and willing to undergo medical, psychological, and genetic screening. The fee for donation would be 'considerable.' She liked the word 'considerable' and had sent her particulars to a post office box. Then she had promptly forgotten about it until an invitation for an interview popped into her email inbox.

The Skype contact was MrsT43644. The woman who answered had perfect make-up, red lipstick and black, wavy hair with a glossy shine. The camera was close to her face. Nothing in the room was visible that might have given some clues about her.

The woman had a distinctly Latin accent. 'Hello, Susan. Very nice to meet you.'

'Please call me Sue.'

'All right, Sue. How are you today?'

'I'm good. You must be Mrs T.'

'I am. Sorry for being mysterious. My client is quite wealthy and is very careful about privacy.'

'Clients,' Sue said. 'Your ad mentioned a couple with fertility issues.'

'Yes! You're right. I misspoke. So, Sue, your résumé was very impressive and you've been advanced to our shortlist.'

'Oh! OK. What does that mean?'

'It means that after I interview you and the other candidates on the shortlist, a smaller number of women will be advanced to the testing phase. Of course, we will pay handsomely for the time and inconvenience, even if you aren't chosen to be the donor.'

Sue fidgeted with her beaded necklace. 'I don't want to seem mercenary but would you mind telling me how much you're paying for the eggs?'

'I'd be concerned if you didn't want to know. It's seventy-five thousand dollars.'

'I'm sorry, did you say seventy-five?'

'Is this less than you expected? More?'

Sue flushed with excitement but deflected the question. 'I had no idea what the going rate was, actually.'

'It's well above the going rate. We're paying a premium for discretion and confidentiality. If chosen, you'd be required to sign a highly restrictive, legally binding nondisclosure agreement. Are you OK to proceed with the interview?'

Sue smiled into the camera. 'Ask me anything.'

When the interview was done, Torres told her she would hear back within a week.

'I look forward to it,' Sue replied.

'One more thing, Sue,' Torres said. 'We're impressed with your professional credentials. My client may require the services of a midwife at a later time. Whether or not you are chosen as our donor, may we keep your résumé on file?'

THIRTY-SIX

Maria Aquino wasn't paying attention to her surroundings. She had walked these alleys of Paradise Village so often that she knew every house, every little night market, every hole in the road that filled with rain water. She knew which corners to avoid – the ones where gangs hung out – and which routes were safest. She was thinking about what she was going to do when she got to her friend Lulu's house on the other side of the slum from her own shanty. Lulu had a new copy of *Candy*, a teen pop magazine, and the girls would hang out, turn the pages together, and laugh until it hurt.

She didn't notice the white van idling by the vacant lot where a house had burned down and no one had rebuilt yet. She didn't notice the door of the van opening and closing.

The light!

The light was so bright it hurt.

She was grabbed from behind. A hand covered her mouth and a needle was expertly thrust into her neck. A thumb pushed on a plunger and a dose of the immediate-onset anesthetic propofol coursed into her jugular vein. She would have crumpled to the ground had another set of hands, a woman's, not caught her and lifted her into the van.

'Go,' the man said.

The driver took off and soon they were outside the slum, parked on a residential side street in Malabon City.

Maria was laid out on a padded examination table. The anesthetist started an IV and began a milky propofol drip to keep her asleep. He stuck EKG electrodes on her chest and clamped a pulsimeter on a finger to check her oxygenation. He bent her head back to keep her airways open and kept a mask and bag at the ready in case he needed to breathe for her.

'She's good,' he declared.

A female gynecologist undressed the girl from the waist down and splayed her legs open.

'She's perfect. Intact hymen and she's not having her period.'

The catheter was set to go, the embryo payload she'd carried in a warming pack in her hand luggage on the flight to the Philippines was inside its fluid-filled delivery chamber. She had practiced the technique exhaustively in Houston for speed and accuracy. Now she inserted the catheter through the small opening in her hymen near her urethra and guided it through the vagina toward the cervix using the fiberoptic camera on its tip. At the cervical opening she moved the tip, just so, with joystick controls and gave the catheter a firm push until it was inside the uterus. From there, she used the camera to lay the catheter tip up against the uterine wall.

'Her endometrium is perfect, her menstrual phase is fine,' she declared. 'We're good to go.' Then she squeezed the trigger and deposited the embryo on to the lining of the uterus.

After she withdrew the catheter she inserted a rectal suppository of progesterone to improve the chance of embryo implantation, dressed the girl, and told the anesthetist that she was done.

'OK,' he said, 'I'm going to slow the drip down until she's almost conscious. Then it'll be time for my line.'

Maria groaned lightly.

The anesthetist had his note card handy. '*Ikaw ay napili*,' he said loudly and theatrically. It was Filipino. 'You have been chosen.' Just to be sure, he said it again.

They took her back to Paradise Village to a spot near where they had snatched her and left her sitting against a wall as her stupor lightened.

Back in the van the anesthetist said to the gynecologist, 'Now what?'

She was cleaning and coiling the catheter for transport. 'Now we go to Peru.'

THIRTY-SEVEN

'Steve, you sound upset. I can hear it in your voice. Look, I'm with some people. No, I'm not blowing you off. On the contrary, I'm going to ask them to leave. Just hang on.'

Anning was in his Houston office with a small group of

employees discussing the geological survey of a new natural gas field. He cleared the room and got back on the line.

'There, you've got my full attention.'

'Look, Randy,' Gottlieb said, 'I didn't sleep last night. You know the last time I missed a night's sleep?'

'That was a terrible night,' Anning said after a memory-laden pause. 'Tell me what's troubling you.'

'I've been reading about this shit in Ireland.'

'I see.'

'You see? Is that all you can say?'

'I'm aware of the situation.'

'It's more than a situation, Randy. This girl's mother is dead. The American priest was kidnapped.'

'Now, Steve, my understanding is that her death was from a medical condition she'd been hospitalized for. As to the priest, that was unfortunate. The people over there decided to do some freelancing.'

Gottlieb was clearly agitated. 'Freelancing? I'm not comfortable where this is headed. It's gone too far.'

'You did your part, Steve. You helped me. And I helped you. I ponied up in a major way as a limited partner in your new fund. And your lady friend, Hartman, got paid damned well for signing over the rights to her catheter and for not asking questions.'

'She still doesn't know what it was for.'

'And that's a good thing. But you, my friend, have done your part. For you, it's over. It's my worry now. And, I've got to tell you, I'm not the least bit worried.'

'I've got a conscience, Randy. I can't turn it on and off.'

'That's because you're a good man. And a good friend. People who've gone through what you and I went through have a bond forever.'

It didn't sound like Anning's words were registering. Gottlieb sounded mournful. 'I don't know what I'm going to do.'

Anning clenched his free hand. 'What does that even mean?'

'It means what it sounds like. I'm feeling a need to unburden myself. The publicity is through the roof. This business with the girls is turning into a very big deal.'

'That's what I envisioned.'

'It's bigger than I envisioned. And there's been violence.'

'Look, Steve, this unburdening sentiment. You've never expressed the need to unburden yourself about Phil Alexander.'

Gottlieb got very angry very fast. 'You told me he was already dead! I was half-crazy that night. We both made the decision.'

'You're the one who did it. Remember? I really want this to stay our own personal and painful memory. So please don't talk about unburdening yourself. It's a horrible idea.'

Later, Anning summoned Clay Carling to his office.

'Clay, you understand how much I've got invested in the success of the New Catholic Church.'

Carling shifted his weight from side to side, digging his cowboy boots into the plush carpet. He nodded.

'The stakes are too high to rely on verbal or even written confidentiality agreements. That's why I had you take care of the folks who worked on the girls – the anesthetist and that gynecologist.'

The security man nodded again. His boss wasn't looking for a comment.

'Steve Gottlieb may also require your helping hand. Before it comes to that, let's send him a message where he lives. Something subtle but not too subtle.'

THIRTY-EIGHT

I t would be called the great unraveling.

When you pull hard enough on a loose end of knitting, the sweater turns into a ball of yarn again.

The New Mexico authorities launched an investigation into Sue Gibney's death by shooting and called in the FBI. Their first interview subject was Cal Donovan.

He had a lot to say.

The first stitch to come undone was Mrs Torres.

A team of FBI special agents from Dallas descended on the ranch. Anning and Carling weren't there. Anning's only senior employee on site was Mrs Torres who was fully prepared for their arrival. She had already retained a criminal lawyer from Wichita Falls who arrived within the hour to attend her interview. Her attorney announced that she was prepared to cooperate in exchange for immunity from prosecution. After a telephonic negotiation involving the Department of Justice, a proffer immunity agreement was faxed over to the ranch.

Torres also had a lot to say.

The next stitch to come undone was Anning's helicopter pilot who was at home in Vernon drinking heavily when the FBI came calling that night.

The following morning a federal judge granted a search warrant for the ranch, the Houston office and personal residence of Randall Anning, and the workplace and personal residence of Clay Carling.

Carling was arrested on a charge of accessory to first-degree murder. The pilot had tagged him as one of the shooters the night that Sue Gibney died, although he said that Anning may have fired the fatal shot. The FBI was in the early stages of linking the security man to the bombing death of Steven Gottlieb and other capital crimes. Carling was promised some vague future sentencing concessions if he agreed to testify against Anning. He didn't require much persuasion. He was angry as hell that he'd been forced to shoot at the RV.

Anning was arrested the next morning in front of his wife. Before the day was out she filed for divorce. His charges included first-degree murder, international kidnapping, and wire fraud related to the public solicitation of donations to the New Catholic Church.

Under advice of the finest counsel money could buy, Anning had nothing to say. He was remanded to federal custody and held without bail.

Belinda Hartman was interviewed by the FBI and before long she was informed that she was not a target of the investigation.

Amanda Pittinger, the reporter from the *Houston Chronicle*, got the bit between her teeth and ran hard with an evolving exposé of the New Catholic Church. A day didn't pass without a new front-page story.

George Pole left his regalia and vestments in the sacristy of the cathedral and returned to the Houston apartment he had rented when he resigned as cardinal. In the fine, classical tradition of Roman aristocrats he drew a hot bath and made deep slits in his wrists and ankles, turning the bath papal red.

In Galway, the Irish authorities had enough probable cause for a judge to issue a second exhumation order for Cindy Riordan. Her repeat autopsy, this one done by the finest forensic pathologist in the country, led to the additional charge of murder to be added to Brendan Doyle's list of pending offenses.

The FBI was given the DNA test results for the girls and their babies. As a special courtesy, the Dallas special agent in charge of the case gave Cal a call one day.

'Professor, I wanted to give you a heads-up on something that's going to come out publicly on the DNA soon,' she said.

'Sue Gibney was the mother,' he said.

'How'd you know?'

'I just did. And the father?'

'Randall Anning.'

Cal was at home when he got the call, surrounded by books, working on a paper about an obscure, medieval pope. He lost all interest in his work and went to his freezer to pour himself a large tumbler of vodka as clear and viscous as tears.

Pedro Alvarado still had a limp from the beating he took from Clay Carling. He knew he wasn't going to get in through the front gate so he parked his truck at the closest point and cut the fence. He didn't want any cattle or horses to get out so he twisted the cut ends back together once he was inside. Then he began the long, painful walk over the prairie.

The stable hands all knew him, of course. He had been well-liked, one of them. But out of fear for their own jobs, no one acknowledged him. But no one stopped him either. They cast their eyes down as he went to the gas pump and filled a five-gallon can and lugged it to the cathedral.

All the doors were locked so he kicked open one near the sacristy. Inside, the cathedral glass had turned yellow from the afternoon light, a shade of green, the color of winter grass. He placed the can on one of the front pews and splashed some gas on the old plaid shirt he'd been wearing. His bare chest and back were crisscrossed with healing scars. He stuffed the shirt into the spout hole, caught the sleeve hanging out with a pocket lighter and ran outside. He was well clear when the explosion turned the cathedral into a big, beautiful furnace.

Hundreds of clergymen and nuns petitioned to have their

resignations rescinded and be reinstated to the good graces of the
Catholic Church. The Vatican was asked to provide guidance and
the matter went all the way up to Pope Celestine. He decreed that
all were welcome back with open arms and without recriminations.

When the time came, Cal lobbied hard to do the honors. The
request went all the way up to the FBI deputy director who
signed off on it.

He and Joe Murphy took the Delta Shuttle from Boston to
Washington and were met at Reagan National Airport by a State
Department people-mover van. Their first stop was the Irish
Embassy where they picked up Mary Riordan and her baby whom
she now just called David.

'It's good to see you, Mary,' Murphy said.

She hugged him. Cal got one too. He hadn't seen her since the
night Sue died.

'You're looking well,' Cal said.

'Can't believe I'm finally going home.'

'There's going to be quite the scene at Shannon Airport, I
expect,' Murphy said.

'I imagine so,' she said.

Cal wasn't sure he was going to mention her but Mary went
there on her own.

'I miss her, you know,' she said.

'Sue would have been really happy today,' Cal replied.

'When he's old enough maybe I'll tell David about her, being
that she's his mum and all.'

'You're his mum,' Murphy said.

She smiled at him. 'I suppose I am.'

The next stop was the Peruvian Embassy. Maria Mollo and baby
JJ – she still liked the name – piled in. She hugged Mary so hard
that the Irish girl yelped in discomfort and delight.

'Eeyore!' she screeched. 'How's my little sister?'

'I am good. JJ is good,' she said in her best English.

Mary tried to pantomime that she was a sight for sore eyes
without luck and Cal's limited Spanish came to the rescue.

At the Philippines Embassy, Maria Aquino and baby Ruperto
climbed in. She too had jettisoned Jesus. She had a new pair of
glasses, even thicker and rounder than the last ones that had gone
missing the night the RV went into a ditch.

'Once a Minion, always a Minion,' Mary said.

'We going home,' the girl said, crying happily.

On the way to Dulles Airport, Cal sat opposite the girls and watched them try to describe to one another what had become of them since they'd been separated, awaiting repatriation. But he wasn't watching them as much as he was watching the babies, three identical, chubby boys with Sue Gibney's lavender eyes.

At the airport, Cal and Murphy stayed with them until the last possible moment and waved goodbye as minders led them through security to their airline gates.

'Well, that's the end of it,' Murphy said.

Cal put his arm around the priest and said, 'You think?'

'You don't?'

'There are people who believe that Elvis is still alive,' Cal said. 'There's always going to be folks who believe the boys are really the sons of God.'

'Well, as long as they don't grow up believing it, I suppose they'll be just fine.'

THIRTY-NINE

'I think we should invite Father Gooseberry,' Jessica had said.

Cal thought it was a terrific idea.

She was going to be attending a medical congress in Milan and Cal had the notion to piggyback on a visit to Rome. After all, Cardinal Da Silva was getting blue in the face with his repeated invitations.

'Really, Cal, the Holy Father is most anxious to thank you personally,' he had said.

The three of them stayed in the same hotel in Rome and took a taxi together to the Vatican. Jessica was looking more decorous than Cal had ever seen her. When he emerged from the shower that morning to see her in a new blue dress that showed almost no skin, he said, 'Who stole Jessica?'

Murphy was dressed in crisp, clerical black and even Cal had on a dark suit and tie for the occasion.

'Excited about meeting the Holy Father?' Murphy asked Jessica.

She faked a yawn then laughed. 'Sure, why not? Bail me out if he asks me any religious quiz questions.'

'He can smell a lapsed Catholic from a hundred paces,' Cal said.

'You leave my drinking buddy alone,' Murphy said, 'or I'll thump you with a Bible.'

Jessica had been reading the *New York Times* International Edition over breakfast while Cal slept. She had torn off an article from the front page and had it folded in her purse.

'See this?' she asked.

Congress approves articles of impeachment against President Griffith – article one: Improper approval of visas for the Marys; article two: Unauthorized wiretaps against the Americans Donovan and Gibney.

Cal grunted. 'You won't see me shedding any tears for him. There's a hundred reasons that creep needed to be removed from office. This is like getting Al Capone for income-tax evasion.'

Murphy nodded and said, '*Sic semper tyrannis.*'

Jessica blanched. 'He's not going to be testing my Latin, is he?'

'George Pole might have,' Cal said. 'Not this pope.'

Sister Elisabetta had persuaded Pope Celestine to pull out all the stops to impress Cal's girlfriend by receiving them in the small throne room of the Apostolic Palace rather than his modest guest-house office.

Jessica flawlessly pulled off the curtsy she had obsessively practiced, Murphy bowed and kissed the pope's ring, and Cal got his customary bear hug.

'What a time you had,' Celestine told him. 'What a drama. How many men can say they singlehandedly healed a great schism within the Church?'

'I was, and will forever be, at your service, Holy Father.'

'And both of you played no small role,' the pope said. 'Father Murphy, you went to Ireland for me. You endured a kidnapping. And Dr Nelson, your expert technical advice and analysis of DNA samples exposed the cynical plot. My profound gratitude to all of you. Now for some small gifts.'

Sister Elisabetta retrieved them from a side table, handed them to a beaming Da Silva, who handed them to the pope.

'For you, Father Murphy, please accept this signed copy of my last book of essays. They are especially helpful if you suffer from insomnia.'

Murphy accepted the book and posed for his photograph.

'For you, Dr Nelson, I would like to give you a simple silver crucifix that belonged to my mother. She received it from my grandfather in Napoli when she was a young girl.'

Cal had never seen Jessica so overwhelmed, but back home she would take the official photograph to a studio to see if the streaks of tears running down her face could be expertly removed.

Then the pope addressed Cal. 'Professor, I thought long and hard about what additional gift I might give to you. You have all my books, you have unrestricted browsing rights to the Vatican Secret Archives and Library. You have papal medals. So, I've decided to simply give you a kiss. Is that enough?'

'More than enough, Holy Father,' he said, bending to receive a generous peck on each cheek.

Later, as a butler was pouring glasses of sherry, Cal's phone vibrated with a text. He discreetly glanced at his screen and saw a selfie of the reporter Amanda Pittinger, which she'd taken outside of their motel in Vernon, Texas. The message was simply, 'Call me,' followed by a small string of heart emojis. Cal pocketed the phone and pulled the pope aside.

'The present you gave Jessica was wonderful,' he said.

'She seemed to like it,' the pontiff replied.

'You know, Holy Father, I can't guarantee that she and I are always going to remain together. My track record in these matters is rather poor. If we break up, will I have to get it back?' He was only half joking.

'Let me tell you something, Professor,' the pope said. 'My mother, may the Lord bless her and keep her, had many, many crucifixes.'